CITY RISING

शहर
कस्बा

CITY RISING

From the Holy Mountain
THE SHANGHAI TETRALOGY | BOOK 1

DAVID ROTENBERG

WINNIPEG

City Rising
From the Holy Mountain

This book is a work of fiction. Names, characters, businesses, organizations, places, events, and incidents either are the product of the author's imagination or are used fictitiously.

Copyright © 2023 David Rotenberg

Design and layout by Matthew Stevens and M. C. Joudrey.

Published by At Bay Press November 2023.

All rights reserved. The use of any part of this publication, reproduced, transmitted in any form or by any means electronic, mechanical, photocopying, recording or otherwise, or stored in a retrieval system without prior written consent of the publisher or in the case of photocopying or other reprographic copying, license from the Canadian Copyright Licensing Agency-is an infringement of the copyright law.

No portion of this work may be reproduced without express written permission from At Bay Press.

Library and Archives Canada cataloguing in publication is available upon request.

ISBN 978-1-998779-08-6

Printed and bound in Canada.

This book is printed on acid free paper that is 100% recycled ancient forest friendly (100% post-consumer recycled).

First At Bay Press Edition

10 9 8 7 6 5 4 3 2 1

atbaypress.com

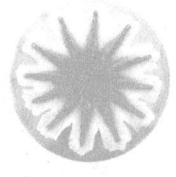

PART I

From the Holy Mountain

Wherein two prophecies are put forward; one proceeds, the other is fulfilled, and a city at the Bend in the River grows.

THE IVORY COMPACT

January, 207 BC

As the late-afternoon winter sun slid behind the towering dark clouds, a shadow swelled across the beautiful but usually desolate foothills of the Green Mountain, the Hua Shan. In the murky light, thousands upon thousands of rebel troops readied themselves to spring a trap that would end the life of the most powerful man the world had ever known, or very possibly would ever know — Q'in She Huang, China's First Emperor.

    A village fisherman raced to the far side of a partially frozen upland lake where his prized eels were supposed to be hibernating in their underwater pen. As he approached, the water was roiling and rich with blood. Females had slithered up onto an ice floe and were giving birth while the thicker, more powerful males thrashed the open water as they gorged themselves on their young. The fisherman watched in shocked silence, then turned his eyes upward toward the darkening sky. Just down the winding mountain path, a hunchbacked farmwife smacked the ice from a blanket she had hung to dry on the bamboo stand the night before and was amazed to find that the coverlet, although frozen stiff, was hot to the touch. Farther back in the foothills, a toothless peasant pinched the night-soil collector's product between his thumb and forefinger and brought it to his nose. To his amazement, the product was as fresh as the man had claimed it to be. He dropped the human fecal matter to the ground and stared at the night-soil collector. Then he looked to the black clouds, sniffed the air, turned, and ran.

Peasants always recognized the distinctive ozone reek that preceded change. But as they retreated to their huts and drew their children close to them, none knew the nature of the change that was beginning, not in the foothills with the rebel troops but on the upper plateau of the Hua Shan, the Holy Mountain. Change conceived and brought into being by the great Q'in She Huang himself.

"You think me mad," China's First Emperor said in a hoarse whisper. "You — all three of you — think I am beyond my wits. That I was tempted here in the depths of winter to this lonely mountaintop to ..." His voice trailed off. For a moment, Q'in She Huang allowed himself to look toward the vine-covered mouth of the cave behind him. He took a deep breath and let it out slowly in a fine line of white mist.

His frosted breath dusted the faces of the three people he trusted most on this earth, his Chosen: his personal Bodyguard; his head Confucian; and Jiang, his favourite concubine. *What are you thinking now, in your secret hearts?* he wondered, then put the thought aside. He knew there was no way to know another's hidden self. There was no way to find the mind's construction in a person's face.

He raised his arms, setting the abalone shells sewn into his silk coverlet tinkling. Then he spoke loudly. "Do you believe that I, who had the Great Wall built, I, who receive personal tribute from the barbarian lands far to the west, from the cruel kingdoms of the south and the arrogant men of the island called Nippon, that I, who united the Middle Kingdom for the first time, am now beyond my wits?"

The Confucian noted the subtle shift in the First Emperor's language. No longer was he using the overblown style of the ancient writers. Now his words were succinct and to the point. More importantly, his thoughts weren't the erratic, unpredictable rantings of a man insanely searching for the secret to eternal life. These were the lucid, considered thoughts of the man who had designed the longest man-made waterway in the world, joining the Yangtze River with Beijing, who had standardized the character writing distinctive to the Black-Haired People and created the Mandarin system of examinations that had led to the world's first organized civil service. This was the First Emperor he had known as a young man, not the one who had burned Confucians along with their books — a madness that he had witnessed and written about in his private journal.

"Do you believe that I am now infirm of mind — mad? That I brought you here to this barren place in search of some mountebank's charade, some alchemist's folly — a stone that would grant me eternal life? Do you believe that is why we now stand here and shiver in the cold while below, the rebel troops surround this mountain? Do you believe that of me?"

Yes, thought the Bodyguard, *that is precisely what I believe. It all began with your madness — your madness within madness. Then its seductive strands slithered beneath the latched door of your chamber and out into the world.* For in Q'in She Huang's madness, his imperial madness, he had somehow eternally bound them all to him. But none of them then understood that. All they knew was his lunacy, his screams for light in the darkness, for them to: "Find it. Find it for me now!" And now these new orders. Two porters to be hobbled and then their flesh slashed so that "their blood will bring to light that which will be."

The sun, almost at the western horizon, broke through the dense cloud cover and instantly banished the gloom. Suddenly the massive clouds were in furious motion, racing away to the north.

Q'in She Huang looked up and marvelled at their speed. Shortly, the sky was perfectly clear — and still, so still. *As if some deity had swept it clean with one great breath*, he thought. Then a cold wind, all the way from the Gobi Desert, swept up the mountainside and blew the long plaits of his lacquered hair against his cheek creasing the wind's sudden howl with a sharp thwap, thwap, thwap.

Jiang, the concubine, wrapped her woven shawl tightly around her, but still the cold entered her, hurt her, like an angry lover. She looked to her last angry lover, Q'in She Huang, and remembered his exacting instructions about the way to reveal a sacred relic. She shivered involuntarily at the memory. More madness!

The First Emperor turned to face the coming cold. "Even nature is in harmony with my intent," he said softly and was tempted to smile — but didn't.

At the western base of the mountain, the rebel general's Mongolian pony stirred beneath him as the desert wind engulfed them. *From the desert. Madness wind*, he thought.

A tear formed then fell from his left eye. The malformation of the socket, like that of his father and his father before him, prevented the eyelid from fully covering the pupil. The gusting wind found the point of access to his eye and the irritation always brought tears. It infuriated him.

He turned to his adjutant. "Are our men in place?"

"Yes, General."

"Their orders?"

"As you commanded, to kill on sight anyone who comes down from the Holy Mountain."

The rebel general was about to retort that there were no holy mountains but was distracted by the commotion of the horses behind him. The unfamiliar desert wind was frightening the animals. "Hold your ranks," he ordered. "Every man is to control his horse on pain of death!" Then he bellowed, "Q'in She Huang either freezes to death on the mountain or is slain as he comes down. His infamy dies with him and his followers this night."

A cheer rose from his men.

As it did, the sibilant voice of the court's Head Eunuch, Chesu Hoi, whispered in his ear, "There are caves, great General." Even with the swirling desert wind, the General smelled the jasmine-scented breath of the half-man. He didn't like the Eunuch to be so close to him, but he managed a smile. The First Emperor's Head Eunuch had powerful allies at court.

"Your meaning?"

"The mountain's white stone is porous."

"What?"

"The Hua Shan is riven with caves and tunnels, General. If Q'in She Huang has a proper guide he could perhaps escape through …"

"You knew of this before but —"

"I was not asked, great General. I am, as you have said so often, merely a court creature," Chesu Hoi said with a barely concealed smile.

The rebel general looked toward the mountain. The sun was setting. The cold seemed to be rising from the ground itself.

He turned in his saddle. His army was spread across the foothills, one great, living thing. With them behind him he was strength itself. China's new emperor. Then why was he filled with such misgiving? Suddenly he was off his horse and shouting orders and running — running toward the Holy Mountain.

The sharp report of snapping branches came from the thick vines that obscured the cave's mouth behind Q'in She Huang. An elderly man hacked through the vines with a short scythe. Behind him, two barefoot porters carried a large, silk-covered object on their shoulders.

The Emperor caught his Bodyguard's eye and nodded slightly. *So these are the two*, the Bodyguard thought as he stepped back and to the side.

Q'in She Huang barked at the porters, "Come forward and put down your burden." The men emerged from the darkness of the cave and then carefully leaned forward from the waist and placed the long, heavy object on the frozen ground.

The Bodyguard leapt forward and in one motion slit the porters' hamstrings. They crumpled to the ground beside their load. The desert wind plucked their cries of pain and flung them eastward, off the mountain, toward the sea.

"Make known the relic," Q'in She Huang said.

Jiang, the concubine, stepped between the two hobbled men and knelt as the First Emperor had instructed her. For a moment she allowed her fingers to luxuriate on the surface of the black silk that covered the long, curved, tubular object on the ground. She took a deep breath, then reached for a far corner with her right hand and pulled it between the second and third fingers of her left. It whispered her name as it moved — *Jiang, Jiang, Jiang* — as Q'in She Huang had so often whispered in her ear as he reached for the clouds and rain.

She pulled at the sheer blackness again and the wind snatched the silk from her hands and lifted it high in the air. And there the silk hung for a moment, like a canopy over all of this.

The First Emperor looked up. Through the black silk, he saw the last rays of the weak winter sun — the last sun rays he would ever see. His role was almost completed, destiny's portal within sight.

"When you leave here, a black trail will appear in the sky. Look for it. Follow it. It will point the way." The three Chosen stared at their Emperor, but before any of them could speak he continued, "Now, cast your eyes down."

At their feet lay a five-foot length of ivory tusk clamped at each end to a square jade stand. At its thickest, it was as big around as a young man's thigh, at its point the size of an infant's clenched fist.

"Narwhal?" asked the Confucian. Astonishment arched his voice.

"Tribute from the far north. It dwarfs the ivories we have from the beasts of Amman. This may well be the largest intact piece of ivory under the heavens. It is beyond doubt the single most powerful object in the world of men and gods." He nodded to the Bodyguard. The man yanked one of the porters to his knees then slid his swalto blade across the man's throat — the man's cry was nothing more than a liquid burble. Then the Bodyguard grabbed a handful of the dying man's hair and pulled hard. The neck wound gaped open and blood, like the falling water upriver from the great gorge, sprayed over the whiteness of the tusk. Quickly the Bodyguard repeated the process with the second porter.

Thousands of slender lines of filigree etched on the tusk's surface guided the blood toward an oblong pool at the thick end of the ivory. Every eye followed its progress. The pool bulged slightly above its lip then overflowed its lower rim in a thin, even, crimson curtain.

Beneath the blood, the surface of the narwhal ivory began to change, from something solid and opaque to something delicate and translucent. Shadows of hundreds of tiny carved figures lurked in the tusk's interior, as if ready to be born.

Then beneath the blood, a crack appeared in the ivory. And another. Then the entire surface beneath the blood curtain fell away, revealing an intricately carved world within.

"Strike a taper."

The flickering light brought to vibrant life what appeared to be hundreds of drunken Han Chinese men with unusually long pigtails and bizarrely shaven foreheads and lengthy reeds coming from their mouths. Some stood, many were lying on pallets. Servants carrying trays and small braziers dotted the tableau. But it was the drunken, pigtailed Han Chinese men that dominated the montage.

The three gasped as one.

"This is the future," the First Emperor said. "This is what I have seen and why we are here. Now, listen to me carefully. For many years to come, the Middle Kingdom will rule supreme. The kingdom will divide, then divide again. Invasions will follow and at times barbarians will sit on my throne, but we will control them — never them us. The great Sea of China will salt every river." He pointed to the scene carved within the tusk. "Until this." He paused to allow his listeners a moment to take in his words. Then, he repeated himself. "Until this." He glanced at the dancing figures. "This is the Age of White Birds on Water. It will be the beginning of the darkness. The onset of China's decline into chaos. With the arrival of the White Birds on Water your challenge begins — your families' challenge begins."

He scraped the long, yellowed nail of his baby finger along the tusk's length, from the blood-filled pool, past the unmarked middle pool, to the far end. He rubbed the surface there. "The Age of White Birds on Water begins the darkness." Then he tapped the ivory sharply and two large panels slid to the frozen ground. Behind the panels was a vista of great structures on the far side of a bend in a river. Structures in shape and design the likes of which had never been seen. Some shot straight up and then curved, others were wide at the base and then rose in two towers, while others seemed to balance magically on almost invisible pedestals. "This is the Age of the Seventy Pagodas. It signifies the end of the darkness, the rebirth." He looked at his Chosen Three. They did not meet his eye.

Q'in She Huang continued, "It is your families' responsibility, when the Age of White Birds on Water begins, to make the darkness come. There will be great resistance. There will be efforts all around you to prevent the darkness, but you must complete your task. The darkness must come or there will be no light. You must make the darkness come or a more subtle, much more dangerous darkness — a contagion — will creep upon our land, and if it does, it will never end. We will be enslaved to others, forever, and the Age of the Seventy Pagodas will never come."

The First Emperor stood and looked down at his Chosen Three. "Each of you must pass down to your succeeding generations the secret of the ivory tusk — of the compact you will enter into on this day on this Holy Mountain. Each family is to give the responsibility of carrying on the commitment to one family member only. That family member is to pass it on to another as age takes him — and so on through time. If any of them fail, then we, the Black-Haired People, will be swept away. China will be no more."

"The period of darkness will be long, but we will find our way through the darkness to the light. To a rebirth the likes of which the world has never seen. One that will dwarf even my achievements — the Age of the Seventy Pagodas."

All three of the Chosen noted that Q'in She Huang had passed by the centre of the tusk.

The First Emperor looked at them and said, "There is a middle window, but it can be opened only when the Age of White Birds on Water is upon the land. Those who experience the darkness will know how to open that portal." He shifted to watch the final rays of the final sun that he would ever see. When the last of the last rays were no more, he said, "Keep the tusk a secret from all others. It is sacred. These are either the words of a madman or a seer — that is up to you." Q'in She Huang looked back the way they had come up the mountain. "Remember that guile is your greatest weapon. People want to believe in whimsy — and madness. I let it be known that I sought the stone of eternal life. I screamed for it night after night from my bedchamber. I sent messengers to the far reaches of our kingdom to find it. I executed hundreds when they failed to bring me the stone of eternal life. I allowed the people to believe me mad to give the Carver time to complete my visions in the tusk — which I now commit to you. You are here to lead, not follow. Use your insight, endurance, and will." He took a deep, wheezing breath, then said, "Now put your hands on the Narwhal Tusk."

Each of the three did. The blood on the tusk was still thick and warm.

"And bind you one to the other — and the leaders of your

families one to the other — until the Age of the Seventy Pagodas arrives, when the rebirth will be complete."

Murmurs of assent rose in the throats of all three.

"Now take the tusk and go. The Carver will lead you down through the caves. Once you are across the river, look for the black trail in the sky to lead you."

"But Emperor ..."

"My voyage is finished. I bound this country together. I united it with canals and laws and language. Now it is yours to see that China enters the darkness so that it will one day see the light. I have been granted a glimpse of the future — it is in the tusk. Make this happen and China will be great. Fail and we will be picked apart by carrion birds, never to taste greatness again." He let out a long, heavy sigh, then said, "Now go." With that, the most powerful man the world had ever known, or very possibly would ever know, turned from his Chosen Three, removed his clothing, knelt in the cold, and awaited his death — like a great slab of rock ready to accept the first snows of winter.

And that is how the rebel general and his troops found Q'in She Huang. A naked, kneeling, frozen figure alone on the high plateau of the Holy Mountain.

Shortly, exhausted runners from the east side of the mountain reported to the General that no one had been seen coming down the mountain. The night quickly took on a tension that loosed icy tendrils of chaos into the air. A leaderless Middle Kingdom was the worst of all possible outcomes, and no one on that desolate mountaintop missed the implication that the First Emperor's Chosen Three had managed to escape.

The rebel general ordered a huge bonfire built. When the fire had pushed back the darkness, he ordered the First Emperor's body thrown on the blaze. The smell of sizzling flesh entered every nostril. It calmed the mountaintop — the First Emperor was truly gone, the new emperor in control.

The rebel general, for the first time that day, allowed himself a moment of calm. Then his teary left eye widened in horror as the First Emperor's head turned on the embers and faced him. Q'in She Huang's dead eyes held the rebel general's until flames engulfed the head in an intense blaze, seemingly of its own making.

A chill ran through the rebel general. "Cut down every tree, burn everything. Build a fire to drive away the night and obliterate for all time what happened here." His voice was thin, girlish. It infuriated him.

The Chosen Three and the Carver sat on the far bank of the river and looked east. The first rays of the cold sun announced a new day — a new, dangerous world. The Narwhal Tusk lay at their feet.

"What now?" asked the Bodyguard.

"Q'in She Huang is no more, hence ..." began the Confucian, but he stopped when he saw Jiang stand and move up the bank away from the river's edge.

For a long moment she stood completely immobile. Then she pointed west, over their heads, toward the Holy Mountain. They turned to see what had drawn her attention. And there, coming from the Hua Shan, was a dense cloud of dark smoke. As Q'in She Huang had promised, there was a black trail in the sky. It was showing the way, eastward, toward the sea and the bend in the river — to a place that would eventually be called Shanghai.

2

APPROACHING THE YANGTZE

The opium addict does not make masterpieces, he becomes one, or rather he becomes the canvas upon which the masterpiece takes place.
    — from Richard Hordoon's letter of August 6, 1837, to Thomas De Quincy

North China Sea
October, 1841

Richard Hordoon holds the pipe in both hands. Its polished cane stem, a dense black from years of use, is silken to his touch; its turned water buffalo horn mouthpiece a pleasure on his tongue; the six inches of silver inlaid with copper at the far end a magical thing in the flickering brazier light. Just past the midway point of the foot-and-a-half-long tube, in a three-inch-wide cavity, sits a turnip-shaped porcelain bowl. The bottom of the bowl is intricately patterned with a series of tiny holes, perfectly placed to convey the smoke to the smoker.

A long needle pierces then plucks a sticky ball of opium from the bronze tray and holds it over the spirit lamp. The black resin pales, softens, then sputters. The needle deposits the bubbling ball in the bowl of the pipe.

A puff, a second, a third, then the process is repeated with the next molten orb from the bronze tray, and the next — until time shimmers, then slips. Rancour crystallizes, then opens and blooms roses and hydrangeas. Richard's neck elongates and his head swivels. His mouth opens and he catches a fine tendril of the far-off scent of desert air. It swirls round and round his teeth, then plunges down his throat.

And his being turns and spirals after it, down and down as a soft wind whispers up into his face and he floats on the gentle draught from the bottom of nowhere.

And the pipe is in his hands again, a cool, sensual smoothness, a swan's neck.

"*Zhangzui*," the voice says in Mandarin. It is the wrong word. The speaker means "*xiqi*," breathe, not "*zhangzui*," which means open your mouth. But Richard knows what is meant. He opens the two large holes in the bottom of his back and draws the serpent smoke down deeper.

Wings sprout from his sides and, filling with air, the skin that joins his ribs and his arms rounds and pulls taut.

And he rises.

He is gliding up a river delta with the majesty of a four-master in full sail, riding with God's breath at his back. He recognizes the waterway. It's the Bogue, the access channel to Canton. The familiar cliffs of Linten Island approach fast. He speeds past the British bark, the *Red Rover*, and the American clipper, the *Water Witch*, at anchor, their sides teeming with pyjama-bottomed Chinamen carrying mango-wood caskets from the English ships to their native bumboats, since no *Fan Kuei* is allowed to set foot on the sacred soil of the Celestial Kingdom.

He holds up a hand — or at least in his mind he holds up a hand — and stares at his palm. For a moment he is lost in the lines of his life.

"Turn your foolish mitt, damn you," he snarls, surprised how quickly his English has taken on a cockney twist. His hand slowly turns to face the other way — and so does he. Now the *Water Witch* and the *Red Rover* are behind him, the deep, navigable passage to Canton straight ahead.

"Up!" he commands, and his palm turns skyward — and so does he.

And the smoke purrs and seeks and finds the hidden entrance within him. His death and the haunting cry of a young girl beckon him to go deeper and deeper into the opium tunnel.

"*Zhangzui!*" The wrong word again.

The smoke turns. It is suddenly angry, liquid fury. Thick leather straps slap across his chest and thighs as iron buckles cinch tight.

"Breathe!" A voice. A different voice. Not in Mandarin. Farsi this time.

"Breathe!"

This time insistent. Calling him back, back from the tunnel. From the cool depths of himself and his search.

"Breathe! Richard, we've turned north toward the bloody Yang-tze, brother mine. No more time for dreaming."

And he was there. Maxi. And it was fading — the secret access to the tunnel lost until the next time the pipe is in his hands ... and he is brave enough to search again.

The Southern Cross was just visible on the western horizon as Richard carefully stepped up onto the midship deck of the flagship of Queen Victoria's Expeditionary Force, HMS *Cornwallis*. His red-haired, white-skinned brother disappeared down a grapple line and boarded the two-man Chinese junk that waited there for him. He tied a red kerchief around his neck, waved goodbye to Richard, then loosed the junk's moorings and headed toward the British steamer *Nemesis*, a mile or so off the port side.

Richard took a deep breath, allowing the salt air to expand his lungs. *Fifteen years in China*, he thought, *and finally it is all about to really begin*. He watched Maxi's junk catch the wind and bolt shoreward, and he laughed aloud. Who would have thought it possible? Richard and Maxi Hordoon in the employ of the British

Expeditionary Force heading toward the mouth of the mighty Yangtze River! Who would believe such a story? Who would dare dream the dream that he and his brother were now living?

On board, mariners scrambled up the rigging to secure the single topgallants, the royals, and even the skysails on the three towering mainmasts. The anchor was secured to the forecastle cleats, the gantry cranes pulled on deck and tied down. As Admiral Gough emerged from the coach house and mounted the steps to the raised quarterdeck, the jib, outer jib, and flying jib were hoisted in the bow and the boat completed its turn into the wind. The men all around Richard worked with a vigour he had not seen before. They all knew that if they could make it to, then up, the Yangtze River to Nanjing there would be riches for one and all. The seamen and soldiers aboard the ships of the armada had already spent more than a year with little to show for their labours. They had seen comrades die in hideous, shrieking agony, poisoned by Chinese cooks; watched helplessly as kidnapped shipmates were executed in public squares as the Manchus led the throngs in cheers and song; stood by while hundreds died from suppurating wounds that would not heal in the tropical heat; and could do nothing as many more shat themselves to death with the dysentery or burned up with the malaria, or both. These seven hundred soldiers and mariners in the Expeditionary Force were battle hardened and disease tested. And despite the Queen's personally appointed diminutive idiot politician, Governor General Robert Pottinger, who had nominal command of the entire enterprise, they still believed in their military commander, Admiral Hugh Gough.

The mariners looked up as the sails momentarily luffed while the ship headed into the wind. Then they passed by the headwind and the sails bloated, the mighty man-o'-war heeled to starboard, and the ship headed due north toward the Yangtze. The men smiled. They were ready for a reward.

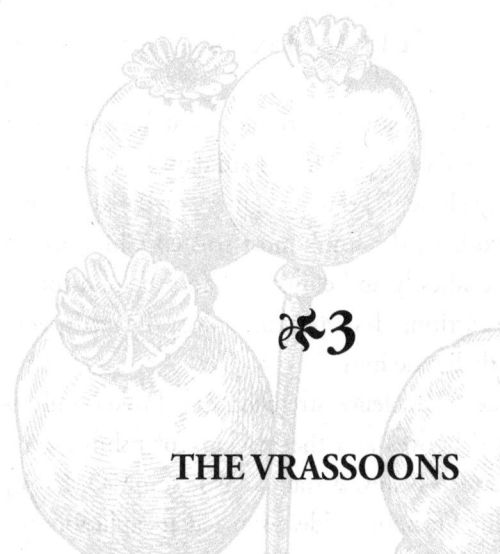

3

THE VRASSOONS

London
November, 1841

More than two thousand miles to the west, the patriarch of the powerful Vrassoon family, the Duke of Warwickshire — Eliazar Vrassoon by name — sat in his London study overlooking the Mall. He, too, was thinking about rewards. "Just rewards for very hard work" is the way he would have put it, had he been inclined to speak his mind aloud — but he wasn't so inclined, and had never been.

Runners were constantly in and out of the enormous outer office carrying messages from the far-flung ends of his vast mercantile empire. But it was one specific message that he awaited.

The eldest of his four sons, Ari, an elegant, perfumed man in his late twenties, entered and assumed his position over his father's left shoulder, his embossed notepad in his immaculately manicured hand. He hoped that this business could be completed quickly, as his man had informed him that a certain young — very young

— beauty awaited his pleasure in the room above the Southwark Inn. Just another kind of reward for a hard day's labour. Ari wanted to smile but wisely chose to keep his lightly powdered face neutral.

Two older workers, the firm's most trusted China hands, slid into the office soundlessly and closed the door behind them. One took his place at a writing desk, pen and ink at the ready, while the other stood silently beside him.

No one spoke. The silence stretched out, broken only by the *clop-clop* of horses' hooves and the hawking of fishmongers from the cobblestone streets below. A train whistle sounded sharply, and for just a moment Vrassoon's eldest son felt inexplicably weak in the knees.

The Vrassoon Patriarch sat with his fingers steepled in front of his face. They all waited. They had all waited many times before for Eliazar Vrassoon to speak. Finally he unsteepled his fingers and scraped the long fingernails of his right hand across his freckled scalp beneath his thinning grey hair. He remembered the glory days in Baghdad, riding with his father to one side of the Grand Vizier — the power around, behind, and through the throne. Then had come the expulsion. Of course, they had known it was going to happen and had already transferred their assets to London and Paris and, most importantly, to Calcutta. *To Calcutta*, he thought wistfully. "Calcutta before ..." he said aloud. He said the word "before" a second time — as if it were a time very, very long ago. Then he cast aside the thought, because now China loomed on the horizon. *The mother of all jewels*, he thought, lapsing into the purple prose of his native Farsi.

It was getting late and Eliazar needed to see the mad girl shortly, as he did at this hour every day since he had taken the baby from her. He owed her at least that — although the meeting always distressed him, and Bedlam was so far away.

He turned to Ari and signalled him to approach. The younger man did and leant down to his father.

"How long after the treaty is signed will the land auction take place?" Eliazar asked.

"There is the hope that it will happen shortly after the conflict ends, whenever that may be. In the early spring, perhaps, but it is hard to know how much resistance the Manchu Emperor will mount. The details of several prospective dates are being finalized by the Foreign Office."

"By *our* people in the Foreign Office?"

"Naturally, father."

"And how long after that to extraterritoriality?"

The younger Vrassoon hesitated.

The Vrassoon Patriarch shook his head. Not for the first time, he wondered if his first-born was strong enough to hold together all that he had wrought. He doubted it. Fortunately, his youngest seemed made of sterner stuff. The Patriarch looked to the elder of the two China hands. "Cyril, your thoughts."

"At first it all seemed so simple, sir. The Chinese took to opium ships in their harbours the way the Scots would take to a freighter loaded down with Glenlivet sailing up the Firth of Forth."

If this was intended as a joke, no one laughed. Finally the Vrassoon Patriarch said, "And now?"

"Now, not so simple, sir."

"Why should it be simple, Cyril? You have been in my employ for almost twenty years. When did we last make an important decision that was not complicated?"

"Granted, sir. But the Chinese are different from the Mesopotamians or the Hindus. They are arrogant. They actually believe that they are winning the war."

The Vrassoon Patriarch thought about that for a moment. He glanced at his watch fob. The mad girl would be waiting for him. "Nothing stops demand, Cyril. If a product is wanted — desired, yearned for — there is no force on earth able to stem the tide." He thought, *The sale of dreams is unstoppable*, and nodded. Then he said, "If governments would only learn that lesson, the world would be an easier place — and more peaceful. Legalize it and tax it and we all win."

"Agreed, sir. But the Chinese do not accept that their populace both does, and will always, demand vast quantities of our opium."

"Fools! Do they believe they can change human nature? That they are gods on earth?"

"Perhaps, sir, perhaps they believe that. More likely they are just practical. They are willing to engage in lengthy wars and to lose in the present in order to win in the future. Their entire history supports that kind of thinking, sir. They have, in fact, been ruled by Manchus, who are not Chinese at all, for over two hundred years. But the Chinese culture long ago seduced the Manchus, who are now more Chinese in many respects than the Han Chinese."

"Then surely these foreign authorities can be undermined."

"Absolutely. For a decade, over a decade, we have all but openly traded our opium at Canton. More recently we have managed to move past the silliness of anchoring off Linten Island and having the Chinese skiffs come out and off-load our product — but, despite all our years of trading and our contacts, we have not moved very far past that. With the exception of the three hundred acres the Manchu authorities assigned to foreigners in the marshes south of the city upon which we have warehouse space — as do the Americans, Scottish, British, and even those damnable Hordoons — it remains an offence punishable by death for any non-Chinese to set foot on Chinese soil. The Mandarins, although they take our bribes, have always resisted our request for real land in the Celestial Kingdom."

"I've warned you not to use that phrase!" The Patriarch's voice was hard. "There is only one Celestial Kingdom and it is not on this earth."

Silence again seeped into the room. The stern religious views of Eliazar Vrassoon were well known and forced upon everyone who worked for the massive, octopus-like company, even to the farthest reaches of the Vrassoon empire.

"Sorry, sir."

"This company has fed you and yours and made you wealthy. It can just as easily impoverish you and yours. Is that clear?"

There was a moment of real shock in the room. The Patriarch did not issue idle threats.

"I want to know when extraterritoriality will be realized."

"Father," his son began, "we haven't even forced a treaty from the Manchu Emperor yet."

"A foregone conclusion," his father snapped. "If Britain can rule the hordes of India, they can force land concessions from these Buddhist heathens."

The son heard the edge of panic in his father's voice. How much of the company's fortune had his father committed to the British expedition that was heading toward Nanjing? Even he didn't know the details of that. He had, in the past, watched in horror as his father endangered the entire wealth of the company, first by a dangerous stock offering and then by vast expenditures in Calcutta. But both had proved, in the long run, to be brilliant business decisions. *Why then am I so concerned about this Chinese venture?* the young man asked himself. And the answer flooded into his mind: because of the Chinese — because of their arrogance, because of their vast numbers, and because there was something else at play here that neither he nor any other person here understood.

A furious knocking at the door sounded loudly in the room.

"In!" the Vrassoon Patriarch shouted.

A dust-covered man, still stinking of horses, held out a fingerprint-stained envelope, then left the room. The Patriarch grabbed it and turned toward the window. The London haze was lifting; for the first time in weeks there was an inkling that the sun might pierce through the fetid air. Eliazar Vrassoon flicked open the seal, read the progress report quickly, and turned to the others.

"Assuming they've kept the same pace reported in this document, our boats should be approaching the Yangtze River even as we speak."

"Our boats, father?" Ari asked.

"The British Expeditionary Force — *our* boats."

4

MAXI

North China Sea
Mid November, 1841

The grease-covered man swore viciously as blood shot from the gash on his hand and splatted against the exposed pistons of the steam engine. His cussing startled the English mariners in charge of the boiler room and engine, not because they were unused to foul language, but because the angry expletives were in a polyglot of Farsi, Hindi, Cockney English, and a language none could identify — Yiddish.

The man's extraordinary linguistic tirade finally ended with a triple denunciation of the female genitalia, all in Farsi, preceded by a very common English verb used in its all-too-common gerundial form. Then the man took the red kerchief from his neck, swiped the blood from his hand across his grease-smeared shirt, and said, "Start her up, gents. See if my blood larded her enough."

Moments later the damnable engine turned over and HMS *Nemesis*, for the first time in a day and a half, began to move. The men gave a cheer for the odd, red-haired Baghdadi Jew whom they knew only by his Christian name, Maxi.

Maxi Hordoon smiled, his large white teeth seeming even whiter in his grease-smeared face. He gave the engine a little kick with his boot and headed for the deck. Under his breath he said, "Fuckin' steamboats almost did us in, they did."

And they had. Years earlier, in a desperate move to increase their opium sales to northern China, Richard, over Maxi's objections, had leased two sidewheeler steamers.

"They're garbage, brother mine," Maxi had said.

"But they can make three round trips from Canton to northern China before the weather sets in," Richard had claimed, "as opposed to the two that's the maximum for even the fastest clipper. Come on, Maxi, think what we could do with fifty percent more profit each year. Fifty percent more, Maxi!"

Despite his reservations and his well-earned fear of monsoon season at sea, Maxi said, "Let me at least take a look at these new mechanical marvels before you throw our money away."

Maxi examined the two sidewheelers, and although they were better than the ones constructed by Miller and Symington, they weren't as secure as Henry Bell's version, called the Comet. Maxi spent almost a week with the boiler men, concerned about the transfer of steam to the pistons. Then he questioned the use of sea water in the boilers but was assured that as long as the boilers were cleaned after each trip the salt residue wouldn't hurt the mechanism. He nodded but wasn't thrilled.

In the end, Richard leased two of the steamships from their agent in Hong Kong, Barclays Bank of London.

Things went well at first, but the turnaround time after each leg of the trip was just barely enough to give the boilers a cursory cleaning, so that the last leg of the third trip took longer — a lot longer than expected. Less than a day's steaming from the Bogue entrance to Canton, the monsoon caught up with them.

Maxi did his best to get more speed from the engine but the salt residue buildup in the boiler proved too much. They just couldn't outrun the storm. It fell on them with a fury that felt personal. The tilt of the boat in the mountainous waves pulled the paddlewheel out of the water over and over again. Then the sea snapped open the hatches and quickly swamped them. Maxi could still feel the swirling water rising around him as he tried to restart the engine of the lead ship. But the water had gotten into the piston shafts and the boiler fires had been snuffed out by the cold sea water.

Maxi was the last to leave the ship. He had actually considered going down with it, then thought better of it. "God'd laugh if I died in this piece of crap," he said as he dove off the sinking vessel.

He and Richard lost not only the two steamships, but also all the silk, silver, and tea they'd accepted as payment for their opium. It almost ended them. The other trading houses circled round them like vultures waiting for a gutted soldier to finally die. But Richard held out, dodging one creditor after another, begging space on one ship and securing it with supposed goods from another. Richard kept them alive. He was smart and shrewd and the Hordoon brothers made it to the next trading season, although they still owed Barclays Bank for both of the steamships.

Maxi would never forget when Vrassoon's man approached them and, with a smile, offered them work at a shilling on the pound. Richard had to hold Maxi back. Maxi wanted to pull the man's head off and cut him into little pieces.

"Liver of blaspheming Jew," Richard said.

"Wha'?"

"Just a quote, Maxi."

Maxi thought about asking where the quote came from but decided instead to say, "You read too much, brother mine. You ought to take care about that. Too much of that reading and yer dick'll fall off, and imagine what our local chefs would make outta that."

Richard laughed. Maxi smiled.

He smiled again now as he watched the Chinese coastline slip past, and wondered at his life. Who would ever have believed that he, Maxi Hordoon, would be standing, legs apart, hands on hips, on the foredeck of the steamer HMS *Nemesis* of the British Expeditionary Force — as it made its way to the mouth of the mighty Yangtze River?

5

THE MASTER CARVER

At the Bend in the River
Late November, 1841

The village of Shanghai's noonday sun streamed through the slatted shutters of his workshop as the Master Carver limped in. Three journeymen carvers were working on different large chunks of third-quality jade, held in place by wooden vises. The sounds of their cutting and smoothing tools produced a gentle whistle in the air. Since he was a boy, the Master Carver had always loved that sound.

Near the south-facing, open window, his older son was completing a large, complex piece carved from the interior of a bull elephant tusk. It had taken him almost five years and now it was nearing completion. The Master Carver put both of his aged hands on the sculpted ivory top of his cane and leaned forward to view the work, and encourage his son. Although it was clear to him that this son did not really have the true carver's gift, fortunately his younger boy did.

The Master Carver hobbled to the very back of the shop to watch his gifted son learning the art of painting intricate country scenes on the interior of small, narrow-necked, glass bottles. Not only did he have to manipulate the extremely slender paintbrushes with great care, he also had to paint upside down. The Master Carver remembered his own struggles with this art. The young man looked up from his labours and grinned at his father. The boy was alive with delight. It lit up every angle of his sharply defined facial features. The Master Carver put a hand gently on his son's forehead and smiled. He would tell this one of the Narwhal Tusk soon. But not now.

The Master Carver left the workshop. From the other side of the high wall, he heard the chatter from the open-air hot-water shop and the distant song of the dumpling hawkers. For a moment he thought of leaving the family compound and calling over one of the street vendors, who would cook up a dumpling-and-soup meal right there for him. But he decided against it and made his way past the storage shed toward the compound's bamboo stand. Pushing his way through the dense front row of canes, he stepped into an open, grassy glade. To one side was a sheer wall of rock covered with vines. He pulled back the dense vegetation and descended the steep concealed stairway there.

At the bottom of the stairway, he used his hands to guide him along a long corridor that was cut from the rock itself. Twice he hit his head on outcroppings from above, but he did not dare light a taper. Finally the passage took a sharp turn to the right, and then a long, gentle curve to the left, and opened to a wide, tall space.

He pressed down on his cane, stood up to his full height, and lit the torch affixed to the wall. The large, beautifully crafted mahogany box, sitting on its stone stand in the centre of the chamber, seemed to draw the light.

The Master Carver took a deep breath of the mineral-rich air and thought, *First the* Fan Kuei *ships sail up our coast, then they dare enter the great river. Maybe now is the time.*

As he slowly walked the perimeter of the almost perfectly circular chamber, he forced his mind — as he had been taught by his father and he would shortly have to teach his younger son — to review the recent history. When the Round-Eyed barbarians had begun to arrive in the south down by Canton, almost four generations ago, some of the Chosen's descendants had believed it was the time of White Birds on Water. But the Master Carver of that time had rejected this conclusion. Although the arrival of the British and their ludicrous desire to trade trinkets was a new reality in the Manchu-ruled Middle Kingdom, it was not the appointed time.

The Long Noses had tried to trade with the Middle Kingdom for many years thereafter but had always been rebuffed. What did these intensely ugly men have to offer China? Their goods were inferior to those readily available throughout the Middle Kingdom. Their manners were appalling, few spoke even the rudiments of the Common Speech, and none could read.

After years and years of their threats, they had finally been allowed to anchor their ships in a remote section of Canton Harbour. Eventually, they were given the right to trade through the good offices of the Hong merchants, who represented the Manchu government. The Hong merchants robbed the fools blind, demanding high tariffs on all traded goods and outrageous fees for the use of warehouse space that they seldom supplied. Bribes made many of the Hong merchants wealthy men. And all this was done with Beijing's blessing, as a healthy percentage of the money the Hong merchants collected made its way up the Grand Canal to Beijing's coffers — the very canal designed by Q'in She Huang, the First Emperor.

"Q'in She Huang." The words slipped from the Master Carver's lips. His words echoed and re-echoed off the rock faces, multiplying and then arranging themselves into sediments of sound. The resonance lifted the Carver's spirits, just as it had, two thousand years before, lifted the spirits of the first Carver who hollowed out this sacred place from the solid rock.

The Carver flipped open the first latch of the mahogany box on the stone pedestal. It made a report like a firecracker in the underground space. He paused and thought back again. The Long Noses were restricted to less than half a square mile in the marsh of Canton Harbour. The only nuisances were the Europeans' Black Robes, who slipped past the guards and peddled their childish version of salvation, which they had evidently found in an old desert book, to the peasants. At first the Manchus had hunted them down, but eventually they were left alone, seen as nothing more than another Round-Eye folly. The locals found them entertaining. The Taoist monks kept them away from any serious centres of population.

The Long Noses wanted to buy silk and tea — but they had nothing to trade but poorly manufactured goods and shoddy cotton garments that even a merchant would not have allowed his servant to wear.

Then came a lethal mixture: Indian-made/British-imported opium and Chinese curiosity.

Finally, the Long Noses had something to trade for silk and tea.

The Carver flipped the second latch and opened the case. The Narwhal Tusk, now deeply yellowed with age, nestled on its plush purple silk pad. Perhaps his talented son would be the one who would have to make a replica of the Tusk. Hopefully he would be up to the task.

The Carver leaned down and looked in the first of the three windows in the Tusk: hundreds of Han Chinese men with shaved foreheads and pigtails seemingly dancing with long reeds in their mouths. "What must have seemed fanciful back then is common now," he said aloud to the empty space.

The arrival of the pale foreigner's opium did not begin the Age of White Birds on Water, although it was surely the precursor of change. The Master Carver of that time had indeed readied himself. But although there was noted change in some of the Middle Kingdom, there was no real change here. Not at the bend in the river, where the black cloud in the sky had led the first Carver. There had even been sightings of a very young, violent, teary-eyed general from Beijing. But not here — not in the agricultural backwater where they had been told — no, *promised* — that the rebirth would happen.

Everyone in the Middle Kingdom felt the creep of the darkness that had begun some three or four generations before.

But Q'in She Huang's order was to allow the darkness in. To foster it. Just as only the brutality of winter cleanses the earth for the spring's planting, so the darkness would have to deepen to permit the arrival of the light.

And the darkness was surely intensifying. The Confucian, who was the nominal proconsul for the district, had lost one of his sons to the drug, and his beloved wife was so addicted that she once sold herself to a cotton merchant to get the money she needed for her daily pipes. The Confucian, no doubt, thought that the predicted darkness had already arrived.

But it was not the Age of White Birds on Water. Not yet. *There is no darkness here*, the Master Carver thought, *but the time approaches*.

The Master Carver allowed his fingers to trace the supple firmness of the ivory, lingering on the centre section for just a moment. Only in ivory could such carving exist. Only its malleable density, its exquisite solidity could permit such work. And narwhal was the purest form of ivory in the world — and so very hard to find. Almost thirty years ago he had secured a tusk and stored it away carefully should it ever be needed to produce a replica. Now he wondered if it would.

Q'in She Huang's vision in the Tusk had last been seen by the Chosen Three over seventy years ago, when the first Round Eye had ventured into the hamlet. His black robe and raving made him a source of laughter for most of the village's residents, but not for the descendants of those who were bound by the Ivory Compact.

Even as this Jesuit was making a grotesque mockery of the

Common Tongue, to the delight of the hamlet's children, the three sought out the Carver and viewed again the "life within" — the vibrant tableau of figures beneath the filigree inscription: *The Age of White Birds on Water*.

But that was so long ago that once again — as the Carver had hoped — the very existence of the Tusk had fallen first into dispute, then into open ridicule. Secrets were best thought to be nothing but whimsy.

I feel it is near, the Carver thought, *and will shortly be upon us. The darkness and pain will begin. We must endure this. The three descendants of the Chosen must force this darkness on the people, if the rebirth is ever to come to pass.*

The Carver took a deep breath, then closed the box and snapped the latches shut. He was tempted to take the Tusk out of its box a second time and stare at the future, but he resisted temptation and walked back into the corridor. There, deep in a crack in the rock, was a large statue. The Carver put the torch in front of it and knelt in prayer — prayer to the man who had first enlisted his ancestor to carve Q'in She Huang's vision in the Tusk and then had protected his ancestors from the wrath of the teary-eyed rebel general — Q'in She Huang's Head Eunuch, Chesu Hoi.

Shanghai was little more than a large trading village at the Bend in the River in 1841. It would soon change — for the worse.

NEAR THE BEND IN THE RIVER

The Yangtze River
December, 1841

The great swaths of white sails draped on the sides of the British man-o'-war, HMS *Cornwallis*, rippled in the breeze with the dawning light. With the rising sun at its back, the expanse of white canvas provided a degree of camouflage for the great fighting vessel — and those that followed. After narrowly avoiding a confrontation near Woosung at the mouth of the Yangtze, the British had taken precautions. They had finally realized the significance of entering a main artery that could lead directly to the heart of China.

The wind picked up and the halyards snapped to. Overhead the mizzen-mast's sails caught the wind first and swelled. They were quickly followed by the fore-course, topsail, and topgallant and the great ship heeled hard to port, its miles of hemp rope drawn taut, its block-and-tackle systems straining to keep control as its starboard canvas and flying jibs flapped wildly.

All eyes on the ship were trained on the water ahead. All but those belonging to Richard Hordoon, the Expeditionary Force's translator. His eyes were locked on the text of a letter from the famous English opium eater Thomas De Quincy. He read the great man's beautifully penned words several times, folded the letter, and placed it carefully in his personal journal. Then he strode to the port rail on the quarterdeck, stared ahead at the approaching bend in the river, and smiled. The wide arc of the mighty Yangtze, as it swung past the mouth of the Huangpu River, was the best natural harbour Richard had ever seen.

A two-man Chinese junk came about and nestled into the side of the ship. Maxi, his face and bare arms covered in engine room grease, pulled himself up, hand over hand, on the rope hung from the quarterdeck, spotted his brother Richard, flung his arms open, and called out, "Mission accomplished! The damned engine works as well as a Baghdadi farts."

Richard shook his head and signalled his brother to follow him astern.

Maxi's antics drew sidelong looks from several mariners and a few of the officers. Two of the senior midshipmen stepped forward, but Maxi turned to them and challenged them in Yiddish, "Something to say to me, gentlemen?"

The midshipmen muttered something about decorum but the red-haired Jew ignored them. Although the British didn't like Maxi, they needed him. Not just because he was a genius in a boiler room — and the new steamships were proving temperamental in China's tropical heat — but also because he led the expedition's irregulars — a fighting unit that in a hundred years would be called guerilla fighters. The British army had learned much since its disgraceful defeat by the Americans in 1776 and the ensuing stalemate in 1812. Its leaders understood that fighting in formation was still a powerful battlefield tactic, but the regimental stand, shoot, kneel, and reload approach to warfare needed to be supported by advance attack teams that had to be local. Since the British didn't trust the Chinese, let alone the Manchus, the next best thing was this noisome Mesopotamian Jew and his band of opium traders — the irregulars.

Maxi's men always preceded the Expeditionary Force on the battlefield. Sometimes they scouted; more often they tested enemy defences and emplacements and reported back to Admiral Gough. Sometimes they didn't bother reporting back. They took some casualties but not many. Maxi knew his men. He even knew some of their children. They all worked for the Hordoon trading company out of Canton. These men were the "unwanted," not good enough for the classier opium traders, like the Dents, the Jardine, Mathesons, the Oliphants, and the damnable Vrassoons. These men owed their very existence to the ingenuity of the Hordoon brothers, and they knew it. They understood Maxi and thought of him as one of them — an outcast. He never recklessly endangered their lives, and yet he never shied away from a legitimate fight. He knew how to lead, and they followed.

Maxi caught up to his older brother near the stern of the quarterdeck just past the gig, the captain's personal boat, which sat on iron deck crutches, its suspension launch wires looped like coiled snakes on a pair of side bollards. Over Richard's shoulder he saw Admiral Gough on the command deck, a full seven storeys above the orlop deck where Maxi and his men were billeted.

Richard was leaning against a deck winch, with one foot on a brass capstan. He stared at the shoreline.

"What do you see, brother mine?"

"Eyes, Maxi. Eyes watching."

"The Chinamen always watch, Richard, so what's so different now?"

These eyes are expecting us, Richard wanted to say, but he stepped away from his brother. Some thoughts were too dangerous, even for family. Family. He allowed himself the luxury of thinking about his twin boys in Malaya, already so strong and wiry at three. They were evidently a handful for their *amah*. Them so strong, and at the end their mother so weak. An image of his wife's final gasps for life in the birthing room came to him, as it did so often.

"Boys, Sarah, two boys," he'd said. But her eyes were wild with fear and pain. She'd grabbed him by the hand and yanked him down to her, then spat out, "Why? What have you done, Richard? What have you done?" He'd pulled his arm free, and her fingernails had left four crimson lines on his forearm. He tried to calm her, "Sarah, please ..." but she'd shrieked back at him, "Tell me, what have you done?" She'd died in the bed, but her pain-contorted face and her terrified question — "What have you done?" — lived on in Richard's head.

Like so many other questions, he thought.

"Do you think they'll fight, or will it be more of that marching up and down *mishagas*?"

"What...?"

"Will the Chinese fight this time or just do that parading nonsense?" Maxi repeated.

Richard remembered the expedition's very first encounter with Chinese warriors and smiled. The extraordinary pre-battle theatrics of the enemy had taken them all by surprise. The Chinese appeared that morning on the battlefield wearing elaborate Chinkiang silks and then proceeded to parade up and down and slap each other on the back as a few of the soldiers pantomimed acts of supposed ferocity. It seemed that the Chinese believed that all they had to do to win a battle was to behave as if they were already victorious. Evidently they felt that the actual details of the fighting were beneath their concern, so they left them to the imagination of their enemy. Why bother with the fine points if you have already won the engagement? Their display lasted for almost ninety minutes.

When, apparently much to the surprise of the Chinese, the British didn't turn tail and run, the Celestials began the second act of their little war drama. Soldiers wielding ancient swords and shouting strange cries and various terms of opprobrium moved forward and performed somersaults and other acrobatic feats — all from a distance, but well within firing range of the fully arrayed forces of the British Expeditionary Force.

Maxi, as the leader of the irregulars, was closer to the show than the army itself and was shocked when he heard shots — six of them — whistle over his head. Instantly the closest acrobat-warrior paused in the air, mid-somersault, and as if someone had cut his strings, crashed to the ground, his ancient sword beneath his body. And lay very, very still. Maxi sprang to his feet to see which of his men had fired, disobeying his orders, and was astounded to see the Queen's man, the diminutive Pottinger, jumping up and down in celebration thirty yards behind him.

"Bagged him. Bagged him like a partridge, I did." The man's upper-class lisp seemed to saw through the heavy air.

Then everything moved quickly. The Manchus' bannered troops raced forward and the battle was joined. But the Chinese weaponry was not up to the task. Many men carried only rattan shields with painted heads of devils or wild animals on them for protection. Some wore tiger-head caps. Neither were any match for a bullet manufactured in Manchester or Leeds. The Chinese had no artillery worthy of the name. Their muskets were of the antique matchlock design and were as likely to send the small-calibre shot backward as forward. Cromwell had used better weapons when he'd forced the King from his throne two hundred years earlier. And although it was the Chinese who had invented gunpowder, they hadn't perfected it. Twice Maxi had set full kegs of Chinese gunpowder alight only to find the damage done was less than what two of his rifle men could have inflicted in five minutes.

After an initial successful foray, Maxi had moved his irregulars to one side. He had real appetite for a fight but none for a slaughter.

"They will fight the way they fight, Maxi. Nothing more," Richard said at last.

"Won't they fight to protect their homes?" "Why should they?

Invaders have come before — shite, Tartars rule them now — but China remains as Chinese as ever, and I think it always will. Eventually the Middle Kingdom opens its legs and simply takes us in."

Maxi wanted to pursue this but Richard turned away, thinking, *Fifteen years, fifteen years to get here.* During that time he had had more direct dealings with common Chinamen than any other foreigner. He spoke their languages better than any non-Chinese except the accursed Jesuits, who were now *persona non grata* in the Middle Kingdom and he and Maxi had ventured up the coast well before the others. A fact that made them no friends in the world of the English, Scottish and American opium traders in Canton.

The first time he'd set foot in Shanghai, Richard had known it was the key to everything for which he had worked. He had performed a full kowtow before the purple-robed chief government official, the Mandarin — the *Ch'in-ch'ai* — and then invited him onboard his ship. The man had declined his offer but was clearly interested in the Foreign Devil who spoke the Common Tongue. Through the Mandarin, Richard met Chen and things had begun — things, plans. For the next two years he'd devoted himself to learning their complex dialect. Even with his tremendous facility for languages, he had found it hard going — but rewarding. And he had kept the glorious harbour at the Bend in the River at the centre of his plans. And now they were here.

"Say that thing about spreading the legs again, brother mine. It's a nice change to hear you talk of such things," Maxi said showing off his large white teeth.

"They'll put up a show. But they don't think they need to defend themselves against barbarians like us. We'll win the battle and get what we think we want. But ultimately we'll do their bidding. It has always been thus here."

"You're a God-eating philosopher, brother."

And you're enjoying all this too much, Richard wanted to say, but he held his tongue. He would need his brother's fury if he were to break free of the detestable House of Vrassoon and trade in the China smoke on his own terms up here in Shanghai. For he had no doubt that once the port was open, once the fighting was done, the mongrel Vrassoons would be there with their self-serving rules and their political friends in London, their damnable monopoly on direct trade from England to China, and their base of power in India. Their cohorts in crime, the Kadooris, might even follow them, using their monopoly on rubber in Siam to wedge their way into the new market — and no doubt this *was* the new market. Not the old Canton routes that were littered with outstretched palms at every turn demanding squeeze. No. Now that the British navy had been lured into war there would be new treaty ports. And these new treaty ports, especially Shanghai, would offer real access to the interior — and the north of China, the heart of the Celestial Kingdom.

He sighed. *Patience*, he thought. *Patience*. It had taken him a decade and a half to get here; a few more years meant nothing. Soon he'd have a foothold, and his twin boys would join him, just up ahead, at the Bend in the River.

7

WHITE BIRDS ON WATER

The Village of Shanghai
December, 1841

The Bodyguard

"It hurts, Papa."

"Don't touch it and it will heal more quickly."

"But it hurts."

Despite himself, the Bodyguard said softly, "Yes, it does." He smiled at his ungainly son. The boy, if left alone, would spend all his time with their baby cormorants. He refused to hunt, reluctantly fished, and only went through the motions of his fighting lessons so he could return to the birds. Often the Bodyguard found the boy in the birds' coop singing to the young chicks. He would have slept with the birds if his father had permitted it. The boy's gentleness won the birds' hearts — and grudgingly his father's as well.

"Ouch!" the boy said as he picked at the scab.

"Leave it alone and allow it to heal."

"But it hurts."

"And it will for the rest of your life."

"For the rest of my life?"

The boy's shocked expression made the Bodyguard laugh out loud. "Come," he said. He held out his left hand. The tattooed cobra on the back of his hand stood out even more starkly than usual in the rising sun.

The Bodyguard's son made his way carefully to the stern of the rocking boat where his father sat, the handle of the wedge-shaped piece of carved wood that acted as both a paddle and a rudder held securely in his other hand. The boy knew better than to ask his father to leave his position of control of the boat while their birds were still underwater fishing.

"Why do I have to have this?" the boy said, pointing at the tattoo.

"Because you are the eldest."

"But what if I don't want it?"

The Bodyguard remembered a similar conversation he had had with his own father almost twenty-five years before. At the time, he had taken some solace when his father said, "It may mean nothing. It hasn't meant anything for more years than anyone can count. It will have meaning only when the White Birds on Water approach."

He reached over and patted his son's cheek, feeling the velvet softness of his skin.

The boy, for a moment, enjoyed his father's touch, then moved his head away from the calloused, rough palm. "It's not funny, Papa, it hurts."

"I know it does, son. Once we call back our cormorants, put your hand in the water. It's cold enough to help."

"Is mine going to be a cobra like yours?"

"Yes, once the scab comes off."

"What does it mean, Papa?"

He was about to repeat what his father had said to him, then stopped himself. The signs were everywhere. The first of the White traders had arrived at the Bend in the River on the very day of his grandfather's birth. Since then, there had been English and Portuguese traders who had anchored offshore from time to time, but none brave enough to break the Manchu law against setting foot on the sacred soil of the Celestial Kingdom. Thanks to the traders, there was now opium to be had in the village. Not much, but some. Through darkened windows, pigtailed Chinese men with shaven foreheads could be seen sucking on long bamboo reeds. The arrival of the raving Black Robe with his stupid book fifteen years ago had raised more alarms — perhaps a further sign. Now there were two of them in the village — but they were not White Birds on Water. Three years ago, Commissioner Lin's men had actually boarded an English trading ship in Canton Harbour and thrown twenty thousand opium caskets into the sea. Afterward, Commissioner Lin had organized formal prayers begging the water's forgiveness for polluting it. The tale was told as a show of Chinese power, but the Bodyguard thought of it as just another sign of the approaching darkness.

The eldest cormorant broke the water's surface not four feet from the boat. The Bodyguard slapped the gunwales twice and the bird approached. Reaching over the side, he carefully plucked his old friend from the cold waters of the Yangtze.

As he put the bird on the plank in front of him he noticed the lack of new moult and the frayed tail feathers. He reached out and touched the metal ring around the base of the bird's neck that stopped the cormorant from swallowing his catch. Then he smoothed down the bird's neck feathers and applied a gentle pressure just above the neck ring. Two wriggling, plump fish burped up the bird's neck, out of his mouth, and onto the bottom of the wooden boat.

The boy quickly picked up the fish and packed them into the reed basket at his side.

The Bodyguard looked from the old bird to his young son — one ending, another just beginning.

He had sculled his slender carrack out farther than usual, past where the Huangpu River emptied into the mighty Yangtze. The current here was strong and the water cold. Good for fishing at this time of year, but treacherous. The light was growing all around them. He had no desire to be caught in the open water when the sun was fully awakened.

He reached into the water and slapped the side of the boat three times, hard. Quickly, his four remaining birds made their way to the boat. He pulled on the rudder and turned the boat so that the side with the birds was away from the Yangtze and toward the much calmer Huangpu. "Come, help me," he told his son. "It's time to bring breakfast home for your mother and brother." He reached into the water and plucked out one young cormorant, then a second. "Pinch out the fish and put them in the basket." He didn't at first notice that his son hadn't responded. He quickly lifted the last two birds from the cold Yangtze water then turned to the boy, who was standing on the boat's single plank seat with his hand over his eyes, looking toward the rising sun.

"Help me, boy."

"Papa, what are those?"

His eyes followed his son's outstretched hand and there, coming out of the rising sun, just taking the large bend of the mighty Yangtze, were four massive ships in full sail — their decks and sides draped with white canvas.

These were not the trading ships he had seen before. These were warships heading up river toward Nanjing. But it wasn't even that which so concerned the Bodyguard. He drew his son close to him and held him tight as their boat rocked in the wash from the four great fighting ships.

"What is it, Papa? Why are you afraid?"

"I'm not afraid, son," he said, although he felt the blood rush into the cobra tattooed on his hand and the one he had never shown his son, that was etched in scar tissue on his back. *So it has begun*, he thought. *All the stories from my father and grandfather of the Narwhal Tusk and a task for our family. Finally, the day has come.* He instinctively rubbed the tattooed cobra and stretched his fingers. Then he thought of his younger brother's son and made a tight fist. The cobra's hood opened as the blood gushed into the veins on the back of his hand — and made the scar tissue on his back turn a flaming red. The cobras were gorged and ready to strike, to choose which of the boys was strong enough to carry the family's responsibility, carved into the surface of the Narwhal Tusk.

"Sit by me, son. Your test is approaching. It is time for me to explain the tattoo on the back of your hand."

The Confucian

He saw them first reflected in his great-grandfather's ebony writing stone, which he had mounted on the wall of his study. The white image glided across the darkness of the stone.

He carefully allowed the ink from his brush to return to the well on his desk then powdered the document he had just finished. He waited for the ink to set then shook off the powder. It sifted to the polished hardwood floor. He rolled the rice paper and sealed it with a wax imprimatur from his ring — the etching of a scholar sitting beneath a tree — then placed it atop a small pile of other scrolls. Few of the candidates would be admitted to the civil service from this lot, he thought. Over the years he had noticed a marked decline in qualified candidates. It had worried him, but looking up at the white reflections moving across the darkness of the ebony writing stone, it occurred to him that his worry was severely misplaced.

He took a deep breath and turned away from the reflection and walked out onto the balcony that overlooked the north reach of the Yangtze.

The glistening of a crane's expansive wings in the first rays of the rising sun drew his eye. He watched as it gracefully descended to the point where the great river made its final turn toward the sea. Shortly, the bird melted into a tiny black dot on the horizon. He leaned against the hardwood railing and smelled the incoming ocean — and waited.

Something came around the bend in the river. Everything shifted. And there they were, four great men-o'-war, four masts apiece, in full sail. Four white birds on water — and he knew they would not be the last. Without thinking, he fell back into the patterns that his grandfather had written of in the ancient journal. *"Do not be fooled by the exterior of a thing but do not ignore it either. See the thing — breathe in the thing — then sense its vital essence. Speak that essence aloud to understand what you have seen. Then write in the book what you have spoken."*

He spoke. His voice was strong and carried on the morning wind. "Ships, within whose cannons is the explosive stuff of change."

"So it has begun at last — the prophecy, the Ivory Compact, is finally in motion. The Age of White Birds on Water is upon us." He took his brush and made an entry in the secret journal that had been passed down to him by the previous Confucians of the Ivory Compact.

The cries of birds drew his eyes from his writing. Below him, in the hundreds of flooded rice paddies that separated him from the river, peasants were attaching long reeds to the feet of hundreds of tiny starlings. The birds screamed in protest. On a signal, the starlings would all be released to fly skyward with their reeds clattering beneath them, in order to frighten away devils that could hurt the tender newly planted rice plants.

The Confucian wanted to laugh. *There are more serious devils approaching than those that would destroy your rice*, he thought. "And these devils will not be frightened away by the silly clatter of reeds beneath tiny birds." This last he said aloud.

In response, an ancient voice sang in his head, and he knew that his ancestors were calling in a debt made all those years ago on a far-off holy mountain. And the paying of that debt would change everything.

Jiang, the Concubine

Jiang carefully disentangled herself from the fat salt merchant and slipped on a silken robe. The scent of opium lingered in the hot air of the stuffy bedchamber. She flung open the wooden shutters of the third-storey room and for a moment thought the opium was still alive in her blood, causing her to hallucinate. But that moment quickly passed. She had seen what she had seen. A great warship, draped all in white, entering the Huangpu River.

She picked up her leather pouch of silk ropes and her two-stringed arhu from the table then quickly made her way down the stairs.

Outside, the morning streets were already alive. The men from the night-soil wagons were quickly collecting the round, red honey-pots from each house, then emptying the contents into the wagons. A second set of men gave the night-soil pots a quick rinse and returned them to the appropriate homes. Jiang knew that although night-soil collection was the lowliest of professions, it also paid the highest financial rewards. Because of that, Jiang's family always married their first daughter into the Zhong clan that controlled this lucrative business. In the meantime, she was happy that she was upwind of the night-soil cart.

She turned a sharp corner and a five-spice egg seller fish-eyed her, then put one nasty finger to a nostril and blew hard. Green snot splatted to the ground inches from the pot. "Missed," the egg seller chortled. "Was his spear big?" she asked Jiang with feigned innocence.

"He would have split you in half, old lady," Jiang quipped.

"Only if he entered the dark passage. In the sacred lotus I can take a stallion." She laughed at her own joke and again blew her nose. This time some of the green mass went in the pot.

"Ah!" Jiang shouted.

"Special ingredient," the five-spice egg seller chimed back.

All around Jiang, the morning smell of porridge escaped from coal-fired braziers. She didn't care to eat at this hour, but the subtle smell of a steamed pork bun drew her down an alley on her way toward the water. The gentle woman selling the buns allowed her hand to linger just a moment too long on Jiang's smooth skin before she took Jiang's half-*tael* piece.

The first bite of the bun filled Jiang with an old joy. *When I get old I can have as many of these as I want. Fat. Fat. Ah, to be free enough and old enough to be fat*, she thought.

She avoided the accusatory looks of the women in the streets as she ran out of the alley, past the fish sellers and the wooden tables thick with wriggling eels ready to be sliced. For a moment she paused in front of the snake seller. Did she need more man in her now? she wondered.

"Cobra?" she asked.

"Man's food," the toothless vendor replied.

"Most days I agree," Jiang said, "but not today."

"Expensive," he prompted.

"How much?"

He quoted an astronomical figure — the laughing price — and she promptly laughed in his face and turned to go. He chased after her and said, "So tell me, how much are you willing to pay?"

She quoted an outrageously low price — the crying price — and he made appropriate protestations.

Five minutes, two threats to leave, and one threat to kill her later and they had settled on a price.

The snake man reached into his burlap bag and withdrew a king cobra, as fat around as a man's arm. He adjusted his hand to secure his grip on the back of the reptile's head.

She nodded.

The snake lashed out with the full strength of its six-foot body but the snake seller was expert at his craft. He knelt in front of a thick log sticking out of the ground. With one quick motion he forced open the cobra's jaws and the fangs scissored out of its mouth.

Just as the poison tipped the end of the fangs the man slammed the cobra's head down onto the cut end of the log. The fangs dug deep into the soft wood. The body of the snake thrashed viciously at the air, but it was firmly secured to the log by its fangs. The snake seller looked up and smiled a toothless grin, then withdrew a slender blade, and made his first cut.

Jiang enjoyed the skinning of the snake. She had seen it done many times before but it never failed to surprise her when the snake seller threw the skin high into the air. It landed on the ground and thrashed — thrashed as if it were still somehow alive. *Very male,* Jiang thought. *With the arrival of the ships, I'll need all the masculine blood in me that I can manage.*

She gave the tail third of the flesh to the beggars standing to one side, who ate it raw. The rest she tucked into a package, and then she raced toward the river.

She got there just as the second ship rounded the west bend.

She watched the great ships — and she knew that nothing would be the same, ever again.

A clatter of birds above her made her look up. The starlings from the rice paddies were falling in ever-narrowing spirals, the weight of the reeds dragging them earthward. A tiny bird crashed to the ground on the path ahead of her. She ran to retrieve it, only to be caught in a hail of hundreds of falling, screaming starlings.

She put up her lovely hands to protect her face, and as she did she looked to the high ridge.

There she saw the Bodyguard and the Confucian, both staring at the ships.

Then she heard the sound of the Chinese artillery — all three did. And all three of the Chosen knew that their job was to usher in the darkness, not defeat it with cannons.

8

SHANGHAI

At the Bend in the River
December, 1841

As Richard contemplated his future at the Bend in the River, the mizzen-mast let out a shriek and the single topgallant sail ripped into shreds like so much tissue. The long canvas strands were quickly picked up by the strong wind and snapped angrily.

A second gingall blast from the shore battery slammed into the bowsprit.

"Cannon on the south shore!" screamed two seamen in unison from their respective crow's nest perches.

Orders were shouted. A sailor's torn body was quickly covered with sheeting, as all hands ran to battle stations and the great ship came about, its massive expanse of canvas luffing in the momentary calm.

The hills on the south side of the river just past the widest part of the arc were lined with long-barrelled, small-calibre cannons: gingalls. But there were enough of them to do some damage. Once the ship was broadside to the land the mariners dropped anchor both fore and aft — then the portside gun ports slammed open.

The grind and screech of iron wheels against oaken floorboards filled the air as the ship's cannons moved forward and stuck their snouts out of their respective gun ports. Then all noise ceased. The wind seemed to pick up but the anchors held the great ship still in the water.

Admiral Gough stared at the shore and, as far as Richard could tell, said a prayer. Then he straightened his waistcoat and gave an order to his adjutant, who promptly called out: "Fire!"

The heavens opened as the thunder of the ship's twenty-six wide-bore port-side cannons transformed the Chinese gun emplacements into the muddy, blooded places where men's lives come to an abrupt end. Richard watched, and the horror of lives lost entered his head. For an instant he thought of his last moments with his mother in the hovel in Calcutta — her life slowly flowing from her emaciated White Russian body, her red hair so thin that he saw more scalp than hair. Then his wife's dying cry of "Why? What have you done!" echoed through his head. He turned — and he was with her again.

"What have you done, Richard?" Sarah asked as she turned slowly in the morning light of their Malay bedroom, showing off her large pregnant belly to her handsome husband.

Richard sat up in their bed and put on a face of mock horror. "My goodness," he said, pointing at her belly, "could I have had something to do with that?"

"Only a very little something — a very, very little something," she said as a lascivious grin creased her full lips. Then she posed demurely, although completely naked, against a footpost of their four-poster bed.

Richard laughed then said, "It's a work day, Sarah," and got to his feet.

"Really?" she asked, pointing at his tented pyjama bottoms.

"That kind of work I could, perhaps, help you with."

"Really?"

"Really, my darling!"

Richard held out his hand and she took it. He guided her onto the bed then stood back. Another aghast look crossed his face. "I do believe that the dirty deed was done on these very premises."

But Sarah knew differently. It had been the day on the south island when she had insisted on a picnic. There on the beach, as the sun set, they had made slow, easy love. And she had connected to the ground and the sound of the waves rolling in and a new life within her. That night they'd slept beneath the stars and she had felt it — the earth spin. And she had spun with it.

Richard positioned the pillows to support her back and she mounted the high bed, then held her arms out to her fine husband, the father of that which grew within her.

"Promise me something, Richard?"

"Anything."

"That you'll write something for me. Just for me."

"I've already …"

"Something new. After I give birth. Something to celebrate me becoming a mother."

"As you wish, Sarah." He breathed the words into her mouth. "As you wish."

Then, as their energies came together and they brought what Asians call the clouds and rain, she whispered in his ear, "What have you done, Richard, what have you done?" But Richard heard more than just a coy come-on in the words. He heard the beginnings of an accusation.

The cannonade lasted for hours, despite the fact that it had been some time since the shore batteries had returned fire.

Before the landing party had fully disembarked, Richard took Maxi aside. Jollyboats, cutters, bumboats, and colourful skiffs were in constant motion between the large troop transports and the landing site. As usual, the Chinese hadn't deigned to defend against the foreigners' landing.

"They may fight as you get closer to the centre of the city," Richard said. "The walls you should be able to scale with no problem. In the first skirmish, head toward the south gate."

"You've told me three times, brother mine."

"Fine, Maxi, but I need you to listen carefully. I don't think the armada is going to stop here. To them, Shanghai is insignificant. It's the mouth of the Grand Canal and Nanjing that they want. And they'll need me to translate when the Emperor has finally had enough and decides he wants a treaty. So I won't be with you in the city."

"On my own, am I, then?" said Maxi with a grin.

"Not really. Chen will meet you there and lead you to the Warrens. There he'll introduce you to the other Chinese power-brokers. You'll recognize some of them from our earlier trips but there are bound to be those you don't know. Let Chen do the talking — even your pidgin is godawful and they'll take it as an insult. Which, by the by, it is. When will you finally — ?"

"Never, brother. It was hard enough for me to learn passable English. This Mandarin is well beyond me. You have the gift to pick up these odd tongues, not me."

"Just keep your mouth shut, but listen carefully, and get Chen to translate everything. Everything. Don't push for anything. Just remind Chen that I am on my way and that we have been good as our word for better than five years with him. We've made him a wealthy man, Maxi, and now it's time for him to return the favour. We want access to any survey plans of the city. We won't be allowed to live within their walls, but then again we don't really want to. We need to know who owns the land next to the river and exactly who has access to the wharves. Get Chen to begin negotiations with whoever that is. He won't sell anything yet, but we'll have our foot in the door."

"Do you want me to stay in Shanghai?"

"Not unless you have to."

"That'd technically make me break my contract with the British Expeditionary Force, brother mine."

"Would it?"

"You know it would."

"Does that bother you, Maxi?"

"Not much," he said as a darkness crossed his face "You'll be with the real action, though, won't you, brother mine?"

"Bureaucrats will decide the important things in the Celestial Kingdom. Battles are just for show, I'm afraid."

"Men die for show?"

"Yes, Maxi, and it won't be the last time for that." Maxi scowled and Richard readied himself for a fight. But none came. "I'll be at the treaty table, since none of our ninnies speak a word of the Common Tongue." He paused, then added, "I'll be there to make the sacrifices of those lives mean something."

Maxi nodded but didn't speak. Orders were being shouted all around them.

"After we take Chinkiang, I think it's just a matter of endless negotiations until Shanghai is opened up — and I want us ready to move as soon as it is."

Maxi nodded again.

"One more thing?"

"What, brother mine?"

"Control yourself."

Maxi gave the smile that had for years terrified his enemies and made ladies swoon. "Knife in its sheath, dick in me pants. Right?"

"Right, Maxi, right."

After the troops were put ashore, steamers pulled two warships up the Huangpu River and the siege of Shanghai began. The mariners and infantrymen, Maxi at the head of his irregulars, made their way overland on an all-night march that swung them all the way around the city, ending at a ridge north of the city gates.

The morning came up fast and caught the British advance contingent unawares. The long march had exhausted the troops, and many had curled up on the ground and slept without taking off their boots.

Maxi never slept the night before battle. He climbed to the far side of the ridge and watched the sun rise. Then he saw them, small, crouched silhouettes coming from the east, not from the city at all. He watched as they skirted the British encampment and flanked out in small groups. He was too far away to give a warning cry and a gunshot would have been lost at that distance, so he began to run.

The east perimeter sentry sighed. His watch was almost over. He thought of good British ale and his young wife. Then he lit a cardboard-wrapped Turkish cigarette and breathed in deeply — and felt the smoke somehow come out his neck! He turned and a wiry Chinaman, clad all in white, smiled at him. In his long fingers a slender, blood-slick knife twirled round and round. *How does he do that?* the sentry thought, then watched helplessly as the knife sank deeper into his throat, then tore sideways.

"Wake up, you slackers!" Maxi screamed as he crested the nearest hill. Quickly, two Chinese assassins were on him, then on the ground writhing in pain. Maxi's second shot awoke the camp and screams quickly followed.

Maxi saw the Manchu banner and raced toward the man carrying it. The man saw Maxi and ran at full speed toward him. Three yards from Maxi he lowered the banner and, to Maxi's surprise, planted it in the ground and pulled himself up and over it as his feet thrashed at Maxi's head. One of the blows landed squarely, flattening Maxi's nose and sending him smashing to the ground.

Maxi hit, then immediately rolled. Only the friction of the banner whistling through the air saved him from the downward thrust of the lance at its end. It stuck several inches deep in the soft ground. Maxi rolled again and came up with a pistol cocked and aimed at the bannerman's head.

The man took his hands from the banner and stood very still. He said something — calmly, totally without fear. Maxi wished Richard were at his side to tell him what the brave man had said, but he wasn't. The man repeated himself. Not arrogant, clearly accepting what was going to happen to him. *The way the opium farmers accepted their lives in India,* he thought.

Maxi reached down and pulled the banner from the ground and handed it to the man. The man canted his head, Maxi matched the head bob precisely, then each turned and left — the bannerman to his army, Maxi to the south gate of the city.

Chen met Maxi just outside the south gate and signalled the *Fan Kuei* to follow him.

Maxi did, through the rickety streets of the Old City, then down a particularly long alley and through a hovel, then down a wooden ladder into a web of tunnels that Maxi knew were called the Warrens. The massive web of underground passages ran beneath the west section of the walled city, all the way to the river.

Maxi knew that above him was the old walled town, with the Huangpu River on the east and the Suzu Creek to the north. To the west were lakes and canals that led back into the southern reaches of the country. Cotton grew down by the delta and rice paddies came right up to the southern walls.

Even beneath the ground Maxi could sense the energy of this place. After the first hundred yards or so, torches were lit in carved niches in the walls. Chen picked up his speed and Maxi matched him stride for stride. The walls were wet to the touch, but the tunnels had been well-tended, and many places were worn smooth from the endless years of running feet.

After many turns and cut stone stairs both up and down, Chen held up his hand and Maxi stopped close behind him. Chen whistled a single, shrill, high-pitched note. Moments later, after the echo had ceased, a low-pitched whistle responded and a rope ladder was lowered from directly overhead. Chen and Maxi climbed it. At the top, strong hands grasped their wrists and hauled them up to a mahogany-floored chamber.

It took a moment for Maxi's eyes to adjust. The room was large and quite cold. A formal lacquered table stood to one side. Behind it stood a High Mandarin and three lesser authorities, all wearing the flowing silk robes and conical hats that were their badges of office. One of the officials, dressed in the purple robe of a scholar, was a certain Confucian.

All eyes were on Maxi.

He bowed low, then got down on one knee and performed the formal kowtow that Richard had taught him. When his forehead touched wooden floor his broken nose sent shards of pain through his entire body but he didn't wince. Finally finished with the elaborate prostrations, he stood.

The Mandarin crossed to the table, reached into his long sleeve, and extracted a map.

As he did, the Confucian thought, *Here is my first deed in fulfilling my family's commitment to the Ivory Compact.*

Maxi accepted tea from Chen — and the planning began.

Later that afternoon, the British, following Maxi's instructions, entered the city by climbing over the roof of a hut built illegally close to the outer wall — and owned by a certain courtesan named Jiang. Resistance in the city melted away as the man with the cobra tattooed on his hand advised against "overt action." The dawn sally of assassins from the walls proved the total extent of the defence mounted by the Shanghainese to protect their city.

By noon a delegation of the wealthiest merchants had come from the city walls and set up a large silk tent. Inside, on shiny black lacquered tables inlaid with designs made from mother-of-pearl, they served tea and fine sweetmeats to the British — then agreed to pay three million silver dollars in return for the safety of their city of 250,000 souls.

Maxi stood in the back of the tent, a cloth to his broken nose. He saw their man, Chen, at the conference table and wondered if he'd had something to do with the ease of the city's capitulation. The entire city had cost the British three dead and sixteen wounded.

The city's Jesuit translator made some final amendments to the document of Shanghai's surrender as the head merchant chattered on, seemingly no more concerned than if he had been bargaining for a slightly better price for the summer's second rice crop.

The money was put on the treaty table. Pottinger's representative, a chubby man named McCullough, didn't deign to touch it, acting as if such trifles were beneath a man of his station in life.

McCullough waited for the head merchant to sign the last of the documents then stepped up to the table and took up the quill pen. He dunked it in the ink and poised it over the parchment. Then he turned to his lieutenant, who fired a shot through the silk roof of the tent. Before anyone in the tent could respond, a loud explosion caused them all to turn to the city.

The south gate of the city flew into bits, killing several Chinese bird and fish merchants whose stalls were adjacent to the gate.

"Just to show these Celestials who runs this town now," he announced, then turned to the Jesuit and ordered, "Translate that for your friends." Before the Jesuit could comply, McCullough placed his pen on the signature line of the peace agreement and dashed off his name with some considerable flourish. When he'd finished, he turned to the interpreter again and said, "Three of my men were murdered this morning before dawn by your heathens. I will expect ten times that number handed over to me for execution by sundown — or the rest of your city will be put to the torch." Then he inexplicably switched to pidgin, despite the fact that the Jesuit's English was missionary-school perfect. "Understandee, boy?

Quickee, go go, chop chop."

When the Shanghai delegation left, the tent flap was momentarily held open by the wind — and there in the bright sunlight stood the bannerman Maxi had encountered that morning. He glared at Maxi — and Maxi believed he had never seen so much hate in the eyes of any individual in his life.

Later, as Maxi lay on the surgeon's table in the belly of HMS *Cornwallis*, he thought that the hate in the bannerman's eyes was totally justified. Then the surgeon yanked the cartilage of his broken nose back into place and the pain that rocketed through his body removed any sentimental feeling Maxi had for the bannerman, the man's children, if he had any, or the lowliest beast of burden in the Middle Kingdom.

Four full decks above Maxi, in the captain's well-appointed quarters, Gough reported on the securing of Shanghai to Governor General Pottinger, who was perched like an old owl over a table covered with river charts.

"We'll leave a battle frigate in this harbour and send another back to here," Pottinger stated, pointing to the mouth of the Yangtze by the village of Woosung.

That made sense to Gough and he nodded.

"Glad you agree, Admiral," Pottinger said, then added, "I want the commander of the frigates to be instructed to intercept and sink any and all Chinese vessels heading up or down the river." He lifted his head from the charts.

"A blockade, sir?" Gough asked incredulously.

"Yes. That's the word I've been searching for. A blockade." Pottinger seemed to be tasting the word. He smiled, an ugly thing to witness as it exposed the diminutive creature's rotted front teeth. Then Queen Victoria's appointed man in China mumbled something unintelligible and abruptly left the cabin.

For a moment Gough didn't know what to do, then he raced

after Pottinger and managed to corner the Governor General on the forecastle deck. "I have misgivings about a full blockade, sir."

Pottinger turned to Gough and a quizzical look crossed his surprisingly large facial features. "Are you questioning my command, Admiral?"

"No, sir. But why can we not allow trade in common goods to continue?"

Her Majesty's representative in China drew himself up to his full five — foot, four-inch height and said, in his fulsome Oxford lisp, "We will take no half measures, my good sir. We have come to this God-forsaken place to accomplish a task and nothing, nothing, will stand in the way of our endeavour. Our period of operations is limited. The government and people of England look to me for decisive results. We will let the monkey Emperor see that we have the means, and are prepared to exert them, of increasing pressure on his damnable country to an unbearable degree." A small smile creased his glistening lips. "Once the armada is fully on the river we will stop and loot every Chinese vessel we come across. Is that clear?"

Gough understood the advantage of raiding Chinese coal vessels to take the coal for their own steamers, but why all the vessels? And had the Queen's representative in China really legitimized looting? Finally he said, "We want to trade with the Chinese, not starve them to death." He added the word "sir" just in time to avoid a formal reprimand.

Pottinger thought about that for a moment, then replied, "A few starving Chinamen might prove advantageous — very advantageous."

9

A VRASSON AT BEDLAM

London
December, 1841

The Vrassoon Patriarch signalled for the matron to take the beautiful madwoman from his arms. "Gently, gently now," he cooed after her as the matron took her and marched her back across the room.

The beautiful madwoman broke free and ran back to Eliazar, clutching at his arm. "Will you dance with me?"

"Surely. Surely I will dance with you," he said, removing her nailless fingers from his coat and turning her to face the matron once again. "Be gentle with her. She's not dangerous."

The matron ignored him and yanked the bedraggled creature by the fleshy part of her upper arm. Two stalwart guards stepped forward and reaffixed the buckles and belts of her outer restraining garment.

Vrassoon looked away. He wanted to wash his hands, but not while she could see him. He owed her that, at least.

"Why bother seeing her at all?" It was his elegant eldest son,

Ari, who thought of the woman as his mad older cousin.

Because she's my heart, Eliazar wanted to say but didn't dare. Then he turned on his son. "How dare you interfere with my privacy?"

"I had no choice, father."

"And why exactly is that? Why are you here?"

"There's news. News that couldn't wait for your return to the office."

Vrassoon raised a single bushy eyebrow. His son signalled him to follow.

Ten minutes later they were in the family's luxurious carriage. The company's two China hands sat across from the Vrassoons. The Patriarch demanded, "They've been authorized by the government to do what?"

"To blockade the Yangtze if they see fit, sir," said the elder China hand, then added, "so that not a single ship can get into the river. And on the river itself they've been given permission to stop every boat — to take the goods and burn the vessels."

"They're fools, Papa," said Ari.

Eliazar Vrassoon looked out the carriage window and thought about that. The men on the British Expeditionary Force were men in search of riches, not so different from himself. He reached out and flipped the latch. The window folded outward. The stink of London entered the carriage. Finally he asked, "Will there be hunger?"

"Surely," the younger China hand replied.

"Starvation?" Vrassoon asked.

"Probably."

The Patriarch tapped his fingers against the leather-upholstered side of the carriage. The rain was coming down in sheets. *So there would be hunger. Much hunger.* He thought about that, then about prayer and faith and the willingness to believe. He thought about the mad girl who had shared his bed, whose daughter was now in her fifth year with the farm family in Hereford. The wind shifted and the rain came at the carriage on a slant. He reached out and pulled the window back into place. The wind shifted again and the rain suddenly beat on the roof of the carriage so loudly that it was hard to hear anyone speak. Eliazar Vrassoon nodded. *There will be hunger and starvation — and the world will change*, he thought. *So be it*. Then he turned to the others in the carriage and said loudly, "Do you think it will ever stop raining?"

The men were actually stunned by the question. Was the Patriarch of the Vrassoon family chatting about the weather? Did he expect them to respond?

Before any of them could speak, Eliazar Vrassoon answered his own question. "Everything stops eventually, gentlemen, and something new arises. It has been and will be forever thus."

There was a palpable sense of relief in the carriage as it raced past the rain-soaked beggars and drunkards of East London on its way to the centre of the Vrassoon company's seat of power, its offices on the Mall.

10

HUNGER

On the Yangtze River
December, 1841

Richard moved silently away from Gough and Pottinger. He knew a great deal more about hunger than they did. He passed by the deck watch unchallenged. As the expedition's translator, he had a temporary commission as a sub-lieutenant and pretty much free rein of the ship, so long as he stayed away from the crew quarters.

Richard stood at the port rail mid-deck and watched the fires on the shore as the great ship headed upriver. He turned his face to the wind and breathed deeply. Then he thought of the people on either side of the great river who might well soon be hungry. Some of whom might, in fact, shortly begin the lengthy process of starving to death.

"*Starving's nothing special, boychick. It's just not eating.*"

Richard wasn't surprised to hear his dead father's voice. Lately, as he neared the completion of his plan, his deceased father's words, spoken in his unique mix of old-fashioned formal Farsi and Yiddish, often popped into his head. Although he had not seen his father for almost twenty years, he remembered exactly when his father had said those words to him.

"They're trying to starve us into leaving, Papa."

"That they are."

"Why?"

"Because they don't want us here, *boychick*."

"You mean the dung-eating new caliph doesn't want us in Baghdad anymore? Because he claims some stupid book said we are monkeys?"

"Dogs and monkeys, actually, Richard. Important to remember that. Not just monkeys, but dogs and monkeys. In fact, the progeny of dogs and monkeys," his father said. The deep cut on his forehead opened slightly when he laughed. The man could find humour in anything.

"We should just rip off the old idiot's beard and shove it down his stupid throat."

"This from a fourteen-year-old? A fourteen-year-old wants violence? Violence! It is my decision to leave Baghdad. Mine. It's a good time."

"A good time? A good time to leave our home?"

"Richard!"

Richard stared for a moment at the fool of a man in front of him, but he chose not to speak. His father might be willing to leave their ancestral home like a beaten mule, but Richard and Maxi were not so inclined. Even as children they had been unafraid. The Baghdadi boys' stones and taunts had never frightened him, and for Maxi they were just an excuse to attack.

There had been fires in the Jewish quarter two Friday nights before — naturally, on a Friday night. The Hordoons had escaped harm because they didn't live in ostentation like the Vrassoons and the Kadooris. The rich had been the first to feel the new caliph's wrath — or rather the rage of the countless Baghdadi poor, ignorant, and gullible. But last Monday while Richard was at school, his father's small leather tanning stall in the bazaar had been set afire — with the old man in it. Luckily Maxi had been nearby. He'd dragged their father to safety and then stood his ground as three grown men tried to loot the stall. Maxi was small in stature but he was a giant in a brawl. Every ounce of him was muscle and sinew, and he loved a fight. When he balled his surprisingly small fists his eyes would go glassy hard, and the smile that the Moslem boys had learned to fear curled his lips. He could take more punishment than any man Richard had ever met, and he was only twelve years old — and extremely pale white, white-skinned and red-haired like their Russian mother. When Richard finally found them, his father had the large gash across his forehead and Maxi was covered in blood — other men's blood. Maxi smiled, his large white teeth showing through his parted, swollen lips. He pointed to the ground, to the three grown men moaning in the dirt — one with an arm bone showing sickly white through his swarthy skin, another with an eye missing, and the third with a reddened crotch that did not bode well for his contribution to future generations.

Remembering, Richard smiled and nodded.

"Why are you nodding? What are you agreeing with, *boychick*?"

"Nothing — everything."

"Good. Agreeing is good," his father said and grinned.

Richard took a deep breath, then asked, "So when have you decided that we leave Baghdad?"

"Tonight — late — after moonset."

So they were going on foot. No trains ran that late. "Where?"

"Where what, *boychick*?"

"Where are we going, Papa?"

"South."

South! Not west to Europe but south! He felt his muscles cramp with anger. Then he thought of Maxi — the wild one — and he knew how they'd spend their last night in old Baghdad.

The two-storey courtyard was centred on an ancient well. The gate in front was made of sturdy metal bars with sharpened tips, but they posed no problem for the Hordoon boys.

Once over the gate they pressed their backs against the wall, in the deep shadow cast by the full moon. Richard sensed rather than saw Maxi at his side, then sensed him gone. Richard reached into the darkness for his brother but he wasn't there. Minutes passed. Sounds of family life from the rooms across the way and the scent of highly spiced chickpeas found their way to his hiding place. Then Maxi was back, as silently as he had left.

"Teacher's home, brother mine."

"You know...?"

"Where he sleeps with his new boy." Maxi pointed toward an ancient stone arch.

"How do — ?"

"Are we here to ask questions or say goodbye to this Jew-hating sodomite?"

"Let's go."

They crept along the compound wall. A dog barked, then fell silent. A few women came to the well carrying stoneware and a large clay pot. The boys went through the arch, turned a corner, and ran down a corridor into another interior courtyard. Across the way was a set of time-worn stone stairs. The boys took a step forward and froze. Something had moved in the courtyard. They both stood completely still. Then a peacock darted out from the shadows.

It took Richard a moment to identify the danger, but Maxi pounced on the animal and grabbed it by its neck. A breathy burp came from the bird rather than the usual piercing cries that would have alerted the whole compound. For a moment Maxi stood in the very centre of the courtyard, in full moonlight, holding the large, squirming creature by the neck. Then he flashed his smile and whipped the bird around his head twice. The bird's neck made a slight popping sound, then its body went limp. Maxi plucked two large tail feathers and threw the limp carcass high over the wall.

Then, he headed toward the stairs.

At the top of the steps a narrow hallway faced the boys. Down the hall, they saw a heavy door barring their way into what Richard assumed was a bedroom. This was obviously a private part of the compound and it was ghostly quiet. No cooking here, no cleaning — just a man's place — and a boy's.

Maxi kicked open the heavy door.

The boy was face down spread-eagled on the bed, his arms and legs tethered by leather thongs to the bed's four posts. Teacher, who always referred to Maxi as the "retarded pig" whenever he called upon him in class, squatted over the terrified boy, whose pants were down around his ankles.

Teacher spun round and squinted toward the door. His thick glasses were on the night table. Maxi jumped forward and, grabbing the man by the hair, threw him to the ground while Richard stuffed yards of the bed sheets into the man's mouth to ensure his silence. Maxi sauntered over to the night table while Richard tied Teacher's hands behind his back. He took the thick glasses and returned to Teacher. Leaning down, he put the glasses on the man's face, "Want you to see us, Teacher. See what the Hordoon brothers are doing to you."

Richard cut the boy loose. "Leave without a sound," he whispered. The boy nodded, grabbed his clothes, and ran from the room.

Once the boy was gone Richard and Maxi lifted Teacher to his feet and frogmarched him to the squatter in the water closet.

The hole in the ground between the porcelain footholds was just large enough, after a bit of tile lifting and prying, to fit a grown man's head — Teacher's head. The boys hoisted squirming Teacher in the air and held him over the reeking hole. Maxi shoved the peacock's tail feathers between Teacher's toes. "Hold these," he ordered.

Richard looked at Maxi. "How did you know where his room …?" But he didn't need an answer, he understood.

Maxi shrugged his shoulders and said, "He would have had either you or me. I let it be me."

Richard nodded, then the Hordoon brothers turned Teacher upside down and shoved him head first into the hole — and left. Perhaps his God would save him. Perhaps, He wouldn't.

A few hours later the Hordoon family snuck out of the city that eight generations of their forefathers had called home. All they took with them was what they could carry on their backs.

Seventeen weeks of hard travelling later, they staggered into the squalor of Calcutta.

The day they arrived, Richard wrote the first entry in the journal that he would keep for the entirety of his life. It read: *How do I explain Calcutta — a dream within a nightmare; a song without end; the glory of darkness and shade while the sun roasts the earth. Then the rain comes. And everywhere palaces — ancient, dilapidated palaces slowly but inevitably falling into the river.*

Richard thought about that first journal entry he had penned when he was barely fifteen years old as he crossed the foredeck of the *Cornwallis,* and the White Birds on Water made their way up the mighty Yangtze River — and changed the course of Chinese history.

⚜11

AT THE GRAND CANAL

The Yangtze at the Grand Canal and farther west
July, 1842

No nation had ever dared to enter the mighty Yangtze in such force as the British did in the last month of 1841. But although the British were virtually unopposed, the Yangtze itself proved a formidable enemy. The British had seventy-five vessels in their armada. Eleven were men-o'-war under sail, ranging in size from the enormous flagship *Cornwallis* to a small ten-gun brig. There were also four troopships, ten steamers, two survey schooners, and forty-eight transports.

The great river, although ten miles across at places, seldom had a navigable channel of any significant width, and Nanjing was two hundred miles upriver. Shallow draft steamers went ahead and attempted to buoy the channel but it proved trickier than anyone had anticipated. Several ships ran aground and needed to wait for high tide to dislodge themselves. Quickly the armada broke into its component parts. Some of the bigger ships needed to be pulled by steamers. Eventually the armada found itself spread over a thirty-mile area, as much as six days of sailing apart from each other. The biggest problems were the flagship, the *Cornwallis*, and a disgusting old tub called the *Belleisle*.

And, of course, Governor General Pottinger insisted that the flagship lead the way.

After the first sixty or seventy miles the banks of the Yangtze suddenly narrowed, sharp bends became common, and the current quickened. The ships found it hard going, and this far upriver the tide was negligible, so any ship that erred in its charting and went aground needed to offload its entire cargo — cannon included — before it could hope to refloat itself.

Not a single ship managed the voyage without grounding at least once; with some it was almost a daily occurrence.

Despite this, the British met little military resistance. The odd shore battery attack was feeble even for the Chinese. However, if mariners ventured ashore — especially if they were ill — they were immediately attacked by brigands or the locals, and these attacks often ended with British heads on the ends of sharpened pikes. So, although the British controlled the water, they were prisoners on their own ships.

Richard stared at the murky water of the great river. They were approaching Chinkiang at the southern entrance to the First Emperor's Grand Canal, which connected Beijing with the Yangtze. *Surely the Chinese will defend the waterway to the heart of their nation*, Richard thought.

As the walls of Chinkiang came into view Richard stood back from the railing and tried to stretch the tension from his muscles. As he did, the railing upon which he had been leaning only a moment before splintered with a crack and the wall behind him flew into a thousand bits. The morning air filled with the high, whistling shriek of flying chain and scrap metal as ranks of gingalls fired from their shore batteries. Richard stood staring at the splintered railing until an officer screamed, "Battle stations!" and the decks and rigging, as if by magic, filled with mariners.

The *Cornwallis* turned into the wind and dropped anchor. Five other ships followed suit. Gough shouted, "Port side gun ports!" and "Siege flags!"

The ports slammed open and battle flags raced up the bowsprit. All around him Richard watched the men of the Royal Navy preparing their positions for battle. He felt his heart race. For a brief moment he wondered where Maxi was, but then he cast aside his concern. If there was anyone who could look after himself in a fight it was his brother. No doubt he was readying his irregulars to lead Her Majesty's troops into battle.

Richard flinched when the first cannon roared beneath his feet. Then over a hundred cannon from five different ships brought the wrath of the British navy to bear on the gingall emplacements that were intended to guard the mouth of Q'in She Huang's Grand Canal. For three hours, without cease, the British shelled the Manchu batteries, and when they fell silent the gunners raised the angle on their weapons and bombarded the walled city itself.

Then, without warning, the guns fell silent. At first Richard couldn't tell since his hearing had left him hours earlier. A sharp slap across his back caused him to spin around. "You're to prepare yourself for a landing in General Gough's party," said the adjutant. Richard looked down. Below him the water was quickly filling with shuttle boats heading toward the shore. Richard thought he could make out the red kerchief that Maxi always wore around his neck on days of battle. Naturally he was in the lead boat, almost at the rocky beach. Maxi was always first to a fight.

A half hour later, seven hundred mariners and armed seamen formed ranks on the shoreline just east of Chinkiang. For some of them it was the first time their feet had touched the sacred soil of the Celestial Kingdom. Shortly afterwards, the horses were brought to join the infantry, and a man from Maxi's irregulars came running up to General Gough.

"It's clear, General, from here to the city. Not a single battery is left, sir."

The man's English was so highly accented that Gough turned to Richard. "What language is he speaking?"

"Farsi-accented English."

"English?"

Richard repeated the irregular's message in his impeccable English, then asked the man in Farsi, "And the city?"

"The gates are closed and barred. No sign of them coming out to meet us in the field."

Richard translated, and Gough asked, "Anything else?"

The irregular looked to Richard and said in Farsi, "Your brother suggests that you tell your British friends to take a close look at the Chinese weapons. There are some surprises."

Richard passed this on to Gough, who turned to a lieutenant and issued an order.

An hour later they were on a battery emplacement hill examining two pieces of Chinese artillery.

"Sir?" Richard asked.

"They're clever. Look at the pivot on that gingall. The weapon itself is poorly constructed and only a little more effective than their shields with the savage pictures and the character writing painted on them."

Richard's ability to read Chinese characters was limited but he knew the characters on the Chinese shields had epithets like "Thief's Judgment," "Red Hair Tamer," and "Subduer of Foreign Devils." He didn't think it was worth telling Gough.

Gough knelt and looked at the iron apparatus on the back of the narrow-barrelled gingall. Two corners of a metal triangle were bolted to the back of the weapon while the third was welded to a large metal ring.

"It's a pivot apparatus," Gough said as he circled the thing.

"Take a large spike and hammer it through the ring into the ground then the gun can be moved on an arc by as few as two gunners. Look at the wheels. They can be set forward and back or in a curve left to right. We need five men to change the basic positioning of our cannon. This is a legitimate advance. Lucky they don't use them strategically or we'd have lost a ship, maybe two."

A lieutenant ran up and saluted. "Sir, the monkeys' handboats are in the western cove."

Richard bridled at hearing the Chinese referred to that way, but he let it pass.

In the western cove Richard watched Gough once again admire the ingenuity of the enemy. In the water, close to the shore, were seven sleek boats with side wheels. "They're hand-powered," the lieutenant said as he showed Gough how a single man could move the boat with a simple arm motion.

Again, Gough quickly realized how fortunate they had been. "If they'd filled these with pitch and then set them ablaze ..." He didn't need to say the rest. Fire on a wooden sailing ship was a frightful thing, and clearly these small boats would have been hard to stop. "If they'd known where our magazines ... well, they didn't," he said, but Richard noted a strong hint of both fear and respect in the man's words.

When Gough turned from the cove he was surprised to see Maxi standing on the rise beyond the beach, clearly waiting for him, his kerchief just slightly redder than his hair.

Gough accepted the man's worth, but he was a gentleman, and this Persian was ... was a Persian. "Report," he ordered.

Maxi smiled. "The city's silent, but I'd watch your flanks as you approach the walls."

"Sir!"

"Sir," Maxi added grudgingly. Richard noted the pulsing vein in his brother's forehead, like a thick worm caught beneath the flawless pale skin.

"No resistance?"

"No resistance yet … sir."

Gough dismissed the Persian.

Maxi turned and headed back the way he had come.

The next day, on the morning of July 21, 1842, General Gough led two full brigades of his men confidently toward the walls of Chinkiang.

As they got within sight of the walls his adjutant said, "There seems to be no defensive positioning at all, General."

Gough didn't like it, but he didn't know what else to do. He needed to secure the mouth of the Grand Canal if he had any chance of forcing the Emperor to the treaty table. Still, the silence was disconcerting, and his own private alarms were ringing like the church bells of his home parish on Easter morn.

He turned back toward his ships and bit his lip, drawing a thin line of blood. Then he reminded himself that he couldn't afford to return to England empty-handed since he had invested what was left of his family's dwindling fortune in the possibility of plunder from this expedition.

"Should we move the brigade forward, sir?"

The land in front of them was hard-packed clay, with grass growing to the height of a man's waist in the distance; to the left were flooded rice paddies. On the right was a grove of tropical trees. Gough didn't like the trees. Even as a child he'd feared the woods. The most frightening threat in his family was to be thrown to the woods — to be "bewildered."

"Divide the brigades in two," Gough ordered. "I don't want a flank exposed to the trees."

Commands were given and the well-trained men responded quickly, with bayoneted rifles at the ready. In the distance the walled city was perhaps two miles off.

The men proceeded carefully, awaiting a response. But there was none. Closer and closer to the walls of the city the troops advanced, in perfect formation.

Suddenly, within two hundred yards of the city walls, Manchu bannermen appeared from the water of the rice paddies.

The brigade wheeled to face the onslaught and weathered the first assault. Casualties on the front rank were high but the second and third ranks held ground. The bannermen retreated toward the city but Gough hesitated to follow, fearing that he would expose a flank as he advanced. Before he could consider his options a second wave of bannermen threw themselves at his troops — this time from the tall grass. The battle rapidly degenerated into hand-to-hand combat, and the superior agility of the Chinese fighters almost took the day. Finally Gough called in his cavalry, and the Chinese retreated toward the walled city.

Gough rallied his men for an attack on the walls only to have a third wave of bannermen attack, this time from the woods. This was followed quickly by a full-frontal attack from the central gate of the walled city.

Neither side gave ground. No quarter was asked for or given. And when the sun finally headed toward the western horizon not a single Chinese soldier was left standing. Not one had run. Everyone had fought to the death. Gough's superior weaponry and military tactics had finally prevailed — although without the surprise attack by Maxi's irregulars from deep in the forest the battle may well have ended British aspirations in the Middle Kingdom.

Gough took stock of his decimated troops and noted the hundreds of swooping vultures that hovered overhead. He ordered burial parties for the dead, then shouted to Richard, "Follow me."

Richard did his best to sidestep the bodies but found his boots quickly slicked with human gore. Looking toward the city he saw Maxi through the gunpowder fog and the fading light. Maxi was on the top of a western wall waving his fire-red kerchief. Gough pointed his troops toward Maxi. His men found the advantageous position that Maxi had marked and scaled the walls. Richard followed them.

Once inside the walls the troops re-formed their ranks and moved slowly toward the centre of the city.

Richard knew immediately that something was very wrong.

The city was ghostly quiet. The Chinese were a noisy people at the best of times — this silence was — it was unChinese — unAsian.

Silence was a rarity in Asia. It was the first thing that had struck Richard when the family arrived in Calcutta: the noise — the constant racket. But it wasn't the noise that bothered Richard. It was the words coming from his father's mouth that he heard above the yelling and shouting of the Calcutta alley in which they lived.

"You'll see, soon the Vrassoons will honour their promise to me," he had said.

"Why will they do that, Papa?" Richard asked sharply.

"In return for a favour I did for them a long time ago, when you were just a little boy ... *boychick*."

"What kind of favour could you do for the Vrassoons? You don't have anything the damnable ..."

"When you're a man you'll understand the hard choices a father has to make to provide for his family. Now go play."

Richard hated his father in that moment but rather than lash out, he wrote.

12

FROM THE JOURNALS OF RICHARD HORDOON: SILENCE

Journal entries, September and October, 1828

After two weeks of desperation with nowhere to live and no money to buy food, the great and powerful Vrassoons deigned to let my father be a night watchman at one of their warehouses. For a night watchman's job, we had trudged across desert and mountain! For a night watchman's job, we had ruined our mother's health! I couldn't believe it.

With little more than a lean-to at the end of the stinking alley in which to live, Maxi and I spent our days in the open. My olive skin turned black beneath the baking sun, but Maxi's White Russian skin turned red to match his flaming hair — then shredded in long snakeskin wisps, which we quickly discovered were of real interest to the locals.

Maxi would approach a crowd and then I would announce, in Hindi, "Mera Bhai khud ki chamri cheel raha hai. — My brother is going to skin himself alive. Kaun itna himmatwala hai jo ek admi, ek ladke, ko khud ko cheelte hue dekh sakta hai! — Who's brave enough to watch a man, a boy, skin himself alive? Step up and watch! Step up! Step up! How much is it worth to see this boy skin himself in front of your eyes?" Trinkets of money tinked into my outstretched hand. When I had got as much as I could from the crowd, I would pocket the cash and step back. Maxi would then take off his shirt and pants and stand almost naked — redder than a sunset. Then slowly he would niggle an edge of skin from the top of his hairless chest and pull it slowly down his body, all the while screaming as if he were in terrible pain. Finally he'd rip off the strip and hand it to me. I would hold the length of skin aloft and call out, "Kaun lal larke ki chamri ka daam dega? Calcutta ki sabse acchi chamri — *Who'll pay for the red boy's skin? The best skin in Calcutta. Fresh skin from a red boy will cure any disease. It will bring happiness to a bad marriage. Make the weak strong, the blind see, and the limp strong like a donkey with a new mare. Eat it raw, brew it into a tea, cook it with your rice. Anyway you want, it will bring you joy.* Isse jyada kya iccha kar sakte ho? Mai kiski boli laga raha hoon is lal larke ke chamri ki — ya jo kushhali yeh malik ko lekaraigie? — *What more could you ask? What am I bid for the red boy's skin — for the happiness it will bring the owner?"*

"You've really picked up the lingo, brother mine," Maxi whispered in Farsi.

"You have the gift of skin, me of tongues, Maxi," I whispered back while I continued to hold up the skin and collect bids. As I did I realized something important — how much a man would pay for happiness, even a moment of happiness, even the illusion of the slightest possibility of happiness.

Most days Maxi and I played a game we called "spy." Through the bazaars, down by the sacred river, into and out of offices and factories and private homes, we learned Calcutta by "spying."

As the weeks passed, Maxi noticed that I concentrated the "spying" on one point in the vast city.

"Here again, brother mine?"

"You don't like offices? It's where money's made."

"I'm more interested in where money is spent."

That you are, Maxi, that you are, I thought, remembering our spying in what I thought of as the "harlot district." We were not ignorant of sex, but transvestite boy whores and castrati whores were new ideas to us — and somehow fascinating to Maxi.

A well-dressed, turbaned man hurried past us. "Him!" I said. So we played spy and followed the man. He proved to be, as I had assumed, a Vrassoon courier. "See, Maxi, another one," I said.

"That makes six in two days," Maxi replied.

"Each taking the same route, you may have noticed."

"If couriers come to the Vrassoon offices, why don't we ever see them leave?"

"Because when they go to the Vrassoon offices they are carrying information — information goes through the front door. When they leave they are carrying money — money goes through the back door. Remember that, Maxi."

Around noon the next day while Maxi "re-spied" the harlots, I decided it was finally time to see what Eliazar Vrassoon looked like. I'd never seen the great man before and somehow felt it was important. I stood amidst a crowd of beggars outside the Vrassoon offices. Two well-armed Sikhs pushed the beggars to the far side of the street. That was okay with me. I wasn't there to beg a handout; I was there to watch — to see.

A carriage drawn by four large horses raced toward the entrance of the Vrassoon offices, the driver shrieking at the wave of humanity that wasn't parting fast enough for his taste. With the shrill neighing of horses and the screech of a handbrake the carriage careened to a stop at the bottom of the marble steps.

I leapt up, and grabbed the stanchion of a gaslight and shinnied up. *The better to see you,* I thought. But before I was able to grin at my own cleverness Eliazar Vrassoon was there on the office steps, two of his four sons at his side and six Sikh guards making sure that his eminence was not touched by the rabble.

The Vrassoon Patriarch descended the steps slowly, as if out for an evening's stroll. At the bottom he looked up. He seemed to be looking straight at me. He was about to smile, when his face suddenly grew hard. He pointed a bony finger right at me. My heart fell in my chest. The hatred in the man's eyes cut through me — and I somehow remembered this man — but in a different place. In a bedroom! Whose bedroom?

A week later as the sun set, I was back at the Vrassoon company playing "spy" when I saw my father standing outside the office. I knew that he should be reporting to work in less than an hour.

Despite the heat of the evening, the men leaving the building all wore top hats and woollen suits. Finally a gaggle of young, curly-haired men left the office, followed by a richly dressed older man: Eliazar Vrassoon.

My father stepped forward and was immediately surrounded by the young men.

"Please," I heard him beg. "Please, just a word, a word, please."

Vrassoon sighed deeply. "Let him speak."

My father smiled. "Thank you. Thank you, sir."

"You have something to say, Hordoon?"

"My girl ... "

"What girl?" There was a moment of stunned silence. "I repeat, what girl? Perhaps the work I have supplied you is too taxing for you. Perhaps a younger man would be better suited —"

"No! Please, your honour, no. It was just a joke. The heat ... just the heat."

The Vrassoon Patriarch smiled, secured his hat on his rather large head, and headed to the waiting carriage. I ran home.

The next day the Vrassoons changed my father's job. They now have him working through the night lifting and moving heavy freight in their warehouse. He has become an old man. I never remember him as a young man. Maybe he never was. My mother is rotting away — sick by the time we arrived and sicker by the day. And now mad as well. Over and over she calls out for someone called Miriam. It is the last straw for Maxi and me. We're tired of begging — me of the paltry take, him of *selling his skin — so we said goodbye to our parents today. Papa was too tired to protest. I'm not sure if mother in her delirium even knew what I said to her. We are heading up the Ganges to Ghazipur. But not before we stock up our larder from the Vrassoons' back door.*

The smell of cooking fires filled the Calcutta night air. The early summer heat had not given up its hold on the vast city, so people were out on the filthy streets. A chanted melody drifted down the darkened alleyway where Maxi and Richard waited.

"Once we do this, we can't come back, Maxi," Richard said. "You understand that."

"Are you asking or telling?"

"Telling."

"No need. I know that if we steal from the Vrassoons that we'd better leave the Vrassoons' town. I think that only makes sense, don't you?" Maxi's white, toothy smile showed through the darkness, then he added, "Especially if the Vrassoon courier should happen to end up injured."

"Maxi, we're looking for seed money to get us up the Ganges to Ghazipur, not violence."

"Aye. So you've said. So you've said," Maxi repeated. "But what say you, brother mine, if by chance this Vrassoon courier isn't interested in being parted from his loot? If, say, he is as frightened of the Vrassoons as he is of us? What if he fights?"

"He won't," Richard said, ending the conversation.

"Okay, right, no violence, just theft."

"Right Maxi, just theft. Just theft."

Four hours later Richard found himself on his knees with the Vrassoon courier's knife pressed against the back of his neck, his face crushed into the filth of the alleyway, and his eyes pleading for Maxi to do something!

And Maxi did. He hurled himself headfirst from the top of a rubbish heap directly at the courier's face. The man was shocked to see this white-and-red thing flying through space at him and released Richard to defend himself against the ghost from the darkness.

The courier's first knife slash cut straight across Maxi's chest, drawing a crimson line of pain. But before the courier could use his knife a second time he felt Maxi's teeth sink deep into his cheek just below his left eye.

Then Maxi was on him — fists like pistons crushing his nose, smashing through orbital bones. Maxi sensed the man's resistance slacken and then he heard a low gurgle come from the man's shattered mouth. He lowered his fist slowly to his side as he sensed the stillness in the body beneath him.

He rose to face his brother, grief etched deep into the lines of his young face. "We did it your way, brother mine. 'Theft, no violence.' A little violence before theft could have saved this man's life — and mine!" Then he turned and headed back down the alley muttering, "No violence, no violence."

Richard ran to catch up to him, but before he could speak Maxi asked, "How much did we get?"

"Enough," Richard lied. "Enough."

When they finally got to Ghazipur it was early May. The temperature was already well into the hundreds and the constant dust in the wind obscured the sun. In order to save the last of their money they hadn't eaten for three days. But their timing was fortuitous. The heat would only break three months later when the summer monsoons swept up from the Bay of Bengal. And it was in these hot months before the monsoons that the raw opium came in from the village farms.

Opium — that which made the Vrassoons wealthy — was the fastest route to riches for the young and strong. Richard and Maxi had determined that they would learn the opium trade from the source. The village farmers around Ghazipur were at the very bottom of the trade — the source of the Nile, the beginning of the river of wealth.

Ghazipur was just up the Ganges from the more famous Benares, but it was a world apart from that ancient city's holy sites and temples. The Government of India Alkaloid Works was the only reason that Ghazipur existed. The Works was a scattered collection of brick buildings sitting on twenty or thirty acres of parched land, surrounded by high brick walls with guard towers strategically placed. Since the river had, of late, shifted south, the Works were almost half a mile of blazing white sand from the north shore of the Ganges. If the Hordoon boys approached the Works from the river they would be shot by the guards in the towers. But if they approached the main gate, they would be granted admission to enter only if they were "of the trade."

Well, Richard and Maxi were not yet "of the trade," so they waited near the front gate until some farmers who had delivered their raw opium to the Works left for their homes. They followed them and used the last of their stolen money to pay for a place to sleep. There they became acquainted with the base of the opium trade and the gentle people who made their meagre living growing *papaver somniferum*, the opium poppy.

While with the opium growers, Richard wrote: *These simple, honest people are changing Maxi. I can see it. He's relaxed around them. He is gentle with them as I've never seen my brother gentle. He laughs with them, learns their songs, cares for their children, and would probably defend them gladly with his life. I've never seen Maxi like this. His wild energy has calmed. The constant tension in his shoulders and hands has vanished. Could it be that Maxi loves these simple people? They certainly adore him.*

Ahmed, the elderly opium farmer, rose early and led the Hordoon boys to the fields. Richard translated his swiftly spoken Hindi to Maxi, who still, after all these months, barely spoke a word of the local tongue. Ahmed never went to school but he had a formal lecture style that would have been familiar to an Oxford don. He began: "The petals of the poppy flower announce their own time of readiness. Once the leaves are at their densest orange they are about to fall. Then you must squeeze the capsule like this." And he reached down and gently but firmly squeezed the capsule between his thumb and forefinger. Then he smiled. "If it is firm like this one then you must be ready. See how it's beginning to grow a coating of white? You must check the flowers every morning. Without fail. Every morning. When the green capsule is finally completely coated with that dusty transparent whiteness it is time."

Then he reached into his pocket and produced a unique knife, called a *nashtar*, that had four slender blades held together with strands of cotton. In one deft stroke he cut the opium capsule. A thick, milk-white juice oozed from the four parallel cuts. Then he handed the *nashtar* to Richard.

Using a *nashtar* was an acquired skill. A skill Richard had yet to acquire.

"No. Your cuts are too deep. See, the resin flows back into the seeds and is lost. Try again."

And Richard did, but this time the cuts were too shallow.

"No. See, the ooze does not flow now." He shook his head and scowled. He took the *nashtar* from Richard's hand and held it out to Maxi, who quickly and accurately lanced ten capsules — just right. Ahmed smiled deeply and put a hand on Maxi's cheek.

Maxi's smile lit up that dry dusty morning.

The Hordoon brothers spent all day lancing the capsules, Richard doing more and more watching and Maxi working with ever-increasing speed, and — to Richard's profound surprise — joy.

The next morning Ahmed took the boys out to the field before sunrise and continued his lecture. "Overnight the ooze hardens into a brown gum, see?" He ran his finger across the sticky substance and held out his finger. "This is raw opium," he announced, then handed both of the boys heavy clay pots and showed them how to scoop the hardened resin into the earthen jars.

As with the *nashtar*, Richard struggled with the task while Maxi seemed to find the inherent rhythm of the process and hence real pleasure in the work.

Two days later the poppy was scored a second time and the process was repeated. A single poppy capsule would be scored up to eight times.

One night Maxi caught Richard writing in his journal.

"What are you figuring, brother mine?"

"How do you mean, figuring?"

"You sit one way when you're writing and another when you're figuring. You screw up your face, like a macaque that swallowed a bee."

Richard smiled, then showed him. Maxi eyed the figures but they meant nothing to him. "Look, Maxi," Richard said, "the eight scorings of the opium capsule yield up to two-hundredths of an ounce of raw opium. Right?" Maxi nodded. "So Ahmed said that twenty pounds are needed per acre to turn a profit — that's about 18,000 poppies lanced eight times each."

Maxi nodded again but this time he said, "So exactly what?"

"So, brother mine, although the opium poppy might be able to grow in many different countries, there are only a few places on earth where the cost of the intensive labour needed to grow the poppy is cheap enough to keep it profitable." Maxi looked at Richard blankly. "Maxi, these people hardly make any money at all, and it's that fact that allows opium to be profitable. I've checked and rechecked the figures."

"You mean they work for nothing?"

"Almost nothing."

"They work for almost nothing, but without them there is no fortune to be made in opium? Is that what you're saying?"

"Yes."

"So these people work so others can be rich?"

CITY RISING

Journal Entry — October, 1828

I didn't answer Maxi's question. How could I? I know from my figures that these farmers are nothing more than pawns in the game where bishops and castles and queens have the real power — the money. And I know that Maxi cares for these people. Day after day he's spent more and more time with them. Of late he's even tried to learn their dances — to the delight of our hosts. And as Ahmed and his entire clan laughed at Maxi's ineptitude, a smile grew on my brother's face. But not the fierce, predatory smile he flashed in Baghdad and Calcutta. This was a smile of pure, simple contentment.

I will never forget the morning when I awakened to find Maxi staring at Ahmed and his three sons, all prostrate on mats, facing west, deep in prayer. I was tempted to make fun of the prone figures until I saw the yearning in my brother's eyes. I retreated and never spoke of it again, so shocked was I by the look on Maxi's face.

It was the hardest day of my life when I had to get Maxi to leave the opium farm. Maxi had been angry at me before — even hit me hard now and then — but never had his rage been so ferocious.

"But we have to go, Maxi," I said to him.

"Why? Why? I like it here, you know that."

It was only by inducing Maxi to chew on some of the raw opium that I calmed him enough to listen. "We are just starting, Maxi," I told him. "This is only the start of the Hordoon brothers. It is only our beginning. This place, this farm and these people, will always be here. If after — but only after — we try our luck and it doesn't work out for you, you can come back here. I'll bankroll you to come back. I promise."

"But I —"

"Maxi —"

"Brother mine, these people's lives seem to have some meaning. They are not wandering. This is their home. And their home is real. You can touch it and see it. It's in them."

I'll never forget his words. But I replied, "I know, Maxi. And they love you here too."

"They do, brother mine," Maxi said in an anguished whisper. "They really do." Then he fell into a profound silence — and I could see the tension begin to rise in him once again.

13

TREATY MOVES

On the Yangtze
July – August, 1842

Richard thought about Maxi's silence now as he confronted the unChinese silence of Chinkiang. He feared that the silence awaiting the arrival of the British Expeditionary Force in the captured city had nothing to do with love of any sort. At first Richard hoped the populace had escaped out the East Gate, but then he opened a door to an ancient courtyard — and his gorge rose in his throat. He slammed the thing shut and gasped for breath. For a moment he was desperate for a pipe, then he found his voice and called out, "Sir, over here."

Gough and his lieutenants approached. "You're white as a …"

Richard pushed open the heavy gate and pointed into the ancient courtyard. Gough stepped in and saw a new horror. An entire family had committed suicide. Grandparents, parents, uncles, aunts, cousins, children all on the ground — a few still writhing in pain from the knives buried hilt-deep in their chests. But no noise — not a sound.

And so it was in the rest of the city. Not a soul was left living. Not a single voice to deride or adulate the invaders. Only the silence of self-inflicted death. And as Richard watched the bodies of Chinese men, women, and children being thrown onto a pile, one upon another by the north wall of Chinkiang, he thought of the love and the vibrant life that Maxi had experienced with the peasant farmers near Ghazipur. He saw in his mind's eye Maxi dancing around the fire as Ahmed cried with laughter. He heard Maxi's hoarse cry, "I like it here, you know that!" Then Richard saw the body of a young girl roll from the top of the pile of bodies and halfway down jerk to a stop as the knife in her belly snagged on another body's belt. She dangled there like a discarded doll on a junk pile. Richard stared at her. For the first time he questioned the very reason he had come to China, all those years ago, and he knew that no amount of prayer or dovening or bowing down to Mecca would answer his question.

The fall of Chinkiang finally set off alarms in Beijing, and a High Mandarin named Kiying was enlisted to slowly and painstakingly investigate the possibility of preparing to begin to think about starting some sort of negotiations or talks or parleys with the *Fan Kuei*, the Foreign Devils.

Yangchow, the city across the river from Chinkiang, chose to pay half a million dollars in silver to be left alone. That gave the British full control of the Yangtze end of the First Emperor's Grand Canal. The British set up camp on both sides of the waterway and proceeded to raid local villages for provisions. They also commandeered junks on the river and used them as houseboats for the officers.

"From here we slowly strangle central China," Pottinger announced over a pheasant dinner on the *Cornwallis*. The officers, except for Gough, nodded their approval. McCullough proposed a toast to Pottinger, who rose to accept the adulation, wiping gravy from his chin, and said, "The Yangtze River is the throat, and as soon as we grab it and squeeze tight, the whole situation of this God-forsaken country will be determined."

There was a momentary silence as those assembled tried to decode the purple prose of their leader. The lull was broken by a tentative, "Hear, hear," followed by a "Well spoken," and then many other such inane affirmatives.

From outside the Captain's cabin, Richard listened to the English congratulate themselves and get progressively more drunk.

The next morning a stifling wave of heat arrived — and stayed. A standoff followed. No junks entered or left the Grand Canal. The British didn't move from their advantageous position, but not a word came from Beijing.

And, oh yes, China began to starve.

The British suffered, too. Sickness — primarily diarrhea, malaria, and dysentery — took a heavy toll on the sailors. Rats had somehow invaded every level of every ship of the entire armada. It was particularly bad on the lowest deck of the *Belleisle*, the orlop, where the soldiers lived in extremely tight quarters.

Rumblings of discontent came from the men, and the dangerous air of mutiny swept from ship to ship.

Finally Gough persuaded Pottinger that they had to do something to force the Emperor's hand. "Nanjing is the key, sir. Once we have it under our control, the Emperor will have to sue for peace. Sir, if we stay here things could degenerate quickly." Pottinger's eyes opened wide and his nostrils flared but Gough continued. "This canal can be secured with less than a third of our ships and the rest could proceed upriver to Nanjing and take her."

Pottinger rose and said, "I'll take your suggestion under advisement," then left for his cabin.

Four hours later he emerged and gave his orders. "Twenty ships are to stay and keep control of the canal. The rest are to follow me on the *Cornwallis* upriver to Nanjing."

Gough, openly relieved, nodded his head and shouted orders.

Shortly afterwards, fifty vessels of the British Expeditionary Force made their way upriver toward the ancient capital, Nanjing.

Halfway there the British were told by a formal delegation that a Mandarin they had dealt with before over the "Hong Kong issue," Ilipu, was on his way.

"So, I see that the Emperor has finally seen the light," remarked Pottinger, scratching the non-existent stubble on his chin in a fine imitation of thought.

"So it would seem, sir," Richard said, after he had translated the last of the courier's words.

"Dismiss the heathen," Pottinger ordered.

Richard did, but in much more conciliatory terms.

As he walked the courier back to his craft he heard Pottinger announce in a loud voice, seemingly to Gough but in reality for the benefit of the sailors within earshot, "The real war on the Yangtze is about to begin. It isn't going to be fought by your soldiers or our great man-o'-war sailing ships, although, I admit those did their part in this tapestry. The real warriors in this conflict — and the heroes, too — will be the diplomats."

Gough stared after Pottinger's retreating figure and scowled. Richard could understand how galling it must be for a real soldier like Gough to hear a strutting popinjay like Pottinger claim the title "warrior" — "heroes" be damned. Real soldiers never believed in heroes.

On land, not three miles from the ship, Ilipu sat with his superior, Kiying. Tea was brought and pickled watermelon seeds. The men sipped their chai and spat out the husks of the seeds.

"The barbarians are pleased that you are here, Ilipu," Kiying said.

"Evidently, sir."

"They also believe you to be in charge of the delegation," Kiying added.

"Only a barbarian would make such a foolish assumption, sir."

"Let them continue in this belief, Ilipu," Kiying ordered.

Ilipu nodded and poured more tea for Kiying.

Both Ilipu and Kiying assumed that, like all other barbarians who had set foot in the Celestial Kingdom, the British had come not simply to trade, but rather they had their sights set on plundering the heart of the Celestial Kingdom, Beijing. And both Mandarins knew that the first duty of every Manchu was to preserve the dynasty. It would be a catastrophe if Beijing fell to these round-eyed monsters. But the two Mandarins were troubled. They did not have real instructions from Beijing, except to make sure that the barbarians removed their ships from the Yangtze, and their powers to negotiate were not clear.

Both also knew that they would be either rewarded or punished based upon how successful they were in getting the *Fan Kuei*'s ships out of the waters of the Celestial Kingdom.

On the 11th of May, 1842, the Mandarins made their first approach to the barbarians — through representatives, naturally.

Richard was called to the deck of the *Cornwallis* and then quickly ushered into the Captain's cabin. There before Admiral Gough and Governor General Pottinger stood three middle-level Chinese civil servants, who delivered their message.

"So?" Pottinger demanded of Richard.

"He says that we are to cease plundering traffic on the river and prepare ourselves for a round of talks."

Pottinger spat out, "Tell these little humbugs that that is precisely what we are *not* going to do. We will continue our war on the river until such time as an acceptable treaty is signed."

Richard relayed the Governor General's message. The three men took it well, or so it seemed. Then Pottinger added, "Tell these three buffoons that they are not to return. That there will be no negotiating — none — with anyone but this Kiying and Ilipu. And that those two scoundrels needn't bother coming unless they have full plenipotentiary powers." Pottinger inexplicably giggled, then repeated in his over-educated lisp, "Potent plenipotentiary powers." An odd smile crept over his face as he added, "There will be no 'I've got no right-ee to agree-ee to' or 'I've got to bring-ee this-ee thing-ee back to my Emperor' bull thwap." He turned to Richard. Richard opened his mouth but no words came. "Tell them, man."

Richard knew that Mandarins, even high-level Mandarins like Kiying and Ilipu, didn't have plenipotentiary powers as they are understood in the West and had no choice but to proceed carefully in any negotiations. He was about to tell Pottinger, when he noted the man's set jaw and decided against offering unsolicited advice. Richard translated Pottinger's message. The Chinese turned ashen and hurriedly left.

Before they were even off the ship Pottinger ordered the flotilla farther upriver and said, "Gough, bombard the south side of the river as we go."

"But there's nothing there ..."

"Precisely."

"To prove a point, sir?"

"What else?" Pottinger demanded. "Bombard the south side of the river, then let's get up to Nanjing. Chop chop, Gough. Chop chop."

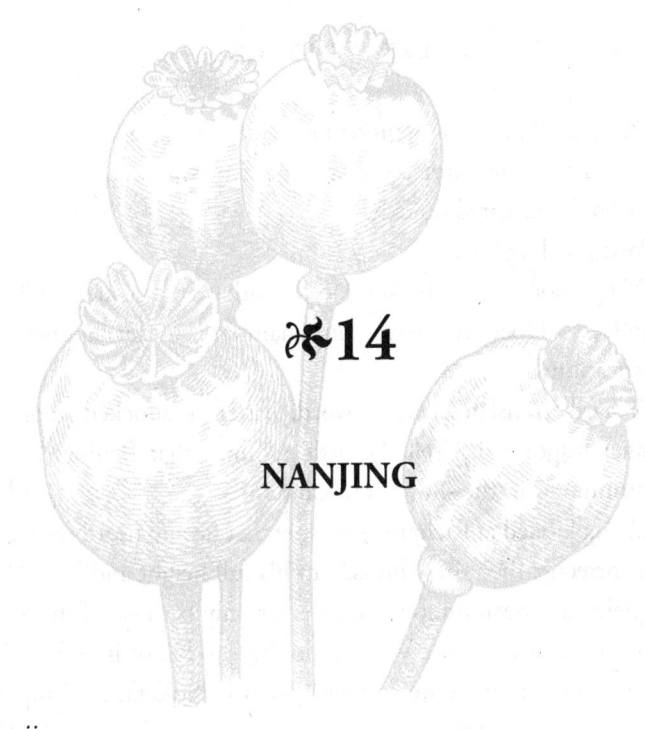

14

NANJING

Nanjing
August 5, 1842

On Friday, August 5, 1842, the steamer *Queen* pulled the *Cornwallis* into position before the walls of Nanjing. Later that day a higher-level Mandarin named Chang, under a white flag, boarded the flagship. Despite Pottinger's claim that he would not see any representative of the Beijing government who did not have full plenipotentiary powers, he surprised his officers by agreeing to meet with Chang. Again, Richard was called.

Chang handed over a parchment text. Richard had only a rudimentary understanding of Chinese writing, so he offered it back to Chang and asked in Chinese, "Would you be kind enough to read the missive?"

Chang smiled, knowing full well that Richard had made this request because, like all other barbarians, he couldn't read. Some barbarians could learn to speak but few could master the writing of the Middle Kingdom. His smile broadened as he read, "Ilipu,

Mandarin and personal representative of the Celestial Emperor, requests that you not attack the sacred city of Nanjing."

Richard translated quickly.

Pottinger laughed.

"Why does the chicken-faced barbarian cackle?" Chang demanded. "Does he have no manners, understanding, or sophistication?"

Richard translated every word. After a shocked moment Pottinger responded, "Tell the little monkey that Beijing, too, is not immune from the shot of our cannons."

Chang looked at Richard to be sure that he had heard the translation correctly, then drew himself to his full height and said, "You foreigners have been unopposed thus far only because of the kindness of the great Emperor, who cannot bear to kill or injure human creatures. But beware, Foreign Devil. If pushed too far the Emperor will call upon his people to rise — every man, woman, and child — every bush will be a soldier ready to kill the hideous barbarians." He turned to Richard. "Translate to the round-eyed maniac."

Richard did — word for word.

"Tell the little monkey to watch his foul mouth," Pottinger said as his face turned a vivid red.

"Enough of the maniacs and monkeys," Gough said quietly.

"What do you expect?" Chang angrily responded. "You kill people everywhere, plunder goods, and act like pirates; disgraceful, disgraceful and completely unacceptable. How can you say you are anything more than bandits? How? You alien barbarians invade our China; your insignificant country attacks our celestial court — how can you say you are anything but common thieves?" Chang slammed his fist on the table and spat at Pottinger's feet.

Gough held a hand to restrain the Governor General. "Ilipu's request is at least a beginning," he whispered.

Two days later, Ilipu sent four officials as his plenipotentiary. Pottinger rejected them outright and the *Cornwallis*, for the first time, opened its gun ports and prepared to assault the ancient city walls of Nanjing.

Quickly another embassy from Ilipu arrived promising a ransom of three million silver dollars and negotiations as soon as Kiying arrived. Pottinger's response was to order Gough to land a full regiment of Madras troops, complete with horses and artillery.

Finally, talks were arranged but not onboard the British warship — rather in a temple outside the town's walls. A commission was handed over by Gough. The Chinese responded that they would need time to examine the document, and while they did, the British should call off their offensive. Pottinger responded, "There has been enough dilly-dallying. The next thing you heathen will hear will be the sound of Her Majesty's cannons as they knock down the walls of Nanjing."

The next morning a messenger arrived on the flagship to tell Gough that Ilipu and Kiying had read the commission and were prepared to appear for formal talks. A skeleton of the treaty was hastily drawn up in both languages and the meeting was set.

At precisely ten o'clock the next morning, Kiying and Ilipu paid a ceremonial visit to the *Cornwallis*. They handed over an agreed-upon version of the treaty and were shown around the ship, offered tea and cherry brandy. It was the first opportunity for the British to see Kiying and they liked what they saw. He had a fine manly countenance, with a pleasant overall cast to his person. But Ilipu, with whom the British had dealt in the past, looked like a broken old man.

When the two Mandarins entered the Captain's cabin they noticed a picture of Queen Victoria. When Gough explained who she was, the Mandarins bowed.

The rest of the negotiations that day were straightforward. It was clear from the beginning that the primary concern of the two Mandarins was the immediate departure of the English fleet. "How many times do we have to tell these heathens that we're not leaving until we have a signed treaty?" Pottinger, ever the "diplomat," spat out in disgust.

Negotiations over the minutiae of the treaty itself finally began.

Two days later Pottinger and Gough received a formal invitation to view Nanjing. They were welcomed to the city by a crudely organized twelve-gun salute. Then, at the very end of a long working session, the real reason for the war was at long last broached — the opium trade. But the Chinese refused to talk about opium in any public forum whatsoever and adamantly rejected any official discussion of the matter.

"If I may, sir?" asked Richard.

"Go ahead," Pottinger said, with an openly bored shrug.

"Suggest to them that the subject of opium is better discussed unofficially. It is, after all, a private matter that needs quiet consideration by men of wisdom."

"More horse thwap."

"Do it," said Gough.

Richard spoke to the Mandarins, who were visibly relieved by the suggestion and quickly entered into an animated conversation. "Why do you English permit the cultivation of the opium poppy in your Indian colony?"

Pottinger offered up the stock British answer. "If we stopped its growth there it would simply move to other locales." From his "figuring" Richard knew the economics of the opium trade and knew this was not necessarily true. "Besides," Pottinger continued, "if your people are virtuous they will desist from the evil practice; and if your officers are incorruptible, and obey their orders, no opium can enter your country."

"This is no answer," said Kiying, "and as you well know neither virtue nor incorruptibility are in vast supply in any society."

"Especially in heathen worlds like yours," Pottinger muttered.

But before Pottinger's slander could be translated Gough asked, "Why not legalize it? At least then you could tax it and your government could collect money to help your people."

The Chinese refused to honour the suggestion with a response.

Richard listened and translated for days and days. In the middle of the seventh day he realized with a shock that the other issue, close to the hearts of all the British negotiators — namely, the opening of China to foreign missionaries — was not even going to be mentioned. As the official negotiations ran their course nary a word was spoken on the subjects of religion and opium! God and opium, the two major causes of the war, never entered the discussions that led to the final draft of the treaty.

The final agreement saw the Chinese paying an indemnity of twenty-one million silver dollars, six of them earmarked to pay compensation for the twenty thousand chests of opium thrown into the sea by Canton's Commissioner Lin. More importantly for Richard, five ports were opened to trade: Canton, Amoy, Foochow, Ningpo, and of course Shanghai. The Hong trading system was abolished. Consuls were to arrive and be treated as equals, and a schedule of customs duties was to be accepted and not amended at the will of any local Mandarin.

Beijing's acceptance came before the end of the month, and the signed treaty was laid out on the captain's table of HMS *Cornwallis* — four silk-bound copies in both English and Chinese.

15

THE WHITE BIRDS LAND

White Birds, October 1842 and Richard's Journal, 1828

Gough immediately ordered the English fleet back downstream — toward the Bend in the River — where Richard and Maxi, their obligations to the British Expeditionary Force completed, fully intended to jump ship and begin life.

The Chinese locals saw the ships heading downstream and assumed the armada had been defeated by the glorious armies of the Emperor. But it wasn't just the uninformed populace who claimed victory. "Why are they celebrating?" Pottinger asked Richard as the *Cornwallis* passed by jeering crowds on the banks of the river. Richard knew that the ruling Manchus believed the treaty they had signed hadn't really cost them anything. They were sure that the extremely restrictive access to Canton would simply be repeated in five other ports. Allowing consuls to come to these ports was fine with Beijing since, as far as they were concerned, *Fan Kuei* should be superintended by a *Taipan—a* business leader — of their own, who should, naturally, report to his Chinese superior. As for the other provisions the English insisted on — namely the acceptance of an English ambassador in Beijing, the demand to dismantle the Hong merchant system, and standardizing tariff rates — well, these were niceties that could be sidestepped as the Manchus deemed necessary. From the Manchu point of view nothing important had changed.

But Richard suspected the Chinese were wrong this time. Terribly wrong. He assumed the western powers wouldn't carve up China as they had Africa. They would not take over China as the English had India, or the Russians had central Asia. What they would probably do was riddle China through and through — like water carves out tunnels in limestone. Shortly, the Europeans would be able to work and live and sell their opium — and proselytize — at will. With, in fact, an absolute colonial confidence.

London's response to the treaty was less than enthusiastic. One newspaper opined: "It secures us a few round millions of dollars and no end of very refreshing tea." Another editorialized that the best thing about the treaty was that the English populace would no longer have to be bothered with reports of "sweeping away whole crowds of poor pigtailed animals with cannon or bayonet." Neither paper ran the story on the front page; both gave several more column inches to the recapture of Kabul.

The Protestant community and their press, however, were joyous. One of their more effusive newspapers stated, "Since clearly God had chosen England to chastise and humble China so He will likely employ her to introduce the blessings of Christian civilization."

The American Evangelicals were equally enthusiastic. They saw God's work as preparing the way for their imminent arrival.

The opium merchants on both sides of the Atlantic Ocean didn't bother expressing their pleasure with the treaty in print, but simply began to plan for the full opening of China. The offices of Dent and Company in London, Oliphant and Company (also known as the

House of Zion) in Philadelphia, Jardine, Matheson Traders in Edinburgh, and of course the Vrassoons' British East India Company were hives of activity as they mobilized to move, en masse, into the new treaty ports.

In Paris a certain Madame Colombe looked at her sternly handsome Jesuit son and asked, "Are you and your order ready for a serious return to China?" He smiled, kissed his mother's hand, then took his leave.

When he was gone, Madame Colombe's other child, Suzanne, entered the room. "Are you and your girls ready for a sea voyage, *ma chérie*?"

"It is time to extend our business, mother, and this *Shan-geh-hi* sounds ideal. Will you be joining me?"

"I'm too old for the travel, but I do envy the adventure that awaits you, my darling."

"Will my brother be doing whatever it is he does in China as well?"

Madame Colombe shrugged her shoulders and smiled. Whores and priests, priests and whores — the women in her family had given birth to both in equal numbers for generation upon generation.

In a far wing of his palatial estate in Hampstead, the Vrassoon Patriarch pocketed the urgent message and took his leave of the staff of Bedlam, who were paid to carefully dress as lords and ladies for what he thought of as his mad girl's Mid-Winter Eve's Ball.

"Don't go now, Daddy!" The girl's shrill voice came all the way across the vast room. He turned and glared at the nurses dressed as duchesses at her side, then quickly crossed to her. She sat in the large chair in her expensive party dress, her eyes alive with pleasure. This was, after all, her yearly treat. The Vrassoons' Mid-Winter Eve's Ball — a falsehood within a secret — the last vestige of

Eliazar Vrassoon's heart's obligation to a creature he once loved.

"Just for a minute or two, then I'll be back, dearest." He looked sternly at her nurses.

"And you'll dance with me, Papa?"

"Of course I'll dance with you. Would a Mid-Winter Eve's Ball in your honour be complete if I didn't dance with you?" He pecked at her dusky cheek, turned, then hurried to his waiting carriage.

Forty minutes later he entered his private office in the British East India Company. There he was met by his eldest son, Ari, and his two lead China hands.

"So?" he demanded.

"It's not ready yet."

"Bollocks!" Eliazar Vrassoon shouted — no longer the Duke of Warwickshire, now simply what he truly was, a bare-knuckled street-fighter protecting his hard-earned territory. Then he turned to his son. "Where are those Baghdadi boys?" Despite the fact that Richard and Maxi were both in their thirties they would always be boys in the eyes of Eliazar Vrassoon. Dangerous boys.

An image flashed into his mind: a young boy's hand pushing open a door to reveal the madwoman as a beautiful little girl asleep in her tiny bed. He remembered exactly what he had said: "Your father has agreed, boy. Your father has agreed."

"Our …"

"Your father … has agreed," he had said sternly.

He shoved the memory away and looked out the window. It was the longest night of the year, but the blaze of light from the thousands of candles in the ballroom would banish the darkness. An eerie chill went through him. Some cultures thought that when you felt that, it was a cat crossing your grave. Other cultures believed that your death had found your whereabouts. But Vrassoon was from neither of these cultures. He shook off the feeling and repeated his question.

"Where are the Baghdadi boys?"

On the very last day of 1842, Richard and Maxi shared a bottle of exquisite
Champagne, then completed their plans for Shanghai's upcoming concession auction.

As they did, in London, the Great Seal of England was affixed to a copy of the Treaty of Nanjing at the Lord Chancellor's house on Great George Street. Six blocks away, Queen Victoria danced in the new year at Windsor Castle.

As Her Gracious Majesty danced in London, Richard breathed the opium deep into his lungs and forced his mind back to how all this began. In the flickering brazier light, through the haze of opium smoke, he read his journal entries, beginning with the night after he and Maxi had left the opium farmers, over fifteen years earlier.

Journal Entry, April 1828

The two small earthen jars, each packed to the brim with raw opium, that Ahmed has given us in return for our three months of labour in his fields will be our entrance fee to the world of the Works at Ghazipur and the second part of our education in opium.

The raw opium arrives at the Works in early April. It is weighed and then poured into wide stone vats in a covered warehouse. The product resembles a molasses-like tar, but smells like fresh-mown hay.

It smells of promise.

Opium absorbs moisture from the air quickly but needs to be thoroughly dried before it is packed for shipment. The dry, dust-rich winds of Ghazipur in late April, May, and June are perfect for the task. Once the dry weather establishes itself, small portions of the paste are taken from the storage vats and spread in shallow wooden trays on raised concrete platforms to dry.

Eventually there are hundreds of gallons of opium in the drying trays, stirred by mechanical mixers that often break down — at which point Maxi and I step in with our spades and rakes. For months Maxi and I have stirred the stuff in the stifling heat, exposing every ounce of the drug to the air.

The monkeys have been our only real distraction during these long hot days. Although the animals have the run of the Works they never eat the opium from the drying trays — but they do drink from the nearby stream, and always seem a bit soused. One day, near the end of our first month, we stopped our stirring and watched a clearly dopy monkey walk on its back legs out along a tree branch that overhangs the Work's wall by some six or eight feet.

He almost got to the end of the slender limb when he let out a screech, teetered forward, and fell the thirty or so feet to the hard ground, head clunking when he hit. He lay there for a moment then got up, smiled at us, gave a toothy chatter, took one step ... and fell over dead.

It was the first thing to put a smile on Maxi's face since we left Ahmed and the opium farm.

I've learned that Maxi wasn't smiling at a drunken monkey. In the monkey's actions he'd seen thought — strategic thought in motion — and physics. As the monkey moved on the thin sections of the tree limb he reached up, grabbing a branch above him, thereby dividing his weight between the branch above and the one below.

I watched Maxi turn slowly in a full circle taking in the entire perimeter wall of the Works. Only three trees were close enough to the wall to have branches that came into the compound. One was close to the caker's hut. It had one slender branch that stretched eight or nine feet past the glass-studded top of the wall. The branch was so thin that the guards must have ignored it since it seemed to present no means of access to the grounds.

"What do you see," I asked him.

Maxi shielded his eyes from the scorching sun and looked above the slender branch. "Many feet above that branch is a cluster of somewhat thicker limbs — too high for a man to reach from the lower branch unless there was a tool of some ... "

Then he smiled as he pointed toward an unwound turban of one of the cakers stretched over the caker's roof to dry in the sun.

"Think about ways to distribute a man's weight between two or even three points — about how to divide a man's weight so a slender branch would not have to bear the full load," he said as he kept looking at the branch over the wall and the unwound caker's turban.

"It's like a puzzle," I said.

"Aye," he smiled back, then added, "I've always loved puzzles. This one is challenging, but solvable."

That night, as the stars ignited the southern sky and Maxi worked through the mechanics of suspending weight through triangulation, Richard finished putting into his journal all he knew about their future source of wealth, opium.

Once it has dried, some of the hardened opium is moved to a shed where it is pressed into blocks wrapped in oiled Nepal paper and sold as Akbari, *which is locally consumed. Akbari is used mostly for medicinal purposes. It is dissolved in water or alcohol. In India Akbari is the poor man's malaria cure, his rejuvenator in old age, his only relief from fatigue and pain.*

"Then why don't we sell this Akbari, brother mine? We could do that here," Maxi said.

"So, you could stay with the opium farmers, Maxi?"

"Why not? Why not just sell Akbari?"

"Because the selling of relief from pain and fatigue is not the same as selling happiness."

"What are you...?"

"Listen to me, Maxi. I agree that there is some money in selling a cure for pain, but not a fortune. Not a future. The real money is in selling the dream of happiness. Smoked opium, Chandra, is where the money is. And no one in India smokes opium — that only happens in China. No, don't turn away from me, Maxi. Listen. At first the Chinese mixed the raw opium with tobacco or betel leaves in what they called Madak. But Madak only yields the smoker little dreams. Some daring smoker must have decided, 'The hell with the chaff, I'll smoke the wheat.' And he did. And the uncut opium granted him a world of dreams. An entire universe of dreams. Try to understand this, Maxi. We're in the business of selling dreams — and once the smoker has visited the dream worlds, he wants to live there. That's what we are going to supply him with, Maxi — access — access to the infinity of dreams."

Maxi stared at me for a long moment, then returned to his "rope calculations."

Maxi and I worked ourselves silly proving to the Works that we could be trusted enough to become cakers. After three months, finally, today, the monsoons arrived. With the rain there is no need for more stirring, and all the opium was hauled indoors to the caking shed. Either they are going to throw us out on our Baghdadi asses or they are going to offer us what we've been angling for — work in the caking shed.

For three months we have been stirring the muck and planning. Sewing false pockets into our britches, watching the monkeys cross over the walls on their tree branches, and digging holes near the one dark corner in the wall that can't be seen by either of the two nearby watchtowers.

So it was that we found ourselves standing in the deserted courtyard of the Works, in the rain. And it rained. And we stood. And we waited in the rain. And the Indian supervisors watched us strange boys from far away and wondered at our endurance. We stood there for two days and two nights, not moving, not eating — waiting.

Finally on the morning of the third day the head supervisor came out under an umbrella held by a lackey. "What is it that you want? Why are you still here? You have exactly one minute to answer my question, then I will have the guards shoot the two of you," he said in a furiously *fast and highly accented rural Hindi.*

I smiled and nodded my head. I had missed some of the first two sentences but got the gist. "Thank you for honouring us with your attentions. We want simply to stay and work for your fine firm."

"But the rainy season has come. There is no more need for stirrers."

"We thank you for the opportunity to learn the art of stirring. Now we wish to learn the art of the caker."

That clearly surprised the supervisor and he had to think for a moment. He said, finally, "We will pay you nothing. In return we will teach you the caker's art."

"That sounds entirely fair," *I replied quickly, knowing full well that the man would be pocketing our salaries. Maxi smiled.*

The supervisor turned on his heel and retreated indoors, out of the rain.

I took a step forward, slipped in the muck, and fell to the ground — and lay there.

"Get up, brother mine, it's wet out here."

"Tired."

"Yes, but this is not such a good place to sleep."

"So tired."

"Your journal's getting wet."

That got me to my feet.

And so we have become cakers at the Government of India Alkaloid Works in Ghazipur — and made our first serious opium trade: our labour for their product.

16

A CALCUTTA DEATH, A CAKER'S LIFE

Calcutta, 1833 and at the opium works, 1834–1836

"He's dead," the warehouse manager announced bluntly. Death was hardly an unusual occurrence in the stifling heat of the Vrassoon warehouses. Although, death of a non-Indian was different — of a Vrassoon co-religionist, almost unheard of.

The Vrassoon Patriarch stood over the body and was momentarily tempted to place the point of his polished shoe against Hordoon's nose and push. But he resisted. "Leave us," he said, and the manager retreated to a far corner.

Vrassoon stared down at the dead man. "So it is over," he said in a low voice. "Our deal is finally done. That which joined us now belongs just to me and awaits me in her bed. As any good girl would. How could someone like you even know someone as precious as her?" He looked away from the body, then back at the prematurely aged man at his feet. He was tempted to say something solemn, then thought better of it and called out, "Contact the family and have them claim the body."

"I don't think there is a family to …"

"Of course. Just get the body out of here," he muttered.

"Shall we hire someone to sit by the body until it is prepared for burial?"

Vrassoon thought about that. Then about the girl. No longer a girl, now a young woman. With sudden rages and unpredictable, sudden lusts. He thought about her docile beauty, then about being with her in London soon, and said, "No. The Ganges is good enough for the locals. It's good enough for him."

The cakers sat along both of the long sides of the dark shed with the tools of their trade lined up in front of them: brass cup about six inches in diameter, several bundles of poppy-petal sheets (made of pressed poppy petals), a pail of inferior opium called *lewah* (a semi-liquid form of the drug), and a box of crushed poppy stems and leaves called "poppy trash." Richard and Maxi watched as the caker assigned to teach them, took his brass cup and lined the bottom with poppy sheets, then adhered it together with *lewah* until he had a base of about half an inch. "Give me a lump of dried opium," he ordered. Maxi did. The caker dropped the dried opium, just over three pounds in weight, on top of the poppy sheets. Then the caker fitted poppy sheets over the top and tucked them into the sides until he had a complete ball.

He held it out for the boys to see. "Do you understand?" he asked. The boys nodded. "Good." The caker dipped the ball into the *lewah* again and rolled it in the poppy trash. "The finished ball," he said, "is then moved from my brass cup to the clay drying moulds."

When the balls were finished they weighed in at just under four pounds — three of smokable opium, one of poppy trash. These were then packed into specially made mango-wood chests, two layers separated by yet more poppy trash. The chest itself, very much like a sailor's footlocker, was then sealed with pitch to keep the water out — and, theoretically, thieves away from the valuable opium within.

Richard and Maxi quickly proved themselves adept at the task. Within the week they had their own spaces against the south wall of the caking shed. And there they worked, fourteen hours a day, seven days a week, for the three months of the monsoon season.

The cool rain pelted down on the roof and often sluiced beneath the walls of the place. One morning a huge coral snake swam in with the rainwater. Maxi had a way with snakes. He was faster than a mongoose. He leapt to his feet, that damned smile on his lips, and danced toward the poisonous reptile. Then, with lightning speed, he reached down and nabbed the snake behind the head and pressed it to the ground. The serpent's body whipped back and forth in the air. The cakers screamed and raced for the doors. Maxi yanked the serpent up, holding its flat head between his thumb and index finger, and quickly bit it behind the eyes. Then, with the snake's blood on his lips, he dangled the thing from his mouth and pranced around like a clown in the bazaar. The cakers applauded wildly.

It terrified Richard.

The opium was shipped to Calcutta on a guarded train that picked up the mango chests every four days once the rains came.

Maxi and Richard simply skimmed. Not a lot at a time. No need. The factory produced almost 6,500 cups a day. A little patience, and the secret pockets in their britches filled by evening. Before they headed to the sleeping room they made a quick trip to their hole between the towers. After several months, Maxi and Richard Hordoon had a stake.

When the monsoon season ended, the Hordoon boys left the Works. They found a deserted alley in a nearby town and waited for a new-moon night. Then they snuck out of the alley and carefully approached the walls of the Works.

Up close the wall seemed huge. Maxi sang softly to himself as he threaded the length of turban cloth through the belt loops on his pants and then around and through his legs, cinching it together over his crotch. He flung the other end, which he had anchored with a piece of chain, over the highest branch of the tree, knotted it, and handed the end to Richard.

"This'll work?"

"Brother mine, do you have a better way of getting back into the Works and getting our opium? Maybe we should just walk up to the front gate and see if they'll understand our plight and just let us in. 'We're sorry to bother you, but we've been stealing from you for months and now we'd like to come in and get what we've taken.' I'm sure they'll understand, Richard."

"Shut up, Maxi."

"Done. Now you pull, slow and steady, when I signal you."

Maxi shinnied up the tree like any monkey and headed toward the slender overhanging branch. Before he did, he fixed the top end of his rope triangle on a high branch, then the apex on the trunk. He took a deep breath and signalled to Richard, who pulled — slow and steady. And Maxi's cantilever worked. As he moved along the ever-thinning branch his weight was held less and less by the branch and more and more by the triangulation of the turban cloth.

Once across the wall he skittered down and hid in the shadows, and when he was ready he quickly raced to their hiding hole and scooped out their swag — almost sixteen pounds of *Chandra* opium. Within twenty minutes the Hordoon boys were racing along the river toward the sea — with their very first opium shipment.

They stopped in a small, dusty town almost twenty miles upriver from the Works, found a dark alley, and fell to the ground exhausted. Maxi curled in the dust and was asleep in a minute, Richard shortly thereafter.

Both awoke with a start. They were being watched.

"Where?" Richard barked.

"Right in front of us, brother mine," said Maxi as he slowly got to his feet.

Richard shook his head and, sure enough, an old man stood

not three feet from them. A cloud moved and a slender beam of moonlight lit the man's ancient features. Sorrow was etched into the deep lines of his face. Then the old man sat in the dust right in front of them and remained motionless, as if he were part of the ground itself. It was only then that the Hordoon boys realized that he was almost naked.

Suddenly the man's head began to shake violently and his voice, an echo from the depths of a vast cave, startled the boys. In Hindi he said, "Angad and Bali," pointing at the boys.

"What's he saying, brother mine?"

Richard ignored Maxi's question and asked the man in Hindi: "Isn't Angad the god who killed his own brother, Bali?"

The old man's head stopped shaking and his eyes welled with dark, viscous tears. "Brother will kill brother," he said, his voice a harsh whisper.

Richard knelt and, in Hindi, spoke directly into the man's face: "You see that in us?" The man did not answer. Richard repeated his question but again the man gave no response. Finally Richard grabbed the ancient by his bony shoulders and shouted, "Do you see that in us?"

The old man's hand came up from the yellow dust of the alley. He touched Richard's forehead, then pointed at Maxi with a spindly, yellow-dusted finger.

Richard swiped his hand viciously across his forehead. Maxi noted that the yellow dust was unmoved by his brother's ministrations.

"Damn it, Richard, what's he saying?"

But the toothless man had stood and was now walking away. Suddenly he bent over double and laughter spewed out of him — the laughter of utter futility. The laughter of one who has seen the world as it is and realized that he is not important, just a tiny part of a deity's infinite jest.

"Why is the old one laughing? What did he say?" Maxi pressed as the man disappeared into the blackness at the far end of the alley.

"It was hard to translate, his accent ..."

"You're a lousy liar, brother mine. Leave that to me. So what did the old fool say?"

"Don't call him an old fool, Maxi."

"Ah, and why is that?"

Richard didn't answer. He thought of a man who would kill his own brother, then looked at Maxi and began to laugh.

"You too? What the hell are *you* laughing at?"

"Us. Look at us, Maxi. We're just kids, Maxi. Just kids."

Over the course of the next two months, the young Hordoons made their way, with their stolen opium, to the smallish seaport of Vishakhapatnam, some six hundred miles south of Calcutta. There they found a merchant willing to buy some of their product and purchased two passages on a clipper ship to China — the Celestial Kingdom, where opium turned to gold.

Maxi loved everything about the ship. He was always above deck, learning all he could about the complex block-and-tackle systems and intricate knots that controlled the acres of canvas that drove the vessel ever eastward.

But by the third day out from port, Richard had still not conquered his seasickness and sat by an open porthole on the steerage deck trying not to retch.

An hour earlier, desperate to overcome his nausea, he had opened one of their four remaining opium packets and thrown some of the drug into his mouth. The grit was still in his teeth as he took in large gulps of sea air through the open porthole.

"Try this, me son."

Richard recoiled at the knurled brown root and the tiny, filthy hand that held it not an inch from his nose. He looked past the root and the hand and saw a very small, crippled man in a stained black cassock.

"It's ginger root, lad. Chew on't. It'll help."

"Thank you, but ..."

"It's part of God's bounty, me son. God provides for every need; all you have to do is look closely. God provides. Chew on't, lad."

Richard did, and was immediately astonished by the intense, unusual flavour. He didn't feel like retching so much but spitting certainly gained a new appeal.

"Don't swallow it, it's nay peeled. Just chew." Then the ugly, foul-smelling little man sat right beside Richard and asked, "On which of God's quests are you, me son?"

"My brother and I are off to China," Richard managed to say.

"To do God's work," the little man said, nodding. It wasn't a question, rather a statement of fact. He rested his largish head against the swaying wall of the ship. "I was much older than you the first time I landed in the Middle Kingdom."

That perked up Richard's interest. "How many times have you been there?"

"Four. God has granted his servant four lengthy stays." He nodded again and smiled. "Yes, He has been very kind to His Brother Matthew," then he added with a further small smile, "S.J."

"S.J.?"

His small hand touched Richard's cheek as he said in a gentle voice, "My poor benighted pagan boy, Society of Jesus." Then without prompting he added, "The *Irish* Society of Jesus."

Richard assumed he was supposed to respond so he said, "Ah."

"I doubt there's any White man alive who knows more about the Middle Kingdom than I do. I even speak what they call the Common Tongue." Then a brilliant smile crossed his face. "It's a long voyage. Learning a new language might help you pass the time."

Richard smiled back, his nausea now in retreat. He wondered if the opium had finally kicked in, or was it the magic of this tiny Irish Jesuit? He didn't care.

Brother Matthew began to speak. He had a vast knowledge of

China and of everything that influenced the Chinese.

Every morning they would meet at sunrise just after Brother Matthew had completed his morning prayers. While Richard prepared their morning meal he had his morning chew of opium. He was aware that each day he was using just a bit more than the day before but it calmed him and allowed him to concentrate. Besides, it wasn't *Chandra*, smokable opium, just bits of the raw product to keep the seasickness at bay.

As soon as the Jesuit finished eating, which he did forcefully and with surprising gusto for one so small, the lesson would begin. Brother Matthew was pleasantly surprised by Richard's linguistic ability, and after three weeks together they were conversing in rudimentary Mandarin.

Although Richard was pleased to learn the local tongue, he was more interested in learning what Brother Matthew knew about the Middle Kingdom — and the opium trade. And Brother Matthew was an enthusiastic teacher. When they got to a topic that he really liked he would leap to his feet and hobble back and forth in front of his ever-attentive pupil, gesturing with his tiny hands and speaking as if a large conclave had gathered to hang on his every word.

"At Calcutta, the government of India — read the government of sodding England, may the fat cow rot in Hell — sells the chests of opium at open auction to the likes of the British East India Company..."

The bloody Vrassoons, Richard thought, catching himself already using the little man's habits of speech.

"... which holds a monopoly on all direct trade from England to China, and whose Indiamen Trading Ships are the largest ocean-going vessels in the world."

That surprised Richard. So the Vrassoons had a monopoly on all direct trade from England to China. It had to have taken some real coin to line enough parliamentary pockets to keep that in place.

"There's also Dent and Company, whose English firm have been

China traders since the mid seventeenth century, as well as Jardine, Matheson, the huge Scottish trading company, and the American Oliphant and Company, who claim to be in the missionary delivery business and whose ostentatious *piety*," — he said the word as if it were a ridiculous joke — "gives rise to their nickname, the House of Zion." At that he laughed aloud and repeated the name "House of Zion" eight or ten times, each with more relish than the time before. "Apostates one and all! Bound for the fires of Hell they are. Poor misguided souls. Without Rome, what are we? I ask you that! What are we?"

Richard didn't know and said nothing. Brother Matthew happily continued. "You might note that their heretical faith and missionary zeal never got in the way of their opium trading. Wha' think you o' that?"

Again, Richard didn't know what to say and was saved by the continuing monologue of his tiny teacher.

"Then there are some smaller independents."

But behind many of them had to be the money the Vrassoons made from the monopoly granted to them by Parliament, Richard thought.

Brother Matthew laughed, a high girlish giggle. "And it's all perfectly legal — in India. But the moment the mango opium chests are onboard ship, the government of India — read England, may she sink in the sea with all the bitch's sterling boys — turns its back, washes its hands like Pontius Pilate, and wonders, 'Goodness gracious, where do you think all that opium is going?'"

This last was done in a whistling, sibilant, Etonian accent that, at the time, Richard didn't recognize. Clearly the little man liked to imitate aristocrats and government officials, and Richard supposed him good at it.

"Perfectly legal opium leaves India and becomes contraband the moment it approaches its intended market — China.

"From the beginning of the process everyone knows that opium is made specifically for the Chinese market. It's totally adapted to Chinese methods and tastes." Then he giggled again and said, "It's the only commodity that the English have to trade that the Chinese want — want for their tea. Tea has, from the beginning, been the end goal for the English. Only Chinese black tea can withstand the long sea voyage and keep its potency, son. And it doesn't hurt that the import duties extracted for that potency fills Her Majesty's cunting tax coffers. All that loot must buy the bitch many a fine frock!

"So there is pressure from all sides to trade: Indian opium for Chinese tea — Chinese tea in England for pounds sterling — pounds sterling for Indian opium from the Indian government — England again. Soon the English won't even bother with pounds sterling to India, they'll make the poor Hindus buy the cotton shirts from their Manchester factories. Shirts for opium. Opium for silver. Silver for shirts. And round and round and round, like the Devil and his whore with a keg of rum."

And at every turn the Vrassoons take their cut, Richard thought.

That night Richard wrote in his journal:

There is always a tremendous demand for dreams. Brother Matthew claims a Chinese labourer, who makes twenty taels *a month, from which he needs to feed, clothe, and house his family of six, will often spend as much as ten of those* taels *for his opium.*

The little Jesuit just can't understand that.

I can.

Only under the effects of the opium is the labourer no longer just a worker living in poverty, without hope of change. Suddenly he is enjoying the luxuries that life grants only the fortunate. He is no longer poor. He is no longer a two-legged mule. He is a proud lord — for as long as the effects of the drug last.

The lesson continued the next morning when Brother Matthew produced a map and pointed out places and names as he spoke. "At the turn of the century the Manchu Emperor in Beijing forbade any European access to the Celestial Kingdom. Twenty years before that, we Jesuits had lost our place of esteem in Beijing and been thrown back into the hinterlands of the vast country, forbidden to approach the big cities. Many of my brethren died in anonymity. Some were martyred. Almost all of us were tortured."

Richard looked at the hobbled little man. Could his twisted body be the result of Manchu torture?

"To be honest, none of us succeeded in converting much of the population." He smiled that small smile again, then changed the topic. "Finally, in response to much British grumbling — as a nation they are snivellers and whingers — an edict was finally issued by the Beijing Emperor. It permitted the Foreign Devils, *Fan Kuei*, access to the Middle Kingdom for purposes of trading, but only through the complex river access to Canton called the Bogue." He pointed out the estuary on the map. "Westerners were not permitted to set foot on the sacred soil of China except deep up the cuts of the Bogue at one small section of Canton Harbour, just past Linten Island." Brother Matthew pointed out the location on the map.

"Is Canton large?"

"Bigger than Calcutta and London put together."

Richard had never been to London, but Calcutta was far bigger than Baghdad so Richard was impressed.

"At Canton the Chinese divided the traders into 'factories' based on national origin. At their factories, the *Fan Kuei* are permitted to meet only with the Hong merchants who have been assigned to them by Beijing. The Hong merchants are both their commercial representatives and their watchdogs. Foreign Devils are never allowed to talk to the real power, the Mandarins, the *Ch'in-ch'ai*. The *Fan Kuei* find the Hong merchants, on the whole, an agreeable lot — but the Hong merchants find themselves between a pillar and a post. They have to deal with the *Fan Kuei and* make money for Beijing. As well, they are personally responsible for the actions of all the *Fan Kuei*, and every servant, translator, cook, or labourer that they supply for the Foreign Devils."

"What?" Richard asked. "How can they be personally responsible?"

"All of China is set up that way. Everyone is someone else's responsibility. If a farmer does wrong, both the farmer and the village official who is responsible for the behaviour of his people are punished by the Mandarin. Public executions are a common sight. Millstoning or boarding is also much in use."

When he said those final words, a real darkness crossed his features. *So that's the form of torture he endured*, Richard thought. He had heard tell of this cruel punishment but didn't know the details, except that a heavy millstone or wooden board was put around an offender's neck and it stayed there for as long as the authorities saw fit.

"Richard, opium strains the entirety of the Chinese system of social responsibility. Since almost everyone of power in China has his hands in the opium rice bowl, who is there to punish the supposed wrongdoer? And make no mistake, opium is the Devil's work, Richard. The Devil's work."

Richard thought about that for a moment, then noticed that the little Jesuit was looking at him in a new way. "Do not do the Devil's work, my son. Do not do the Devil's work."

Suddenly the Hindu man's words — "Brother will kill brother" — screamed deep in Richard's mind. He heard it a second time, then a third, until his whole body vibrated with the old man's curse. He closed his eyes tight and balled up his fists — and hoped it would pass.

"Are you all right, sir?" the owner of the opium den asked.

Richard nodded slowly and pointed a shaky finger toward the empty bowl of his pipe. The owner deposited a heated orb of opium in the centre of the bowl and then she tilted the pipe over the brazier. Smoke curled upward and Richard inhaled deeply.

Richard didn't see her deposit the third ball of opium in his pipe, but as he inhaled its sweet smoke a maniacal grin crossed his features. By the fourth ball he couldn't hold back his laughter.

"What?" Jiang, the owner of the opium den asked sweetly.

"I was just wondering."

"Wondering what, sir?"

"Wondering if anyone in England — or anywhere else in the world for that matter — has informed, her Royal Majesty, the most powerful woman in the world, Queen Victoria, that by putting her signature to the Treaty of Nanjing she has become the Sister to the Manchu Emperor and ... and ..." He began to splutter then regained control, " ... and the Auntie to the Moon."

The laughter that flowed from Richard's mouth filled the den.

Jiang retreated behind a silk curtain, where the progeny of the First Emperor's Bodyguard and the Confucian waited. The three listened to the hoarse laughter from Richard Hordoon and it pleased them.

The White Birds had landed — the first part of the Ivory Compact had been completed.

PART II

17

THE BODYGUARD, HIS BROTHER, AND HIS NEPHEW

Village of Shanghai, 1842

"You know who I am," said the tall man with the cobra tattoo on the back of his hand. It was not a question.

The young woman, his sister-in-law, moved her baby boy so he could suckle from her other breast, then nodded.

The tall man looked at the array of furniture and the dark, polished wood floor of this house. *They have amassed wealth*, he thought. "Where is he?"

"My son ..."

"My nephew," he interrupted her. "My nephew belongs to me, just as ..."

"... my husband could have belonged to you."

"If the time was upon us when he was younger, yes, it would have been him. It is the compact, agreed upon long ago."

The young mother held her baby tightly to her. At least this one was hers to keep, to raise, and, if necessary, to set out to avenge his brother.

"Where is the boy?" The man's voice snapped in the stillness of the room. The young mother looked up and to one side.

The boy was perched atop a tall, beautifully inlaid, lacquered armoire.

The tall man smiled. *Good*, he thought. Then he called out in a stern voice, "Here, boy."

Without hesitation, and with the elegance of an acrobat, the boy slid from his vantage point and approached the man.

The woman started toward her son.

"No, mother, it is my destiny. As it has been the destiny of all the first-born males of this family stretching back into ancient times."

"Your father …"

"Prepared me, mother. Now my father's older brother will test me, and if he finds me worthy he will finish my preparation."

"For what?" she screamed

"To kill, mother. To kill. Am I not right, uncle?"

The boy reached up and took the hand of the ancestor of the Bodyguard. There was already strength in the boy's grip. It frightened the man with the cobra tattooed on the back of his hand — frightened him for the safety of his own son. Only one of the two boys would be entrusted with the obligation of the Ivory Compact. Only one of the two could begin the resurrection of the ancient Guild of Assassins. The other would … he would not let himself complete the thought.

The boy's father entered the room and nodded toward his elder brother.

He saw the cobra tattoo on the back of his brother's hand. So he had finally come — as the legend said he would. And, as the legend stated, his brother had insisted that his firstborn go with him and challenge for the right to restart the ancient Guild.

His wife began to sob and the baby at her breast joined her cries. Her husband ignored her entreaties. "It is our place on the Ivory."

She'd heard of the prophecy but there had been no demand since — since forever, and now this man came and demanded her son. She protested again.

"Quiet, now. It is what I began his training for," her husband said. "It is what I was trained for by my father, and my father by his father. It is the role we must play."

His wife visibly stiffened and, holding her baby tightly to her, hissed, "And now I will have a role to play too. If my son dies, my people and I will be revenged upon all of those, I say *all of those*, who had anything to do with taking his life." Then she spat on the floor and stomped on the spittle with her left foot. "A curse into the ground will grow a branch of evil."

Her husband nodded slowly, knowing she was not wrong, then said, "As it may be. Now dry your tears and leave us." Then he turned to his brother. "I need a few moments with my son. I do not deny your right to him. I need a moment, that is all."

The Bodyguard left the two — father and son — alone.

The young assassin stood by the window, feet wide apart, head held proudly. Silhouetted against the setting sun he was the most beautiful thing his father had ever seen.

His father grunted, then held out his left hand with the thumb and baby finger held apart from the three centre fingers, which were tightly bunched. The boy put his right hand over his heart and splayed his fingers.

"There will be death soon."

"I am ready, father."

He nodded at his boy. Every morning for ten summers they had trained together before going to the fields. "Do your duty," he barked.

"I will, sir," the young assassin responded.

Then there was silence broken only by the wind outside and the breathing of the two men within.

"This pledge goes all the way back to the First Emperor's

Bodyguard, who is your revered ancestor, of whom you must beg a blessing. He was the beginning of all this."

The young assassin had heard the story many times. The phrase *kai shi* (beginning) had been the very first words he had spoken. It had caused a terrible stir in the village. And now, almost eleven years later, the portent of that day had come to fruition.

"Honour your weapons and they will serve you well."

"I will, my father, as I honour you."

"Do your duty as it has been prescribed and do what you need to do to take the position and restart the Guild of Assassins, for my brother's presence tells me that the time has come."

"I will, my father, and help our people out of the darkness into the light."

They had spoken this litany at the end of every training session, but this time there was a quaver in his father's voice and tears in his eyes.

The young assassin stood very still and allowed the image of his father to burn into his memory.

Then the door opened and the boy's uncle, the Bodyguard, strode in. "It's time."

"He'll live with you and your family until …"

"Until I must choose. You know this, brother."

"Can his mother and I…?"

"Visit him? No. And you knew that as well." Then he grabbed the boy's Manchu-dictated pigtail with his cobra-tattooed hand.

"This goes first." With a single slash of his swalto blade, the hated symbol of Manchu domination fell to the polished wood floor. "Leave it there," the cobra man said to his brother. "It will stay until your son's work is done, as a reminder of him and the duty he owes his people."

⚜18

THE SELLING OF SHANGHAI

Village of Shanghai
June, 1843

It was hot. July in Shanghai was always hot, and humid, and mosquito-infested — no place for men in wool suits and top hats. But that was what the assembled were wearing that sultry morning of June 17th, 1843, as they awaited the arrival of Queen Victoria's land auctioneer.

"Why are we dressed like this, Richard?" Maxi squawked as he scratched his thighs beneath his gabardine trousers.

"Because *they* are," Richard said, as a maniacal smile creased his handsome face. Then he broke out in an almost hysterical laugh that caused all eyes in the room to turn in his direction. Maxi gave him a sharp look. Under his breath Richard whispered, "Don't worry, I'm sober as a churchman." This last word he spoke loudly. Then he added in a whisper, "Look at us, Maxi, two kids with all these toffs!"

"Why are heathens allowed to bid in this auction?" asked the short, pot-bellied, bald-headed leader of the American trading firm of

Oliphant and Company, out of Philadelphia. He clutched an aged family Bible to his chest. Not for nothing was the Oliphant trading house called the House of Zion by most of the other traders. Then, of course, there was also the Oliphant claim that they were in the business of spreading the word of Christ — which they did while they sold opium to the heathens. "They're not Christians, are they?" Jedediah Oliphant asked.

"No, sir, they're Hebrews from Mesopotamia," Oliphant's elderly China hand replied.

"Mesopotamian Hebrews? Whoever heard of…?"

"The Hordoon brothers, sir."

Jedediah Oliphant paused and adjusted his spectacles. His already florid face reddened. "Those are the Hordoon brothers?"

"There are no others, sir."

"Handsome in an odd, Hebraic sort of way, I'd say."

"Some of the women agree with you, sir."

"Where's Rachel?" Jedediah asked quickly.

Rachel, his daughter, would have caused quite a stir at the Bend in the River. Jedediah might have been nothing much to look at himself, but his daughter, through some genetic fluke, was a true beauty. She had pale skin, a thin waist, dark auburn tresses, and startling green eyes. To the men of the opium trade, who for years had not been allowed to bring Caucasian women into their settlement at Canton, she would be a shock — a breath of pure air — a startling burst of light in their midst.

"As always, safely on board the *Water Witch*, sir."

"Hate that name. Blasphemous name. Can't we change it?"

"Not without risking a revolt amongst the crew. Sailors are superstitious, sir. The *Water Witch* has made more trans-Pacific voyages than any bark in our fleet. Not a single crewman has perished in any of the crossings, so —"

"It's through Christ's will that the ship arrives safely, not the actions of the ship's captain or any of its —"

"I don't advise changing the name, sir. I really don't."

The head of the House of Zion looked at his China hand. The man seemed to know what he was talking about. So he simply harrumphed. "Where are the other heathens?"

"The Vrassoons?"

"Yes, those."

"Their representative will be less obvious but far more significant. After all, Vrassoon is a knighted lord of the British Empire."

"Codswallop," the head of the House of Zion announced. "Just codswallop. We should sit them down and talk to them of the Good Book. Now *there* would be a conversion!"

The China hand looked at his boss and wondered if the man realized the danger that Vrassoon and Company, with its monopoly on direct trade between China and England, posed to the Oliphants' opium assets. But he chose to say nothing.

"Codswallop, I repeat," Jedediah repeated — this time loudly enough for everyone in the room to wonder what in heaven's name a codswallop was, or did, or meant.

"The American looks like he's swallowed a large toad," said Percy St. John Dent, second in command at Dent and Company of London.

"Aye, or perhaps a lizard," replied Hercules McCallum, co-owner of Jardine, Matheson out of Edinburgh, as he adjusted the shoe on his left foot to relieve the pain from the gout nodule there. He and Percy had become fast friends during their years at school together in a weather-blown stretch of land on the Scottish east coast, just north of Sinclair Castle — the coldest damned place in the coldest damned country in the world. Although they relished disagreeing with each other on almost every other topic, on that point they were in full agreement.

"The head of the House of Zion does sputter, doesn't he?" Percy asked rhetorically.

"It's an American trait, I believe, typical of Evangelical speech over there."

"Just Evangelical speech?"

"Aye."

"And why would that be?"

"It's my belief that it is caused by their erroneous conviction that they are the sole recipients of the Lord's final wisdom."

"And why would that make them sputter, you northern barbarian?"

"Because, my self-satisfied Oxonian, it should be clear to all — even Americans — that God would not choose to bequeath His final wisdom — I do love the presumptuousness of that phrase, 'final wisdom' — well, be that as it may, God would not permit His 'final wisdom' to be housed in such a ramshackle backwater as America."

"Have you ever been, Hercules?"

"No."

"And yet you feel confident calling it a ramshackle backwater?"

"I've never been to Sweden, but I know they're all blonds."

"I rather like blonds."

"As do I, Percy — as long as they don't sputter."

"Well, that depends."

"Depends on what?"

"On whether they sputter before or after," Percy St. John Dent replied with a grin.

Hercules looked at his English counterpart and said, "And here I thought you were a God-fearing, chaste gentleman!"

"Hercules, I am a businessman not unlike yourself."

"Aye, Percy, a businessman but not really like myself. You'll see what I mean when the auctioneer arrives."

Percy turned to Hercules. "What are you planning, you detestable Scot?"

"Wait and see, Percy, wait and see."

Percy St. John Dent shook his head but resisted laughing. He and Hercules might have enjoyed each other's friendship at their Scottish boarding school, but the two had been trained there to lead men and nations — and through their opium trade they were actively competing with each other to do just that.

A shuffle at the front of the warehouse drew their attention. The auctioneer entered, swatting mosquitoes as he did.

Vrassoon's man noted the pallor of the auctioneer's skin and leaned forward just slightly to get a good look at the man's hands — the signet ring on the middle finger of the left hand caught the light from the overhead window. *Good*, the Vrassoon man thought, *so he made it.* The Vrassoon man checked his list of properties and the double columns of figures beside each. The figures in the left-hand column were considerably lower than those in the right-hand column. He folded the paper, removing the more expensive figures from his sight. *No need to consider paying that much*, he thought.

"Gentlemen." The auctioneer cleared his throat, then coughed heavily into a linen handkerchief that had evidently received many similar deposits, since it crinkled when he folded it before replacing it in his breast pocket. "Gentlemen, I hereby open the initial land auction in the village of Shanghai."

He had just turned to a large surveyor's map affixed to the wall when over his shoulder he heard Percy St. John Dent, with his elegant Oxonian accent, say, "If I may, sir? I don't mean to halt the proceedings, but since the spoils we are now about to divide were won by the actions of Queen Victoria's Expeditionary Force, I feel it only right to sing her praise before we begin." He turned to the other Englishmen and Scots, who all stood, removed their hats, and launched into a spirited rendition of "God Save the Queen."

Instantly the entire assemblage from Oliphant and Company slid back their chairs and headed toward the doors. They signalled to the other Americans to follow them. Most did, but the representative of the large trading firm Russell and Company, a man with the odd last name of Delano, remained — although he did not stand.

The Vrassoon delegation stood, but refrained from removing their hats on religious grounds.

The Hordoons had already put aside their top hats and so they just stood. As they did, Maxi remarked, "They could sing 'Fuck Me on the Stairs, Molly' as far as I'm concerned."

"Or not sing it," replied Richard.

The assembly proceeded to sing the praise of a fat lady thousands of miles away with gusto, if not skill.

Jiang and the Bodyguard stood in the crowd of people at the back and watched in amazement as the *Fan Kuei*, in their ludicrous dark wool suits, held their hats and seemed to scream in unison some doggerel verse they evidently all knew. Why they stood or removed their hats to say the verse neither the Bodyguard nor Jiang knew or wanted to know.

The Confucian watched the proceedings from the safety and secrecy of a side chamber that he was able to use since the auction was taking place in a warehouse belonging to one of his brothers. He made a note in a small, but well-used, book.

When the *Fan Kuei* screeching was over, the Americans returned. And the auctioneer turned to his map, but he was interrupted a second time by the arrival of tea that the Confucian had ordered for all the traders.

"Can we just get on with this?" bellowed Vrassoon's man.

Richard stood up and with a broad smile suggested, "We are in China and tea is our business. Surely we can pause for a moment to partake in the leaf's freshness."

Expensively gowned young Chinese men and elderly women quickly appeared and pushed beautifully made carts with inlaid mother-of-pearl tops through the room distributing tea in translucent porcelain cups. Richard smiled as he raised his in a toast to the

Vrassoon representative.

The tea was wonderful. Light, open, and refreshing. Maxi and Richard savoured the fine delicate southern blend, just momentarily wondering why this particular tea was never available for sale. But then again, the Hordoon boys had been in China for almost fifteen years and they knew full well that even with Richard's fluency in the language and all his contacts through Chen they had only been introduced to the thinnest upper layer of Chinese topsoil — never allowed to dig beneath the surface to find the true riches. Richard took another sip and wondered at the taste. After all, it was the appetite for tea in England and the Americas that had started the whole China trade. He took a final sip and looked around him. Richard smiled.

"What, brother mine?" Maxi asked.

"The brocades and topcoats, the waistcoats and watch fobs, the swish and bravura don't hide the scoundrels beneath."

"Save the fancy talk for your journals, the auctioneer's about ready up there."

The auctioneer had rehearsed his approach to the proceedings for several months with the help of the Vrassoons back in London, settling on a strategy that should put the prime pieces of Shanghai's property in the Vrassoons' hands with little trouble. The first parcel of land put up for auction was a seemingly insignificant wedge with its point on the Huangpu River and its large base well to the north of the Old City. The Vrassoons were concerned about the piece since it could cut off access to the Suzu Creek. It also encompassed a potentially valuable path used by traders that they called the Bubbling Spring Way. After much debate in London, it was decided that this piece should be put up first and made light of.

The auctioneer cleared his throat again. "Mornin', gentlemen. Tea was very good, very good indeed. Now, I would suggest we begin with something small just to get us started." He pointed to the wedge-shaped plot on the survey map. "What do I hear for this oddly shaped little parcel?"

Maxi sensed Richard tense at this side, but before he could say anything, the auctioneer banged his gavel and stated, "We'll start the bidding at two hundred pounds. Do I hear two hundred?"

Maxi saw the Vrassoon man about to raise his hand, then he heard Richard's voice beside him, "Five thousand, five hundred pounds."

There was an audible gasp in the room. Five thousand pounds was 30 percent of a clipper's take on a successful trading run up the China coast.

"Five thousand, five hundred pounds. Very generous of you, sir. Five thousand, five hundred pounds." The auctioneer said, obviously not knowing what he should do next.

Richard shouted out, "Five thousand, five hundred pounds going once."

The auctioneer intoned, "Going once," then took a deep breath. Sweat popped out on his forehead as if he suddenly had an attack of hives. "Going twice …"

"Six thousand pounds!" The annoyed voice belonged to Vrassoon's man.

The auctioneer smiled and turned back to Richard. "Six thousand pounds to you, sir. Do I hear six thousand, five hundred pounds?"

Maxi looked at Richard. His brother stood completely still.

"Six thousand, one hundred pounds, sir?"

Again, Richard didn't move a muscle, although Maxi sensed his brother smiling.

"Six thousand and fifty pounds, sir?"

Richard's smile broadened and Vrassoon's man suddenly shouted, "Do you want the damned wedge of property or not, man?"

Richard turned slowly to the older man then said a single word. "Not!"

Vrassoon's man paled. Mr. Vrassoon did not care to have his money spent recklessly.

The auctioneer clearly didn't know what to do so he went back to script. "Six thousand pounds bid from the House of Vrassoon, going once, going twice — sold, for six thousand pounds to the House of Vrassoon, excuse me, to the British East India Company."

Richard turned and walked to the back of the large room and Maxi followed closely. "Hey! What was all that about, brother mine?"

"It's rigged, Maxi. I just made sure that the Vrassoons paid top dollar, that's all. They were going to get that piece no matter what — I just thought they ought to pay for it. The auctioneer's their man. The order of presentation is their idea. The whole thing's a fixed game."

"So aren't we going to bid on any of the land? I thought we were going to set up shop here."

"We are, Maxi, but not by the rotting Vrassoons' rules. Besides, until we pay off our debt to Barclays for those sodding steamships we lost we don't have much cash to work with. You have to trust me, Maxi. We don't need prime property now. We have Chen to act as our comprador and he'll give us all the access to the water we need through his wharf property. Right now we need our money for other and better things. Maybe in ten years, we'll buy back this expensive real estate at a shilling on the pound. Now, we conserve our funds and buy only the odd cheap property."

And as the afternoon made its way into early evening that was exactly what Richard did. The Dents and the Oliphants bid against each other. Jardine, Matheson went head-to-head for prime land with the Vrassoons. Even the old schoolboy ties between the Dents and the Jardines didn't stop them from viciously bidding the prices up on parcels of land they coveted. And coveted was the right word for this exercise.

Just as they were ready for a dinner break, the blare of horns and then the crash of gongs and cymbals filled the warehouse. Suddenly, all the Chinese in the room threw themselves to the ground. The door opened and, to the hammering of percussion, a Mandarin, wearing a conical hat and with the tiles proclaiming his high office strung from his neck, entered the room. Of the traders, only Richard knew that his purple Chinkiang silk gown announced that he came directly from the Manchu court in Beijing. Beside him was a young, fair-faced Han Chinese man.

The Mandarin's voice was full of fury. The young man at his side did his best to translate his words into English but his skill wasn't up to the task.

All that was clear was that the Mandarin was displeased — extremely displeased — with something.

Vrassoon's man ran over to Richard. "Explain it to His Mandarin Excellency, or whatever he calls himself, that this is a legally sanctioned auction and he has no right to interfere with —"

"You explain it to him, or have you lost your tongue? He's right over there, tell him yourself," Richard replied.

"He doesn't speak —"

"English. No. Neither does his translator, it seems. But then why should they? We're in their country, not they in ours."

"Tell him, Hordoon! Mr. Vrassoon will not be pleased with any delay."

"You'd like me to speak to His Excellency?"

"You're the only one gone native on us, mate."

"Ah." Richard smiled and then slowly approached the emissary of the Manchu court. The Mandarin's guards quickly stepped in front of their charge; their weapons drawn. Richard slowed his pace. The room had gone silent; only the street noise through the open door broke the so very unChinese quiet. A breeze picked up and whooshed into the room. Richard smelled the river and the mud flats of the Pudong across the way. Then he scented something else. Something extremely familiar. The sweet reek of opium — and it was coming from the Mandarin himself.

Richard smiled inwardly, then bowed and offered his thanks for the appearance of such an eminent man in their midst. The Mandarin stared at him and then pointed to the floor.

An air of tension cut through the room. The Mandarin was demanding a formal kowtow, something that none of the Europeans had ever agreed to do.

Richard sensed the anxiety in the room and then looked at his Christian counterparts. "It's just kneeling down," he muttered, and in quick, elegant movements he completed the complex prostrations of the full kowtow.

The Mandarin barked a command. The guards parted and the Mandarin stepped forward. "Stand!" he ordered, and remained impassive as Richard got back to his feet. Then he nodded. As he did, Richard asked in fluent Mandarin, "Will this suffice? The procedure is new to me and I need much practice. I apologize if it was not fully correct."

The Mandarin gave a dismissive grunt and stepped closer to this oddly scented, grotesquely coloured man.

When he got close enough, Richard whispered in Mandarin, "Excellency, there is more money to be made from those who refuse to kowtow than from those of us who will. If you permit me, I can show you how this can be done. As a fellow dream traveller I can show you the way."

Richard thought the man was going to order his immediate execution, but all the Mandarin said was, "And your name would be?"

Richard told him his name, and twenty minutes later, much to Richard's surprise, the Mandarin left without ever saying what had caused him to interrupt the proceedings in the first place — and the bidding continued.

The common front the traders had shown in the presence of the Mandarin disappeared the moment he left the room, and the prerogatives of business, the opium business, reasserted themselves.

Later that night, the Manchu Mandarin was led by the Confucian to the door of Jiang's establishment.

Jiang bowed low and, with her eyes still averted, said, "As we agreed, my house is at your service." Jiang felt the scrape of cracked finger nails as they moved across her cheek, and she stepped back.

The Mandarin's smile had a disconcertingly easy cruelty to it.

"Excellency," she said as she stepped aside to allow the Mandarin ahead of her into the main hall, where she had arrayed her best wares. The Mandarin entered the chamber and stopped. His long fingernails came out of the sleeves of his gown as he slowly scanned Jiang's finest courtesans, posed on couches, against columns, and on leather stools. Although courtesans were used to being wooed by suitors before offering up any sort of sexual favours, for the Manchu Mandarin, the *Ch'in-ch'ai*, the rules were broken. The women held their poses as surely as any statue despite the pain of putting pressure on their tiny bound feet. Jiang had guessed that the Mandarin's tastes would run to the visual and the controlled, but he gave no indication that he saw anything that pleased him. Jiang nodded subtly and the women, as one, rose, turned, then repositioned themselves, the youngest, as if by accident, now in groups of two and three.

The Mandarin didn't move and, more troublingly, didn't speak. *Could it be that his tastes run to boys?* Jiang thought as she came up beside the man and said, gently, "Choose, it is the price we agreed upon for you to permit the auction to proceed. If there is nothing in this room that pleases …"

"Oh, there is something in the room that greatly pleases," the Mandarin said in a hushed voice. His voice was surprisingly light, like smoke in the wind.

"I'm glad," Jiang said, "they are all most expert —"

"No doubt they are," he cut her off, "but …" the Mandarin's eyes left the array of elaborately dressed young women and turned to Jiang, "… I doubt that any match the mastery of their mistress.

It is my right. It is my right to choose a whore from this group of whores." His voice curled with a rage that somehow seemed personal. "So I choose you," he said, touching the brocade on Jiang's dress. "You. My whore," he announced loudly. Then he smiled that cruel smile again.

The Confucian didn't know what to do. The girls were relieved but embarrassed for their "mother." The Mandarin remained silent, staring at Jiang.

Finally Jiang canted her head slightly then announced sweetly to all assembled, "It is my pleasure to bring the clouds and rain — to such an esteemed man."

Early the next week, Maxi came running into the leaky wooden shed that served as the Hordoons' office. "Richard. They're here!"

Richard looked up from his calculations and for a moment didn't know what had brought the blush to his red-haired brother's face. Then he understood and let out a cry of joy, grabbed his hat, and raced his brother to the docks.

There, standing side by side holding hands, were his twin four-year-old sons, both dressed in short pants, knee socks, caps, jackets, and ties. Their Malay *amah* stood behind them, her white-gloved hands holding her bag. Behind her, two Chinese men were stacking suitcases high on a long-handled wheelbarrow.

"Hello, boys," Richard said in Farsi as he stepped toward them. "Who is who?"

The *amah* started to speak but Richard put a finger to his lips. Then he asked the same thing in Mandarin and, to his pleasure, one of the boys stepped forward and responded in kind, "I'm Milo, sir, and this is my brother Silas."

Richard beamed. He hadn't seen the boys in three years. He put out a hand toward Milo and said, "Welcome, son."

The boy took his hand then leapt into his arms and shouted, "Daddy."

But the other boy, Silas, stepped back behind his *amah*, and despite her best efforts, he wouldn't come out from behind her skirts.

From Richard's arms Milo turned and called in English, "Come, brother mine, come to Daddy."

Maxi laughed out loud and shouted, "Brother mine! Where'd they get that?"

Richard gently put Milo down, although he held his hand tightly. Then he reached out toward Silas. "Come, son, I'm your father."

Milo crossed over, took Silas's hand, and walked him back to Richard. "Father, this is my fine brother, Silas," he said, with his surprising command of Mandarin.

Richard extended his hand. "Proud to meet you, Silas." Richard's hand hung in the air for a long, embarrassing moment, then he reached for his son. The boy hissed at him and bit his hand.

Richard let out a short shout that drew many eyes.

The boys' *amah* put her gloved hands over her mouth. Milo ran to his brother's side. "Don't be angry, father."

Then Maxi stepped forward. "Angry? Why would he be angry at a little nip? The boy's got spunk, he does. Good lad. I've bitten your father several times myself, and enjoyed it every time. Truly." Maxi extended his hand. "I'm your Uncle Maxi, proud to make your acquaintance."

Slowly Silas reached out and shook his uncle's hand. "Myself as well, sir."

The boy's formality made them all laugh. For a moment there was a family unit, father and two sons — an idyll. Then Chen came running up with Richard's man, Patterson, who looked after his stables for him.

In furiously fast Mandarin, Chen said, "I'm sorry to interrupt, sir, but we need your signature on the waybill now or the ship won't sail on the tide. Please sir, you must hurry."

"Patterson, take my sons back to the warehouse. Show them our horses. I'll be back as soon as I can." Richard quickly turned and ran after Chen, with Maxi at his side, toward the harbour.

The *amah* indicated the luggage but Patterson ignored her and turned to the boys. Then, under his breath he said, "Come, me little heathens, welcome to the monkey kingdom."

⚘19

TROUBLE IN THE OPIUM TRADE

Village of Shanghai
August, 1843

Two months later, Richard was stunned when he stepped into Chen's stifling warehouse. The hastily erected structure on the docks about a mile south of the Suzu Creek was filled to overflowing with goods, some en route to England, others intended for various locales in China. Richard, as he always did when he came to the warehouse, marvelled at Maxi's handiwork, which was evident in the building's ingenious pulley system. A series of intricate knots and pin-rails permitted items hung from the rafters to be labelled and returned to the ground with a minimum of confusion and fuss. Richard nodded as he thought, *While I was learning from the little Jesuit, Maxi was learning from the sailors.*

Teas in twelve-foot-long woven hemp bags hung from every rafter, scenting the air with a dense, exotic tang; the wooden shelves were stacked high with bolt upon bolt of silks dyed blue and red and green and opal and puce, brought from Chinkiang and Canton and secret farms farther upriver that, of the Europeans, only Richard had found. The locked wire cage area on the far side of the tall space was completely filled with mango-wood caskets crammed with India's finest opium. Even in the area outside the lockup, the mango chests were piled six deep almost to the ceiling.

The warehouse was stuffed with goods — but there wasn't a single worker — not one. Not a single item was being moved, or being readied to be moved, or even inventoried

Richard turned to Chen, his comprador, but before he could speak the smaller man answered the obvious question. "Because they won't work for you. They won't cross into your concession. I've tried. They won't lift or carry or load your goods, no matter how much money I offer them."

"They won't work for me?"

"No. Not for the *Fan Kuei*, not for any of you."

"Since when?"

"It was hard to get them before, but now it's impossible."

"Why now? What's happened now?"

"The Manchu Mandarin has brought in Taoist monks who tell the people they and their entire families will be cursed if they work for the *Fan Kuei*."

Richard took that in, then looked at Chen, with whom he had worked for years. It crossed his mind that this small man might have paid a heavy personal price for his contact with the Foreign Devils. But then he cast the thought aside. He had paid Chen well, and never looked too closely at the man's books. Richard had made Chen a wealthy man, and there was always a price for wealth — Richard could attest to that.

"This is bullshit," he barked.

Chen found it humorous that Europeans made cuss words out of valuable substances. The manure of a bull was very useful, both as fertilizer and in many different medicines; in fact, there was an active market in quality bull excreta in which Chen had speculated and made a handsome profit — one of his few good bets.

"Fuck," Richard muttered.

Another one, Chen thought. *Why would sexual intercourse be a subject about which one could or should cuss?* Chen had watched the opium traders spend a large proportion of their energy in trying to get local beauties to have sex with them. Why, then, should an endeavour that seemed to be at the forefront of their concern be a thing about which they cussed? Chen shook his head. He had known this strange foreigner for almost twelve years and he still didn't really understand the first thing about him.

They had first met when Chen's personal fortunes were at a low ebb. His gambling habit had cost him his finest consort and was threatening the quiet of his home and even his livelihood. He was the second-ranking scholar in the village at the Bend in the River, having passed the first three civil service examinations before his twenty-second birthday — a feat accomplished by very few. As such, he had status in the community, a secure job, and a land allotment. Only his eldest brother, the Confucian, held a higher rank. The combination of Chen's obvious abilities and his gambling habits had brought him to the attention of the Manchu-appointed Mandarin who was responsible for all conduct at the Bend in the River. The Mandarin ordered him to make contact with any *Fan Kuei* who were brave enough to venture this far up the Yangtze. The Mandarin controlled the gambling house to which Chen was most indebted and had landed on a plan to get the money Chen owed him, and much more.

Chen could still feel the weight of the ancient writing stone that the Mandarin had put in his lap, and in his mind's eye still saw the legal document, which he had had no choice but to sign, that gave 60 percent of all of his earnings to the Mandarin for the next twenty years of his life.

At first Chen had thought of refusing to sign the document, then he'd reconsidered. He had already made contact with this strange opium trader that he thought of as "Lee Char Or'oon" and the man seemed in need of "representation" at the Bend in the River. Chen made a quick calculation. If he reported only 80 percent of his earnings to the Mandarin — not a hard thing to do, and in some ways expected of him — and he stole, say, 30 percent from the foolish *Fan Kuei*, then signing this legal document would cost him nothing — and his gambling debt would be forgiven. He thought about it for a moment, smiled as he thought of getting his favourite consort back, then took the proffered brush, dunked it in the exquisitely dark ink, carefully rolled the bristles on the writing stone's incline, allowing the excess ink to drip back into the reservoir, and drew the characters of his name carefully on the bottom of the agreement.

The Mandarin's long fingernails scraped along the rice paper as he drew it toward him, powdered the document, then allowed the powder to drift to the teakwood floor.

Then the Mandarin smiled at Chen and said, "I'll expect the first payment and your accounts on the third day of each new moon." His smile broadened as he added, "If that is convenient." He pointed to the floor, then the door.

The man was demanding that Chen perform a full kowtow, then back out of the chamber on his knees.

As Chen knelt for the first section of the formal bows he wondered about people with position and power. Wondered how they could be so foolish. So concerned with things that were unimportant — appearances, rather than realities. So he grovelled his way out of the room as the Mandarin turned his attention to "more important" business.

To refuse to grovel if it will get you what you want or need struck Chen as … well, as "bullshit." Chen turned to the man whom he still thought of as Lee Char Or'oon and said, "It's bullshit, but it's the way it is."

"How much did you offer them to work for us?"

"Half a *tael* of silver every other month. And still there were no takers."

"I never authorized —"

"They think you smell bad ... and more importantly, that you bring bad luck. So they don't think, even for half a *tael* of silver, it's worth the risk."

Even knowing that Chen would exaggerate by at least 15 percent, which he would then pocket, Richard knew that the price was still over three times what a normal worker would make in any of the menial jobs in the place Richard was beginning to think of as Shanghai.

"Have the Taoist priests been —"

"Stirring them up?" Chen smiled. "That's what priests do, stir things up."

Richard agreed with that assessment. He left the warehouse.

A dense rotting smell came from the Huangpu River. Richard saw the large tandem junks pulling a dredge net just to the north. They had probably passed where he stood about a half hour back, so the water was still roiling with its rich bounty of silt and nutrient decay. He looked across the river to the Pudong and a shiver went through him. The area was still wild in its own way. Even the Chinese were concerned the odd time they needed to access the place. If one were to believe the rumours, the Pudong was home to whores and pirates and mountebanks and ancient martial arts cults and sorcerers. Experience had taught Richard to respect the Middle Kingdom's version of rumours. Mesopotamians were fabulists. Everyone in the Middle East was a ludicrous fabulist. But the people of the Middle Kingdom were practical, very practical. When they were frightened of something — anything — it was worth taking note. Richard had had only one experience with the Pudong — and it was not something he wanted to repeat.

He turned from the river and headed east along the Suzu Creek. The creek itself was Chinese territory, not given over in the Treaty of Nanjing, so it was dotted with small family junks. The odd one was larger and moored away from the houseboat junks. The creek was deep enough to float several larger vessels. One was a favourite restaurant of Maxi's, another a favourite opium den of Richard's. But it wasn't the river vessels that interested Richard as he crossed the smallest of the creek bridges and entered the American Settlement. He wanted to know if it was just the British that had scared off Chinese workers — or all non-Chinese.

Crossing the bridge, he came to a small contingent of American marines. They eyed him carefully. For a moment he thought they were going to bar his way but they stepped aside. The American Settlement was as clear of Chinamen as the British Concession. The only overt difference was the flying of the Stars and Stripes instead of the Union Jack, but Richard didn't salute any flag so he didn't see that as very important. The streets were still little more than muddy lanes, the buildings hastily put up shacks, and the whiff of sewage wrapped itself around cooking smells — just as in the British Concession.

The Chinese referred to the area north of the Suzu Creek along the Huangpu River as Hangkow. It had traditionally been a fishing centre. Several small Chinese junks were at anchor just off the partially completed jetty. Two American clippers, owned by Russell and Company, rode the swell farther out in the river. The Americans had thrown up a dozen two-storey wooden shacks along the shore. Goods were stored on the first floor while dormitories for the White workers were on the second. In the back of the rickety buildings were rudimentary cooking and toilet facilities. As in the British Concession, wood planks sufficed for roads — where there were roads of any sort. The old Chinese cart paths were used more often than not as the demarcation of streets. Some of them even had fancy names — way too fancy for dirt paths.

As in the British Concession, there were only men — and now evidently all of those were White. There was not a Chinese face in evidence.

Richard was about to enter the American administrative offices when he stopped cold in his tracks. At first he didn't believe what he'd seen — a woman — a White woman — a White woman here, at the Bend in the River? There had been no White women allowed in Canton for all those years. The Chinese strictly forbade it. Married men left their wives behind in Hong Kong or Malay, as Richard had. But here?

He ran quickly down the wobbly steps into the mud path, then dashed around a corner — and there she was, lifting her skirts to step over a large puddle. He stared. Deep purple outer frock, a taupe lace bonnet, white white white skin, and flashing green eyes that turned to him and held his with a kind of invitation. Then she hopped over the puddle in a graceful leap and quickly stepped up on the board sidewalk before heading down the block of rickety buildings.

Richard followed.

The woman disappeared into a particularly austere building with a small bronze plaque by the door: Oliphant Trading Company, Philadelphia, Pennsylvania.

Richard grinned as he recalled rumours that Papa Oliphant was such a protective father that he was unwilling to let his daughter out of his sight. "The House of Zion has a Jezebel," he said aloud.

That drew harrumphs of indignation from the frocked and top-hatted men around him who were evidently heading into the Oliphant Trading Company (aka The House of Zion) as well.

Richard dusted off his britches and followed the crowd.

Inside the main entrance he turned to the left, and there was a modest hall in which the men all stood, hats in hands. A pump organ began to play and the plump, bald leader of the House of Zion, Jedediah Oliphant, stepped forward. The small man wore a black woollen waistcoat and sweated profusely. He pulled at the watch chain looped across his round little tummy and pulled out a large pocket watch that he flicked open with a fleshy thumb. After a brief examination of the watch face, the head of the House of Zion said, "Open your prayer books to page 212 and we will sing together 'Our House is Built on His Foundation.'"

All around Richard, men turned pages and quickly raised their voices in song.

Through the heavy voices Richard heard the sweetness of a light soprano that seemed to float on the breath of the men. He stepped slightly back and there she was, the green-eyed woman. She smiled at him, and he felt his heart skip a beat — then another one.

The service or song-fest or whatever it was (Richard hadn't attended a religious ceremony of any kind in almost twenty years, and even then only when his mother had insisted) ended with a flourish and the senseless shaking of hands. Then the participants dispersed and returned, Richard assumed, to their jobs.

Richard looked for the woman at the end of the service but didn't see her, so he approached Jedediah Oliphant, as he had initially intended.

The head of the Oliphant and Company knew Richard and heartily disliked him — as did all the other opium traders. But Richard had known real hate since his childhood and was not put off by mere dislike. He put out his hand as he approached.

Oliphant declined the offered handshake. "Have you come to this place to investigate the one true faith?"

For a moment Richard had no idea what he was talking about, but when it struck him, he smiled. "No, but I did enjoy the singing."

"God's songs they are, my son."

Richard let that go. "Can I have a word?"

Oliphant grudgingly led him into a hardwood-panelled room and closed the door. The board floor was carpeted with a quality Persian rug whose pattern Richard immediately identified as coming from the Takrit area. A small fireplace was embedded in one wall and three leather wingback chairs dominated the room. Oliphant sat in one but didn't offer Richard a place in one of the others.

"So?"

Richard ignored the slight. "I want to talk about Chinese workers."

"Do you have any?"

"No. Do you?"

Oliphant waved a chubby fist in front of his chubby red face as if smoke had somehow entered the room and bothered his nose. "No," he said slowly.

"And this is not a problem as far as you are concerned?"

"God will provide."

Richard snicked his teeth and said, "Absolutely." He turned to leave; the hypocrisy of Christian opium traders was too much for him just now. But before he could get to the door it was flung open, and the vision from the street with the soprano voice appeared. With a quick curtsey she said, "I'm sorry to interrupt, father, but the Bible translator is waiting for you."

Richard stepped aside and she passed by, a step closer, he thought, than was absolutely necessary. A whiff of rosewater came off her. He smiled and turned back to Jedediah Oliphant. "Your daughter, here, in Shanghai?"

Gruffly the older man said, "She's a fully qualified missionary who has come to this dark place to bring the light of the Word of the Lord. Haven't you, my dear?"

The green-eyed creature smiled and retreated from the office.

"I've found her a suitable husband, a classmate of mine — two years ahead of me at the seminary, a pastor from Massachusetts. They'll be married once her missionary work here is finished. She hasn't met him yet, but they're a good match."

Richard couldn't resist asking, "And she'll be happy with you choosing a husband for her?"

"My daughter is a good girl."

Richard wondered about how long a "good girl" remained a good girl with a husband older than her father, but he didn't speak.

The silence in the room seemed to draw itself out. Finally Oliphant broke it, saying, "Rachel listens to her father."

So her name is Rachel, Richard thought, and although he'd never bothered with the Bible, he thought that perhaps he'd spend the evening figuring out exactly where in that dusty old book the name of this "good girl" originated.

Rachel Elizabeth Oliphant was not a "bad girl," but nor was she the "good girl" her father believed her to be. She had for years privately questioned her Church's teaching. Not only had she found her own urges as powerful as anything she had ever felt in prayer, but her ability to read Hebrew and Aramaic gave her access to part of the "Good Book" that flew in the face of American Evangelical thought.

She was shocked when she painstakingly translated the story of the rape of Lot by his daughters, not to mention the horrors she found in the Dinah story, or Abraham's questionable behaviour with his wife while in Egypt. But perhaps most revealing to her were two passages from the Bible at what she thought of as opposite ends of desire. The first, the openly erotic poetry of the Song of Solomon, was so surprising to her that at first she couldn't believe her translation was correct. The second challenged everything she had ever thought about faith — it was her translation of the story of Job. She had often been told the story of the good man put through horrifying tribulations to challenge his faith in his God. The way she'd always heard the story was that Job bowed down and accepted the power of God. But her translation from the original Aramaic stunned her. Nowhere did she find Job accepting the totally unjustified punishment that he was forced to endure. In fact, as far as Rachel Elizabeth Oliphant could translate, the final thing Job said to God was: "I have seen You and I am appalled."

When she realized that in its original form Job was the last book of the Hebrew Bible — not a middle book of what Christians call the Old Testament — she literally began to shake. The whole Old

Testament did not lead to the arrival of the prophets that acted as precursors to the arrival of Christ, as she had been taught. It led to Job — and Job's assertion of his right to reject God's arbitrary, capricious use of power.

So, as her mother went first blind then slowly insane while the tumour grew in her head, Rachel thought of Job's response to God, not her father's relentless platitudes about God's unfathomable plan for man.

And yet she did not openly criticize her Church or resist her father's insistence that she do missionary work. How else could a Victorian girl get to see the world — and hold off her father's impulsive desire for her to marry a man over twice her age?

She found much of Asia to her liking, although, being a woman, she had been kept away from China for almost a year, and when she finally was allowed ashore, she was closely guarded by her father and his men. Yet she had still managed, often from the covered interior of a carried sedan chair, to see much. She loved the sights and sounds of the open-air markets and the street hawkers who produced delicious hot food at almost any hour of the day. She often forced her escorts to stop and, although she was seldom allowed out of the sedan chair herself, she would have her father's men buy her freshly cooked dumplings stuffed with pork and shrimp in a ginger sauce, sticky rice balls with a cooked egg yolk in the centre, or long, thick noodles in a sweet brown sauce. She was anxious to try to eat with the sticks that the locals used, but she was not allowed to try.

There were things that were less pleasing. The few women she saw — since the Chinese, like their American counterparts, kept their women behind locked doors — all waddled painfully on their bound feet. The tiny appendages were an obscenity to her.

Then she met her very first courtesan, who, she later learned, was probably on her way to one of the eight or ten dinner parties thrown in her honour by various wealthy men interested in her amorous attentions. The runners carrying Rachel's sedan chair slowed in the narrow street of the Old City as the courtesan's sedan chair approached from the opposite direction. The street was not quite wide enough to allow the two sedan chairs to pass, and as her sedan chair scraped against the wall, Rachel heard a shriek from the other chair that caused the courtesan's carriers to bump her sedan chair into Rachel's. When they did, the rungs of her privacy curtain caught on the rings of Rachel's drapery — revealing one woman to the other.

For a breathtaking few moments, beauty from the West examined beauty from the East and vice-versa — and each found the other both enchanting and hideous, at the same time.

The one overriding impression that Rachel came away with was that this woman who spent her time with several different men did not strike her as any less a child of God than the ostentatious virgins of her native Philadelphia.

About a mile to the north on the Bend in the River, in the three-storey stone headquarters of the British East India Trading Company, heart of the Vrassoons' empire, Cyril, the Vrassoons' elder China hand began the first of his two attacks on the Hordoon brothers.

He raised a glass of sherry to the Manchu Mandarin standing in his office and took a deep sip. The scribe by the Mandarin's side and his personal bodyguard didn't move a muscle.

Cyril's command of Mandarin was not perfect but it was serviceable, and he had one of the very few Mandarin/English dictionaries in existence, with which he spent an hour every evening no matter how long his day had been. Ownership of the dictionary had been a result of one of the more delicate negotiations into which he had entered upon his arrival at the Bend in the River. But he wasn't thinking of that just now.

"May I congratulate you on a fine proclamation, sir. I look forward to it being made public." Cyril saluted the Mandarin a second time and once again drank alone.

The Mandarin just held his drink and waited — for the rest.

Cyril smiled. "You await *my* proclamation?"

The Mandarin didn't smile. Didn't move. Just listened.

Cyril retreated to his leather-topped partner's desk and slipped a key into the lock. He pulled out the central drawer until he heard a click, then he gently pushed it forward about an inch and heard a second click — that unlocked the bottom drawer. From that drawer, he withdrew a document written in English. He put it face up on the desk and resisted smiling.

The Mandarin clearly didn't speak let alone read English. He gave a quick, short shriek and the office door slammed open. Two of his armed guards entered, followed by a tall, elderly Jesuit.

Cyril noted the man's sallow pallor and the fire in his rheumy eyes. The Jesuit wheezed when he exhaled and had a pronounced limp. But he was clearly a believer. Cyril had seen such fire in the Vrassoon Patriarch's eyes when it came to matters of religion and practice. Cyril handed over the document.

The Jesuit pulled back the sleeves of his Chinese-style outer gown. Cyril had forgotten that one of the great fights between the Jesuits and the other Catholic orders in the Middle Kingdom was the willingness of the Jesuits to adopt the clothing and habits of the local population, a choice that was totally resisted by the other Catholic orders (especially the mendicant orders) and thought to be out and out blasphemy by the Protestant Evangelicals.

The Jesuit finished reading the document and turned to the Mandarin. "It is as you agreed. Once your new tariffs drive the Hebrew brothers out of business, you will be given 50 percent of all their property and opium assets."

The Mandarin nodded, then reached for the paper and with one move tore the thing in two and dropped it to the floor. "Sixty percent," he said in Mandarin.

Cyril contained his smile. He had authorization to go to 75 percent. He did the appropriate harrumphing and muttering then counter-offered. They settled at 58 percent, and everyone was happy. Perhaps this deal would pacify Mr. Vrassoon, although he doubted it. Cyril glanced at the calendar on his desk. Eliazar Vrassoon would shortly arrive in Calcutta, and not too long after he would no doubt make his triumphal arrival in Shanghai.

The Mandarin stepped forward and held out his long, elegant fingers. On his left pinky, the ring bearing his chop glinted in the light. He dunked it in the ink the scribe proffered and affixed his sign to the scroll. Then he turned and thought of rewarding himself for completing this unsavoury business with the *Fan Kuei*. Perhaps a session of clouds and rain with Jiang would cleanse him of the distaste.

Even before the Mandarin could sample the delectations of Jiang's brothel, Cyril completed his note to the Vrassoon Patriarch with the words, "*Your first plan is in place and the second about to begin. The Hordoons may soon be no more, and these new tariffs will undoubtedly raise a cry from the traders to seek extraterritoriality — as you predicted.*" He called in his most trusted aide and gave him the handwritten note. "This is not to leave your sight, and you are to deliver it personally to Mr. Vrassoon in Calcutta. I will expect it to be in his hands by the end of the month. If I find it hasn't arrived in that time I will personally see to it that you and your family never see another penny from this fine company. Do I make myself clear?"

The young Jew nodded, took the letter, and ran to the docks — the tide was going out.

Then Cyril called the two hard men into his office and set in motion the second part of the Vrassoon's two-pronged attack on the Hordoon boys.

"So, which of you has the stomach for violence?" he asked.

The two young men looked at each other before the taller of the two stepped forward. "I'm y'r man, Gov."

Ah, our co-religionist from the hard streets of east London, Cyril thought, then added to himself as a reminder, *No matter how successful we get, we'll always need you and your muscle. You were with us at the beginning and you'll be with us at the end.* Then he quickly amended his thought, *If there is such a thing as the end for us.*

He held out an official-looking document and said, "Do you know where the Baghdadi boys do business?"

The rough man nodded.

"Good. Take this to them, and don't leave until you can tell me exactly how they took it."

Well, the Hordoon brothers didn't take it well.

"The Vrassoons have bought our note from Barclay's Bank and are calling in the debt," Richard told Maxi, while the hard man waited for his response.

"The one from the sunken steamships?"

"The same."

"But we had years to pay off that debt."

"Not now that the Vrassoons have bought it."

"Can they do that?"

Richard's hands flew up like two doves suddenly loosed from their cage and a high-pitched laugh came from him. The formal document slipped from his hand and fluttered to the floor. "The Vrassoons, it would seem can do whatever they damn well want to do."

"Is there an immediate demand for payment?"

"What do you think, Maxi! They want to drive us out of business. Naturally they're demanding payment."

It was then that Maxi threw himself on the Vrassoon messenger and smashed him to the floor.

"Let him go, Maxi. He's just a stupid messenger," Richard said.

"Thanks, Gov," said the man, who dusted himself off, and then in one quick move lunged at Maxi.

Richard let out a sigh. *When would they finally learn about Maxi?* he wondered as he looked away.

It took less than a minute for Maxi to rearrange the features on the man's face so that even his own mother would not recognize him.

Richard leaned over the prone, gasping man and said, "Tell your master that we received his message and you, my friend, your present condition is our response. Tell him that." Maxi yanked the bleeding man to his feet and then turned him to face Richard. "Do you understand me?"

The man nodded, and Maxi ran him out into the filthy alley. When he returned he saw Richard sitting on a wooden stool in the corner staring at nothing. Then he reached for his opium pipe.

Maxi caught Richard's hand and held it tightly. "No, brother mine, not now."

The next morning Richard was awakened by a loud knocking. Maxi was already on his feet, pulling on his britches, as Richard pushed aside the mosquito netting over his bed. He felt a heavy weight on his chest and pushed it off. The old Bible in which he was researching the origins of Rachel Oliphant's name fell from his chest to the plank floor with a thud. Richard took God and His Son's name in vain several times, each a slightly different, and often colourful, variation on the basic theme.

The knocking got louder. Richard reached for the Bible and found his balance awry. More and harder knocking from the front door. "What's the time, damn it?" he called.

"At least a couple of hours before sunrise, brother mine. Maybe close to four," Maxi called back as he headed toward the barred front door of their temporary living quarters.

"Who is it, Maxi?"

Maxi withdrew the bayonet he kept hidden between the joists above the door and lit an oil lamp. The flame came up quickly, casting a sallow glow. Maxi slid open a panel and held the lamp up to it. The mirror at the end of the panel reflected the light to another mirror that brought back the image of Chen, wrapped against the morning cold, standing at their unmarked door.

"It's Chen," Maxi called back.

Richard was suddenly fully awake. Chen wouldn't venture deep into the Concession, especially at this hour of the night, unless there was an emergency.

Shanghai was a no man's land between eleven bells and sunrise. Most of the sedan-carried courtesans were safely ensconced for the night, either having decided to reward their patrons with their sexual favours or not, by that hour. With the exception of the hot-water shops, almost every merchant had closed their doors. Those too poor to find housing for the night often bought the required two cups of tea in the hot-water shop and slept at their tables. It was worth the price to avoid the violence on the street, where cheap liquor was consumed by sailors, opium inhaled by the hard-muscled Chinese labourers, and the hands and mouths of lowly street whores were much in demand.

"Let him in, Maxi," said Richard, as he struggled into his clothing.

By the time Richard was dressed he found Chen and Maxi in the cookhouse, the brazier throwing heat into the dank room, the smell of brewing tea no doubt about to enter the air.

"So?" Richard demanded, looking at Maxi.

"I don't know, brother mine. It's something technical. I have marketplace Mandarin and he has, well, about the same in English."

"After all these years, Maxi ..." Richard shook his head.

Chen held up his teacup and said in Mandarin, "*Ni de cha do hao, hao cha* — Your tea is very well brewed, very good."

"What's very good?" Maxi asked.

Richard sighed. "He says your tea is well brewed, very good. Say thank you."

"Thanks," Maxi said to Chen, who gave him a quizzical look.

"Jesus! *Shieh sheh*"

"I know that. *Shieh sheh*," Maxi said.

Chen stared at him, stone-faced.

"Fine, now we've got that out of the way, what are you doing here, Chen?"

The smaller man straightened his back. Richard could clearly see he wanted to say, "This is China, I am Chinese, I can go anywhere here!" But the moment passed and Chen said, "You should be prepared."

"For what?"

"The Mandarin's newest proclamation." Chen took a rice paper scroll from his sleeve and handed it to Richard, who unfurled it and tried his best to make out the meaning of the characters. For a second he wondered at his own genius with spoken language but his almost complete inability to decipher character writing. He did recognize the characters for "all men" and "immediately" and "new," although he understood that the "new" was attached to another character that he couldn't decipher. "Would you read it to me, please, Chen?"

"Surely," Chen said, and reached for the scroll. "The following proclamation comes into effect immediately and concerns all men in the Concession territories. New tariff rates on all goods are published below …'"

"What?" Richard's voice bounced off the walls, "The Treaty of Nanjing explicitly states that tariff rates on traded goods can only be changed after full consultation with the —"

"They consulted with the Vrassoons representative, who agreed," Chen said, and then he went on to explain that the Vrassoons' representative had also suggested an upfront payment scheme.

Richard swore softly, and Chen saw in the flickering oil lamp light something he had never seen on the face of the *Fan Kuei* he thought of as Lee Char Or'oon — fear.

Maxi saw it too. "What? What's he saying?"

Richard explained. Maxi swore too, but not softly.

Chen watched the red-haired maniac and resisted the impulse to run. Not only was the man's violent nature clear, but he was also the ugliest thing that Chen had ever seen. Red hair, fish-belly skin, blue eyes — a devil if ever there was one.

"And the Vrassoons agreed to an upfront payment," Richard repeated.

"Explain," Maxi demanded.

"Rather than paying as items come and go from the warehouse, the Vrassoons agreed that every trading house will put up 100,000 silver pieces as credit from which the Hong merchant will keep accounts. When the trading company has used 50 percent another 100,000 is due."

"That's crazy, what kind of business deal is that?"

"The kind designed to drive us out of business, Maxi — that kind of business deal. It makes sense. The Vrassoons are the only firm in Shanghai that has enough money on hand, and they can afford to piss it away."

"But why? Why piss away money just to hurt us?"

"Because they hate us Maxi."

"I know that brother mine, but why? Why do they hate us?"

Richard had no answer to that, but he took the dual threats seriously. He grabbed his hat and headed toward the door.

"Where are you going?"

"To see the Vrassoons. Maxi, it took us fifteen years to get here. Fifteen years, and now it can all be taken from us. All of it, Maxi. All of it."

"Don't beg, brother mine. We've never begged. Never."

"I won't. I'll see if the Vrassoons will take our remaining clipper as partial payment of the debt."

"But what will we use to ship our goods?"

"What goods, Maxi? We have no Chinese willing to load or

unload our ships. So, what goods do we have? Think Maxi. Now's the time to think. Not beg. Not fight, either. We're in a box and we need to find a way out. The Vrassoons think they have us ..." He didn't speak the end of the thought which was: ...*and they just might*.

Richard hurried toward the Bend in the River, where the wealthy trading houses had their ostentatious head offices. From across the road he eyed the head offices of Dent and Company. Its large Union Jack flapped in the early summer breeze while its two stone lions stood guard on either side of the large bronze doors. Richard looked to one side of the stone lions and saw Dent's real guards — men seemingly doing nothing more than lounging a few yards down the alley, smoking pre-packed cardboard Russian cigarettes and outwardly uninterested in the traffic along the river. But when a rickshaw pulled up and disgorged a portly man in a top hat, the lounging men were quickly on their guard, one with a hand inside his shirt, perhaps with the butt of a pistol in his palm.

Richard smiled at them; they didn't smile back.

Beside Dents was a construction site whose foundation hole was only partially dug. The river water had seeped through the boarded barrier and was quickly refilling with the mud that had, no doubt, been laboriously removed. After the hole in the ground, the path bent quickly to the right so that a traveller was suddenly confronted with the imposing façade of the head offices of the Scottish trading giant, Jardine, Matheson. The heavy oak doors looked as though they'd never been opened. *No doubt their major business goes through the back door*, Richard thought. *Nothing much has changed.*

At the end of a series of lower buildings was, naturally enough, the tallest building in Shanghai — The British East India Company — the Vrassoons' private fiefdom.

Security was not hidden here. Four Sikhs in full regimental uniform flanked the doors and scowled as only Sikhs can. Richard walked up the steps and immediately the men stepped forward to bar his way.

"I have an appointment," Richard said in English.

They did not move.

"I have an appointment," Richard repeated, in Hindi this time.

The Sikhs didn't move, although their scowls intensified.

"Fine," Richard said in Punjabi. "I have an appointment."

Something in the smile family, perhaps the second cousin of a smirk, crossed the leader's face and he replied in rapid-fire Punjabi, "With whom do you have this appointment?"

Richard breathed a sigh of relief. The Punjabi word for "appointment" was close to the Hindi word so he got the gist of the question. "With the chief," he said in Punjabi, knowing that "chief" wasn't the right word.

"Man in charge," the Sikh soldier corrected him.

"Thank you, the man in charge is who I wish to see." The Sikhs didn't seem to realize that Richard had moved from having an appointment to "wishing to see" in all of thirty seconds.

The leader shouted an order to one of the others, who disappeared through the tall mahogany doors. Then the Sikh folded his arms and turned to the street. So did the other soldiers. So, eventually, did Richard.

And they waited as the day got hotter — and the Hordoon brothers, by the minute, fell further and further into debt. Finally the door opened and Richard was ushered into an office that was a perfect replica of a London men's club — unnecessarily stuffy, with the windows closed and draped. The leather of the chair stuck to his shirt the moment he sat. "God damn it!" Richard muttered.

"It is inadvisable to take the Lord's name in vain in these premises. At least swear in Yiddish if you insist on cussing."

The older man stood in the doorway, his woollen suit clinging to his skinny body, sweat visible on his pockmarked face.

"The guards say you claim you had an appointment with me.

You don't but I've been expecting you."

"Ah, you got my message?" Richard smiled.

"Our badly beaten man, that message?"

"The very one. I see he held his wits together long enough to …" Richard suddenly stopped speaking. He found himself momentarily wobbly on his feet. "He was rude to my brother — an inadvisable thing to do."

"Really?" the Vrassoon man said, "Well, Mr. Hordoon, I've been expecting you because my employer has prepared an offer to you and your miscreant brother."

"And that would be?"

"Mr. Vrassoon is graciously prepared to cancel the debt of yours he bought from Barclays Bank in return for you and your brother handing over the paltry assets you presently hold in Shanghai and agreeing not to return to this country, either in person or in proxy, for a period of fifty years."

"Have you got a name, old man? You're not a Vrassoon, you don't have the swagger for it. And besides, you have something that no Vrassoon has ever had."

"And that would be?"

"A sense of humour. Surely you know that offer is a joke. So what's your name, friend?"

"I am not your friend, and my name is my business, not yours." His foot reached for a button on the floor. "Now you claimed to have an appointment with me. So what exactly is your business here?"

Richard noticed the silhouettes of the Sikhs behind the elderly man. Even in shadow, Richard could sense their scowls.

"Perhaps a street rat like yourself has no business in the offices of the British East India Company," the elderly man suggested, with a wry smile on his face.

Richard began to nod. "Perhaps, old man, you're right. No business with the likes of you or your master. Would you tell him something for me?"

"Perhaps you'd like to write down your message for Mr. Vrassoon. If you know how to write, that is."

"Ah, a slander ... very good. No need to write it down. It's short, and I think even a dotard like yourself could remember it. So, you ready? Good, here it is. Tell Mr. Vrassoon that Richard Hordoon tells him to fuck himself up the arse with a crowbar."

The older man's face fell.

"Ah, perhaps you didn't understand my English. How's this?" Then Richard repeated his charming message in Farsi, in Hindi, in Punjabi, in Mandarin, and finally in Yiddish. By then he was face down in the dusty street, having been lifted and then thrown some fifteen feet by the Sikh guards.

As Richard spat the dust from his mouth, it occurred to him that he had eaten dirt before, and no doubt he would eat dirt again before his time on this earth was done.

"So how successful was your brainpower in getting the Vrassoons to change their minds about our debt or the new tariffs, brother mine?"

"Take that fuckin' smile off your face, Maxi, and get the boys."

That indeed took the smile off Maxi's face. "Why do you want to see the boys?"

"Just get them, Maxi. I'm leaving."

"What?"

"Tonight. I'm going upriver. We need workers and new markets. We have to set out in new directions. The fuckin' Vrassoons already own this place."

"And you want to say goodbye to the boys?"

"Yes, Maxi, get them. I've got a lot to do before sundown."

Silas and Milo stood side by side in the shed waiting for their father, whom they heard outside giving orders to the men. The sound of horses approaching made Silas step back. Silas didn't like horses.

Patterson stuck his head in the door. "He'll be here shortly, so scrub your tears from your eyes, me little heathens."

Outside the boys heard their Uncle Maxi saying, "Not enough men, brother mine. Not enough even to carry what you need."

"I'm not carrying a lot. Just enough to prove to them that I can deliver. This is a search mission, not a trading mission."

"I wasn't talking about that. You may be able to speak their language but you've got no fist with you — a language that everyone understands."

"I can't afford to have you come with me. I need you here to press Chen to get us workers. Press him hard. When I get back I want to see Yellow men everywhere around our warehouses. Besides, I want you to look after the boys."

Milo smiled when he heard that and turned to Silas. "Uncle Maxi to look after the boys!" he whispered.

Silas smiled. He liked his Uncle Maxi well enough, but there was something just beneath the skin that he didn't understand.

The door burst open and Richard got down on one knee and held out his arms. Milo flew across the floor into his father's grasp. Silas didn't fly, but he snuggled up to his father too.

"So, can you figure out what I'm up to?"

"You're going to find new markets," Milo said confidently. Richard ruffled his hair. "And make the House of Hordoon the greatest trading house in all of Asia."

Richard let out a laugh and then turned to Silas.

The boy resisted the impulse to pull back from his father. The strange sour odour that opium imparted was constantly on his father's skin, and it made Silas want to throw up. But he put his hands on his father's face and said, with an odd dispassion, as if he'd rehearsed what he was going to say, "Be careful, Papa."

Richard heard the distance in the boy's voice but chose to ignore it. He looked right back at his son and said, "Can't be too careful if you want to live your life. You have to take risks now and then.

If you want to be a businessman you have to live with risk, Silas."

"I don't want to be a businessman, Papa."

"Do you want to live your life? Or do you just want to be dead a long time before you stop breathing and they put you in the ground?"

Silas thought about that. He was afraid of dying but he intrinsically understood what his father was saying. "I want to live my life, sir." The words came out stiff and formal. He backed a full step away from his father.

"Good lad. Me too. That's why I'm off upriver."

"Bring us back something spectacular, Papa," Milo demanded.

"I'll bring you back a whole new inheritance."

"I don't want an inheritance, I just want you to come back," said Silas. Although his words said concern, his tone was purely practical — cold.

Richard stared at his serious son. "I'll come back, Silas."

"Or I'll fetch him back," added Maxi, coming in the door. "Time to go, brother mine, the darkness should cover your exit." Richard looked at him. "Don't want you followed, now, do we?"

Richard turned and headed toward the door. His horse had been brought to the front of the building. He mounted quickly, then looked back through the door. Milo was holding Silas's hand and reassuring him that "Papa will be home soon." Silas nodded, but it was as if he had been told to do so.

 20

A FIRST FORAY

Up the River
September 1843

Richard and three of Maxi's "irregulars" made their way down to the Bend in the River, then headed west. As they skirted the American Settlement, they turned in their saddles to look back at the beginnings of the great city of Shanghai. Then Richard pulled his cloak more tightly around him and they headed out through the west gate and passed the last of the Chinese sentries, whom Maxi had bribed only an hour before.

Early that night, after Maxi was sure the boys were comfortably asleep with their Malay *amah* curled up on her mat outside the bedroom door, he headed down toward the docks. He was usually accompanied by at least two of his irregulars, since Shanghai after dark, even for Maxi, could be a dodgy place.

Maxi passed by Jiang's ever-growing establishment and turned right into the heart of the Old City. The smell of cooking surrounded him and many staring eyes — often angry eyes — watched his progress. On the sidewalk a street doctor applied a thick, wriggling leech to a large growth on a young man's chest. The young man turned to Maxi and sneered. He was missing both of his front teeth. It didn't surprise Maxi.

Clothing was hung out of almost every window on bamboo poles. Older people sat on three-legged stools, their pant legs rolled up to expose their shins to the evening air. A woman sat calmly on the curb as a young man cut her hair. Three grizzled men shared a hand-rolled cigarette whose smoke hung in the fetid air of what the Chinese ironically referred to as the Chinese Concession. A scrawny, bearded man picked up his little girl and shook the remainder of the pee from her before sliding on her sacking pants. He didn't smile at Maxi. The girl didn't smile either. This was the Old City — Chinese didn't have to pretend to smile at the hated *Fan Kuei* here.

Maxi passed by a river stone seller who held up her very best bloodstone. Maxi shook his head then ducked into an alley. He counted four wooden doorways then entered the fifth and quickly found himself at the south entrance to the Warrens.

He climbed down the ladder, as he had done that first time before the British invasion of the city.

A hand touched the small of his back. He froze. The icy tendrils of fear, not something he was used to, slithered up his spine.

"You're late," the voice from the darkness said. Then a taper was lit and Chen stepped into the light. His translator stood beside him. "Follow me."

As Chen led the way, Maxi wondered why they needed to meet in the Warrens rather than in Chen's Hong warehouse.

Chen was happy not to enlighten the red-haired devil. He led him to a small chamber where the sound of the river was easy to hear through the east wall. On the other side of the south wall, Jiang, the Confucian, and the Bodyguard waited and listened.

Chen's interpreter stepped forward silently.

"So where is your brother?"

"Upriver trying to find us markets and workers."

Chen sighed, then made Maxi go through the exact nature of the problem — not that he didn't know it, but he wanted the Chosen Three to hear what seemingly stood in the way of the building of the Seventy Pagodas. He was especially interested in his eldest brother hearing the problem — his eldest brother, the Confucian.

Later, Maxi left the Warrens by its most northerly exit and did not head toward the British Concession. Instead, he retraced the steps he had taken two nights before, when he had first found his way to Rachel Oliphant's bed.

And the Chosen Three sat and reviewed the problem they had heard from the red-haired *Fan Kuei*. They knew that new Taoist priests had been installed up and down the river and were all reporting directly to Manchu Mandarins. Workers were terrified by these new priests into believing that working for the *Fan Kuei* would bring them terrible luck that would bankrupt a family for generations. These superstitions were backed up by the threats of real punishment issued daily from the scribes of the Manchu Mandarins who now held sway in the village at the Bend in the River. How, then, could they induce Chinese men to work in the British and American Concessions — induce them without betraying why they wanted their fellow countrymen to work for the enemy?

On the morning of the second day of sailing, Richard's junk crossed to the north side of the Yangtze to a village he had used as a depot three times in the past. Chen had set up the arrangement that provided a way to keep the opium away from the authorities. When Richard ordered the junk turned into the wind and headed toward shore, he saw the villagers approach the riverside en masse — with pikes and old muskets at the ready. Just outside of musket range Richard ordered the captain to come about.

"What, sir?"

Richard didn't answer.

"Sir?"

"Tell your men to lower a bumboat, I'm going ashore."

Twenty minutes later Richard sat in the bow of the bumboat, his arms extended to show he had no weapon. When the boat entered the shallows, strong arms grabbed Richard and dragged him through the water to the shore. He didn't resist. He kept looking for Chen's contact man in the village, but couldn't see him. The man was either no longer in the village or no longer on this earth. Richard was afraid it might be the latter.

Then Richard was thrown face down on the pebbly beach. When he turned and looked up, four pikes were aimed at his heart. He slowly got to his knees and in flawless Mandarin said, "Is this the greeting for an old friend? Has courtesy disappeared from the Celestial Kingdom?"

"You are no friend here."

The breathy voice belonged to a young man in full Taoist robes. From the deference offered to him by the villagers, Richard realized that he was the equivalent of a mullah or a parish priest.

"Why is that? I have always been a friend to these people."

"Friends don't bring poison to friends."

"I have brought no poison. My intention is only to trade."

The young Taoist monk made a mocking sound in the back of his throat, then spat. It was at that moment that Richard heard the swoosh of boats. He turned. Dozens of swift village carracks headed toward the junk that had brought him — the junk that carried the four mango chests of opium.

Soon the mango chests were lying empty on the beach, the junk was sunk, and Richard and his men were set adrift in the river in the bumboat with the screamed admonition, "You and your poison are not welcome here or anywhere on the river!"

Three days later Richard and his men got back to the point where they'd left their horses. The horses were nowhere to be seen — so much for trusting the locals.

"Horse meat is very tasty," the captain of the junk said, then muttered something about this being the last time he'd risk his neck or his property for the stupid Round-Eyed monsters.

Two nights later, Richard arrived back in Shanghai.

Maxi lit an oil lamp and looked at his brother. "You look awful."

"That doesn't surprise me." He told Maxi of the utter failure of the trip, then added that he'd lost four horses and owed the junk captain for his vessel.

"He'll have to get in line. There're a lot of creditors ahead of him."

"What're we going to do, Maxi?"

Maxi had never seen Richard so utterly lost. "Now? Now we're going to sleep." He took his brother's hand and guided him toward his bed, then wrapped the sheets around him and lowered the mosquito netting.

Three hours later Maxi heard Richard rise from his bed and head toward the door. Maxi stopped him. "No opium tonight, brother mine. Sleep tonight — we have much work to do tomorrow."

The brothers were awakened next morning by the shriek of horns and the clash of cymbals. Maxi woke the boys' *amah* and had them secreted out the back alley, then he and Richard opened the door of their Shanghai home.

There, in full regalia, was the Manchu Mandarin, the *Ch'in-ch'ai*, his tile of office dangling from his neck, purple silk robes to announce that he was directly from Beijing, his hair braided and stacked atop his head and neatly tucked beneath his tall, conical cap. Richard remembered his first meeting with a Manchu Mandarin almost fifteen years ago. He had been tempted to laugh at the outlandish costume. Then the Mandarin, with the lifting of his hand, had had three men brought forward and executed while he washed his hands and ate sweetmeats ... and smiled at Richard all the while. It took all the laughter out of the situation.

Although this was a different Mandarin and the foreigners were in theory protected by the provisions of the Treaty of Nanjing, the smile on the Mandarin's face was frighteningly familiar.

Richard bowed to a middle position. Maxi at his side did the same.

The Mandarin ignored the courtesy and said in his high, nasal voice, "I have come to look at my future property." Then he tilted his head and six guards rushed forward, pushing Richard and Maxi aside. The Mandarin, like a great clipper ship under full sail, floated past the Hordoons and entered their home.

Richard sensed Maxi's growing tension. He took him by the arm and pulled him to one side.

"Are you going to just let that — ?"

"*Zai xiang*, he's a *zai xiang*, a Mandarin, Maxi."

"And he has soldiers with him?"

"That too."

Maxi looked at Richard. "What, brother mine?"

"Did you see his smile?"

Maxi nodded. "Didn't care much for it myself."

"Knowing, it was, Maxi. A bloody knowing smile. As if all this had come to pass just as he thought it would."

"I don't follow."

"As if all along he knew what would happen here at the Bend in the River. Maxi, they let us build up their village, spend our money on it and our expertise, and all along they were just waiting to take it back from us."

Maxi didn't like that, nor did he like the way the Mandarin's grossly long fingernails probed the sheets on Richard's bed.

21

A SECOND FORAY

Up the River
December, 1843

Early the next morning Richard sat with Percy St. John Dent in the back room of Dent's formal offices by the river. Richard knew Dent was an old China hand who had worked his way up in his father's company from the very bottom. Rumour had it that his father had never lent him a penny or given him any leniency when he fell short of expectations. As well, it was common knowledge that his father had forced an unloving marriage on his son to solidify a business arrangement.

Percy St. John Dent was perhaps five years Richard's senior and still carried the sinewy muscle that hard work had built up on his long frame. The man was also a mathematical wizard, keeping massive columns of figures in his head. He was famous for his ability to spout data at a moment's notice. And now he was quoting the declining numbers of Chinese workers in the Concession and its direct effect on profits.

"If we worked together," Richard said, "we might be able to force extraterritoriality on the Chinese."

Percy St. John Dent looked at this handsome, swarthy man and thought, *Together with you? Never.* But he smiled and said, "I don't actually need your clipper ship, Mr. Hordoon."

"But at the price I offered it to you, I assume it would be hard to pass up."

Percy St. John Dent nodded and turned away. He didn't like dealing with the Baghdadi Hebrew but he had a grudging respect for the man and his maniac brother. The respect one real worker has for another. The price the man wanted for his clipper was more than fair. *So, the rumour about the Vrassoons calling in some sort of debt is true*, he thought. *Interesting. Well, no reason not to profit when the shoals shift beneath a competitor. We are businessmen, after all, and here is a substantial profit right in front of me.* He turned back to Richard and said, "What form of payment are you looking for?"

"Chinese silver or American gold coin." Richard took a breath, then said, "Now, this very moment, or I offer it to Jardine, Matheson."

The mention of Dent's historic rival brought the desired effect. Two hours later Richard handed over the writ of ownership of his last clipper ship and received his compensation in Chinese silver.

"It's heavy," he said to Maxi.

"Yes, but it's not enough to pay our debt."

"No, but under the provisions of the contract we can buy ourselves some time by producing 10 percent of the debt in currency — this is currency, Maxi."

"Fine, but it only buys us time. What are we going …?"

Richard spun the chambers on his floor safe and opened it. "Maxi, here are the deeds for the three properties we have in the Concession. Bring them to Chen and get us buyers — Chinese buyers. Take the money and buy cheaper land, then build, Maxi, build. Keep 5 percent of the currency and leverage that. Call Patterson and get him to deliver the rest of the silver to the Vrassoons, and call in the boys."

"Why the boys?"

"Because I'm heading back upriver."

"Tonight?"

"Or earlier. The key to this whole thing is getting Chinese labour into the Concession. Without them, we're doomed."

"We still owe the 100,000 silver *taels* in tariff to the Mandarin."

"Stall. It's a language he'll understand. The money's on its way, the money got lost, the money is up your arse ... you're a Baghdadi, God damn it, so like every good Baghdadi lie, Maxi. Make it up, just stall him — then start building. All those workers who're coming into this city need places to live."

Richard didn't bother with horses this time. He took Maxi's second-in-command, an almost silent man named Phillips, whose loyalty to Maxi was beyond question. The two of them took Maxi's much-loved and much-used two-man junk and sculled out into the waters of the Huangpu River. When they got to the treacherous confluence of the Yangtze they stayed on the south side of the great river.

They made sure they passed by the hostile village that had set Richard's first team adrift well before dawn on the second day. Phillips watched the shoreline warily as they passed.

At noon on the third day Richard pointed to a prosperous-looking village on the south shore.

"You sure, sir?" They were almost the only words Phillips had spoken since they had begun their journey.

"No, Phillips, this is China, what could be sure?"

But their greeting was cordial, if cool. No guns, no Taoist priests, and by late afternoon two rice merchants who had done business with Richard in the past — using their good auspices and warehouses as covers for the opium trade — showed up. Orders were given and the women prepared a meal. Not a feast as a show of welcome, as is customary, but a large meal.

Richard watched carefully where he was seated at the round table. Well, to be more exact, he watched carefully where the head of the fish was facing. The head of the fish always faced the guest of honour. The old woman who shambled in and placed the fish platter on the table turned it so that the head faced Richard. He gave out an audible sigh.

The food was fresh and gently seasoned with soya and ginger. The steamed buns, stuffed with pork and nuts, and a plant that the Chinese referred to as green vegetable were cooked in some sort of light, white sauce. The rice was unusual. Richard remarked on it.

"Basmati," the rice merchant answered, "best rice in the world. If the gods ate rice, they'd eat only Basmati. Unfortunately, we are just beginning to grow it in the delta."

Before the meal was halfway through Richard broached the problem of the lack of Chinese workers willing to work in the *Fan Kuei* Concessions. The rice merchants pondered, or appeared to ponder, Richard's problem. Then Richard said, "Basmati may be the rice of the gods, but this," he produced a palm-leaf-wrapped ball of opium, "is the dream of the gods."

A full night of smoking later, the rice merchants had agreed to move two hundred chests of opium for Richard. They still had no solution for the lack of workers in the Concession, but Richard was happy with their commitment as a start. They also agreed to come to Shanghai and get the goods themselves when they next arrived to pick up rice shipments from the delta. This, after yet another evening of fine smoke. On the third evening of smoke, Richard broached the idea of the rice merchants recruiting other rice merchants farther upriver to continue the chain of opium sales farther inland.

But Richard's timing was bad. The men wanted to smoke and dream but Richard, feeling the need to get back to Shanghai, pushed when he shouldn't have. The presence of two courtesans in their midst and too much opium flashing through Richard's veins didn't help. When the younger of the two rice merchants suddenly retracted his offer of sale and assistance altogether, Richard lost his temper and pushed the man. He tripped over the opium brazier and let out a yelp as the hot coals fell on his foot. He hopped away and lost his balance, hitting his head hard against the stone floor — and lay very, very still.

Richard didn't remember much after that. There was some yelling and much commotion. He felt a sharp pain on his left temple — then darkness.

He awoke with the oddest sensation. He was on his knees but his head was propped off the ground and his hands were tied to something ahead of him. It was completely dark so he couldn't tell what had happened. He leaned to one side and found himself suddenly rolling until his face was pointed to the ceiling — or whatever was up there. His back was bent at an awkward angle and he had no choice but to stay that way until mercifully daylight came.

There was no mercy in the light of day, however. He saw the millstone, about four and a half feet in diameter, had been, like stone stocks, clamped down around his neck, and smelled the deep reek of urine that he finally figured out was coming from him. His hands were through two holes in the millstone and chained in place. He tried to lift the thing, and it took all of his considerable strength to get it off the ground. He quickly allowed it back to the dust. It had to weigh in excess of two hundred pounds.

He turned and the damned thing rolled, putting him face up again. He gave a heave and it turned again so that he could put his knees down. He tried to control his panic. He was in the village's central square. Peasants carrying earthenware jugs to the well for the morning meal began to arrive. At first, he tried to talk to them but it soon became obvious that they would not respond to him in any way. Even his entreaties for a sip of water were ignored.

He calmed himself and took stock of the situation. The man he'd pushed in the opium den — maybe he'd died. Perhaps he himself had been sentenced while unconscious. *Not exactly due process*, he thought. Then he thought of his partner, the silent Phillips, Maxi's second-in-command. Where was he? He tried to remember if the man had been with him smoking opium. No, he hadn't been there. Richard remembered him sitting silently to one side, then leaving before the argument.

Richard knew that any punishment meted out to him would also apply to his man. By Chinese thinking, each of them was responsible for the actions of the other. Richard tried to lift the millstone to see if his comrade was in the square with him but his knees buckled under the strain, allowing the millstone to clunk to the ground again. This thrust his head forward and drew blood from his shoulders. He took a breath and looked straight forward — east into the rising sun. He strained to look left and right but couldn't move his head enough to get a good look at whatever was or wasn't to his north and south. He didn't see Phillips. He dug in his knees and pushed to the right. The millstone rolled, allowing him to see, although upside down, to the west side of the square — no Phillips. He shifted his weight and the stone rolled, allowing him to get his knees down. He needed the stone to make a circle so he could see north and south. He took three deep breaths, arched his back, and pushed with his feet — the millstone lifted off the ground and turned about thirty degrees to the east. He allowed himself to catch his breath and looked again. No Phillips. It took him almost an hour and all of his energy to lift the millstone over and over again so that he could complete a full circle. Phillips was nowhere to be seen in the square.

Richard allowed himself a moment of hope. Phillips was smart, resourceful, and loyal. He would have headed back to Shanghai to get help — if he wasn't already dead. Richard refused to allow himself to consider that possibility.

The heat was increasing by the minute. He needed water and

the well was almost thirty yards away. He reminded himself that in the heat, without water, a man could easily die. His shoulders ached and the millstone continued to cut deep into them but he needed water. He set his feet and pushed to his right. The heavy stone moved grudgingly in the dirt. He looked to his right. He wanted the line of the millstone to lead him straight to the well. He was off by a little. He regrouped and pushed again. The well was pretty much in a straight line to his right. He steadied his breath, dug in his left foot, shifted his body weight to the right, and pushed. The millstone did a complete revolution and a half and came to a stop with Richard facing the blazing sun. He shimmied his weight and the thing finally turned enough to allow his left foot to touch the ground. He pushed hard and the stone rolled, this time just a bit more than a full turn, so that his knees once again touched down. He looked to his right. He was off-line. He planted his right foot in the dirt and pushed. Nothing. He tried a second time. The thing wouldn't move. He looked down. A damned pebble. A pebble stopped his progress! He planted his left foot and shifted his body weight and the thing turned a full revolution.

By this time, he had generated an audience of gawking children, most of whom had never seen a White Devil, let alone a White Devil in a millstone. He ignored them and pushed to straighten the line of the millstone. This time there was no rock to impede the movement of the stone. He rested for a while.

He must have slept, because when he looked up the sun was already past its zenith and the children were gone. He felt the blood on his cheek where he must have scraped it against the stone in his sleep. He looked to his right. The well was only ten yards away and, miraculously, directly in line with the trajectory of the millstone. Richard managed to roll the thing seven more revolutions in the next few hours and found himself right beside the well.

He slept for a bit to get his strength together. When he awoke he gave a mighty heave and lifted the millstone onto the ledge of the well. It almost tipped over into the abyss, but he managed to control the weight.

Now that he was there he faced an even more daunting task. How was he to lift the water to his mouth with his hands chained a full two feet away from his mouth? Even if he could pull a bucket of water up to the ledge (how he could do that he hadn't even begun to consider), how could he then get the water from the bucket to his mouth?

He felt a hand on his back and turned his head as best as he could manage. A figure was silhouetted by the sun — a small figure of a man in what Richard could only make out as a filthy black robe. A voice he thought he recognized said, "Are ye doing God's work, me son? Or the work of the Devil? Ye must nae do the Devil's work, son."

The heat was intense and he knew he was already badly dehydrated. He could not tell if he was delirious or if somehow the dwarf Jesuit from the ship all those years ago was actually by his side, nursing water into his parched mouth and telling him that he must sleep, that he needed his strength for the challenge ahead.

Richard wanted to say thank you but his mouth was full of water, and he swallowed it gratefully. Then he found himself on a gentle slope that allowed the weight of the millstone off his shoulders. Sleep, deep sleep, found him, and he retreated gratefully into its safety.

The next day Richard was pulled to his feet and marched, every part of him aching, to the local Mandarin's office. The man never looked at Richard, who swayed precariously with the weight of the millstone on his shoulders, knowing full well if he fell the Mandarin would have him executed. Finally, the Mandarin pronounced his sentence, a hundred days, then called out the words: "*Dai nu ren shang lai, xi ling* — Bring out the woman and the bells."

Quickly the Mandarin's supernumeraries attached tinkling

bells to the locks of the millstone so that every movement produced a giggling burp of jingles. Then they looped a rope around Richard's waist and a small woman, wearing a deeply cowled robe, stepped forward. On a sharp order from the Mandarin, she lifted her head and pulled back her hood. Her nose and ears had been cut off. Richard had to make himself stay still. Somehow he knew he mustn't look away from this woman. She approached him and took the free end of the rope. She gave a tug and led him out of the chamber.

I'm the end of the punishment for her that began with her disfigurement, Richard thought as he staggered behind her. *I'm this poor woman's final disgrace.* He knew his very life depended on this woman. He thought long and hard before he said his first words to her. They were, "Thank you for your kindness."

She responded by screeching insults at him.

Not a bad start, Richard thought. *With other women I've done worse."*

Richard slowly learned the delicate balancing act needed for the basics of survival — like how to squat to defecate with the weight on his shoulders (like most Europeans, he didn't bother with the niceties of hygiene), how to build up a slant of dirt to allow himself to sleep without wrenching his back or having to sleep on his knees, how to find support for the weight on his neck when he stood, how to beg the woman to feed him, as he had no earthly way of getting his hands to his mouth.

It took time and effort but Richard was able to get the woman to tell him her name, Yuan Tu, and slowly he began to read the expressions on her butchered face. By the third day, he was sure that he saw concern there. Even sympathy. That night she helped him build the mound he needed for sleeping and fed him the scraps she'd collected from the village's rubbish heap.

On the fourth morning Richard found himself awakened by a strange dream. He thought his brother was there beside him telling him that everything was going to be okay. When he awoke Maxi was nowhere to be seen — but there was a shred of rag tied to the fingers of his left hand. He strained his head to see it better and waited for the early-morning light. When the first of the sun's rays cast their milkiness into the darkness, Richard allowed a smile to come to his lips — the bit of rag was red, flaming red.

Yuan Tu approached him with the morning's ration of food, a thin rice paste that she gently spooned into his mouth. All around him the town was coming to life. The smell of real cooking from the nearby houses almost drove him mad with hunger. To his left, three Manchu guards, who periodically checked in on him, swaggered forward. The Manchus were the only Celestials who didn't have to shave their foreheads and wear their hair in a long braid down their backs. Despite the best efforts of the Chinese to incorporate these impositions into their culture, they still stood out as the overt sign of the conquered.

One of the Manchus leaned down toward Richard and held his nose.

"No doubt you'd smell rosier in my position," Richard said.

It surprised the Manchu that Richard was willing to speak. The Foreign Devil had never spoken to them before. Then a quizzical look crossed the guard's face and he tugged the bit of red kerchief free from Richard's left hand. "What is this?" he demanded. Without waiting for Richard's response, he turned to the other soldiers and said, "Red rag for the Red Devil. The —"

He never got out another word as the bullet from Maxi's rifle pierced his larynx. The other guards whipped around. Richard heard a sharp slap and six rifles snapped out from around the corner of the wall. The sun glinted off strands of silk that somehow joined the weapons. The guards looked at one another — then were almost cut in half as the six rifles fired at the same time.

Richard tugged at Yuan Tu to get behind him. She cowered into his side.

The villagers shrieked and ran for cover.

Richard heard Maxi shout something and then the sound of hooves clattering on the hard ground.

A cart pulled by two horses raced toward him and dropped its back gate to the ground. Maxi and Phillips ran to Richard, rolled him up the slanted ramp into the bed of the cart and slammed the gate shut as the horses took off at a full gallop.

"Take the woman — they'll kill her if we leave her," Richard shouted.

"Get her," Maxi yelled at Phillips, who leapt down and grabbed the woman and tossed her into the moving cart. As he did, Maxi braced himself against the side of the moving thing and pulled hard on a strand of silk in his hands. The six rifles that had magically snapped into position against the wall of the building clattered to the ground and then followed in the dirt, dragged by the cart.

Richard thought he heard more gunshots behind him but couldn't tell as the millstone rolled wildly in the back of the bouncing cart sending him twisting and turning, slamming into the sides of the cart several times, until one sharp turn sent the wheel rolling and his head smashed into the gate of the cart. With a kind of gratitude, Richard accepted the coming darkness. The last thing he remembered thinking was that he really, really wanted a pipe of opium.

Richard awoke to a gentle rocking motion.

"You done with the sleeping, brother mine?"

Richard looked up and Maxi was standing over him. Phillips sat silently against the port rail.

Richard went to adjust the millstone and realized it wasn't there. He almost flew to his feet, and he was lucky that Maxi was near at hand because without the excess weight he almost flung himself overboard.

"Time to sit and get your sea legs. We've a day's sailing before we're back in Shanghai."

Richard sat and stared at his brother. The horses and the cart moved slowly to the rhythm of the river. The six silk-tethered rifles leaned against the port rail of the large junk.

"What?" Maxi asked.

Pointing to the rifles, Richard asked, "Your invention?"

"A little something I'm working on."

"Well, it worked."

"This time," Maxi replied, then added with a smile, "it's never worked before." In response to Richard's grimace, Maxi asked, nonchalantly, "Is that a problem for you, brother mine? They could just as well have shot you, to be honest."

Richard said, "No, Maxi, no problem," but he was thinking about the dwarf Jesuit, about doing the Devil's work, and about the prophecy of the old Indian outside the Opium Works in Ghazipur: "Brother will kill brother." *Well, not this time*, Richard thought, *not this time.*

The earless, noseless woman approached him and knelt by his side, keeping her disfigured face away from the eyes of Maxi Hordoon, a man she was convinced was a red-haired devil.

"What's her name, brother mine?"

"Yuan Tu are the first of her many names. But why don't you call her Lily."

"I'm safe back in Shanghai but this firm is no better off," Richard barked. His voice was still hoarse from the days with his neck in the millstone. He looked at Maxi and Phillips and the other loyal "irregulars." "All we are is several days deeper in debt, gentlemen. We still have no workers and no new markets."

"Not to mention the 100,000 silver *taels* we owe the Mandarin, brother mine."

"Thanks, I really needed to be reminded of that. I want us all to ante up. Sell everything we have, Maxi — the horses, the food stuffs, the cooking utensils, everything. I need to go back."

"Back out there? Upriver? Are you mad, brother mine? Has that thing you wore around your neck squeezed all the reason from your silly head?"

"No, Maxi. What do you suggest we do? Sit here and let everything we've worked for all these years be taken from us? Or should we run, like Papa did?"

Maxi turned from his brother. Richard was surprised to see Maxi doing something that appeared to be calculating. "Maxi?"

"You need cover when you travel inland. A way to be there but not attract the attention of the Manchu Mandarins or the Taoist monks if they get a bee up their butts."

"I agree."

"What about travelling with the House of Zion? They're planning to Bible-thump their way into the hearts of the Middle Kingdom."

"When?"

"In three days. The expedition is already outfitted, they're just waiting for transport."

For a fleeting moment it occurred to Richard to ask Maxi how he knew all this, but the possibility so intrigued him that he let it pass. "Fine, but why would they allow me to go with them?"

"Because they need a translator, surely, if they are going to win the souls of the heathens."

"They already have a translator, Maxi, that flake McKinnon."

"Yes, but what if something should befall Mr. McKinnon that put him into the bad books of the Evangelicals at Oliphant and Company?"

Richard smiled and shook his head. "I sense a plan."

"Yes, brother mine, you're not the only Hordoon capable of planning."

"I grant that."

"Fine. Now, I would assume that Jiang's little establishment is a dire temptation to the likes of such men as Mr. McKinnon, wouldn't you think?"

Richard's smile broadened and he clasped his brother to him — the Hordoon boys were at it again!

It wasn't hard to convince the Chinese hooker to play along. Madame Jiang gave her permission, for a modest fee, and the trap was fully baited. Richard almost felt sorry for the man when he ran out into the streets without his pants or underclothes, with the hooker running after him all the way to the American Settlement ... almost. But Richard never had much sympathy for hypocrites. If a religious man claims there is only one path upon which a righteous man must tread, then he had damned well better not stray from that path himself. And paying to be fellated by a whore instructed to dress as a nun would, in most circles, be considered to have strayed from the traditional path to a heavenly reward.

McKinnon's comeuppance was swift and dire. He was expelled from the House of Zion and set adrift. That left a vacancy for a translator on the Oliphants' next missionary voyage into the Celestial heartland — and translators were both vital and hard to come by. Richard, as luck would have it, was available.

Then magically a larger, better-equipped junk became available. The vessel, which Maxi had arranged already, had a crew of five men who had worked for him in the past, and the far forward section of its hold concealed forty-five mango-wood chests containing enough opium to intoxicate the population of a small city.

The sun was rising as Richard boarded the junk at the Suzu Creek wharf. He had tried to get Phillips passage with him, but the House of Oliphant had refused. Richard nodded slightly to two of the junk's sailors, whom he recognized, and traded simple pleasantries with a third as he awaited the arrival of the traders of the House of Zion.

Something niggled at the back of Richard's mind. The sudden availability of the junk, the sailors who were loyal to Maxi, the fact that Maxi had known of the Oliphants' imminent travels — how had Maxi ... ? But suddenly he didn't care, because Rachel Oliphant was climbing the gangway to the junk, and she was looking right at him.

Maxi watched the proceedings from a distance with a scowl on his face.

The warmth of Rachel's smile as she boarded the junk almost matched the passion of her love making the night before. And yet Maxi knew he was somehow moving away from her — from all of them at the Bend in the River.

22

THE ARRIVAL OF THE PATRIARCH

Village of Shanghai
Late December, 1843

Eliazar Vrassoon received Cyril's message in Calcutta and within days was onboard the swiftest available British East India clipper ship — all sails unfurled — headed toward Shanghai. If Cyril thought extraterritoriality was possible, he wanted to be there to move the possible into the probable.

The Vrassoon Patriarch knew that extraterritoriality was the key to securing the family's fortune. His eldest son was safely ensconced in London playing nursemaid to the family's political contacts while he oversaw the textile mills in Liverpool and Manchester. His competent second son was looking after the family's operations in Calcutta with a sharp eye kept on opium supplies out of the Works at Ghazipur. Sons three and four were heading Vrassoon operations in Paris and Vienna, protecting the family's banking interests while branching out into textile works whenever they could manage it. The market for Chinese tea, silk, and porcelain was growing exponentially but the key remained full access to the Chinese opium smokers — something that only extraterritoriality could assure. Vrassoon opium was sold in China for silver, which was used to buy tea, silk, and porcelains. These were then sold in England for more silver and cotton goods from Liverpool and Manchester, which were in turn sold for opium in Calcutta, which then went to China — a closed circle of sales, the holy grail of commerce. And round and round and round it went, generating more wealth than some nations possess. But it could all fall apart without extraterritoriality. Hence, Eliazar Vrassoon was willing to deal with almost anyone and do almost anything to secure extraterritoriality — to close the trading circle.

After a difficult and oft-delayed crossing, the Patriarch of the Vrassoon family watched the new buildings of the European trading companies slide by as his ship approached the Huangpu docks. He drew his muffler around his neck. The damp cold of a Shanghai January had penetrated his expensive clothing, but he had a smile on his face. *Things are in place*, he thought. The Vrassoons' impressive building greeted the clipper as it took the bend in the river. Vrassoon sighed. *All we need now is extraterritoriality here in Shanghai and our trading empire will be assured to last and last.*

By the time the great man actually set foot on the soil of the Middle Kingdom, there were very few people of importance who did not know of his coming.

Cyril had arranged an elaborate greeting party for his boss that representatives from both Dents and Jardine, Matheson had agreed to attend.

The Hordoons, naturally enough, weren't invited, but they were in attendance that brisk morning nonetheless. Richard, freshly returned from his voyage upriver with the House of Zion, wouldn't have missed it for the world. Six years before he had spent a lot of money that he could ill afford to find out what had happened to his parents in Calcutta. The Pinkerton man had reported his findings.

Richard never told Maxi — and now here before him was the man who had ordered his father's dead body thrown in a river like so much rotted fruit.

Eliazar Vrassoon stared at the ragtag group of Europeans who stood at an odd sort of attention. When Cyril stepped forward to give his speech of welcome, Eliazar held up a hand for him to stop, muttering, "What is this foolishness?"

"Just a welcome, sir, for …"

"I'm a businessman not a showgirl. Now put an end to this nonsense right now and take me to the company's office."

Maxi tapped Richard's shoulder and whispered in his ear, just the way he used to when they played spy back in Calcutta, "Ugly, isn't he?"

"That he is. I bet he works at it."

Suddenly Sikh guards were moving quickly through the crowd pushing open a path for the Vrassoon Patriarch.

Richard sidestepped a Sikh and planted himself right in front of Eliazar Vrassoon.

The man was nonplussed. "So we meet again, young man. What have you to bargain with this time?"

The Sikh guard pulled Richard out of the way and by the time Maxi got to his brother, Richard was visibly shaking and, despite the cold, covered in sweat.

ૐ23

EXTRATERRITORIALITY

The Village of Shanghai
February, 1844

Hercules McCallum, the leader of the giant Scottish trading company Jardine, Matheson, stretched his massive shoulders and cursed the cold as he propped his bare left foot on a cushion and adjusted the canvas hot-water bottle upon which he sat. *Shanghai is even colder this February than last,* he thought, then noted for the hundredth time that the Glasgow-quarried flagstones covering the floor of his office on the Bund didn't help the problem. He glanced at the massive but empty fireplace. Too many Concession buildings had burnt to the ground because of faulty chimney work, so most Europeans simply put up with the cold — and used hot water bottles.

Hercules picked up a surprisingly dainty silver bell and gave it a ring. After a moment, a panel, made from Scottish border county oak, slid back smoothly and his personal secretary came in carrying a bronze tray upon which sat both a large tot of single malt

Scottish whisky and a cloudy draught meant to combat the painful gout nodule on the big toe of Hercules's left foot.

"Have we had any responses yet, James?"

"Aye, sir. Everyone, even the Persians, have agreed to meet."

That didn't surprise him. The Hordoons were heathens but they were nothing if not practical. He was surprised, however, that the American traders had agreed. "Do we not have to undergo an Evangelical dunking in order to be honoured with the presence of the House of Zion?"

"They haven't stipulated religious conversion as a prerequisite of their attendance, sir."

"Could we suggest they leave their Bibles at home or would they consider that ill-mannered, do you suppose?" He chuckled, but it caused the gout nodule to glance against the leather of the footstool, which sent shards of pain raging up his leg.

James saw his employer's discomfort but knew better than to acknowledge it. Hercules, at forty-two, still had a body to match his name. In his earlier years, the man had been a seemingly unstoppable force of nature. Women loved his physical prowess and men followed wherever he led. And then had come the debilitating gout. James made himself smile and replied, "Perhaps, sir."

Hercules took the draught of foul-smelling stuff then washed it down with a big gulp of the single malt whisky — and sighed. "Confirm with all of them for this hour tomorrow night."

James nodded and returned through the oak panel whence he came.

Alone in the room, Hercules stood and walked carefully toward the windows that faced the Huangpu River. He looked across to the Pudong, with its incantatory mysteries, then up the street to the House of Vrassoon, and then in the other direction to the offices of the English traders, Dent's. They could lose it all, he knew. Every one of them could lose everything. All the work. All the time. All the money could go away if they couldn't convince Chinese labourers to come into the Concessions and work.

His left foot brushed against his right shoe. Again, the pain, like splinters of glass racing up his leg, took his breath from him. He waited for the agony to subside, then looked down at the small red bump on the big toe of his left foot. Such a small thing to incapacitate someone as powerful as himself. Like the little matter of Chinese workers bringing the greatest trading companies in the world to their knees. He wondered what would happen if he took a knife to the gout nodule and simply cut it out. His doctors had, in no uncertain terms, warned him against that. He took a sip of his whisky and thought that the nodule might have to stay on his foot, but this Chinese labour problem had to go away.

The meeting itself did not start well. Hercules's proffered whisky was pronounced "spittle of the devil" by Jedediah Oliphant, who then added a few choice words that sounded like a biblical quotation. But Hercules, who was as Bible-learned as any minister, couldn't for the life of him identify from where in the Good Book the man's vituperative admonition against alcohol came. The food was put aside on the basis of some sort of hocus pocus dietary restriction by the newly arrived Vrassoon Patriarch and his skull-capped retinue. Percy St. John Dent sipped his liquor and nibbled at the edges of his food. Only the two Persians ate and drank heartily, the red-haired one smacking his lips loudly.

Hercules ignored these warning signs and rose from his seat at the head of the table. "Thank you for joining me, gentlemen. Please accept my apologies if my humble offerings have caused offence. None was intended, of that I can assure you."

The men around the table nodded. Maxi reached for a fat turkey leg that oozed reddish juices down his chin as he chomped down on the flesh.

"We are competitors," Hercules continued, "but we are now

confronted by a common problem." The faces around the table stared back at him. No one spoke. The red-haired Persian set down his turkey leg and wiped his chin. Hercules waited for someone to respond. This was clearly going to be more difficult than he had anticipated.

"All right," he began again, "we've had years of undercutting, outdoing, and outsmarting each other. We're traders, businessmen, opponents. I acknowledge that, and I think the rest of you around this table have no quibble with those definitions." Again, no one spoke. At least no one contradicted him, he thought. "But if we fight each other now, if we don't come together and speak with one voice against our common enemy —"

"And who exactly would this common enemy be, in your esteemed opinion?" asked Percy St. John Dent with an open mischievousness. Then, with a breathless sarcasm, he asked, "Would you by any chance be referring to the British East India Company's Vrassoon family with their parliamentary monopoly on direct trade between China and England? Would *they* be the common enemy, Mr. Hercules McCallum?"

Eliazar Vrassoon spread his arms magnanimously and said, "As simple traders, none of us here has the wisdom to question the noble actions of Her Majesty's duly appointed Parliament. The law is the law. We are law-abiding traders, not brigands or pirates. We all here obey the law, do we not?"

"The law!" Maxi spat out. Richard put a hand on his brother's arm to restrain him.

"Yes, the law," Hercules jumped in. "The law," he repeated. Then he asked pointedly, "Why are *we* not the law here, in our own home? Why are the Manchus the law in our Concessions? Surely our Concessions should be ruled by our laws." He paused for a moment, then said, as if it were nothing significant, "Why do we not work together toward extraterritoriality? Speak with one voice for it?"

Extraterritoriality was the end goal of every colonizing power. With it, the colonizers could control the laws within the bounds of their jurisdictions. No longer would the Concession be a small enclave within the mass of China. The Concession would be a piece of England — or America — a sovereign power governed by the trading houses, who would make and enforce the law as they saw fit.

"But we're *not* the law here." Jedediah Oliphant stated the obvious.

"Aye, but we could be," Hercules said, and smiled. "If we unite. Uniting is the key to gaining extraterritoriality."

Everyone agreed with that. They would have to ask their respective governments to force the Manchus into granting extraterritoriality — perhaps with some substantial loss of life, and definitely with a momentary loss of tax revenue. Anti-colonial forces in both England and America were growing stronger. If they sensed any wavering in the traders' resolve they would pounce.

Maxi reached for his drumstick and took another bite. His bright, hard teeth hit bone with a clink. He looked at his brother and then reached for a second piece of turkey. But before he could get it into his mouth the discussion had degenerated into squabbling.

Richard knew the head of Jardine, Matheson was right. Only if they were united could they hope to get their governments to force extraterritoriality on the Chinese. And only with extraterritoriality in place could the traders secure Chinese labourers to work for them. With extraterritoriality, they could offer the workers places to live and, most important, protection from the Manchu Mandarins' retribution. But too many years of animosity and distrust separated the men in the room, and Richard knew that Hercules wasn't the one to unite the traders. He looked at the irate faces around the table as the voices grew in both volume and anger and his eye kept landing on the calm visage of Eliazar Vrassoon. Finally, the man turned his bulbous eyes toward him, nodded, and then said in Yiddish, "Meet me tonight."

The foreign words stopped the English-speakers around the table. Quickly accusations flew against the "heathens in our midst." "English," Percy St. John Dent suggested, "is the language of this meeting."

The Vrassoon Patriarch nodded. "My apologies, gentlemen." But Richard read no apology in either the man's tone or his demeanour.

By the time Richard and Maxi finally got up to leave, the leaders of the great trading houses of Shanghai were sitting in stony, angry silence.

Late that night, Richard entered the very heart of enemy territory, the private study of the Patriarch of the Vrassoon clan. He stood with his cap literally in hand and waited for the older man to join him.

The room bespoke power and money — both understated, but very much in evidence. Throw rugs from the Punjab, milk-soft leather chairs to rival any found in the finest salons of Paris, delicately leaded windows overlooking the beginnings of the promenade along the Huangpu River, original oil paintings that seemed to feature the same female model at different ages, all in gilt frames, a silver menorah to one side and other telltale artifacts of Judaica.

Without fanfare or apology for making him wait, Eliazar Vrassoon entered the room followed by Cyril, his China hand. The Patriarch dismissed Cyril with the pointing of a finger then waited until the man was out the door before he turned to Richard.

Richard guessed Vrassoon was in his middle to late fifties, probably about the age his own father would have been had he lived that long. A surge of anger raced through Richard but it quickly dissipated as something else — something urgent — tugged at the sides of his memory. The head of the British East India Company extended his hand. The words *What are you doing here?* flew into Richard's mind but he couldn't find the rest of the thought. For a moment he felt as though he were falling, somehow only a child again — and there was wetness between his legs! Then he was pointing, showing this man something. What?

Richard finally noticed Eliazar's extended hand. It felt good not to have reciprocated the courtesy.

"As you will," Vrassoon said as he returned his hand to his coat pocket. "Well, our Christian counterparts seem intent upon fighting one another," the older man said.

"Unlike us Jews, who always love and honour each other," Richard spat back sarcastically.

The older man nodded and poured himself a small glass of sherry from a crystal decanter. He didn't offer Richard a drink. "Indeed," he said, "but we at least won't squabble over religious niceties."

"Only because I have no religious niceties," Richard responded.

"No, you don't." Eliazar Vrassoon's voice was suddenly cold as ice. "No, you're not any kind of a Jew. In fact, if they didn't hate us all so much you'd have no identity whatsoever. You're only a Jew because the goyim hate you."

Richard accepted that. "I live my life by my own values."

"That assumes you have some."

"I reject your medieval darkness in favour of finding my own light."

Vrassoon shook his head slowly and then said, "You are a lonely man, Mr. Hordoon."

"Better lonely than idolatrous."

"Idolatrous!" The Vrassoon Patriarch's voice arched in a high crescendo that surprised Richard.

"Yes. Now, could you skip the preamble and tell me whatever it is…?"

Vrassoon hesitated. Did he really need this boy's assistance? Didn't he have enough power on his own? No. If it was just a man or two or three from his own company the other traders wouldn't care. Why should they? But if it were men from two different companies, then it would imply that the next could be from their firms. It would become a real threat to their safety. Enough of a threat, Eliazar hoped, to force all the traders to speak with one voice to their governments to force extraterritoriality on the Manchus.

He looked at young Hordoon. *We are partners, you and I, and have been for a very long time,* he thought. *And only now will you begin to know it.* The Vrassoon Patriarch took a deep breath and then began.

"I hold the note on your debt to Barclays Bank."

"This is not news to me."

"Would you like an extension on the payment schedule of that note?"

Richard stopped himself from speaking. His time with the House of Zion in the countryside had taught him that he could open large markets that none of the other traders even knew existed. Those markets could generate large sums of cash. Maybe not enough to pay off the whole debt, but certainly enough to make a sizable dent in it. But it would take time to set up his networks. Time that, until this very moment, he'd had no way of finding. He made sure his voice was nonchalant when he spoke. "I'm listening."

Walking home that night Richard knew that the Eliazar Vrassoon's plan was the only way to get the traders to unite. He had made as good a deal as he could, although he was shocked when, at the end of their haggling, Vrassoon had said, "You drove a harder bargain when you were younger." When Richard had pressed for the meaning of that cryptic remark the older man had just laughed and asked, "So we have a deal?" And Richard had taken the old man's hand — the hand that had ordered his father's body tossed into a river — and the deal was sealed. He knew that he must never tell Maxi about the details. *If Maxi ever found out what I did to get the three-year extension on the debt repayment from the Vrassoons he would kill someone. Well, many people. Eliazar Vrassoon first,* Richard thought, then added, *After that, he'd probably come after me.*

The Vrassoon Patriarch's generous financial offer to the Manchu Mandarin assured the heathen's cooperation in this matter. The Mandarin, in fact, seemed only too ready to write a proclamation that would call on all civic officials to "Enforce our local laws, to their full extent, on *all* the citizens of Shanghai, without exception."

Mr. Norman Vincent dipped his quill in the inkwell on his highboy desk and marked a bill of lading "Paid," then rubbed his hands together to revive the feeling in his fingers. The cold here in Shanghai was different from his native London, and he had been sick often since his first arrival in the Far East just over three years before. He took the locket from around his neck and opened it. The broad, honest features of his wife stared back at him. In her arms, she held their baby girl. *She won't be a baby anymore,* he thought. *She must be walking and talking by now.* He sighed, and his breath misted in the office.

He'd worked hard this morning and wanted to reward himself. The Old Shanghai Restaurant in the Chinese section — the Old City — was technically out of bounds for foreigners but the food there was wonderful, and a bowl of soup, *tong,* was just the thing he needed on a cold day like today. *Maybe with those wonderful dumplings in it.* The thought made him smile as he signed out with his supervisor and, grabbing his muffler, headed out of the Vrassoons' British East India Company offices.

On the partially built raised promenade along the Huangpu River he looked across at the Pudong and gave a little shiver. He needed to control his urges and save his money, he reminded himself. That's why he was here in this far-off place — to make money. But the sexual offerings across the river were a great temptation to him. Only in the Pudong could a man get sexual satisfaction at a price a shipping clerk could afford.

He turned away from temptation and toward the rewards of the palate as he headed east along the river then south into the heart of Old Shanghai.

Just moments after Mr. Vincent turned toward the Old Shanghai Restaurant, a fellow *Fan Kuei*, this one a bookkeeper in the employ of the Hordoons, also made his way toward the forbidden Old City. This man had a new girl and his new girl needed a present. Something special. Only in the Old City could a bookkeeper like Charles David afford a special present — for a new girl. He whistled as he walked, his step jaunty, a smile creasing his attractive young features. It would be the last smile that would grace his countenance on this earth.

The Manchu authorities arrested both men, as had been agreed upon, strapped chains to their wrists and then threw them literally into a hole in the ground to await their fate. By entering the Old City, they had, after all, broken the law — the Manchu law, and Manchu courts would decide their punishment.

Richard felt a momentary pang when he heard of the arrest of Charles David. He had put forward the names of three men in his employ, as had Vrassoon, so that neither would have directly "condemned" anyone. He comforted himself by thinking, *Someone has to make the sacrifice. At least it wasn't one of Maxi's irregulars.*

The Confucian was surprised when he was asked to sit as judge in the trial of the two Europeans. Usually, such cases would go directly to the Manchu Mandarin, but he sensed that something was afoot in all this. He hastily sent messages to Jiang and the Bodyguard. They met late that night in his study. He laid out the facts. Two Europeans had been taken into custody and charged with treason against the state for doing no more than almost all Foreign Devils had done in the past in Shanghai. The Manchu separation law had been ignored from the beginning. But now, seemingly out of nowhere, the law had been put into full force.

"Why?" asked the Bodyguard

"Who cares why?" said Jiang. "There may be an opportunity here for us to advance the prophecy."

"How?"

"What is the greatest problem in the Concession?"

"What it's always been. Our people won't work for them."

"Right. So if you were in the traders' position, what would you do?"

"I'd call upon my nation's navies to force extraterritoriality —"

"So would I." Jiang cut off the Confucian. "So why haven't they done that?"

"That one I can answer," said the Bodyguard. "They hate each other more than we hate them, so they can't unite themselves. They are like children unable to see what is right before them."

"True. So what can we do to unite them, to get them together, and bring in their countries' great ships?"

The Bodyguard nodded. Jiang canted her head. The Confucian smiled. "Death can bring together the living."

The two men standing before the Confucian, heads bowed, seemed pitiful specimens of their races, but then again, a full week in a dark pit had broken stronger men than these. One was on his knees begging for forgiveness. The other stood very still and said nothing, strangely dispassionate. *These people are so short-sighted. They have no view of themselves as part of the continuum of history, as we do*, the Confucian thought as he held up his hand and the guards roughly silenced the blubbering man.

The packed court fell quiet. Maxi stood at the back and demanded a translation of the proceedings from Richard.

The Confucian rose and, allowing the old-fashioned singsong to come into his voice, pronounced his sentence on the men: "*Xuan shou shi zhong* — Death by public strangulation."

Mr. Norman Vincent had wet himself and couldn't control his

shaking. The mumbled prayers of the Evangelicals only seemed to make it worse. He couldn't focus. This couldn't be happening to him. Not to him. He looked at the cracked paving tiles upon which his knees rested. Then vomit spewed from him and he voided into his britches — and he felt the bite of the rope on his neck.

Charles David caught the whiff of human excrement from the man beside him. He was strangely calm — or so the watchers felt. Some called it brave. Charles knew better. It was the normal detachment that he had been able to cloak himself in since he was a boy.

He looked up at the crowd. Every non-Asian in Shanghai had been forced to come view the strangulation. He scanned the faces, recognizing some. Then his eyes landed on the face of the young Hordoon boy named Silas. The boy was staring at him, but not with the fear and disgust that was so evident on the faces of almost all the non-Asians. The boy had a detached curiosity … a detached curiosity that Charles recognized as akin to his own. When the rope slid around his neck he continued to stare at Silas Hordoon and as his lungs screamed for air and his eyes bulged, he stared steadily at the boy and forced his mouth to form the words, "Despite it, do great things, boy, great things."

"Barbaric! Beyond any sense of law!" Jedediah Oliphant exclaimed, and for the first time in a very long time, he envied those who could indulge in the calming effects of alcohol.

"At least demand their bodies," shouted Maxi.

For a moment Richard wondered if Maxi had found out about the ill-treatment of their own father's body, but then he dismissed the idea. If Maxi had known, Eliazar Vrassoon would not have been able to hire enough Sikh guards to keep himself safe. No, Maxi was only responding to the death of the two men.

Richard appreciated Maxi's sentiments but he didn't want to deal with them now. Now, with all the traders upset and together back in the offices of Jardine, Matheson, was the time to act. To rally the troops, not get bogged down in niceties like the disposition of dead bodies.

"Outrageous, beyond the bounds of civilized behaviour — well beyond it," added Percy St. John Dent as he topped up his glass with Hercules's fine whisky and took a seat.

"Never again must this be allowed to happen to our people," stated Hercules, ignoring the pain from the new nodule on the baby toe of his left foot.

The Vrassoon Patriarch stepped forward, caught Richard's eye briefly, and suggested, "Then we are agreed that we must take our fate into our own hands. That these heathens must be shown a lesson. That we will speak as one voice to be free in our lands to do as we see fit." He looked around for a moment, then lifted the glass in his hand. Slowly everyone in the room lifted theirs — even Jedediah Oliphant grabbed an empty glass and held it aloft. "To extraterritoriality, gentlemen."

The men drank to their pledge, then retreated to their offices to contact their highest government sources to begin the process that would bring on what history would call the Second Opium War.

✤ 24

THE ARRIVAL OF THE PATRIARCH

War
March, 1844

It proved to be not much of a war, as wars go. The arrival of the six British man-o'-war and two American fighting vessels in the Shanghai harbour was remarkably effective. A slight hesitation from the Manchu authorities induced an out-and-out shelling of the Chinese section of the city from the ships. Before the sun set that day the basics of an extraterritoriality agreement had been proposed by the Manchu Mandarin himself.

Richard translated, and with Hercules and Percy St. John Dent pushing the traders' points, the agreement got more and more specific. The relentless squirming and conniving of the Mandarin to make the agreement porous was resisted at every turn. Eventually, six days later, when the document was signed, it was the most inclusive, restrictive document on Chinese power that had ever been written, or, more importantly, signed.

The party began that night at sunset in the British Concession and shortly thereafter in the American Concession. Oliphant tried to begin the festivities with prayer but only managed to get through an opening hymn before the revelry took over. Guns were fired in the air and liquor flowed freely as midnight — the appointed hour for the beginning of extraterritoriality — approached.

As the merriment increased, Richard retreated to the Old City and knocked at an unmarked door at the end of a dusty alley. Jiang opened the door and canted her head toward Richard — a very good customer. "Is the woman with you?" she asked.

Richard nodded and called for Lily. From behind packing crates in the alley, the woman without a nose or ears approached with her head down.

"Your usual accommodations are ready for you. Your pipe is cleaned, your dreams await," Jiang said.

Several miles up the Huangpu River, Maxi stood by two shallow graves. Milo and Silas were at his side. "These men sacrificed their lives for us," he said. "You must honour men who fall in your command, boys, or no one will follow you." Maxi bowed his head. He didn't know prayers or care about them. He cared about lives lost for no good reason. He turned to the boys and said, "Honour these men in your thoughts. Now put your flowers on their graves."

The boys knelt and put their flowers down. Silas allowed his hand to touch the cold, sandy earth and wondered what it felt like to lie beneath the ground.

Maxi watched his nephew and sensed the boy's distance, something that he himself had been feeling more and more. And now these two senseless deaths. Two murders. He suspected they were two sacrifices but had no more than suspicion upon which to base this. He looked around at the river and the growing city behind them and knew in his heart, for the first time, that this was not his home, nor would it ever be. A strong gust of wind from the west drew his eye. The Taiping rebels were upriver. He knew that. But he wondered why that particular thought had sped through his mind as he stood on the windy hillside beside his two nephews and the two graves.

The midnight bell sounded and the town crier called out "Midnight Hour!" and shouts of joy came from the mouths of the non-Asians.

In the Old City, Chinese parents smelled the ozone reek of change in the air and pulled their children close to them.

The third opium ball did the trick for Richard. He opened the holes in his back and spiralled down the deep well to himself and the dark secret that lurked there.

As he did, a sleek sailing ship came about in the harbour. The French had arrived — with Suzanne and Pierre Colombe, madam and priest, side by side on deck.

The sounds of revelry from the land moved across the water and greeted brother and sister on the upper deck. "A party," Suzanne said with a smile. "How appropriate a welcome. You'll have to do something about that, brother. Parties aren't good for churches, are they?"

"No, my sister, they are not. Although I believe they are good for your commercial enterprise." His words were sharp.

"Nice of you to notice," Suzanne replied. Then she turned her eyes to her new home, Shanghai.

25

THE ARRIVAL OF THE PATRIARCH

Shanghai
1846 to September 1847

Extraterritoriality immediately solved two problems facing all the traders. With the protection that it provided, they were able to recruit and keep enough Chinese workers to run their businesses and households, and under the terms of the treaty, the traders could avoid the 100,000 *taels* of silver demanded by the Manchu Mandarin. Extraterritoriality worked surprisingly well in other ways, as well. Percy St. John Dent was appointed head of the newly formed Governing Council with the understanding that the position would rotate through the four great trading houses (the Hordoons were not included) on a six-month basis. On Fridays, from sunrise to just before sundown (out of consideration for the Vrassoons), petitioners to the Council would be heard. Also, each of the trading houses (this time the Hordoons were included) was required to provide six men to act as constables. These men were to report directly to the head of the Council.

It all seemed so civilized. What, in fact, this arrangement did was ensure that no trading house would have any power over the others. The 'police officers', in fact, never reported to the head of the Council before they had reported to the head of their own trading company.

The one notable advance was the breaking down of the border, at the Suzu Creek, between the American and British Concessions. The two sides adopted the name "the Foreign Settlement" for the merged territory. However, the French — being French — declined to join their English-speaking Protestant counterparts and settled on the novel name "The French Concession" for their lands bordering the Chinese Old City. Shortly after the name became simply "The Concession."

The Foreign Settlement and the Concession were divided by nothing more than an invisible line down the centre of a street, yet they had different governing bodies, different laws, different police forces — all of which made it very convenient for a felon from one side or the other to cross that invisible line and suddenly go from wanted man to free man.

Within the Concession boundaries and under the protection of the guns of the French flagship, the *Casini*, the Colombes — Jesuit and madam — thrived. Within three months Suzanne had managed to open the House of Paris on the central road of the Concession, and Father Pierre had the foundation completed and some of the walls up for Asia's largest Christian house of worship, the Cathedral of St. Ignatius.

Much to the surprise of the English and Americans, the *Cassini* was quickly becoming a permanent fixture in the harbour. The Foreign Settlement failed to realize that the commander of the *Cassini*, Captain de Plas, was a devout Catholic who believed it was his duty to protect both the Concession and all Catholics in this "heathen hellhole," hence the positioning of his ship so that his stern port guns could reach the government building on the western edge of the Concession and the bow port guns could reach the Cathedral on the east.

It never occurred to good Captain de Plas that his guns offered as much protection to Suzanne's house of pleasure as they did to Pierre's cathedral.

Father Pierre finally approached the red-haired Jew who had been coming by the cathedral construction site almost every day. "Are you attracted to our house of worship? It is open to all," Father Pierre said.

For a moment Maxi thought he understood what was being asked, then he made the international signal for "I don't speak the language" — a large shoulder shrug accompanied by an "ain't — I — a — fool?" face.

Father Pierre nodded slowly — a Jew *and* a non-French-speaker. He couldn't decide which was more offensive. But he made himself smile and rephrased his question in torturously slowly spoken English.

Maxi began to shake his head before Pierre had even finished. "No, I don't want to come in."

"Father," Pierre prompted congenially.

"Excuse me?"

"You can call me Father. Father Pierre."

Maxi smiled, showing a lot of large, white teeth, and said, "I think not."

"Fine." Father Pierre's smile seemed to harden on his sharp features. "Then why are you here if not for God's word that can only be received within the walls of Mother Church?"

Maxi waved a hand, as if it were keeping smoke from his face. He wasn't going to be drawn into this sort of argument.

"What do you want here, Jew?"

Pierre's tone was one that Maxi had heard often enough in his life. In a certain way, Maxi preferred hatred out in the open. At least that way the rules were clear. "I want nothing inside your church … Father … just knowledge of how the building is put together."

That surprised Father Pierre. "Are you interested in building design?"

"No. I'm interested in how buildings are made." He didn't bother adding that he was actually interested in the mathematics behind the construction, and how the mathematics sometimes led him to understand the meaning of things, and that without the meaning of things Maxi felt somehow adrift. As if any day of the week or year could be any other day of the week or year. As if there was no forward motion. With Ahmed the opium farmer he hadn't felt that way; when he attended the Chinese opera he didn't feel that way. This Church, with its arbitrary rules and dogma, didn't hold out the possibility of meaning to Maxi. But the building itself, that which encased the religion, might.

Father Pierre's smile returned. He knew that every angle, every construction idea behind the building of the great cathedral had come directly from God, so he thought that the Jew's interest in the building techniques might very well lead to an interest in God who had made the rules that governed all the principles of nature — and the building of His great churches.

Pierre called over his master builder and instructed him to answer Maxi's questions. Maxi wanted to know about the flying buttresses, their respective weights versus the weight of the section of the roof they supported, the mathematical calculation involved in finding the pivot point for the buttress, and the depth to which the buttress had to be sunk into the ground.

Father Pierre stood back and watched him soak up the proffered information. He was impressed with Maxi's quick comprehension of the information and his ability to deduce problematic issues arising from the facts he had heard.

The master builder moved on to the actual machinery used in the construction, but Maxi already knew the basic principles involved. Even the complex knotting systems used for the block and tackle were nothing new to him.

"Would you like to step inside?" Father Pierre asked. Maxi hesitated. "It is not yet consecrated. Besides, there are few walls. God's buildings require walls," he joked.

Maxi nodded and followed the Jesuit.

"Over there will be the front door of the cathedral. And where we are now is the main aisle — the nave."

Maxi looked around him. The flying buttresses on the west side were already levered against wall stanchions and holding sections of roof aloft. He could imagine the walls in place and the feeling of weightless lift given by the buttresses, which were massive outside the walls but slender inside, like the branches of the trees that fell over the walls of the Government of India Alkaloid Works at Ghazipur.

They walked side by side down the central aisle toward the high altar. About two-thirds of the way down other aisles branched out left and right. Maxi looked at Father Pierre, who replied, "The transept. To the east," he said, pointing, "and the west, à la Rue des Juifs."

"Pardon me?"

"Just the name for the street outside the west transept door." Father Pierre wasn't interested in explaining that the Rue des Juifs was the only place where Jewish moneylenders were allowed to enact their savage trade. Since Mother Church seldom had enough money on hand to build the necessary buildings to glorify God, the money was often raised by borrowing it from the Jewish moneylenders just outside the west transept door. Convenient for business. And in cases where the congregation could not raise the money needed to pay back the Jews, they could be riled up on an Easter Sunday and sent to chase away those who happened to hold the debt note for the Church. No moneylender — no money lent. Very convenient.

While her brother occupied himself with the construction of his great cathedral, Suzanne had business of her own to attend to. She decided it was finally time to see what the local competition had to offer. Accompanied by two of her bouncers, she entered the anteroom of Jiang's establishment. Her men wore a consistent scowl, but Suzanne knew that this was just a mask. Right at that moment they couldn't have been happier, because they were about to sample the wares of Jiang's pleasure house, and Suzanne would foot the bill. Who wouldn't be smiling, especially since the bouncers were not allowed under any circumstances to touch the women in Suzanne's House of Paris?

Suzanne was impressed by the understated elegance of Jiang's establishment. Her discerning eye caught the carefully planted clues to the erotic, despite the fact that most were cloaked in a classical Chinese formality. The women wore Manchu-style robes, *hanfu*, and hair dressings but a few ribbon ties were always left open to reveal the curve of a breast or the length of a finely defined calf muscle. All of the women had beautifully painted mouths, and tiny feet — the result of binding when they were young.

"You are troubled?" Jiang asked.

"No," Suzanne lied smoothly, then decided to be honest. "Yes. Have all their feet been bound?"

Jiang nodded. "Absolutely. It is a sign of respect from their parents. After all, who would marry a woman with unbound feet?"

"But your feet were not bound."

"Yes, but that is my family's tradition."

"Do the women in your family marry?"

"The eldest daughter, yes. She is always an artist."

"And the others?"

"One of my younger daughters will succeed me. She will not marry but she will produce at least two daughters. It has always been thus here. So, now look at the beauty arrayed before you and choose."

To her surprise Suzanne felt an old stirring deep within her as one of the tall beauties tilted her head and gave her a lascivious smile.

Jiang's silky voice spoke a series of Mandarin words that were quickly translated into French. "Her name is Tu Yeh. She is most practised in the pleasuring of women like yourself."

Suzanne turned and looked into the high-cheekboned, flawless-skinned face of the famous Jiang. "Is she indeed?"

"She is." Jiang's round-faced translator stood behind her mistress and did her job with remarkable ease.

"Does she perform with accoutrements? Both receiving and delivering?"

Jiang needed a moment to sort through the difference in euphemisms, then understood the question. She looked closely at this *Fan Kuei* woman, allowing her eyes to examine openly the fine white skin, the petite curves, the devilish, thin-lipped smile — and tiny, very sexy ears. She knew from her many spies that this was Suzanne Colombe from the House of Paris. She leaned forward. Suzanne's delicate perfume wafted up and surrounded her. Then she kissed the woman on the neck.

Suzanne was startled by the kiss, then allowed herself to move with the touch. She reached up a hand and pulled the lovely lips from her neck. Then she looked into Jiang's unfathomably deep eyes. The women both smiled at the same time, their eyes expressing even more pleasure than their mouths.

"And how much do you cost?"

"The same as you do. Too much for paying customers."

"How about this Tu Yeh creature?"

Suzanne didn't bargain. She paid the price demanded and retreated with Tu Yeh to a back room that they accessed through a narrow hallway. On either side of the corridor, two bunks high, were pallets upon which men reclined and smoked their opium. Some were alone. A few were with partially clad girls.

Tu Yeh noticed Suzanne's interest. "Would you like to partake … before?"

Suzanne allowed a smile up to her lips and said, "Before what?"

When Suzanne emerged from the expert ministrations of Tu Yeh she was surprised to hear a kind of high-pitched singsong colloquy of voices. She followed the sound through the main greeting chamber, through an interior courtyard, and into a high-ceilinged room with a set of raised platforms at one end. Across from the platforms sat an attentive audience on low chairs and three-legged bamboo stools. On the platforms were four Chinese men in elaborate costumes, singing. The crash of a cymbal froze them in space and a delicate woman, wearing a costume with sleeves that draped all the way to the floor, moved quickly — it seemed to Suzanne that the woman floated on air — to the centre of what was clearly a stage. A cymbal crashed and a screech came from the woman that shook the crystal chandelier. Then she threw her arms up in the air, causing her sleeves to float up like yards of silk caught by the wind. When the sleeves were at their full extension the actress struck a startling pose, The horns blared and cymbals crashed and then crashed again. And the audience went wild. Shouts of "*Hao*!" which Suzanne knew meant "good," rose from the room. People sprang to their feet and cheered. None louder, it seemed to Suzanne, than an attractive red-haired man whose applause led the room.

"Do you like?" It was Jiang whispering in her ear again. Suzanne didn't know if the woman was referring to the red-haired man or the performance. Before she could answer, a tall, handsome Chinese woman in her mid-twenties came onstage and readjusted the actress's position, turned to the other actors, and shouted, "Again."

Quickly the actors moved offstage and the musicians rearranged themselves. The Chinese woman then counted down from three and said "*Kai shi*," which Suzanne recognized as meaning "play."

"So, I ask again, do you like?"

"It's a play?"

"My daughter's newest opera. She is thinking of calling it *Journey to the West*."

Suzanne had often had opera singers and concert violinists perform in her establishment back in Paris, so she appreciated the odd symbiosis of art and sex. "The handsome one in charge is your daughter?"

"Yes. I named her Fu Tsong."

"Fu Tsong. Very pretty."

Jiang pushed Suzanne's shoulder just a little more than gently and said, through her translator, "She's a widow, but actually she's married — married to her operas." Suzanne turned to face Jiang. The woman was smiling. "Besides, she's too good-looking for an old bird like you."

Suzanne smiled back and nodded. "Absolutely too young for me. But that one over there isn't," she said, indicating the red-haired man who had returned to his seat and was watching the stage intently.

"Ah. The true Red-Haired Devil." She stopped for a moment and tried to wrap her tongue around the strange name, "Maxi Hordoon." Her pronunciation was close to perfect.

"Ah, the Jew. Is he a frequent visitor to your house?"

"Yes. He is unmarried. At first the girls were frightened of him, but once they saw his spear they changed their tune. Now he comes more often for the plays my daughter stages than for the girls. Be careful with him."

"Why careful?"

"There is violence there."

Suzanne had already seen that. But violence was also passion, and as Tu Yeh had proved to her in no uncertain terms, she needed some passion in her life just now. She also needed a partner, so she turned to Jiang. "Would you be available for tea tomorrow afternoon? I have a business proposition that might interest you."

Jiang looked at the slowly lengthening shadows outside the window as she gently put the dark, hot beverage, untouched, to one side of the table. Suzanne had proudly presented it, through her translator, as a drink called coffee. Jiang had taken a sip and found it bitter. Suzanne had immediately ordered that tea be served.

When the tea arrived Jiang smiled and said, "Very considerate of you."

"My apologies. I thought the coffee might be a treat."

"Perhaps, like certain positions, it is an acquired taste."

"Perhaps."

The two women drank their respective beverages in silence. Finally Suzanne said, "The men in this city have no idea how much money there is to be made in our trade."

Jiang didn't totally agree but she nodded and said, "Let us hope they stay so blind."

"You and I both make our living off the folly of men."

Jiang didn't completely agree with that statement either, but she nodded.

"As long as men feel they are in command they can be manipulated in any manner that a smart woman — or two smart women — want."

Jiang agreed more with this statement.

"But men can also be the enemy. They can sense that we are making money and insist upon taking a portion for themselves."

"In return for their protection," Jiang said sarcastically.

"Yes. Extortion. And it never ends. And it always increases. It is the one serious downside of our business."

Jiang agreed completely with this assessment.

"What if there were a circumstance under which this extortion could be regulated? In which the government, not gangs of thugs, offered us protection? And what if the extortion money were an agreed-upon percentage of our gross income?"

Jiang looked at the long tea leaves, like tall sea grass, moving with invisible currents. She knew, as all Chinese knew, that change was a serious part of life. She allowed herself to breathe deeply. Beyond the heavy smell of the coffee and the gentle aroma of the tea she detected the unmistakable reek of ozone in the air. Change was near.

"What percentage?" Jiang asked.

"Three percent, delivered at the end of each month in cash. Never taken out in trade on our girls. Never varying. Based upon figures that we supply for them at the end of the third week of each month."

"We supply the figures upon which the percentage is based?" Jiang asked, trying to keep the excitement out of her voice.

"We do," Suzanne affirmed. "You see the advantage of this regulated system to us, I assume, over the randomness that we put up with presently."

"I do," Jiang offered carefully. "But we would need a powerful government person with whom to deal."

"Absolutely. I have a very loyal customer at the House of Paris who happens to be the head of the governing unit of the Concession — the French Concession. Do you think that would be powerful enough?"

Suzanne proceeded to outline her plan. It would work only if Jiang moved into the Concession, where the protection could be offered. Jiang could either keep her house in the Old City and open a new house in a building just down the road from the House of Paris, or she could move her entire operation into the Concession.

"I need to think about this," Jiang said.

"Absolutely. Take all the time you need. But this evening, let my house entertain you."

Jiang angled her head slightly and asked, "At what time would you like me there?"

A mere six weeks later, the Foreign Settlement and the Concession were abuzz with the opening of Jiang's new house. The name was taken from ancient Chinese literature and was understood by very few. It translated as "It will happen at the Bend in the River," but the house, from its opening, was known simply as "Jiang's," the finest house of ill repute and opium den in all of Asia.

Jiang's opened on a beautiful spring evening in late April, when the wind moved softly up the Yangtze, bringing the scent of the sea into every room of the elegant house. French opera singers mingled with buccaneers who stood to have their portraits taken by a thin-faced Englishman who was showing off the newest of new inventions — the photographic camera. Two French painters mocked the newfangled thing as blasphemy, claiming that it would never replace their art.

The centrepiece of the evening was the premiere of a selection from the first act of Jiang's daughter's *Journey to the West*. Maxi was completely entranced by the singing, dancing, tumbling miracle of what would eventually be called Peking Opera. He was completely incapable of escaping the power of *Journey to the West*. Over and over he rose with the others in the audience and howled out "*Hao!*" then whistled and shouted his pleasure.

As Maxi fell into the heart of *Journey to the West* and found himself wanting to meet its creator, Richard signalled to the English photographer to follow him back to his office. He had already had an interesting conversation with the man, and there was more he wanted to know.

"Show me the pictures you mentioned earlier," Richard asked.

The young man reached into his leather satchel and drew out a neatly wrapped package. Untying the string knot, he folded back the brown paper and spread out the twenty photographs of which he had spoken.

"This is Eliazar Vrassoon's eldest boy?"

"Well, he's a man, sir, not a boy, but it's him."

"How did you get these?" Richard demanded.

"He paid me to take them."

"Yes, but how is it that you have them and not him?"

"He has the originals, but I have the negatives." He laughed. "He neglected to demand them from me."

Richard doubted the Vrassoon heir even knew there were negatives. "Where did you take these photographs?"

"In the anteroom of his favourite whorehouse in London."

"He let you …?"

"Shit, yes! He wanted to pose with the little thing but she cried and refused."

That stopped Richard for a moment, and he asked, "Little thing?"

"His whore."

"How young was she?"

"Ten. Maybe twelve."

Richard spread out the photographs. Three showed the Vrassoon's eldest son without a shirt and a leg up on a stool, flexing his not-inconsiderable muscles.

"Is it possible to put two pictures together?" he asked.

"You mean rip one or both and paste them together?"

"No, I mean take the subject of one photograph and include it in another photograph. So that it looks to the viewer as if the two were photographed together at the same time and in the same place."

The young photographer scratched his head. Richard was glad to see nothing living crept out of the man's curls. "In theory I guess it's possible, sir, but the two photographs would have different backgrounds, so it would be obvious that the picture had been monkeyed with."

"Really?" Richard said, as he took a pair of nail scissors from his desk and proceeded to cut the figure of the eldest Vrassoon son from one of the photographs. Then he turned to the younger man and said, "What if you took a photograph of someone else and kept that person's figure on the right side of the image. Then you could paste this figure of the Vrassoon boy here on the left side of the photograph, and then re-photograph the pasted picture to get an image with both figures against the same background."

"I guess I could do that, but why would — ?"

"Because I'd pay you more for that one photograph — and its negative — than you've been paid for all the photographs you've ever taken."

The younger man smiled and said, "I'm listening, Mr. Hordoon. Who's the other figure to go with the Vrassoon boy?"

Richard turned toward the large window and stared out at the wave of Chinese men and women moving past on the street outside his office. "How young was the bastard's whore?"

"Ten, maybe twelve, as I said."

Richard thought again. "And she cried?"

"I got the feeling that he hurt her, sir."

"Ah," Richard said. "The second figure will be a girl. A ten- or twelve-year-old girl. A hurt girl. A naked, hurt, Chinese girl. I'll send her to your hotel room to photograph."

The young photographer blushed. "I'll not hurt her, Mr. Hordoon."

"Nor will I. It'll be pretend. Only your photograph will make it appear real."

"But in my room, it's —"

"Improper. Certainly. This girl will have a chaperone, naturally."

The next morning the young photographer was awakened by a loud knocking at his door. He opened it and stepped back in horror.

Lily was used to people being startled by her noseless, earless appearance so she ignored the young man, reached behind her, and shoved forward what looked like a ten-year-old Han Chinese girl — a beautiful ten-year-old Han Chinese girl.

When the girl stepped into the photographer's room she pulled on the ribbon tie of her robe and it fell to the ground. As Madame Jiang had instructed her, she played at being a young girl — a hurt young girl — while the flustered photographer began the complicated calculations that could produce a picture that might send the Vrassoon boy directly to hell.

The next morning Maxi paid the photographer to take pictures of his young nephews. Dressed in Chinese silk robes, pantaloons, and slippers, Milo and Silas were photographed with huge smiles on their faces and their arms around each other. Within weeks the pictures appeared in newspapers around the world and, along with dozens of the young man's other photographs, gave the outside world its first views of the Wild West of the East — Shanghai. Silas loved the photograph of himself and Milo and wanted it framed and hung in their room. When he mentioned it to Patterson, though, the man turned on him and, ripping the photograph in half, screamed, "You're not fuckin' monkeys, heathen!"

ॐ 26

OPIUM — DREAMS AND NIGHTMARES

Shanghai, 1847

Rachel stood just inside the doorway, unexpectedly taken aback. Lily, instead of Richard, had opened the door to her knock.

"I'm sorry, she frightened me ... her face ..." Rachel's voice disappeared into a whisper, then was nothing more than breath.

"She's ... excuse me," Richard replied, then gently instructed Lily to leave them alone.

After a slight hesitation, the woman left the room.

"Careful of her, Mr. Hordoon, I think she cares for you," Rachel said.

"Foolishness."

"Not so foolish. Take care. After all, what could be more dangerous than a woman scorned?"

Richard smiled and said, "A fallen woman, perhaps?"

"Perhaps," Rachel said with a slow smile as she thought of her time with this man's brother.

Rachel hadn't seen Maxi for over a month. And the last time

they were alone he'd spent their precious time either brooding sullenly or talking excitedly about some play he had seen called *Journey to the West*. She sensed that he was trying to tell her something, something important to him, but he couldn't find the words. Then after that, nothing — not a single word for almost five weeks. She needed to see him but had no way of contacting him. She did, however, have a way of getting in touch with his brother, Richard.

They had grown close on their three-month trek upriver but they had never been free of the ever-watchful eyes of her father and his men. When they were together they talked of books and writing. He had shown her some of his journals and she had been helpful in editing certain passages. She also had a vast knowledge of Shakespeare, and they'd enjoyed many a lively conversation on what both agreed was the most problematic, although fascinating, of the Bard's plays, *Cymbeline*.

"And you are here now, Rachel to …?"

"Continue my work on your journals, naturally," she replied.

Richard took her wrap, showed her to his desk, and handed her his journal. She turned to the page they'd left off at and began to read. Richard watched her from across the room and said her name, silently, over and over again.

Rachel came to an entry wherein Richard responded to Thomas De Quincy's final letter, and after reading it carefully she corrected a line.

"What have you excised?"

"Your use of several subordinate clauses back-to-back lacks elegance."

"Ah," Richard said as he turned down the flame in the oil lamp.

"How am I to edit without the light?" she asked, putting down her pen.

Richard couldn't take his eyes off her. Her pale skin and green eyes were somehow luminous even in the half-light. He had trouble restraining himself from reaching over and touching the strand of auburn hair that had fallen across her face. After what seemed a very long silence, he said, "And you came over here, to my home, just to edit my writing, did you, Rachel?"

"Why else would I be here, Mr. Hordoon?" She met his eyes and held them. "You are staring, Mr. Hordoon."

"It's just the light," he said, as he reached over to turn the flame up — but her hand stopped his.

"There's more than enough light now." Then she said the most extraordinary thing. "We all must live a little before we die, don't you think, Mr. Hordoon?" The light glinted in her hazel eyes.

"Oh, yes," Richard responded, "before we marry a man twice our age, I think it wise to live a little."

Her face took on a sudden, hard cast. She turned the light up full and stood. "I think it is time that I left."

Richard reluctantly left the room, saying, "I'll get you a carriage to take you home."

Rachel thought about that for a second and she began to laugh. No carriage could take her all the way home to Philadelphia. With Richard out of the room she took the opportunity to search for signs of Maxi — but saw none.

Richard returned shortly and walked her outside to her conveyance. He was surprised to see two of her father's men, whom he recognized from his trek upriver. As the carriage drove away the two men continued to watch Richard, who mumbled under his breath, "Shit."

Returning to his room, Richard sat in a corner and knocked gently on a panel. Lily came in with his ivory pipe and three balls of opium heated and ready. He arranged himself on the pillows and Lily placed the first molten opium ball in the pipe's cup. He inhaled deeply and began his voyage.

The disfigured woman saw Richard's eyes turn back and knew he was beyond feeling, so she reached over and ran her fingers through his thick hair, leaned in close, and breathed in his maleness.

Richard was travelling. Alive inside the smoke. He tilted his hand up and he soared; then breathed down and his feet touched the ground. Looking down he noted that he was wearing expensive leather shoes and his leggings had been changed to elegant corduroy. He heard a tapping to one side and noticed that he held a pure ivory walking stick. He willed the stick up and his eyes followed. A large stone building faced him. In response to his command the end of the stick moved slowly around him in a wide arc. As the stick moved, he turned.

He was on a wide street filled with men and women and carriages and horses and large mercantile emporiums selling all the goods of the world. A sputtering sound drew his attention. A metal carriage moved slowly toward him. A man with goggles held a wheel in his hands but there were no horses to pull the vehicle. Richard felt his face crease with a smile. "Opium folly," he said, or thought he said. He'd certainly experienced opium folly before. He turned around, pointed his stick forward, and moved down the elegant avenue. Then he recognized the old Asian oak tree that demarcated the end of his property line. He was on Bubbling Spring Road, but no longer was it a dirt path, prone to icy patches in the winter and mosquito-infested bogs in the summer. Now it was a high street to match any in London or Paris or Rome, filled with stores and fancy women and hotels.

Suddenly the thunder of horses' hooves at his back caused him to turn abruptly. And there, charging right at him, were a dozen thoroughbred horses with men in their saddles whipping the horses into a lather. Richard held his hands in front of his face preparing for the concussion and marvelled as the horses swerved around him on all sides, leaving him completely untouched. He whooped and bent down, then sprang from his knees. And up he went. He was above a large racetrack, floating. Below him the thoroughbreds charged toward a large water jump on the back stretch of the track. The vast viewing stands were filled with people cheering. And he was there amongst them, shouting his heart out, screaming "Milo! Milo! Milo!" as his son guided his horse over the far jump.

It was a dream, he knew — but as Thomas De Quincy had implied in his early letters, sometimes the smoke dreams were precursors of the truth.

He sensed the weight of another molten orb of opium in his pipe and breathed deeply. He wanted to explore further the future that was right in front of him.

"Wake him up! Wake him up this very minute," Maxi shouted at Lily. But Lily spoke little English and Maxi's marketplace Mandarin always abandoned him in a crisis. Still, they understood each other well enough — not what was said, exactly, but the intent behind the words — the safety of the dreaming man.

In his stupor Richard watched a man and a woman yelling at each other on the elegant, paved streets of Bubbling Spring Road. The man was White, the woman Chinese. The Chinese woman's face was covered by a large floppy hat. The White man wore a top hat that bobbed as he spoke. "No Chinese or dogs, the sign says. Can't you read?"

Richard turned in the dream to see the sign. Who would post such a thing? But he'd lost control of the smoke and he found himself racing into a huge dry goods emporium. All around him people were shopping. Dresses, hats, high lace-up women's boots, corsets, and the other paraphernalia of an expensive ladies' shop climbed the walls in leaps and bounds of colour and fabric. Suddenly he was face to face with another sign, this one on a store wall. He was too close to read it so he stepped back. Slowly the sign came into focus: "Upstairs Ladies Have Fits."

Richard began to laugh, and couldn't stop.

"What's he laughing about?"

The voice startled Lily. Its profound anger transcended language and made her scuttle away from the laughing man on the pillows on the floor.

"I repeat, what is the heathen laughing about?"

Lily blanched. Rachel's father and the two men from Oliphant and Company stood in the doorway. One carried a firearm, the other a massive club. Jedediah Oliphant carried no weapon but his fury made him easily the most dangerous of the three.

"I didn't raise my daughter to end as a whore in the bed of a —"

He never got the last word out as he slumped forward and all hell broke loose in the chamber. Two gunshots sounded so loudly that Lily lost her already limited hearing, and the raw smell of gunpowder filled her nostrils. Then something red. And moving fast. A cry from a man. Another man hitting the floor with a thump, blood spurting from a third's nose as he fell to his knees.

Finally things seemed to clear and Lily saw Maxi, his red hair on end, standing alone over the three prone bodies.

"Now collect your foolish asses and don't come back here again. And if I even hear that you so much as raise your voice to your daughter I'll be there — your worst nightmare. You hear me?"

Oliphant nodded as he and his men beat a hasty retreat.

Maxi slammed the door behind them then stepped forward and held out his hand to Lily. She took it and got up from the floor.

"It's okay, Richard is safe."

She was grateful that there was no anger in his voice. "I'm …"

He put a finger to her lips. "It's okay. He's safe, Lily. Richard is safe."

She felt the weight of his calloused hand in hers and found herself holding onto it tightly.

The widow seamstress looked at her son, sallow, bone-showing thin, craven-eyed — lying in a pool of his own sweat on the floor mat. His shaven forehead was thick with stubble, his Manchu-required braid ratted with dirt and what looked like bits of floor tile. She leaned in. His mouth opened and formed the word: *ya pian* — opium.

She remembered that mouth clasped around her breast sucking gently and the baby who looked up into her eyes, his chubby hands kneading and kneading her soft flesh. His sweet baby smell rising to her as she stroked his head.

So long ago, she thought. *Forever ago.* She looked closely at her grown son trying to find that child again. To find a remnant, a trace, a hint of what he had been before the smoke — so long before the smoke.

She shivered.

Crossing to the brazier she poked the embers with a stick, then noted that the coal she had bought only yesterday was almost all used up. *No, not used up*, she thought, *sold. He sold it.* He had already stolen everything else of hers that could be sold and had converted it into the dream smoke.

The sun was rising, another winter day was about to dawn. It would be the last day she dealt with the addiction of her son.

The young man moaned and the air filled with the acrid smell of his urine as it wet his pants then found its way through the matting to the floor.

She nodded and for a moment wondered what would happen. Not here. No one would care here. But there — beyond. What would happen to her beyond?

The young man's mouth opened again and pleaded for *ya pian*.

She sighed. *Ya pian*, damnable opium. *Damnation fall upon those that brought this scourge here to the Bend in the River.*

Then she reached for the silk pillow that had been a gift from her mother on her wedding day and placed it over her son's face — and pressed with all her might.

She was surprised that he didn't struggle much. Surprised how easy it was to extinguish the life flame in an opium addict. Then, one more surprise, she began to cry. She watched, as if they were someone else's tears landing on her son's very still face.

She walked over to her bed. From beneath the mattress she withdrew a Taiping pamphlet she had been given at the Bird and Fish Market almost two years ago. It was entitled: *The Ways of God Explained to Man*. She folded the pamphlet carefully and put it in her belt. People had been talking about the success of the Taiping Rebels from the mountains in northern Guangxi province. Talking about how they were going to rid the Middle Kingdom of the foreigners — and their damnable opium. How they needed every able-bodied person in their efforts. A woman who could kill her addict son would certainly be of use to such people.

She closed the door to her small home for the last time and took the first step on a long journey that would bring her to the attention of the largest rebellion in the history of the world — the Taiping Revolt.

She was not the only person at the Bend in the River who was influenced by the Taiping pamphlets. It had taken Maxi several days to get the document translated since he didn't want to use Chen or his men, and somehow he knew not to ask Richard's help. When he finally read the translation of the Taiping pamphlet an old familiar feeling took him. A feeling he had encountered on an opium farm, years ago, in far-off India.

27

THE RISE OF THE PROPHET

Shanghai
Summer 1848 to Late Fall 1852

"Because I had no food for my family," the prisoner replied. Then he bowed his head, his chains rattled, and the muscles rippled across his broad back.

The Confucian had heard it over and over again in the past few years.

Just another thief, the Confucian wanted to think, but he knew differently. He'd seen too many of them lately. Strong men — men who had fed their families and been loyal to the state and paid their taxes — now out of work. Judicially he didn't really have any choice. The man would be executed. Thieves, when caught and brought to the Confucian, were always executed. He was about to pronounce his sentence when it occurred to him to ask, "What work did you do?"

"Canal work, your honour."

"On the Grand Canal?"

"Yes, the First Emperor's canal."

"And what did you do there?"

"I pulled barges. But there are no more barges." His voice began to trail off as he repeated, "No more barges."

The man is well-spoken for a labourer, the Confucian thought, but all he said was, "At dawn, you will journey to the Hereafter," as he had said so many times recently.

The guards hauled the condemned man to his feet and then, much to their surprise, the Confucian asked, "What's your name?" The canal worker offered up his name. The Confucian turned to the guards. "Keep him in custody. I don't want him executed, yet." Before he could be questioned, the Confucian stood and left the chamber.

In his study later that day he pulled the ancient journal from its hiding place and added to the knowledge there. He was deeply troubled.

The arrival of the White Birds on Water had certainly changed many things at the Bend in the River. The darkness was intensifying. In fact, the village, no, the country itself was afloat (perhaps it would be more accurate to say "adrift") in opium dens, opium users, and opium addicts. But it was not just the addicts or the addiction that caused such serious problems for the Middle Kingdom. Huge sums of Chinese silver left the country to pay for the opium. With the loss of so much of China's national treasury, the Manchu powers in Beijing had begun to tax the peasants harder and mete out punishments more liberally to those who couldn't pay. Seldom did a day go by when the Confucian did not come across some poor man whose hands had been cut off, or who had been blinded, or locked into a heavy wooden board, his head and hands imprisoned through crudely cut holes. These pitiable souls were invariably led by a daughter or a wife who did her best to share the bolted and shackled weight, but to little avail.

As well, the countryside was filled with labourers who had no work. Q'in She Huang's Grand Canal, joining the mighty Yangtze River to Beijing, was virtually unused. Although Shanghai had not grown markedly, British manufactured goods, principally sold through Hong Kong and Canton, flooded almost every Chinese market, driving local producers out of business. Manchester's factory-made shirts, even after a three-thousand-mile sea voyage, were less than a third of the price of a locally milled and sewn garment. Thus, thousands of strong, sometimes very strong, Grand Canal workers, used to pulling barges with their long cables for mile after mile, were now without work, without a way to feed their families.

Despite that, and the granting of extraterritoriality, not many of these workers made their way into Shanghai — just enough to run the *Fan Kuei*'s businesses. Shanghai was still little more than a large town at the Bend in the River. There were more and more *Fan Kuei* every year but few more Chinese. "Only Chinese can build the Seventy Pagodas. But there are so few of us here," the Confucian said aloud to his empty room.

The Confucian lifted his eyes from the civil service examination papers that littered his polished wood desk. Something about the paper he had just graded tweaked a memory. He allowed his mind to drift.

The White Birds have come. They brought the Europeans who built up our village at the Bend in the River. Europeans brought the beginnings of power. Without that, what possibility of rebirth is there? But bringing the Europeans must be only the first part of the plan, he thought.

He knew that on the Holy Mountain blood had opened the first window of the ancient Narwhal Tusk — but what would open the second, and further, what would make the prediction of the third window, the Seventy Pagodas, come into being? He thought again of the second window. Why was it closed to them? He knew that a previous Carver had tried to force the window open but had achieved nothing more than damaging the surface of the Tusk. Like so much else, the contents of the second window would have to wait "until the time was right." He sighed, then looked at the civil service examination paper again, and now he knew of what it reminded him — a paper he had marked some ten or twelve years ago and failed outright. Then another exam four or five years after that, which he'd clearly seen was written by the same candidate. Once again he'd failed the incompetent, but this examination paper he'd kept. And now he extracted it from the hidden drawer in the side of his desk and looked at it.

The calligraphy was harsh — crude — full of fury. He turned the paper so it better caught the light. The childish way that the candidate made his characters was surprising but the content of his answers was astonishing. The Confucian had been marking civil service entrance exams since he was admitted to the upper echelons of the civil service himself some twenty-eight years ago. Usually inadequate answers were filled with apologies and excuses, but the answers on the paper in his hand were nothing of the sort. They were angry — an outraged exegesis on the unfairness of the examination system itself. He finished reading the first two answers then sat back in his chair. He had never heard anyone claim to be the brother of Jesus Christ before. Let alone claim such a thing on the entrance exam to the civil service. He sat very still for a moment, allowing an idea to percolate upward from his depths. He was a Confucian scholar but he respected the promptings of his heart. Chinese people did not speak of intuition; they knew these instinctive promptings to be a truth. They knew that intuition was nothing more than knowledge in search of words.

He checked the access number on the paper and cross-referenced it with the district in which the exam had been written. He knew the proctor and no doubt, with a little money, he'd be able to find this "brother of Jesus Christ," should he want to. But why would he want to? The Confucian remembered the ancient adage:

"Two thoughts in one place, like two fruits in one garden, often share a parent." But what shared parent was there between this "brother of Jesus Christ" and the Narwhal Tusk's vision of Seventy Pagodas? Seventy Pagodas would need thousands upon thousands of workers to build — many more than those presently working in the Foreign Settlement and the French Concession. Where could such a vast number of workers be found? There were legions of unemployed in the countryside. He posed himself a simple question: What could cause those peasants to leave the countryside and chance living near the *Fan Kuei*?

He put the paper down and crossed to the window of his study. The Huangpu River turned just to his right. Below him, to one side a small wharf on the Bund was doing modest business. His own small warehouse, run by his youngest brother, Chen, was at the edge of his view. He took the exam paper and hurried out of his room.

Quickly crossing the dirt path down by the water he made his way northward toward the British Concession — the Foreign Settlement. Although he usually took his walks in the Old City, that day something pushed him toward the *Fan Kuei*'s territory. The streets, often little more than mud paths (at best rows of boards), were, as always, pretty much empty. He thought of signalling for one of the rickshaws that always awaited the command of the British warehouse managers but decided against it. He needed to walk. To think.

Bubbling Spring Road was hardly worth the appellation. The only traffic it had was due to the fact that it connected the British and the French Concessions to the Bend in the River. There were a few carriages closed up tight in an effort to keep the British women they carried free of malaria. *Good luck*, he thought. *Better to chance the malaria than die of the heat in one of those devices the British insist on painting black*. A few European men on horseback and several Chinese men bent beneath heavy loads passed him as he made his way.

A European riding a fine-dappled mare tipped his hat to him. The Confucian bowed his head slightly. The Europeans knew him as the nominal authority of the town but had no idea that this day he was bent on figuring out how to make this town into a bustling city — bustling with thousands and thousands of Chinese workers from the country.

A Black Robe approached from an alleyway with three young Chinese men trailing behind him. The Confucian had to choke down his initial disgust with these self-righteous Christians who endlessly tried to bring their God to his country. One of the young men was wearing a filthy robe like the Jesuit. Ridiculous. Hot black sackcloth in the dead of summer heat. What fool doesn't know to wear light cotton or silk in the depths of a Shanghai summer? These fools, evidently.

He stood still, tickling an idea forward, and allowed his imagination to generate the hundreds — no, thousands of peasants needed to complete the dream of the Seventy Pagodas.

Pieces began to fall into place. Bubbling Spring Road — Seventy Pagodas — peasants flooding in — and the fury of a young man rejected by the civil service who believed himself to be the brother of the Black Robes' God — at the very least, interesting.

That night the Confucian's wife couldn't find the right things to say or the right food to present him. She put a small bowl of sweetened rice outside his study door and headed toward her sleeping mat.

In his study the Confucian carefully reread what he was beginning to think of as "the prophet's paper." Such anger. Such incendiary rage. Many had led with much less. But before he did anything, he needed to understand the man's bizarre religious claims.

He had no real contact with the Black Robes and didn't know anyone who did but Jiang, through her connections with the French. Most of the brothels and opium dens were in their Concession. It was the French who had brought the Black Robes to Shanghai.

He carefully folded the exam of "the prophet" and placed it in the interior pocket of his robe, then took his lacquered umbrella and headed out into the nighttime drizzle.

His polite knock was greeted with giggles from the women within. Then a harsh "shush" and the giggles stopped. The door opened. Jiang, the courtesan, stood with one hand on her hip and the other held high up the side of the door. Behind her, the Confucian heard the muffled sounds of merriment and smatterings of a language he assumed was French.

"You can stand out in the rain if you wish or enter along with all the other clients of this establishment." Jiang's Mandarin was already becoming the strange argot that would eventually become known as Shanghainese. Her features were truly beautiful but her smile was such that, with the movement of even the smallest muscle, it could well turn cruel.

"There is a tea house down at the end of this alley. Would you permit me to purchase you a cup of tea there?" He noted that his always precise speech was even more so when he spoke to her.

"Sure, why not?" she said, noting in turn that her language took on a whorish tinge when she addressed the Confucian.

At the tea house, both refused Indian tea in favour of the dark, musky mixture grown in the south near Amman. The tall, capped cups arrived with their long, slender tea leaves dancing erect in the liquid, like eels in a pond.

Finally, he said to Jiang, "You know the French."

"Yes. I know them. They are in business with me, as you well know."

"Indeed, but it's not that part of the French that interests me."

Jiang looked at the Confucian for a long moment. What kind of man was this? Power and distance, but no joy, no release. She had heard rumours that his family had been badly hurt by the easy availability of opium. Something about a youngest son and a wife, she remembered, but that would have been this man's mother and his brother, not his wife and his son — or maybe his grandmother and grandson. Then she took a closer look at the Confucian. Already his face was older, much older than just five years ago when he had first come into her brothel with the Mandarin from Beijing on the day of the auction.

"I have many contacts in the French community here."

"From opium and ..."

"Women. Yes, from my trade in opium and women."

"Ah," he said, clearly uncomfortable.

She reached across the table and touched his hand. He looked up and almost fell into her eyes. Then she smiled. "What can I do for you?"

"You know the French?"

"Some, yes, as I indicated."

"The whores or the priests?"

"Both."

"Ah, I had heard as much."

"And you're interested in a priest, not a whore?"

"I am."

Now it was her turn to say, "Ah." She lifted the hot tea to her lovely lips.

"A specific priest — a powerful priest — who would be willing to talk about a young Chinese man who believes himself to be the brother of Jesus Christ."

She put her teacup down and looked at him. He wasn't fooling. There never was, nor would there ever be, any jest in the Confucian. "So you have interest in the rebels?"

The Confucian was surprised by Jiang's quick surmise and nodded slowly but didn't elaborate. That was fine with Jiang. She too had an interest in the rebels, some of whom frequented her house to watch the Peking Opera performances that her brilliant daughter, Fu Tsong, wrote and directed. The rebels never drank or went into the back rooms with the girls but they seemed almost transported by the players on the stage who nightly performed their unique magic for her clientele.

"You would like to meet the powerful priest from the big church?"

"Yes."

"Why?"

"For him to explain how this Jesus, who was born so long ago, could now have a brother who lives amongst us."

"As dogma it couldn't be more wrongheaded," Father Pierre said through his translator, putting the Taiping religious pamphlet that the Confucian had given him far to one side of his desk, as though it should not infect anything else of value on the teakwood surface.

The Confucian took note of that. He'd had limited dealings with what the *Fan Kuei* called "priests." He was himself, at times, treated as though he were a priest by the *Fan Kuei*. He was no priest, no fanatic Taoist monk! He was a civil administrator, a literate man versed in the classical works of the Middle Kingdom and hence a follower of the only logical system of thought and social organization in the world: Confucianism.

The Confucian picked up the pamphlet and said, "Ah."

Father Pierre rose from behind his large desk and strode to the window, his hands clasped firmly behind his back, his whole body vibrating with anger. "I thought you were a man of intelligence and learning," he said.

The Confucian was both of those but had no desire to discuss such matters with a man who wore a black wool cassock in the midst of Shanghai summer. And such an arrogant man. To be so sure of one's opinions while living in someone else's country was beyond the Confucian's comprehension. So the Confucian rose and simply repeated, "Ah."

Father Pierre turned to him. "You do realize that this is blasphemy and will not go unpunished?"

The Confucian wanted to ask, "Who will do this punishing?" but was afraid that the silly *Fan Kuei* priest would invoke some sort of deity who took words as personal insults. What kind of God could care what a human being wrote or thought about Him? What God could be so insecure in His own power that He could waste a moment of His time over such irrelevancies? Perhaps the same God that didn't seem to care that opium was destroying the lives of millions of people, or that millions were caught and in danger of losing their lives between the forces of the Taiping and the fury of the Manchus. Finally he said, "So these texts are not of your faith?"

"They are the inevitable product of those who have lost their way."

The Confucian hoped that Father Pierre wasn't going to launch into a tirade about sheep. What was it with Catholics and sheep? Sheep were particularly stupid animals. Why did Catholics insist upon calling the people who followed their faith sheep and those who led the faith shepherds — perhaps the job requiring the least amount of skill or intelligence in the entire Middle Kingdom.

"… Who have turned their backs on Rome." Father Pierre completed, or at least believed he had completed, his thought.

Ah, yet another reference to that village in the midst of one of the barbarian's insignificant countries. It had been explained to him that Rome was a city in a place called Italy. When he'd asked for further information about this fabled place he was surprised to learn that it was just a small town, that China had fifty or sixty cities that were far bigger. When he mentioned that, he was told that Rome was really a metaphor. When he inquired, "A metaphor for what?" he was given the answer that these Christians always seemed to fall back on — "For faith" — which naturally enough, was then followed by the Christian catch-all, "God's ways are beyond our comprehension." The Confucian found such convenient elliptical thinking beneath contempt, so he smiled at Father Pierre and asked, "Would the Americans believe the matters discussed in this pamphlet?"

Father Pierre harrumphed. Something about Americans seemed to particularly gall him. Finally he said, "It is incomprehensible to me what American Protestants believe, if anything. They strike me as closer to Jews and pagans than to Christians."

This confused the Confucian, but what was evident to him was that Father Pierre was distressed — about something or other. So he took his leave of the man.

Two hours later, in the American Settlement west of the Suzu Creek, he stood patiently in the outer offices of Oliphant and Company, the place the other traders referred to as the House of Zion. The Confucian had asked about that reference and been told that Zion was a place called Israel that was mentioned in the pamphlet that he held in his hand. When he had asked about this Israel he had been told that, like Rome, it was small and actually just a metaphor. This time he'd decided not to ask what the metaphor stood for.

When the door opened he was surprised to see a *Fan Kuei* woman dressed in a long black dress with a bonnet of some sort that covered her head. But the effect of the bonnet was not to hide the woman's beauty so much as frame her remarkable facial features, as a fine filigree hem does a silk robe. The Confucian found most *Fan Kuei* faces almost grotesque in their size and shape — gross in both volume and composition. But this woman's features struck him as understated and pleasing. Then she smiled and the room grew a moment brighter. He smiled back then followed her into a dark, stuffy office that had much more furniture than was necessary, and ridiculous heavy velvet curtains. The Confucian picked lightly at his silk robe to pull it away from his skin while he waited for Jedediah Oliphant, the head of the House of Oliphant, to turn from the window. *What is it about the Fan Kuei and their desire to look out windows?* he wondered.

When Jedediah turned to him, the man's face was awash in sweat, his colour a florid red, and his anger something to behold.

"Where did you get this abomination?"

"Abomination," "blasphemy" — his religious vocabulary was increasing mightily, although he assumed these words were esoteric irrelevancies.

"It is from the Taiping. They have published much of this material and I"

"Apostasy!"

Another interesting word. How many words did these foolish *Fan Kuei* have for…?

Then the chubby man ripped the pamphlet in two, and in two again.

The Confucian stared at him. Didn't the man understand that there were probably hundreds of thousands of that exact pamphlet in existence? What did ripping one into quarters accomplish?

The head of the House of Zion threw the pieces of the pamphlet into a bucket at the side of his desk then said, "You do understand that you can go to Hell for reading material like this."

The Confucian had trouble not laughing about that, but he nodded, thought about leaving this fool's presence, then decided to ask his question. "Did this Taiping writing come from your religious beliefs?"

After much to-ing and fro-ing, eventually the man acknowledged that what was written in the pamphlet had its origins in his faith. Then, without prompting, he elaborated, "It began with Reverend Edwin Stevens. He was a Yale man caught up in the great religious revival that swept through New England in the 1820s. He took a post in Canton in 1832 as the head of the American Seaman's Friends Society. He initially spent his time trying to keep English and American sailors from the temptations while on shore."

This, the Confucian thought, was a foolish way to spend one's time. These poor men had been at sea for months and months, twenty men to a room — how would you keep them from alcohol and women except by shooting them?

"But Stevens eventually realized that his real audience was the Chinese. Millions upon millions of lost souls awaited the Good Word. But getting the Book translated was not simple. The authorities blocked his every effort, until he found a Chinese Christian named Liang, who was working as a printer for a Scottish Protestant, named William Milne ..."

And on and on he talked. The Confucian got the basics of the story. This Liang, who had been a devout Buddhist, converted to Christianity, probably to keep his job, and produced précis of text from the American Bible which were then brought to the Chinese. Evidently one of them must have fallen into the hands of the leader of the Taipingers, Hung Hsiu-ch'uan, and it was from this that he had extracted his unusual approach to Christianity.

The Confucian continued to listen. He didn't believe anything of this "faith" had any personal value but he understood the need for men to escape the drudgery of their lives, to believe that there was some reason for the suffering, and in the end, relief. He couldn't help making the obvious observation that opium offered much the same rewards — escape from drudgery, a reason to work and suffer to be able to get the money to find that escape, and finally a relief from this life altogether.

The Confucian was surprised that the man was still talking. Didn't this silly little fat man realize the danger of peddling dreams? Evidently not. The Confucian thanked the American for his time and made a hasty exit. When he emerged, the sun was shining and the junks on the Suzu Creek were ready for business. He signalled to a bumboat and made his way out to one of the larger junks. He was helped onboard, then sat down to a fine dinner. As he ate the tender pork dumplings he took out another copy of the Taiping pamphlet and carefully reread it. By the time the main course of jumping shrimp — live shrimp, slightly pixilated because they had been marinating in strong Chinese wine — arrived, he had made up his mind. He tapped the side of the bowl and one of the shrimps leapt upward; he caught it between his chopsticks and watched it wriggle. "I have you," he said softly. Then he dunked the shrimp into the piquant sauce and popped it into his mouth, where he expertly snipped off its head, swallowed the body, and then spat the head and carapace to the junk's floor.

Hung Hsiu-ch'uan smiled at his followers. Only three years ago he had been literally a voice in the wilderness. A failed scholar, seen by many as a religious fanatic. Now he was a leader.

Years ago, he had received a religious tract from an American Protestant missionary. He'd put it aside as senseless rantings of white-faced barbarians. But shortly thereafter he'd suffered a serious illness during which he'd had many dreams of a heaven and a man in robes referring to him as his younger brother. In his convalescence, he reread the religious tract — and was shocked to see that the man described in the tract was the man from his dreams. That he had talked with Jesus.

It was suddenly clear to him that he was not just another Chinese worker struggling to survive under the pressure of the Manchu Ch'ing Dynasty. He was different. Blessed. Kissed by Heaven — the younger brother of Jesus Christ himself.

His father did not find this amusing, and after Hsiu-ch'uan failed his civil service entrance exam for the second time his family disowned him. He left home and made his way back into the Hakka territory. There he found a Jesuit mission, where he told his dream and asked to be baptized. The Jesuits refused. It was the turning point in his life. He abandoned his desire to be part of any *Fan Kuei* organization and adopted a stance in rigid opposition to all of them. Amongst the dispossessed Hakka peoples, he found a ready audience for his vision — to establish the Heavenly Kingdom of Great Peace, of which he was going to be the Heavenly King, with five of his followers named as Kings.

The Manchu authorities laughed. The Europeans were

unimpressed. But the Confucian, in Hung Hsui-ch'uan, believed he had found a means to an end.

Jiang arranged the introductory meeting with one of Hung Hsui-ch'uan's rebels. Not a simple thing in Shanghai. Since the revolt of the Small Knife Triad that gave the secretive Tong Society control of the city for the better part of a year and a half, security had been very tight. The British had attempted to impose a curfew but the French refused to abide by it. They had business interests that required free movement after dark. Daylight brothels were, for obvious reasons, not all that financially successful.

The Confucian was surprised by the modest appearance of the young man that his wife led into his study. Then he looked closer. The man had the scars of age in his eyes despite his fine, smooth skin and glossy hair. The Confucian chose to stand when the young rebel entered.

The young fighter looked at the Confucian and a snarl curled his lip. "You have words for me, old man?"

The Confucian bridled at the discourtesy but reminded himself that he had a long road to travel and it was foolish to be waylaid by insults. "Thank you for honouring me with your presence. I have a message I'd like you to carry to your leader, Hung Hsui-ch'uan."

The younger man sat heavily. His dirt-stained smock left a slurred mark on the silk of the upholstered chair. Then he looked at the Confucian's desk and sprang to his feet.

The Confucian, confused, backed off as the young fighter kicked over the desk. "What are you — ?"

"Are you an examiner, old man? Do you grade the entrance papers of those attempting to be part of the Manchu civil service? Do you work for the oppressors of our country? Are you nothing more than a foreigner dressed in our clothing, sleeping with our women and despoiling this sacred land?"

The Confucian stood his ground. "I have a message I want

sent to Hung Hsui-ch'uan, leader of the Taiping rebels."

"You mean the Heavenly King."

"Do I?"

"If you refer to Hung Hsui-ch'uan, you do."

"Fine, for the Heavenly King."

"What is your message for the Heavenly King?"

"Please tell him that I can be of service to his cause."

"Why?"

"Excuse me?"

"Why would you wish to be of service to the Heavenly King? He will bring equality to this land. No more Mandarins. No more Confucians. Women will have equal rights. The great landowners will give up their lands and divide it amongst their serfs. Why would you support this which would rob you of your position of power and prestige? Why would you do that?"

Without missing a beat the Confucian said, "Because his cause is just and the Manchus must be taught a lesson."

The young rebel looked at the Confucian. "Why is it that I don't believe you?"

The Confucian took a breath then let it out slowly. "Who am I addressing?"

"Can you not guess?"

"Hung Hsui-ch'uan?"

"The very same Hung Hsui-ch'uan that you people refused entrance to the civil service twice."

"Perhaps we did you a favour. Rather than one scribe amongst millions you are now a man of great power." That hung in the air like something hot and volatile. The Confucian knew that his life could end momentarily if this were taken the wrong way.

Hung walked back to the podium and tilted the writing stone there. The ink dribbled down the side of the mahogany desk and dripped to the hardwood floor. "I repeat — what do you want, old man?"

"I want to support your cause."

"Why would you want that?"

"Because your victory would support my goals."

"Which are?"

"None of your business."

The rebel turned on him, his hand raised, but the Confucian did not back down.

"Think practically for a moment. You believe in your cause. I do not. But I have the means you need to help your cause succeed. Why does it matter what there is for me in this?"

The rebel allowed his hand to come down to his side. "What do you have to offer me?"

"Access to the society of the canal porters. Perhaps half a million men without work, without hope, and with very strong arms."

The Confucian wanted to smile, but he wisely chose not to as Hung Hsui-ch'uan, the Heavenly King, took a seat and said simply, "I'm listening."

The Confucian's visit to the prison was brief. They had expected his coming since the arrival of the thief who was not to be executed. The Confucian had the man unshackled and took him by the arm and guided him out of the prison. The stunned man didn't know what to say and did his best to express his appreciation, but the Confucian stopped him.

"Can you read?"

"Some."

"Enough to read this?" the Confucian asked, handing over the Taiping pamphlet.

"I already know about …"

"The Taipingers?"

"Yes."

"And?" The canal worker was suddenly wary. The Confucian

put his hand on the man's shoulder and said simply, "The Heavenly King is expecting you and your people."

With the canal workers swelling his ranks, the Heavenly King launched his first major strike against the Manchu overlords. With his goal of a Kingdom of Heaven on earth set as firmly as frontlets between his eyes he aimed his troops toward the same vulnerable point in the Manchus' defences that the hated British had attacked in 1841 — Chinkiang, the City of Suicides.

It was in the late fall of 1852 when Maxi found himself admiring the craftsmanship of a nail-free construction. Perfect tongue-and-groove wooden planks fit one into the next to form a remarkably pleasing whole. Through his interpreter he asked the cost of building such a structure. Upon hearing the outrageous quote, he laughed. But he knew that even after real bargaining the price would not come down enough. He was here to create a secure depot for the Hordoon brothers' products, not a work of art like the one in front of which he now stood. Maxi changed the subject by asking, through his translator, "Where did you get the fine silk robe you're wearing?"

"A half day's journey up the river at Chinkiang. They have the finest silks in the whole of the Middle Kingdom." He paused and a smile came to his face as he added, "I have a brother who could get you the best price for ..."

Maxi smiled back. He'd heard such offers since he was a child. This one he'd accept — and it would change his life.

A day later Maxi acknowledged the stares of the women in the streets of Chinkiang. He was happy with his purchases of fine silk robes for his nephews, Milo and Silas, and pleased that his business dealings had gone well. He was well fed and pleasantly tipsy from the strong beer brewed in the German enclave at Qintao, and the night was redolent with the promise of a cool fall after a long hot summer.

He walked along the west wall of the Old City, the farthest from the Grand Canal. Torches stuck in wall niches periodically broke the darkness. He was happy to be away from the intrigues and infighting of the Foreign Settlement in Shanghai.

He looked up at the catwalk high up on the city wall and blinked himself out of his reverie. Where were the guards? City walls were always patrolled by guards. He hurried around a squalid building that obscured his view, then down an alley to get a glimpse of the farthest section of the wall. It was empty of protectors too. He pressed himself against the alley wall and calmed his breathing. Then he heard them. The telltale clicks of feet on ladders — many feet. Then they appeared, dressed in black from head to foot with dark cloths around their faces. Their weapons must have been dulled with lard because they didn't glint in the bright moonlight. They formed up and waited in complete silence. Then a slender, taller man joined them and raised a hand high into the night air. The moonlight glinted off the large silver cross he held. The men in black all knelt in prayer, then rose ... and unearthed holy hell upon the unsuspecting citizenry of Chinkiang, the City of Suicides.

Although taken by surprise, the Manchus had two full regiments within the city walls and a third outside the east gate down by the Grand Canal. Maxi retreated to a rooftop and watched — watched in rapt fascination as the very first major battle of the Taiping Rebellion unfolded before him like something that had awaited his coming all these many years.

Four days later Maxi allowed the fine hair of the horse's mane to move smoothly through his grooming comb. He breathed in the earthy smell of the animal, then put his head against the horse's neck and allowed the animal's warmth to calm him.

"You're awfully quiet this evening," Richard said.

"Thinking. Just thinking."

"Of what are you thinking?"

"What I saw in Chinkiang."

"Let it go, Maxi. The Manchus put the rebels back in their place. The revolt is over."

Maxi took a coarse brush and began to work on the horse's flank. "It's not, brother mine. The Manchus had three full regiments yet they just barely won. The Taipingers fought like madmen — like men possessed. They fought for something. They fought from their hearts."

"What? Are you suggesting that the God freaks can beat the Manchu Emperor?"

"Not that they can, but that they will. I saw one of their soldiers throw himself in front of a Manchu gingall at a roadblock. The man gave up his life so the others could overwhelm the battery and escape."

"So, he was following —"

"No, brother mine, he wasn't following orders. That's the point. He gave up his life voluntarily without being ordered. Listen to me! And he wasn't the only Taipinger willing to die for their cause. That's why they're going to win. They're going to win because they believe in something. Even from that rooftop I could feel it. They're going to win because their beliefs give their lives meaning."

Richard watched Maxi turn and leave the stable. In all his years with his brother, he doubted he'd ever heard him string so many words together.

Later that night Jiang approached Maxi as he watched the actors rehearse parts of the second act of *Journey to the West*.

"You seem sad," she said.

"I'll miss this," he said.

"This? Not the girls, just the plays?"

"Just the plays. Your daughter is an artist. She touches the hearts of simple men like me."

Jiang was about to protest that he was far from simple, then she stopped herself. The monkey king character had just made an entrance, to the accompaniment of horns and cymbals, and Maxi jumped to his feet to cheer, just as any child might.

The night was late when Maxi crept down the alleyway that was the unofficial back entrance to the American section of the Foreign Settlement. Maxi had used a section of the Warrens to be sure that he wasn't followed, then exited the underground tunnels through the back courtyard of a tailor's shop before heading down the alley. As he moved through the darkness he remembered another night excursion, this time with his brother at his side as they left their parting gift to old Baghdad.

And here he was, parting again.

He had not made this circuitous trip in several months but now he wanted to say goodbye to Rachel.

"You're leaving," she said. "I can see it in your eyes."

Maxi hung his head for a moment, then nodded.

"Why?" Her hands flew to her mouth to stop her sobs.

He gently pulled her hands down from her beautiful lips and kissed her on her forehead. "Because I need to find a place to call home before I die. Because this place is not of me. Because I yearn for something that is mine and has meaning. Real meaning. Like you find in your Bible."

"But I …"

"I know you have your doubts about that book, but you basically believe in what it teaches, don't you?"

Now it was her turn to hang her head. After a long sigh, she said, "I do."

"That's good, Rachel. That's good. But I don't have anything like that in my life and I need it. Everyone needs it." He put a finger under her chin and raised her face to his. "You understand that. I know you do."

"When…?"

"Tonight."

There were tears and clutching and desperate lovemaking as they tried to remember each other's warmth. Then lips and godspeeds and parting with understanding, but no sweetness.

An hour later Maxi spotted Anderson with his travelling gear, gave the man the key to his private living quarters, wished him luck, and headed down the deserted streets to the west gate of the city. There he was halted by guards. He smiled at them and reached for his purse but was stopped by a familiar voice from the darkness.

"You'll have to fight to leave here."

"If necessary, brother mine. I've clubbed the daylights out of you before and I'll do it again if need be."

"You're all geared up. Where are you heading?"

"You promised me, promised in India, that if things didn't work out you'd let me go back."

"To the opium farmers?"

"Not necessarily to them, but to something simple. You promised not to stand in my way. But here you are. Things haven't worked out for me. I want something simpler, and I know where I can find that."

"With the Taipingers."

Maxi nodded and hoisted his pack on his back.

"Nothing I can say …"

"To stop me? No. Not a thing."

"As it must be?"

"As it must be, brother mine."

"He went where?" Silas demanded.

"He's gone now, son."

Milo put a hand on Silas's shoulder in warning.

"Things change in the world, boys. You change. I change. Your Uncle Maxi changed, and now he doesn't live here anymore. Don't ask me where he is because I can't tell you without endangering him." He thought suddenly of the old Indian's warning: "Brother will kill brother!" Richard allowed the voice to fade away then said to the boys, "And I won't endanger my brother. Is that clear?"

Patterson came in with a stack of waybills. Richard took them, then said, "Milo, come with me, I could use a hand."

Father and favourite son left the room.

Patterson looked at Silas. "Crying? Of course not. The young heathen doesn't know how to cry, does he? Just snivel. Oh, you're good at snivelling, you are. Well stop it! Your uncle is nothing more than a monkey-lover."

Late that night Richard summoned Anderson and Patterson to his private study. The two men waited while Richard paced. Finally Richard stopped and turned to Anderson. "How goes our building?"

"Fine. We've almost filled your properties with those four-storey buildings your brother designed."

"Good. Patterson, I want an accounting of everything in our warehouses."

"Certainly, but —"

"Then sell it. Sell it all. Every last mango chest of opium, every bolt of silk, every porcelain cup, every leaf of tea. All of it, and I really don't care how much you get for it."

"And do what with the money?"

"Buy land. Cheap land anywhere in the Settlement, land for Anderson to build a hundred more of Maxi's four-storey buildings. And then a hundred more after that."

Six weeks later, just before dawn, there was a knocking on the door of the House of Paris. An unusual time for a client, even in Shanghai. Suzanne's serving girl answered the door and didn't know what to do with the missionary woman standing on the top step.

"May I see the mistress of the house?"

It took a bit of translating, but after a few misunderstandings Rachel was led to the inner office of Suzanne Colombe, who poured coffee for the two of them.

"So if you're not here to convert me, why are you here?" Suzanne said in her accented but textbook-perfect English. Rachel hadn't touched her coffee. "Do you prefer tea?" Suzanne asked as she looked more closely at the woman's slightly sweated complexion. *Could it be?* she wondered. Then she reached to a sideboard and pushed a large platter of morning meats across to her guest, and the woman blanched. *Ah*, Suzanne thought, *ah, so that is the problem.* Then she had a second thought. *Will Maxi Hordoon come back and marry this girl or not?*

ॐ 28

MEETINGS

Shanghai
Winter 1852, eighteen Months after the start of the Taiping Rebellion

The stone thrown at his window drew Richard back from the edges of his opium dream.

Since Maxi had left he'd found that even with the serpent smoke alive in his veins he'd been unable to find rest. The deep rumble of danger kept churning in his guts. He had never been separated from his brother for more than a few weeks. Now Maxi had been gone for months — and Richard had no idea if he was ever going to come back. Maxi had instructed his man Anderson in all that he was working on for the Hordoon Company, so the business didn't miss a step. But Richard found himself feeling that if he stood quickly from his bed he'd fall — as if his very equilibrium had been tampered with. Every time Richard entered a room he sensed that Maxi had just left it, that somehow Maxi was just around every corner — but he never was. Nor had there been any word from his brother.

Maxi was gone and Richard was alone, so when a second pebble struck the windowpane, he reached for his Belgium flintlock pistol and slowly peered out. There, to his surprise, was a woman, standing in the alley. When he pulled open the window the figure turned her face up to his. In the moonlight Rachel Oliphant was a luminous presence. A godly gift of beauty in this rough world.

When he opened the door she pulled her shawl tightly around her and came quickly into his drawing room.

"Rachel ..."

"Don't look at me. At my shame."

It was only then that Richard saw that she was pregnant. "Rachel."

She turned to him, her face picking up the flickering light from the oil lamp. She pushed a tendril of hair from her forehead and her beauty filled the room. Her face creased in a humble smile as she said, "Are you well, Mr. Hordoon?"

"Yes," Richard said slowly, "I am well. And you?"

She pulled aside her shawl to reveal the full extent of her belly and said, "Very well."

"You look lovely ..."

"I don't."

"You do."

Richard reached out a hand to her and she backed away. "Don't."

"I'll marry you, if that is what you want."

For a moment a quizzical look crossed her face, then she smiled. A laugh squeaked from her pursed lips and she shook her head, finally saying the single word, "No."

"I will if —"

"Where is Maxi?" her voice pleaded, and for the first time Richard understood how Maxi had known to come and save him from the attack of the Oliphants, and why the Oliphants may have attacked him in the first place. "Where's your brother, Mr. Hordoon? I need to see Maxi."

The night was uncommonly cold, even for January. The wind howled in Jiang's face as she put a foot up onto the small plank that joined the junk bobbing on the filthy waters of the Suzu Creek to the small carrack that she had hired.

"What are you staring at, old man?" she demanded of the ancient creature who rowed the boat.

The man spat in the water and mumbled something about being paid.

"You'll be paid when you come and get me."

Again the man mumbled; this time the country word for "harlot" slid into the cold air and hung there like something dark and ugly.

Jiang ignored the insult. She'd heard far worse. What she wanted from this man was his silence. "Do you have a daughter, old man?"

The man stared at her, then slowly nodded.

"I could use a new maid. Have her appear at —"

"I know where," the old man grunted.

"Good. She'll make enough money to keep you and your wife comfortable in your ... old age." She had wanted to say "dotage" but decided against it.

"How long?"

"How long will she work for me?"

"No. How long are you here on this junk?"

She told him, and he helped her up the planking to the deck of the ship. She waited until the old man's carrack was lost in the darkness downriver before she headed below decks and found some relief from the piercing cold.

The family who owned the junk was nowhere to be seen but the smell of their cooking brazier tainted the air. She followed the source of the smell down a narrow set of steps and into a passage. There to one side was a closed door. She opened it.

Inside, the other progeny of the Chosen Three awaited her — and of course the Carver. She noted that the Carvers seemed old even when they were young — as if they were born old men. The Bodyguard never seemed to age, but the Confucian had sent his youngest son to represent his family. She nodded slightly and removed the plain woollen blanket she wore around her shoulders and as a cowl over her head — no need to advertise her beauty on the dark and dangerous streets in this part of the city. But when she shook out her long hair she didn't miss the admiring looks of the young Confucian. She had known his father, but not this young man — although both had that disconcerting way of staring.

The boat lurched momentarily and she steadied herself against an overhead timber. The Carver stepped forward and offered her a seat. She refused his offer with a curt shake of her head, then added, "I got here as quickly as I could." Before the men could comment she added evenly, "We all have our labours, gentlemen. The fact that mine bring pleasure make them no less valuable than yours — as some of your family members will attest."

"Enough," the Carver said. "The threat of the Taiping Prophet has to be understood in light of the Ivory Compact."

Jiang looked to the young Confucian. "You didn't tell him about your father and his meeting?"

The Confucian quickly gave the bare details of his father's meeting with the extraordinary young man.

"And that was how long ago?" the Bodyguard asked.

"Twenty months, just before he took to his bed."

"He didn't bother consulting us?" complained the Bodyguard.

"He consulted me," Jiang broke in. "Nothing in the Compact states that all decisions must be made jointly."

"Be that as it may, now we must act," the Carver said as the wide-bellied boat once again listed dangerously in the screaming wind.

Jiang steadied herself against a ship wall, as did the Carver and the Confucian. But the Bodyguard's balance was such that he counteracted the motion by shifting his weight. *Like an acrobat*, Jiang thought. She looked down at the planks and thought of them as a platform that danced beneath her feet. *I think more like my daughter and her Peking Opera every day.*

The boat righted itself.

"Have you tried to open the second portal? There must be information there that we need," said the Bodyguard.

"In all likelihood there is, but I've been unable to open the window," replied the Carver.

"So we work with what we have," said Jiang.

"Agreed," said the Confucian, who then turned to the Bodyguard and said, "Time to stop fishing and make your selection."

"It will be done."

"Have you chosen?"

The Bodyguard thought of his son — and then of his powerful young nephew, who now lived in his home. "The choice will be made soon."

"Don't hesitate, we may well need the services of a master assassin shortly," said Jiang.

A silence greeted that.

"So be it," said Jiang.

"But aren't we a little ahead of ourselves?" the Bodyguard asked. "How does the rise of the Taiping Prophet fit into the prophecy of the Seventy Pagodas?"

"Simply," said the young Confucian.

"Explain," demanded the Bodyguard.

"If the Long Noses declare their Foreign Settlements neutral in the struggle …"

"…and manage to get the Prophet to agree to that neutrality," added Jiang.

"Yes, and get the Prophet to agree, then the one vital thing most missing from our village at the Bend in the River will be addressed."

"I don't follow," said the Bodyguard.

"People," responded the young Confucian. "This extraterritoriality that the Long Noses received has enabled them to induce local Shanghainese to work for them. But we are still almost nothing more than a large village. We need to become a great city to build the Seventy Pagodas. Even Beijing and Canton and Nanjing have nothing like seventy. But if Shanghai is safe while rebellion rages through the countryside, then ..."

Somehow the howling wind entered the room. Papers riffled on the table and a tablecloth flapped. A scythe of cold cut through the room, like a warning.

"It takes many people to build seventy pagodas," agreed the Bodyguard.

"Many people."

"So we must see to it that the Long Noses approach the Prophet?"

"Yes."

"And once they secure Shanghai's neutrality, we support the Prophet?"

"Yes."

There was another long silence. The slapping of the waves against the ancient timbers of the junk grew loud. They knew that there would be death — much death — and they would support it, all to fulfill a prophecy. None of the progeny in the room had ever been free of doubt about the prophecy. None had refrained from questioning and railing against the demands set upon them so long ago on the Holy Mountain. But none of them dared stand in the way of the future greatness that was promised. Much of the rest of the prophecy had come to pass: foreigners invading; foreigners sitting on the Celestial Throne but always succumbing to the luxuriance of China; the arrival of the White Birds on Water and the ensuing darkness. And here was yet more darkness — and so much death.

"What if the Prophet wins?" asked the young man whom the

others had already begun to think of as the Confucian. "If he takes over all of China, won't he then turn and demand Shanghai as well?"

Jiang thought about that. Finally she said, "That mustn't happen. The Prophet is a means, not an end." She knew that the Prophet would be more inclined to burn Shanghai to the ground than to build seventy pagodas.

The Confucian recited his father's admonition: "How, once launched heavenward, can an archer be sure of the landing place of his arrow?"

Jiang laughed and turned to the Bodyguard. "That is your job. It is time to begin the Guild of Assassins so that when we need the Prophet ended — he will be ended."

The Bodyguard thought again of his son and his nephew.

Jiang surprised the others when she asked, "Would your chosen assassin be able to juggle and tumble?"

"Yes, but …"

"Good," Jiang said. "When you have selected the one to begin the Guild, send the assassin to me."

29

THE SETTLEMENT AND THE TAIPINGERS

Summer 1852, twenty months after the start of the Taiping Revolt

Richard watched and tried not to laugh, although he understood perfectly well that there was nothing very funny going on in this private room in the back of the famous Yu Yuan Gardens. The harmonious lines of the polished mahogany wood, the deep, still pool with its bright-orange carp and its arching bridge, as well as the peaceful orderliness of the immaculate gardens did nothing to mediate the open anger in the room. Even getting to the damned place was a challenge now that the Manchus had been defeated in the city proper by the Han Chinese Triad of the Small Knives.

It didn't matter to the traders if they dealt with the devious Manchus or the openly thuggish Triads. No one believed that the Triads would rule Shanghai for long. Already they were fighting amongst themselves.

None of the English, French, or American powers cared. The Triads would disappear back into their rat holes on their own. But these religious rebels, these Taipingers sitting across the table from the committee of opium traders, they controlled almost a third of the Middle Kingdom, including the ancient capital of Nanjing, and were a significant power — and in total opposition to the use of opium by their people, all their people.

Every time one of the traders spoke, and Richard translated, the Taipingers responded with increasingly surly scowls.

The head of the Taiping delegation was not their leader, Hung Hsui-ch'uan. This man, who sat directly across the table from the Vrassoon Patriarch, referred to himself as the West King. There were apparently five such kings. Richard wondered which direction had two kings. But there was nothing else very humorous about the rebels. The Taipingers had come raging out of their mountain retreats just under three years ago, and although initially they had lost their battles with the Manchus, their numbers had swelled quickly and victories followed.

Richard wondered how much his brother had to do with their military successes.

The Taipingers' particular religious approach was so stern that men and women were strictly separated and not permitted, upon penalty of death, to have sexual intercourse until the Manchus were driven from Beijing. All of their people were organized into fighting and working battalions under military commanders, who reported to captains, who eventually reported to one of the five Kings, who then reported to Hung Hsiu-ch'uan, the Heavenly King himself. The rebels quickly routed local warlords and large landowners, distributing the land and wealth to their followers, which further swelled their ranks. Then towns began to fall to them, and eventually cities. Just the year before, they had routed the Manchus and taken Nanjing, which they now proclaimed as their Heavenly Capital.

Every Taipinger was required to bear arms — everyone except the very young, of which, for obvious reasons given the separation of the sexes, there were very few. Even the old were taught to use weapons. Taken lands were divided amongst the fighters, and food was distributed to people according to their need. The Taipingers treated women as equals to men. As well, they banned foot binding in all its forms, and the Manchu-imposed long braid and shaved forehead were outlawed. It was one of the many things about the men sitting across the table from the traders that differentiated them from most other Chinese.

There was also a requirement to memorize long religious tracts from the writings of the Heavenly King. The failure to recite on command could lead to summary execution. Sabbath started on Saturday evening, when large banners were strung across the streets and all activity stopped. Attendance at church was mandatory. And of course, alcohol and opium — especially opium — were forbidden upon pain of death.

The Taipinger West King put the palms of his hands on the beautifully inlaid table and stood. "We have nothing more to discuss, it seems." He shouted an order in what Richard assumed was Hakka, since he couldn't discern the meaning, then turned to leave.

"We have *much* to discuss," Eliazar Vrassoon said.

For an instant Richard thought of the doctored photograph of Vrassoon's eldest son that was so carefully hidden in his desk.

The West King turned and hissed into Vrassoon's face, "You are nothing more than thieves and pirates. You poison our people. You do not believe in the one true God."

Richard translated slowly to give the room a moment to calm down. Then Jedediah Oliphant rose to his feet and said to Richard, "Translate this accurately so the heathen will understand." Richard nodded. "Tell him that Oliphant and Company came to China for one primary reason, to spread the word of Jesus Christ and his Father, the one true God." Richard hesitated. "Tell him, man."

Richard did.

The West King turned on Oliphant. "Do you not sell opium to my people?"

Richard translated.

"We do nothing of the kind. We trade for goods, as all traders must, and spread God's Holy Word."

"Which words, exactly?" the West King demanded.

Oliphant produced his vellum-bound family Bible from an old leather case and handed it to the Taipinger. The man handed it to his translator, who flipped it open and spoke in Hakka to his King. The man smiled, then shook his head as he tossed it, like so much garbage, onto the table. "This book is not the true Word."

Oliphant's fat neck bulged out like a bullfrog's and his bald head turned a bright red. Richard thought the man's eyes might pop out of his stupid face. Then Anderson came running into the room.

Richard signalled him over to one side. "What?"

"Their soldiers have cut off access to the Huangpu and they are massing at the east gate."

"How many?"

"Thousands upon thousands."

Richard turned to the Taipinger, who openly smiled, evidently understanding the news that Anderson brought. "Could you excuse us for a moment, please?" Richard signalled the traders to join him in the next chamber. Once there, he quickly told them Anderson's news.

Anger immediately flared, but it was Hercules McCallum who spoke calmly. "We don't want anything from these rebels — just to be left alone. To keep the town at the Bend in the River neutral. We can be of use to them by keeping the Manchus out of Shanghai — at least for the moment, with the Triad in control, that's no real problem. In return, we want nothing from them. Not a blessed thing. We should promise that we will trade only in the Manchu's territory and make motions toward closing our trading routes up the Yangtze. We would be protecting their eastern flank, and we also keep at least some of the Manchu navy nearby watching us, not up there fighting them."

Vrassoon nodded and Oliphant grudgingly agreed, then the traders returned to the negotiating room.

The Taipingers listened to Richard without interrupting as he laid out the deal. For a moment Richard thought he'd swayed the Taiping King, then something dark crossed the man's face. "But you would still trade opium? Do the Devil's work?"

Using the phrase the dwarf Jesuit had used all those years ago sent Richard into a moment of interior fall, vertigo, and he reached for the table to balance himself. The room was strangely quiet, he thought. Then he looked at the Taipinger and asked, "Have you met the red-haired Long Nose from the Bend in the River?"

That completely stopped the Taipinger, who slowly nodded.

"He's my brother."

Something akin to a smile crossed the Taipinger's face. "He's a very brave man."

"Is my brother all right?"

"He is by the side of the Heavenly Leader."

When that was translated, the ripple of shock amongst the traders was palpable. So that was where the maniac went. There had been rumours for months that he had gotten himself killed on a trading expedition or in a whorehouse. But now this!

Oliphant cursed under his breath. First the Jew assaulted him and his men, then he had to send Rachel back to his sister in Philadelphia to prevent a scandal, and now the red-haired crazy man was fighting for the Taiping rebels!

So the red-haired Jew is working for the God rebels, Hercules McCallum thought. *Surely the oddest of bedfellows.* Then he looked at Richard Hordoon and the Taiping King. *Yet another unlikely pair*, he thought.

With Maxi's image secured between Richard and the Taiping King of the West, the negotiations that would eventually lead to the guarantee of neutrality for the Settlement and the French Concession began. The talks went on for six more days, at the end of which time a declaration of peace and support was signed by both sides.

With that done, Richard turned his attention to the issue of the Vrassoons' monopoly on trade between England and the Middle Kingdom. He had a weapon in the doctored photograph, but no way to deliver the damning thing to the people that counted — the House of Lords.

NEUTRALITY AND PROSPERITY

*The Lands of the Heavenly King and Shanghai
1854*

The Heavenly King allowed his fingers to trace the elegant hem of his fine Chinkiang silk robe as, from a hill, he watched the movement of his troops across the plain below. Huge banners distinguished one Taiping regiment from the next. He spotted a black line in the ground across which his troops hadn't crossed. He wondered what the cut in the ground was, but being the Heavenly King and brother of Jesus made it difficult to admit that there were things he didn't know. Then he noticed what looked like long, earth-toned silk runner carpets meeting up with the black trench. In the distance the Manchu forces of the Q'ing Dowager Empress were massed in formal battle array. Augmented by mercenaries from many countries, the Q'ing fighters were the best-trained soldiers in the whole of Asia. And they fought for personal plunder, so they really fought.

The Heavenly King turned his head and lifted a finger. His

adjutant, a young man with a pockmarked face who spoke fluent Hakka, Cantonese, Mandarin, and — in this case most importantly — English, leaned in with head bowed and asked, "Majesty?"

"The red-haired *Fan Kuei*?" he demanded.

The young man pointed to a stand of trees at the extreme west side of the battlefield and held out the British-made spyglass. The Heavenly King took the instrument and panned the formation of the Beijing devil's troops, then past them to the small thicket. "The *Fan Kuei* is in the trees?" he asked.

"Yes, Majesty."

"And what is he doing in the…?" But his words ceased as, through the glass, he spotted movement in the thicket. Movement, then suddenly men on horseback broke through the treeline and headed toward the black trench on the right flank of the Q'ing formation. The black trench! Then he saw them. The earth-coloured runner carpets being pulled away by thick silk cords, revealing more black trenches beneath them. He followed the course of the darkness on the land. He hadn't noticed before that the dark path completely encircled the Manchu forces.

As the Manchus wheeled to face what they thought was an onslaught from the thicket, a single figure with a red kerchief around his neck raced from the opposite side toward the black trench. The Heavenly King gasped as he saw the red-haired *Fan Kuei* touch a lit torch to the side of the black circle. For a moment nothing happened, then the fire spirit leapt up from the ground and raced with ever-increasing speed down the length of the dark trench, encircling the Manchu forces in flame.

Maxi spoke softly to his horse to calm him in the presence of the fire, then stood on the animal's back, took off his red kerchief, and waved it. The five Taiping regiments, one composed entirely of women, swung in two wide arcs around the outside of the flaming trench.

As the disoriented and gasping Manchus leapt through the

ring of flame the Taipingers opened fire — and the slaughter was appalling.

Upon hearing of their defeat, the Q'ing authorities immediately attacked twenty villages thought by them to be Taiping centres. Men, women, and children were burned alive in the courtyards of their living compounds. Only the aged were spared to spread the Manchus' message: *This will happen to anyone who offers food or support of any kind to the Rebels.*

On the rivers, the lifeblood of China, the war was carried by the Taipingers to the Q'ing with a vigour that took the Manchus by surprise. The willingness of Taiping soldiers to offer up their lives was new in the Middle Kingdom. Then the South River pirates left their looting ways and joined the Taipingers, adding vast knowledge of the rivers and many ships to the rebel cause. And just as the British had done a decade earlier, the Taipingers began to strangle China by blockading its great rivers.

The Manchus counterattacked with particular viciousness and initially drove the Taipingers back towards their mountain aerie. But as serfs swelled their ranks, the Taipingers organized them into more and more regiments and finally drove the Manchus back toward Beijing. The viciousness of the fighting surprised both sides. There were never any prisoners taken. The soil of China was quickly drenched in the blood of its people. The initial deaths only hinted at the final death toll — some thirty million, who would lose their lives as the Heavenly King established his heaven on earth.

Those who found themselves under Taiping rule were forced to convert to the Heavenly King's particular variant of Protestantism, the one true faith, and obey strict rules about the separation of the sexes, religious observances, and military service. Not everyone found the Taipingers' way of life easy to tolerate. Meanwhile, ethnic Chinese under Manchu control were taxed unmercifully and were constantly under suspicion of being rebel sympathizers.

However, it was in the disputed zones that things were the

worst. Villagers never knew if they were going to be punished by the Manchus or the Taipingers. Life quickly became unbearable. And people began to move — to safety — to the Foreign Settlement in Shanghai.

There, Richard's land purchases, crowded with four-storey tenements designed by Maxi and built by Anderson, were awaiting their coming. Literally thousands of people arrived at the Bend in the River every week for almost two years — and Richard had places for them to stay. Sometimes five to a room, sometimes ten. For the wealthy from Chinkiang and Nanjing he had single-family dwellings.

Finally he had more workers than he could use, and so much money in rent that he could claim the title of Asia's richest landlord.

Maxi looked at his pregnant Hakka wife and her two young daughters and smiled. His long day of labour in his fields had finally come to an end. Although he could have moved into Nanjing and lived in luxury, closer to the Heavenly King, as a reward for his exploits in the field of battle, he didn't want that. The only things he requested were to work in the fields with all the others, and be permitted, unlike the others, to live with his wife. His requests were granted by the Heavenly King himself.

One of his adopted daughters took his big, calloused hand and he looked down into her doe-like eyes. Then he reached for his Hakka wife and said, in Farsi, "I am finally at home." He wanted to touch her rounded belly, to feel the life within, but it was forbidden for men to touch their wives in public, just as so much else was forbidden, in the lands of the Heavenly King.

"Vrassoon! Open the door to your God-forsaken house!" Richard's voice sounded foreign to him, as if it came from the other side of some great divide. He banged at the heavy door again, this time the leather satchel he carried with him. The door opened and two well-muscled blond men stepped out. One put a bearpaw of a hand on his chest and pushed him firmly away from the door of the Vrassoons' private residence.

"Mr. Vrassoon doesn't see visitors on the Sabbath."

Richard almost laughed. His smile was enough to draw a threatening look from the second of the two. "So you're his Shabbos goys?" Richard managed.

The men looked at each other, not sure if they had been insulted or not.

"You're more like his Shabbos apes, wouldn't ya say?"

That they understood unequivocally, and the blow that landed squarely on the point of Richard's jaw sent him careening down the polished steps. Even as his face splatted against the bottom stair he wanted to yell out, *Hells bells, these steps are marble. Marble in China! Who in fucking hell needs marble in China?* Richard found himself on his feet, blood streaming down his face. "Get Vrassoon out here. Get his slimy eminence out here. We have some business to transact. Business enough to get him away from his imitation of religiosity." The men stared at Richard. "Get him, now, you hunk of baboon turd!" It felt good to make a fuss in the lair of the Vrassoons — or even outside the lair. It felt good to muss their feathers. It felt good, but it didn't get him anywhere.

In fact it wasn't until the following Thursday that he was granted an audience with the Patriarch of the Vrassoon family.

The man's neatly trimmed beard and comfortable clothing belied the fury in his dark eyes. "You were rude at my door, and on the Sabbath. I would expect that from —"

"Yeah, yeah, but not from a Jew like me. Well, I'm a Jew like me, not a Jew like you, so can we skip that crap." Even Richard was surprised by his own insolence, but it felt good. *Why did it feel so good to abuse this man?* he wondered. He thought of the doctored picture and it was about to make him smile when an image came up in his mind. Himself as a boy giving something to this man. Not something — someone — who? He shook his head and noticed the man looking at him, through him.

"Do you need a drink? Your other vice, I'm afraid, I can't supply for you."

Richard thought about that and nodded, the irony of the world's biggest opium trader having none of his own product in his home made him smile. Richard looked at the man's clear, hard eyes. He'd never experienced the dream. He didn't even know what he was selling — yet he sold it by the ton. He shook his head, "Thanks, but I only drink with friends, and as for my other vice, I ... never mind."

"Fine. What brings you here with such a heavy satchel? Another bargain you wish to strike?"

Richard hefted the satchel he had brought with him. "That's right, a bargain ..." But he never completed his thought. He crumpled forward as laughter took him. It rolled up his throat and spat out into the room. Through his tears Richard saw the Vrassoon Patriarch eyeing the door of the room. "Don't leave, old man. Nah. The show's just beginning." Richard reached for the heavy satchel, unbuttoned its clasp, and dumped the equivalent of 250,000 pounds sterling on Eliazar Vrassoon's desk.

The older man hadn't moved a muscle. "And this would be?" the man asked, his voice suddenly rife with sibilance.

"The remainder of the money the Hordoon boys owe you, every last fucking penny of it."

Vrassoon lifted a heavy eyebrow.

"Now give me back my debt note."

The hand Richard held out shook. Something was wrong and he knew it. He repeated his request, but the Vrassoon Patriarch didn't move.

"You've done very well, son."

"I'm not your son," Richard shouted. "Just give me back the debt note you bought from Barclays."

"The lawyers need to look into a few things, but you should have your note by Thursday next."

Richard wanted to ask *What things?* but he was suddenly exhausted. And there was something else he felt he needed from this man — something he had given him a long time ago.

Before he could think, he found himself out on Bubbling Spring Road, his noseless, earless, female companion, Lily, offering an arm to steady his walk to the opium den.

Patterson answered Richard's summons first thing the next morning.

"So what do you think, Patterson?" Richard asked.

"Think of what, sir?"

"Of horses," Richard said enigmatically.

Patterson resisted sighing. Was the heathen opiated again? Finally he said, "I'm quite fond of horses, sir."

"Racehorses?" Richard asked.

Patterson stared at his employer. Was he drunk? "Racehorses? I would go so far as to say that I am extremely fond of racehorses."

"Good, let's buy some."

"They can run a pretty penny, sir."

"Even better."

Patterson didn't know what to make of the skinflint actually wanting to spend money. He mentioned, "Fine idea, sir. But there's no racecourse in Shanghai."

"Racetrack," Richard corrected him.

"Be that as it may, a place to race horses, sir. There's no such place here."

"Aye, as you would say, Patterson, aye, that is true. Be that as it may, let's buy some racehorses, Patterson, spend a bit of our hard-earned profits."

Patterson liked the idea of spending money. Especially money that was not his. But why did the addicted heathen want to spend it here in this God-forsaken place? Why not take it home and spend it? Then again, maybe this heathen had no home except here. God help him, if that was the case. But then again, spending a bit of scratch could be fun — and he liked horses. "Where will we find the animals, sir?"

"The horses? Arabia, Scotland, and Kentucky, I expect. I rather thought you'd look after that."

Patterson resisted smiling. Oh, he'd look after that all right, and skim the appropriate amount of money to buy that final parcel of land just north of Kelso in the Scottish border country, to which he was looking forward to retiring from this hellhole.

"Patterson?"

"Sir?"

"Teach young Silas about horses. Maybe that will catch his fancy."

The horses didn't much interest Silas, but they became Milo's obsession. Every new animal that arrived Milo insisted on riding — and, although Silas didn't want much to do with the animals, he was always there to cheer on his brother. Now in their middle teenage years they were closer than ever, but very different young men. Milo was close to his father and anxious to learn everything about the family business. Silas was often silent and withdrawn, but brilliant with languages and fascinated by the Chinese culture around him. Hearing about the Peking Opera at the House of Paris, he even managed to sneak in twice to watch before being ushered out with a hand on his shoulder, the kind but firm hand of Jiang, who whispered, "Soon, but not yet, my fine colt."

Richard built a fine new stable for his racehorses, and the day it was completed he took Silas aside.

"It's time for you to become part of this family."

"I am part of this family. I'm your son."

"Yes, but this family runs a serious business, and you have to become a part of it."

"Why?"

"Because, son, a man needs expertise in this world to make a living. Time to learn the horse trade. Patterson'll show you what needs doing."

"But why me?"

Richard didn't know what to say to that and found himself suddenly shouting, "You're a Hordoon, son. One of us. Me and your Uncle Maxi, we built this business from nothing."

"And where is my uncle now?"

"Gone, Silas. Gone. But you're still here, and it's time to earn your keep."

"Ye're an odd one, ain't ye?" Patterson asked as he handed Silas the shovel.

Silas didn't answer. It wasn't really a question anyway.

"It's called shit, lad, and that thing in yer puffy, soft hands is a shovel." Patterson laughed. "Shovel shit, me odd little heathen."

Silas turned to look at Patterson.

"Don't give me that Persian stare, boy, or whatever the fuck it is on your kiking face."

Silas hefted the shovel and slid it beneath a pile of fresh horse dung, keeping his distance from the Arabian steed who eyed him from the far side of the stall.

Silas was afraid of horses. The taut, quivering muscles in their thighs and the sidelong violence in their eyes, put together with their rock-hard hooves, terrified the young man. He was so small compared to them. Milo had assured him that as long as he didn't show fear the horse wouldn't hurt him. Often enough he'd said, "Give him a big swack on the butt, Silas, and he'll know who's the boss."

Patterson laughed again for some reason.

Silas wanted to turn to the man but he couldn't. It wasn't Patterson's cruel tongue or violent temper that scared Silas. It was as if the man knew his secret. His hidden shame. It was the reason Silas never said anything, even to Milo, about the way that Patterson treated him.

"The shit's on yer leg," Patterson said with a chortle.

Silas looked down and the man was right. The load had been too big for the shovel blade and some of the riper matter had slid off onto his tweed pants and come to rest in his cuffs.

"Not the perfect clothing for the job, lad."

Silas just nodded and backed out of the paddock with his shovel piled high. The manure pile was on the south side of the stables and steamed in the morning sun. Silas heaved his load onto the pile then looked around. It was silly to carry what he thought of as horse poop, one shovel at a time, out to the pile. He grabbed a hand dolly, fitted a wooden bucket to its base, and rolled it back to the stalls.

As he passed the horses he remembered how his Uncle Maxi had fawned over his own animals. Maxi seemed, like Milo and his father, to have a real affection for them. His father spent hours stroking and talking to the new Arabian pony they'd just purchased.

He'd also seen that same look on his father's face sometimes when Milo was at his side. He'd seen the look on Uncle Maxi's face when he worked out his intricate knots and inventions.

But Silas had never felt anything like that. He'd heard rumours about his father and the missionary woman and he assumed that Uncle Maxi felt strongly for some woman — although there were few non-Chinese women in Shanghai. Silas had listened in rapt attention as Uncle Maxi told them of working on the opium farm in far-off India. How he had "loved those people, loved them through and through."

Silas had never loved anybody or anything. He knew he was incapable of it. So he pretended. But he couldn't pretend well enough to fool Patterson. Patterson knew his secret, his shame. Silas tried to make himself feel things. He cared about Milo but he suspected that this was only because Milo had always been there for him. Some nights Silas would creep from their bed and snuggle up beside their *amah*, who slept on the mat outside their door. But even then, it was just for warmth.

Silas knew that it didn't matter to him who offered him warmth or comfort or even love — he couldn't return it. There was something wrong, and he knew it. Unfortunately, Patterson knew it as well.

31

DEATH AND BIRTH IN THE BAMBOO

North of Shanghai, across the Huangpu River, in the Pudong
1854

Somehow the Bodyguard knew it would end up in the bamboo thicket — that death and decision would come in the bamboo — so he had avoided it for as long as he could. But now they were in there, obscured from his view — only the movement of the elegant stems in the crisp early-morning light gave a hint as to their whereabouts. And now the screams of "Help me, father! Help me, father!" over and over again.

They had completed the rituals in the previous two weeks, during which time his son and his nephew had grown even closer, as only those who need each other to survive can. But the ancient rule of one leader for the Guild of Assassins was firm and he dared not break it for fear of betraying his family's oath, sealed in the Narwhal Tusk.

"Help me, father! Help me, father!"

He had thought about resurrecting the Guild himself but knew he was too old. Already the rot had set in, he could feel it, and soon every eye would see it — as one sees a small black blotch on a peach slowly eat into the centre and attack the pit.

"Help me, father! Help me, father!"

The Bodyguard

I wanted to put my hands to my ears to block the sound from punishing my heart but I couldn't allow myself that luxury.

This is my duty — as it is my son's duty, and my nephew's.

The Son

"Help me, father! Help me, father!" The sharpened bamboo cane is sticking out of my skin just below my right shoulder. Blood is coursing down my side but I've shallowed my breathing, as father taught me. I realize that the pain is bearable. But I am scared and I know that Loa Wei Fen will be in the trees, up in the bamboo — "Kill from above; always find a way above."

The Nephew

My cousin fell into the pit trap I set for him. One of the sharpened bamboo stems pierced his right breast, but has not cut into the sac that holds his heart. I wish it had killed him — so that I would not have to.

The Son

I am reaching for the swalto blade in my belt, but when I move the pain suddenly floods me. But I need my blade to defend myself. For he will be coming. Coming soon for my heart.

The Nephew

I taste the cobra skin that wraps the handle of my swalto blade as I put it between my teeth. I need both hands free to descend from the tall shoots. I've never been so high in the bamboo before and the tassels sing to me in the morning breeze. I want to go higher to hear the clear voice of the morning's song, but below me — in a pit — lies my destiny.

The Bodyguard

I begin to run. The bamboo tears my clothes, cuts at my skin — one lances a deep cut just below my left eye. But I run as fast as I can to my son — my gentle son.

The Son

A lone cloud races across the morning sky, moving a circle of darkness beneath it as it runs toward the horizon. So beautiful! So beautiful! But now I see the snake in the bamboo — my cousin, the snake.

The Nephew

The swalto turns in my hand and nestles into place — as if it is a living thing — its keen edges and point a thing of immaculate purpose. Then I am moving — down, down, down the largest of the bamboo stems — my legs controlling my descent — as I move head-first toward my destiny in the pit.

The Son

The sun glints off the snake's swalto blade — its deadly tooth — and I look away. The blood has stopped flowing from my shoulder. The breeze is cool. It is going to be a beautiful day. A day to spend with the cormorants — my cormorants — on the water. And suddenly I am there, in the boat, the youngest cormorant in my lap. I hold up the cruel metal ring that I was supposed to tighten around my bird's neck so he couldn't swallow the fish he caught and I look to father sitting by the rudder and say, "Do I have to?"

The Bodyguard

The bamboo patch in front of me yields quickly, much to my surprise, and then I see them. My son pinned in a shallow pit and my nephew pressure-gripping the bamboo stem with his knees as he descends head-first for the kill.

The Nephew

I arch my back and the cobra carved there uncoils. I feel its strength, its massive fury — and then I drop on my prey.

The Son

"I won't do it, father. I won't. This is a good bird. A good bird. My bird. He won't swallow the fish. He'll bring them back to the boat. I promise."

"It is the cormorant's fate to be ringed. It is its purpose. Now put the ring on his neck — and don't be gentle or it will fall off."

"But this is Kiwa — my cormorant — he loves me."

The Bodyguard

I thought I heard the word "love" come from my son's mouth as I approach. And it pierces my heart. "Help me, father! Help me. father!" My gentle son — but I look away. I look away.

The Nephew

Then I am there. Overtop of him, my swalto ready for the initial cut. His mouth opens and a bubble of blood comes to his lips. Then I hear him. He is saying my name.

The Son

"Loa Wei Fen, Loa Wei Fen, help me. I cannot put the neck ring on Kiwa. I cannot."

The Bodyguard

I see my nephew hesitate and I shout, "Don't falter. It is your destiny, Loa Wei Fen. Either you kill him or I kill you — the choice is yours."

The Nephew

Uncle is yelling at me and my cousin is pinned by the bamboo stake and the sun is rising and the cobra on my back is hissing in my ears and the swalto blade flips to the killing position in my hand — and I ...

The Son

The cormorant bites me. He's never bitten me before. Blood is coming from my chest. From my chest? Why from my chest? Kiwa bit me on the hand.

The Bodyguard

Loa Wei Fen's first cut isn't deep enough. "Strike again!" I scream.

The Nephew

I didn't need to be prompted. Everything in me wants the warm gush of blood to rain on me and change me and allow me to become the thing I was meant to be — an assassin.

The Son

"Help me, father! Help me, father!"

The Bodyguard

"Strike or I will strike you!"

The Nephew

All the practice, all the training — I open the cobra's hood on my back and my *chi* flows out from my centre to my arms and the swalto leaps for joy as it digs deep into my cousin's stomach then rips up and up. Then there is a sudden stillness. Above me the bamboo sways to my *chi*'s motion and the sun turns to warm my back and the world stands very still — I can hear the smallest animals in the thickets, and the wind catches its breath and the very motion of the planet — as I cut open my cousin's chest, slice free his heart from its bonds, cut it in half, and bite deep.

The Bodyguard

Loa Wei Fen's face is smeared in the blood of my son as he spits the piece of heart high in the air — as the ritual demands. I can see his *chi* finally retreat into its den and the boy turns to me — now, no longer a boy.

The Nephew

"We should bury your son."

The Bodyguard

"No. I now have no son. Leave the carcass for the jackals."

It is the final lesson I had to teach Loa Wei Fen. Pity is not part of an assassin's work — nor is honour for the dead.

The Fisherman

As I hold out my hand to my blood-soaked nephew I know that something important in my life has ended. I am no longer the progeny of the First Emperor's Bodyguard — and my nephew is no longer my nephew. The young man is now the founder of the Guild of Assassins and his name, Loa Wei Fen, will be the stuff of History Tellers' tales for ages to come.

The Bodyguard was now, simply, the Fisherman — a simple man who had lost a much beloved son.

PART III

⸲32

THE HISTORY TELLER

Shanghai
1856

Jiang nodded as she listened to her tall, brilliant daughter, Fu Tsong, explain her most recent version of her opera, *Journey to the West*. Despite being impressed with her daughter's talent, her attention wandered as she thought of the communication she had received that morning from the Fisherman: "A new leader of the Guild has been chosen. He awaits your instructions."

"Then, mother, after all the trials and tribulations, all the miles of walking and the constant danger — and the love that has grown between the Princess from the East and her manservant — they finally arrive in the palace of the King of the West. The Serving Man is shocked to see that no one is there to greet them — no banquet of welcome awaits them. Then the Princess, his Princess, is unceremoniously taken from him and, without even seeing her new husband, is sent to the house of the King of West's concubines. They both realize that she was nothing more than a pawn in the politics of peace and war between the King of the East and the King of the West. No one cares about her or what happens to her, except the lowly Serving Man, who brought her two thousand miles across rivers, mountains, and deserts."

"It is very sad, Fu Tsong, but duty takes us all to places that we do not expect."

"Indeed, mother. But that is not the end of the play."

"Really? What more story can there be?"

"The final image is the Serving Man, bereft of his Princess, turns toward the East and takes the first step on his two-thousand-mile journey back home."

Jiang smiled. Of course her daughter would see the possibility that she had not seen. She reached out and touched the strong features of her daughter's face. She was, Jiang knew, despite her mother's profession, a conservative woman. A woman whom she had helped marry into the industrious Zhong clan. A woman who had survived the sudden death of her young husband and had assumed his assigned role in the Zhong family hierarchy. A woman whom many had begun to call a History Teller.

Jiang told her so.

"History Teller?" Fu Tsong asked, puzzled.

"It's an old tradition that has faded from memory in many, but before the Manchu courts ruled in the Middle Kingdom there were always two historians in the Emperor's court. The History Chronicler gave the dates, times, and numbers of an historical event. The History Teller found the small, personal truth behind the facts of the historical event and told that story. It is rumoured that Q'in She Huang himself said, 'Abide the History Chronicler for he delivers facts. But heed the History Teller for he sees and tells the truth of what really happened.'"

Fu Tsong was suddenly cautious, and, keeping her eyes from her mother, said, "You are an endless surprise, my mother."

Jiang smiled at that. "You are the History Teller, my daughter.

It has been obvious to many of us for a long time. May I call you by that title?"

History Teller, Fu Tsong thought. *I'd be honoured to be called the History Teller.* She nodded.

"Are you and your troupe ready to travel, History Teller?"

Travel where and travel why? The History Teller wanted to ask, but she knew better than to demand answers from her mother. She also knew that her mother was never whimsical in her requests and always had the interests of Shanghai at heart. And anything that was good for Shanghai was good for her and her troupe. "This is important," she said. It was not a question.

"I wouldn't ask unless it was. You know me, History Teller."

"You honour me, mother, with the title and your trust."

"You honour me, daughter, with your talent and loyalty. You strengthen your family. Your play is lovely and I would not ask you to amend it in any way unless it was important. You know that."

"I do. Is there something that gives offence?"

"Nothing. Truly nothing. I only need you to include an actor in your company whom you have not used before."

"Is this an actor I would know?"

"No."

Suddenly the History Teller was afraid. "Am I permitted to ask who this actor is and why you wish...?"

"No."

After a moment the History Teller nodded. "As you wish, my mother. But can I ask about this actor's abilities?"

"I have no idea if he can sing or dance. But he can tumble and juggle as well or better than anyone else in your company."

"Good. He needn't sing or dance as long as he is athletic."

"Oh, he's very athletic. Very."

"Fine. May I cast him as I see fit?"

"Such decisions are yours, but I think he would make a fine Monkey King."

The History Teller's eyes opened wide. Had her mother known how displeased she had been with the present Monkey King's performance? Perhaps. "When can I meet this young athlete?"

"When you begin your journey."

"To Beijing?"

"No, to Nanjing."

The History Teller paled. The Taipingers controlled the ancient capital.

"I have secured you safe passage from the Heavenly King through one of his senior generals. Someone you've met," Jiang added with a strange smile.

The History Teller wanted to ask who this man was and how her mother knew him, but Jiang kissed her on the cheek, then left.

That night a client at Jiang's reached for his whore. But the drunken Frenchman's aim was off target. And his hand knocked over a brazier, whose coals lit the woman's silk kimono. Which set alight the bedding in the room which torched the walls of the brothel which began a conflagration that in one night burned nearly one in ten of the buildings in Shanghai, the city at the Bend in the River, to the ground. But it was of only minor concern to the Chosen Three, who had finally launched their arrow high into the night sky.

The History Teller gathered her clan by the north bank of the Huangpu. In the distance, the eerie glow of the huge fire in Shanghai cast a further strangeness on the night. A fat pig sizzled on its spit over the coal pit. The moon was already high and the cold of the night intense, but not even the youngest had returned to the housing compound. The women, the strong women of her deceased husband's clan, the Zhong clan, stood and waited for her to speak. She poured more of the powerful Chinese wine and held up her glass. The entire clan stood and looked at her. "Drink then spit," she ordered. They all did as she commanded. She felt the bitter liquid momentarily clench her throat.

The smell of the hundreds of pails of curing night soil — her husband's family business — were somehow sweet on the cold air.

"And again." And they all drank then spat a second time.

She nodded. "Good. My mother, Jiang, has insisted that we talk of great things." She laid out the basic plan of bringing the troupe to the Prophet's stronghold in Nanjing. She never mentioned exactly why and quickly silenced any dissenting voices. "The Long Noses' neutrality treaty with the Prophet is in place so we will not be held back in the city. We will, however, not trust the fates or the *Fan Kuei*'s word, so we'll leave tonight."

"Will it be safe?" her mother-in-law asked. The older woman looked at her daughter-in-law and wanted to reach over and touch her hair and tell her how proud she was to have her as a part of the Zhong clan. But there had never been outward demonstrations of affection between the two. Even in private they were subdued. The History Teller saved all of her affection for her one true love, since the death of her husband: her work on the operas.

"I don't know," she said, turning away from the question. "I just don't know." She turned toward the rest of the large clan. "You will not see me or the troupe for some time. Don't take to heart what you hear of us. I may need to gain the Prophet's trust." Then, turning to her actors, she said, "Get your things. It is time for us to leave."

The actors hesitated.

"What?" she demanded.

They looked at the crackling pig, and the History Teller smiled, then nodded. *Actors and food*, she thought, but what she said was, "There will be no meat for us for some time, so we'll await the completion of the roast — then we will leave. We will be on the river before moonset."

Late that night the History Teller hoisted the last of her bags up on the wharf railing. As she turned toward the large river junk that awaited her on the north shore of the river she was startled by the appearance, as if from the ground itself, of a young man, scarcely more than a boy. The fresh cobra tattoo on his hand stood out in the last rays of the setting moon. "I am to come with you, History Teller," the boy/man said.

The History Teller took a breath and steadied herself. The boy/man's athleticism was obvious, but his silence was disconcerting. There was blood on the sides of his shirt. Blood newly dried.

"Did my mother send you?"

The Assassin shrugged.

"Did she?"

"My uncle gave me the order. I don't know if it came from someone else."

"And this uncle's order said?"

"To meet the History Teller by the upper bend in the river and follow what she says."

The History Teller nodded and reached for her satchel. As she pulled it off the railing the bag's handle snagged and the contents fell toward the ground. Toward, but not quite to, because the strange boy/man leapt forward, and with an unworldly speed he caught each and every article, one by one, before any of them touched the earth.

Then he looked up at the History Teller and something dark and sad crossed his face. Something the History Teller saw but made herself forget.

The History Teller indicated that the things were to be put back in the satchel. The Assassin returned the articles to the case.

Then the History Teller reached into a much larger case and threw its contents at the boy/man.

The Assassin saw the glint of metal in the moonlight. Then, as he had been taught, he shallowed his breathing and the objects — cymbals, drums, drumsticks, horns — slowed in their twirling, spinning paths toward him.

He caught each of the seven objects, the last, a large cymbal, in his teeth. Then he stood there on one foot and awaited the History Teller's orders. They finally came.

"Pack those up and carry them onboard the junk."

33

INTO THE COUNTRYSIDE

The Real Middle Kingdom
1856–1857

The heavily armed Manchu patrol boats were on their windward side. "When did they show up?" asked the History Teller.

"While you slept," the one-eyed Captain of her junk replied as he spat into the muddy water of the Yangtze. "They'll stop us before we get to the narrows. Are your papers in order?"

"Naturally. We are on our way to Beijing to entertain the Dowager Empress."

The Captain's single eye widened. He'd been paid enough money by the whore madam to get this handsome woman and her troupe of players to Chinkiang at the foot of the Grand Canal — no farther. He spat overboard a second time and said, "You are aware the Middle Kingdom is at war."

"How far are we from the narrows?"

"An hour, maybe a little more."

The History Teller nodded as she turned to her assistant, a

competent but entirely boring middle-aged man. "Tell the new actor to get into makeup." Before the pedantic man could question this, the History Teller said, "I want to work on the fourth act. Maybe the morning light will bring some clarity to that mess."

The man threw up his hands and headed below decks. Waking up actors in the morning wasn't his idea of a good time.

The one-eyed Captain had been correct. In just under an hour a Manchu war junk hung a spinnaker sail and crossed their bow with gingalls openly displayed and shouted at the Captain to turn into the wind. Without hesitation, the Captain pulled the long-handled tiller hard against his body. The junk's thick mast swung slowly across the deck and the ship turned smoothly and with remarkable speed into the wind — and there it stayed.

The Manchu Commander stepped onto the junk's deck after twenty of his armed men had rousted the History Teller and her players. The man strode across the deck as if he were reviewing his troops on a battle parade. He stopped in front of one of the older actors and shouted, "Remove your mask."

The older man did.

The Commander turned the actor around quickly and pulled the man's long, braided hair from beneath his robe. "It is the law for you to wear your hair out!" He turned the man around to face him and ran his hand over the man's badly shaven high forehead. Then he hit him hard across the face, drawing blood from the man's mouth. "It is the law for Han Chinese to shave their foreheads up to the line of the top of their ears. It is the law."

He didn't bother turning to the History Teller. He just held out his hands and shouted, "Papers!"

The History Teller handed over the documents her mother had supplied. She had no idea if they were good forgeries or in fact the real thing. All she knew was that they claimed the troupe was on its way up to Beijing to entertain the Dowager Empress, Tzu Hsi.

She glanced over at the boy/man. All she knew about him was

that his name was Loa Wei Fen, or at least that was the name he used. She canted her head slightly in the strange young athlete's direction. Loa Wei Fen nodded and pulled the headdress from his head. He still had a hastily painted approximation of the Monkey King makeup on his face.

The History Teller heard a harrumph from the Manchu Commander, then he snarled, "Nonsense. Men are dying and this crap is given free passage." He shoved the papers back at the History Teller, then turned to the one-eyed Captain. "Papers!"

The Captain produced the documents for both the junk and his personal passage. The Manchu Commander was not much impressed. He shouted an order that the History Teller couldn't translate, then moved back toward his own ship.

As the war junk disappeared in the rising sun, the History Teller thought of a small white bird disappearing into the past. She said the words aloud, and something deep within her resonated with them. Something old was near her, and she knew it. Something that touched her — or her mother — or both of them. Then she turned to her troupe and shouted, "Act Four is still a mess. Let's work."

They rehearsed for another hour, but it was clear the boy/man was completely lost.

"Look. It's not complicated. The storyline has to do with the Monkey King killing a family as they try to make their way through his mountain territory," the History Teller explained again.

"I just kill them?" he asked.

"Yes, Loa Wei Fen, you just kill them."

"Why?"

The History Teller turned to look at the other actors. "Already he wants to know why he's doing things."

"That shouldn't bother you, ma'am. It's what you've been asking me for years," said the actor who played the Serving Man.

"Well, you need to be asked that. He …" She turned to Loa Wei Fen and said, "It's territorial, from your point of view, but the storyline has to do with the Princess from the West and her Serving Man. Your threat to the peasants presents a dilemma for the Serving Man. Does he leave his charge, his love, the Princess of the West, and do what is right in trying to protect the peasant family from you? Or does he ignore his duty as a human being — namely, to help the helpless — and thus keep his charge, his love, safe from danger?"

"So I am no more than a dilemma to you?"

The History Teller heard something hidden behind the boy/man's words but ignored it and threw up her arms. "We are all no more than a dilemma. At least your dilemma has an interesting character and a good costume. Count yourself lucky."

Loa Wei Fen shuffled his feet a little, then said, "All right."

They started with the scene in which a family escapes the wrath of their overlord when they can't afford to pay his outrageous tax demands. The father, mother, and child make their stealthy entrance from downstage left and begin their cross to the upstage right riser. The History Teller worked with them for almost an hour trying to get the relationship between the couple clear, then the exact nature of the danger they anticipated encountering in the mountains.

She was finally happy with their performances and was about to call Loa Wei Fen to the stage when the young man leapt to the top of the high platform. His sudden presence was so unexpected, so shockingly, vibrantly alive, that every eye turned to the strange boy/man. But the History Teller just nodded slowly as a smile grew across her features, bringing an intense light to the beauty there.

The next morning the History Teller came up on deck and saw Loa Wei Fen balanced on the port-bow railing without the assistance of a spar or halyard line. The boy/man effortlessly adjusted for the swell and ebb of the waves. Seeing her, he pointed upriver toward the south shore. The History Teller came over to him and shielded her eyes in an effort to see what had attracted Loa Wei

Fen's attention, but it was a full fifteen minutes of sailing before the History Teller finally saw what Loa Wei Fen's keen eyes had already seen — hundreds upon hundreds of heads on pikes planted on the shoreline.

As their junk slid by the ghastly display there was an eerie silence, broken only by the threatening caws of the carrion birds as they feasted on eyeballs and cheeks and esophageal parts. Some of the vultures perched on the heads stared at the passing junk as they dug their claws deep into the flesh beneath them.

One of the young actors broke into tears; another threw up over the side of the junk.

"It's recent," the one-eyed Captain said.

"Manchu or Taiping?" the History Teller asked.

"The victims or the attackers?"

"Who did this?" demanded the History Teller.

"Manchus. As I said before, there is war in the Middle Kingdom. Can't you smell the reek in the air? It's the smell of change. This is not Shanghai — this is the real Middle Kingdom, and the stink of change is everywhere. Write about that if you can, History Teller."

The History Teller watched as the heads stared past the birds that pecked at them and challenged those onboard the ship to avenge this outrage. For almost a half an hour they sailed past the silent cry. Then came the final outrage. On shorter pikes, as if to emphasize the offence, were the heads of children — dozens of them. The History Teller's eye was drawn to one little girl whose hair hung down all the way to the sand. The wind picked up and the girl's hair lifted from the ground. *Like a kite*, she thought. Then lines came to her:

> *The hair as its tail,*
> *The head pulls at its pike bond,*
> *To enter the sky and fly to heaven.*

Later that day, from the vantage of the junk, they saw their first large group of peasants trudging east along the river's stony shore carrying the entirety of their lives' possessions on their backs.

"Where are they headed, Captain?"

"To the safety of Shanghai. You'll see many more soon. The Manchus have blocked all the roads from Nanjing to just east of here. That's why these people use the riverbank. Once they get a few miles farther they'll head inland to the traders' paths. That's why you haven't seen many of them up until now, History Teller."

"And they'll walk to Shanghai?"

"Unless they are wealthy enough to own a cart or hire a horse. Some of the wealthy from Chinkiang are carried all the way to Shanghai. But not these souls."

"How many days…?"

"Would it take to get to Shanghai from here, on foot? If they manage to avoid bandits and the roving bands of Taipingers or renegade Manchus, six, maybe eight. But many of these people travel with babies and old people. For them longer, maybe ten days."

The History Teller looked at the man at her side and finally asked, "How did you lose your eye?"

"Looking for a story, are you?"

"Perhaps. I have a real interest in stories."

"Indeed you do."

"So?"

"In the Arab lands."

The History Teller's knowledge of geography was extremely limited. With the exception of a few travellers and merchant mariners, no one in China knew much about the lands beyond the Middle Kingdom.

The Captain hacked out a coarse laugh and said, "They tell stories there too, History Teller. Those Arabians love their stories."

"Was this far away?"

"As a story would say, far away and long ago. When I was

nothing more than a boy onboard a great ocean-going junk. We had circled the world itself and seen many foreign lands. In fact, we were following the same route that our earlier mariners took, two hundred years before the Manchus came to our land."

The History Teller knew that the Manchus' Q'ing Dynasty had started in the early years of the 1600s, so the Captain was referring to a time around 1400. She'd heard rumours of great ocean-going junks circumnavigating the world even earlier than that. One story had it that the maps made by the sailors on the early junks were later sold to Arab traders who came across the Silk Road, who then sold them to the Spanish, who used them to stumble upon the Americas. The History Teller didn't know if this was true or not, but then again, her interest was not really in facts.

"So what happened?"

"A woman. No, a girl."

"So you weren't that young."

"Just old enough to want, and I was full of juice back then. Full of it." He let out a coarse chortle. "I lost my eye for a girl," he said softly.

The History Teller was willing to listen, but it quickly became clear that the one-eyed Captain was adrift in his memories and was not going to complete the story. That was fine with the History Teller. "I lost my eye for a girl" was an entire world of a story, as far as the History Teller was concerned.

That evening they stopped at the wharf of a large estate. Servants, hundreds of servants, hustled onboard to bring the actors' props, costumes, and set pieces ashore.

The History Teller was met by an elderly man wearing rich robes, with two young women at his side. "Welcome, most welcome," the old man said. As he spoke, the long wisp of hair on his chin bobbed up and down in a weird pantomime of his words. The two young women were careful to keep their eyes down and contented themselves with smoothing out the old man's garments as he moved.

The History Teller noted the angry red rash on the hands of one of the girls — then saw how carefully she kept it hidden beneath her sleeves.

"You will perform for us, I hope," the old man said.

"Indeed," she responded, "and we have a surprise for you."

"A surprise!" the old man exclaimed as his wisp beard danced up and down. "I love surprises!"

As darkness fell, torches were lit in a wide circle and chairs brought out. With the Yangtze River as their backdrop, the troupe performed the first few scenes of *Journey to the West*. The large crowd was enthusiastic, often leaping to their feet and filling the silent night with their cries of "*Hoa*!"

Loa Wei Fen was disappointed that they stopped before his section of the play, and then was surprised when the History Teller called him out onto the stage. He stepped out in his Monkey King costume and makeup and stared at the people amassed on three sides of the raised performance platform.

"Now for the special surprise that I promised," the History Teller announced to the audience. She turned to the stage and ordered, "Take a stance, Loa Wei Fen."

The young man kicked off his slippers, shallowed his breath, allowed his testicles up into his abdominal cavity, and floated his hands forward. He noted the tension increase in the audience. Then the History Teller called out, "Group one!"

Immediately six men in the audience stood and threw objects, ranging from heads of cabbages to a slender dagger, right at the young man on stage.

To the joy of the audience, Loa Wei Fen caught all the objects, including the small knife, upon which he skewered both heads of cabbage.

The old man cheered "*Hoa*!" so loudly that the History Teller thought he might collapse. Then the History Teller called out, "Group two!"

This time eight men stood and hurled objects at Loa Wei Fen. Again the young man caught all the projectiles, this time one knife behind the crook of a knee and another between an elbow and his ribcage.

Again wild cheers greeted the feat. The process was repeated twice more, ending with twelve objects thrown and caught.

The History Teller watched closely. She saw in this boy/man the results of years of training. The History Teller had an idea what the only profession was that would demand such a regimen — and it sent a slither of fear up her spine.

Three days later they approached the southern end of the Grand Canal. On the northeast shore, the city of Chinkiang — the City of Suicides — loomed up in the darkness.

The one-eyed Captain called out, "It's open," in response to the knock on his door. He swung his feet out of his hammock as the History Teller and her boring assistant entered.

The Captain lit an oil lamp and looked at the two. But he didn't speak. He waited for them to begin.

"We approach the Grand Canal," the History Teller said.

For a moment the Captain wondered why the woman never seemed to sweat or feel the cold, then he let that pass and, putting on his sternest face, said, "So what? You're bound for Beijing."

The History Teller stepped forward, laid a hand on his, and said softly, "We are not."

This came as no surprise to the Captain. Nothing about this troupe seemed likely to entertain the Manchus' Dowager Empress: the accent on Han Chinese in the play, the open criticism of power, the adulation of personal love over duty — none of this was destined to find favour in the court of the Manchus. But all he said was, "Really?"

The History Teller smiled, withdrew her hand, and nodded. "You knew."

"Perhaps." The Captain pulled on his britches and snapped the buttons on his flies, then said, "So where are you bound?"

"Nanjing."

The Captain almost choked on that. "My ship goes nowhere near the Taipingers."

"We don't expect you to. Just bring us past the Grand Canal and under the secrecy of night set us ashore."

The Captain's head snapped up and down like a puppet's and he spat out, "Oh, that's all? Risk the wrath of the Manchus. Perhaps you didn't see the miles and miles of heads on pikes? Well, some of those people broke fewer Manchu laws than you are asking me to break. I have no papers to land you there. And what am I to do if I am stopped and you aren't onboard? What am I to tell the damnable Manchus, that you jumped overboard?"

"No. You are to tell them that we took control of your ship and at knifepoint forced you to put us ashore."

"And they'll believe that?"

"They will after Loa Wei Fen finishes his work on you."

The young assassin didn't like it. It wasn't what he was trained for, but after the History Teller explained their predicament he agreed.

The Captain had been sedated with strong wine and opium when Loa Wei Fen entered his cabin. With a single stroke of his swalto blade he cut away the man's robe, exposing a barrel chest and a slightly bloated belly. Loa Wei Fen put his hand on the man's chest. Instinctively the Captain's strong hand reached up and grabbed Loa Wei Fen's, but the Assassin was stronger and very skilled. He hit the man hard once just below the left ear and the man's eyes rolled back in his head. The Assassin needed the Captain to be very still. Any movement and this effort to save the man's life could cause his death.

The door opened behind him and the History Teller entered. "Bring the lamp closer," the Assassin said.

This boy is my death, too, the History Teller thought as she moved the lamp.

Loa Wei Fen reached up and pulled the lamp closer to the Captain's chest. He put the thumb and forefinger of his left hand on the man's ribs, gently forcing the skin between the ribs taut. Then he leaned in and placed his ear to the Captain's chest. He forced himself to ignore the man's heartbeat and instead listened carefully to the pull and push of his lungs. His fingers crept across the ribs to the right side of his chest. No need to enter the left side. Then he sensed it: the place where the lung expanded, and to the left, the place where the viscera moved to allow the expansion. It was not so different from the way he would have tried to find a wall beam beneath a wall covering.

Satisfied with his placement, he withdrew his swalto blade and rested the point at the exact place on the man's chest. Instantly blood welled up and began to pool. Loa Wei Fen quickly stilled his breath and made himself hear the entirety of the room. Then, with an elegant thrust, he pushed the swalto blade through the Captain's chest and retracted it instantly. He was happy, when he looked at his knife, that no hint of the bedding came back with the blade. Any foreign matter left in the wound could be fatal. Quickly he reached in his bag and crushed the healing herb into the wound, then wound it tight with silk.

"Will he…?"

"Live?" Loa Wei Fen asked. "Perhaps. Perhaps not. But if he does, he will have a very convincing wound to show the Manchus. Where are the rest of the crew?"

"They've been tied up and put in the hold."

"Who will guide the ship?" "A man from Chinkiang who owes my mother a favour should be here shortly. He'll lead us to the horses."

Six hours later the last of the actors and their equipment were ashore several miles west of Chinkiang, and the junk was set loose to attract attention on the Yangtze. Travelling on horseback and walking, the troupe made their way through what the one-eyed Captain would no doubt have called the "real China."

And the "real China" was a place of real danger. North of the Yangtze, where they were, was disputed land. One week the Manchus controlled it, one week the Taipingers. The farmers were terrified. The large landowners had armies of their own to protect their property. Many of the merchants were the first to leave for the safety of Shanghai. The roads were not well tended and the horses were often skittish in the foul breezes.

The first two days of travelling were relatively uneventful. The troupe stopped to admire the ancient pillars erected by villages in honour of their famous sons and the feats of engineering that allowed rice paddies to rise like stacked lily pads up the sides of sheer mountains. As well, they stopped and offered their respects at graveyards and Buddhist temples. Twice Taoist priests stopped the troupe, but once it was established that there were no Christian missionaries, they were permitted to proceed.

> *Beside the mulberry trees*
> *the women,*
> *wrapped in scarves,*
> *move like shadows in the dawn.*

Those were the opening lines that the History Teller penned when the troupe approached the first of many silk farms on the gentle slopes of the Hua Shan. As she watched, thoughts kept moving across her mind as if imprinting themselves there like acid on a bronze plate. So unlike Shanghai. So ancient compared to the world in which she lived. But so much of who she was.

The troupe once more performed for their lodging, but this time in a large interior courtyard surrounded by wooden balustrades. This night they began with the play's fourth act, the arrival of the Monkey King in the mountain pass. The History Teller watched closely as

Loa Wei Fen made his way through the moves they had practised, leading to the entrance of the Princess and the Serving Man.

The History Teller was not pleased. Although the moves were all technically correct — in fact immaculately so — they were lifeless. The young man was trying to duplicate exactly what he had been taught. There was no sense of making the leap from the notes to the music. The actual killings seemed so formal that they caused hardly a ripple in the audience watching.

The History Teller thought of the word "ripple" and wondered why that had stuck in her mind, then she mouthed the word and her head turned and there before her was a group of peasant women with their children, sitting quietly watching the play — but *rippling*. For an instant, the History Teller thought it must have been a trick of the fading light, but as she looked more closely she realized that these women and their children were alive with the pupa form of the silkworm. On their clothing, beneath their clothing, in their hair, in their ears — one gently pulled a creature away from her nostril and put it back beneath her quilted coat.

The History Teller knew that the pupa stage of the silkworm was the most delicate. In that stage, the worms had to be kept warm and dry for almost three weeks before they completed the weaving of the cocoon, which was done with the silk they excreted. The only way to assure the warm and dry conditions was for the workers on the estate to each "wear" thousands of the worms.

That made the History Teller shiver — three weeks with living things on your body, day and night! But that was almost nothing compared to the women's crippled hands. The threads of silk were held together by a gummy substance. The only way to remove the substance was to submerge the pupae in boiling water. That could be done with a stick, but retrieving them from the boiling water required real delicacy and care that only a human hand could manage. As a result, not a single woman or girl could pick up a teacup without pain and tears. She wrote:

*The tears of the women
fall on angry red hands.*

But the silk was beautiful, she had to admit. And she thought of two more lines:

*Women's tears
Bring beauty to the world.*

She turned back to the stage — to the artifice she had created. And she frowned. *There needs to be more truth. This young man has to learn how to dance, not just do the steps; make art of juggling and tumbling, not just fulfill the task. He must take the art of it, the truth of it, and, like these people, put it under his clothing and in his ears.*

The next day, when the troupe finally left the silk farm, the History Teller went through her possessions and discarded any made of silk. Although the characters in her plays would continue to wear silk to represent the figures in the dramas properly, she, herself, would never again allow "the beauty that came from tears" to touch her body.

The next evening the Taipingers arrived, in force. They had been warned of the movements of the History Teller's troupe and were positioned and ready when the troupe turned west off the northbound trail. Quickly a second force came up behind the acting troupe so that there was no way out of the trap.

The History Teller dismounted and signalled that the rest should do the same. The Taiping soldiers looked confident, well-fed but none too friendly. When the History Teller stepped forward to speak to the head of the Taiping patrol she was surprised to sense an agile movement in the tall trees to her right. She caught just the slightest glimpse of a figure scaling a tree and knew it was Loa Wei Fen. She took a deep breath and made sure not to look in the boy/man's direction.

"We come in peace," she began, but the Taiping Commander strode past her, followed closely by ten of his armed guards. They quickly but thoroughly emptied the contents from the wagons and the horses' saddlebags.

The commander picked up a long, black wig and demanded, "What's this?"

"A king's wig."

"And this?" he asked, holding up a mask painted a bright red and black.

"A courtier's mask."

"And this?" This time he had a woman's costume with long sleeves that fell all the way to the ground, despite the fact that he held it up over his head.

"The dress of a saddened woman," the History Teller said.

That seemed to interest the Commander and he turned toward her. "Are you a saddened woman?"

The History Teller held her ground and kept her voice level, although she sensed Loa Wei Fen leaning out toward her from above in the tree. *Is the boy going to do something stupid?* She wondered. *God help me, if he feels he has to protect me.* She forced her eyes away from the stand of trees and looked at the Commander. It was clear that the man was taken with her features. She allowed herself to smile. He smiled back. Finally she said, "I am not a saddened woman, Commander."

"I could make you a very sad woman indeed."

"Or a very happy woman, by bringing me to the court of the Heavenly King."

The Commander was clearly surprised that this tall, handsome woman wasn't afraid of him. He stepped quickly toward her but she didn't retreat. She did, though, suddenly look up at the trees to his left. He was about to turn when he caught a glimpse of a red kerchief, then shortly after heard the thundering of a horse's hooves.

He stepped back from the woman, a curse rising in his throat that he quickly swallowed.

The horse entered the clearing and reared as its rider pulled hard on the reins. Then the man took the red kerchief from his neck and wiped the sweat from his face.

Maxi Hordoon smiled at the History Teller.

And the History Teller smiled back at the white-skinned, red-haired *Fan Kuei* who had sat so often in the back of her rehearsal room in her mother's brothel. Words again flew into her head:

A barbarian emerges
From the darkened woods,
Like an angel on a horse.
And the world, once more, turns.

As her smile broadened she sensed something cold near her and turned. The boy/man, Loa Wei Fen, was standing behind her looking at the red-haired *Fan Kuei*. And for an instant the History Teller thought she saw rage cross the young man's face.

More words bloomed in her mind — but these words were dark blossoms of blood and pain.

34

JOURNEY TO THE WEST

Nanjing, the seat of the Heavenly Kingdom
1857

The flames from the torches within their porcelain reflectors cast a cool light in the warm spring evening. The only noise was the hum of insects moving about the interior courtyard where the Heavenly King himself, Hung Hsiu-ch'uan, sat on a raised chair. To his left, a delicately featured young girl fanned away the bugs from the lower half of his body. To his right, another fine-boned Han Chinese girl protected the upper reaches of his person. His feet had not touched the ground for more than five years — and he never waited for anything. Yet here he waited. Waited for the play, *Journey to the West*, to begin.

The other five kings of the Taiping empire were already in their assigned places with their respective retainers, concubines, and children. And they, too, waited.

Behind them were the heads of Taiping brigades, amongst them Maxi, who stood out like a dumpling on a bed of eggplant.

At last the musicians entered and bowed to the Heavenly King then took their places downstage left.

All was still for a moment. Then, with a cymbal crash, the play began.

From upstage right twelve women in perfect step move effortlessly onto the stage and float in quick circles, chanting their sorrow. The patterns they make vary, then vary again, eventually revealing the figure of the small Serving Man standing very still all the way upstage. Horns sound, then more cymbals and a long, sustained note on the two-stringed arhu follows. Then silence. Then more horns, and the Lord of the East makes his entrance with his full entourage. They come to a dramatic stop and the Lord of the East steps forward, then strikes a startling pose and sings, "Bring her here, to me, my daughter. Bring her to her father. To accept her duty to her father and her kingdom. Bring my daughter here."

But rather than the daughter, the daughter's nurse glides forward and in high-pitched wails presents the distress of the Princess. Several times the Lord of the East silences her and commands her to get his daughter. Finally the nurse relents and in a beautiful aria sings of the sorrow of duty when one is "married to the kingdom and a daughter of the state." Once more the Lord of the East commands her to get her charge. Before she does, she approaches the Lord of the East, challenging his wrath, and reminds him that his daughter is the "very jewel in your crown" and her leaving "will plant a tear in your heart."

The Lord of the East orders the Nurse to get his daughter. Then he and his counsellors sing of the onerous task of bearing the weight of state on their shoulders, ending with, "Even a loved daughter is not more to us than our love of our land."

The horns give way to a chopping snarling series of echoing notes from the arhu. In syncopation to the beat, the young Princess arrives. She wears a headdress with two tall feathers, and the sleeves of her Chinkiang silk gown are rolled up to expose her hands. She glides across the stage with such grace that the audience literally gasps. The tilt of her body shows the weight of sorrow on her back, her floating entrance her high status, and her two-feathered headdress her sensual allure. She turns as she comes to centre stage and looks out at the audience, then reaches up and pulls one long feather down into her mouth, strikes a pose on one foot, and opens her mouth — as in a scream — but all that is heard is a single sustained note from the arhu. Her sorrow is music itself.

The ensuing scene is surprisingly sweet. The daughter professes loyalty to her father, he his love to her. Then he commands her to go to the King of the West as a new wife to seal the treaty of peace between the two kingdoms. She bows. All seems well until she races downstage and throws her arms up in the air. The rolled-up sleeves climb the air to the top of the stage and seem to hang there, as if waiting to be told what to do next. The horns' sorrowful moans fill the stage as the Princess of the East sings her song of parting.

At the end of the song there was not a dry eye in the audience. The Heavenly King, Hung Hsiu-ch'uan, shouted "*Hoa!*" which was echoed throughout the courtyard. The actress waited, collected herself, and when the cheering crested she once again stepped forward.

As imperious as the Manchu Dowager Empress, the Princess demands to know how she is going to be escorted to her new husband, two thousand miles away.

A cymbal crashes, then horns sound in discord, and the small Serving Man at the back of the stage steps forward. He doesn't dance, or glide, or juggle, or tumble — he simply steps forward, and bows low.

The Princess shoots a look at her father and throws her sleeves out toward him. But the Lord of the East is unmoved. "Trust him, daughter. For I trust him, with your life."

The stage erupts in motion as the entire court moves in a scatter pattern about the stage. Forty bodies in seemingly random patterns, which are anything but random, producing the effect of a whirlwind, blowing the beloved daughter away from her father.

Maxi held his breath. He'd watched the History Teller work on this section for hour after hour. Rehearsing, changing, retrying — searching for the pattern of bodily motion that was random but exquisite, like the woman herself. And Maxi saw the beauty and stood to holler, "*Hoa*!" Every eye in the audience turned to him. Stunned. Few had ever heard him speak a single word of the Common Tongue in public. They shouted "*hoa*" back at him, this time cheering his use of Mandarin as well as the performance. But Maxi didn't care. He saw the beauty of the History Teller's work and hollered "hoa" again — for both her art and her person.

This scene is followed by a tearful goodbye with the nurse, whose attendants are all there to strew the way with rose petals for the departing Princess.

The journey of the Princess and the Serving Man does not begin well. She is not pleased to be going, not pleased to be virtually unescorted, and furious that her only companion is a peasant. Silence, so rare in Peking Opera, dominates the opening dance between the two — and indeed it is both a physical and emotional dance that ends with the Princess pointing toward the floor and the Serving Man kowtowing to her.

Then the journey begins in earnest. By taking a small bamboo shoot with cornsilk attached to it in her right hand, she indicates that she is riding — while the Serving Man walks. They venture across rivers, over mountains, through open plains and blistering deserts — all without the use of scenery, just the adjustment of the body position of the actors and the music — and the dance and the juggling and the tumbling — and the magic of Peking Opera. They encounter rogue soldiers that they fight off, merchants with whom they bargain for water and food, other nobles who refuse to meet their eyes, Taoist monks who bless their travels, mad-eyed mullahs who attack the travellers, and other pilgrims who join them on their march to the West. The companions change, the dangers increase — the closeness between the Princess and the Serving Man grows.

Finally in crossing a swift stream, the Princess is saved from falling by the Serving Man, who in turn is hurled down the river where he smashes into a large rock. It breaks his leg cleanly between hip and knee. The Princess dismounts and insists that he ride. When he is unable to bear the pain anymore they make camp and the Princess nurses him. That night (in a scene that brought the entire audience to its feet) the Serving Man cries out in pain in his sleep and the Princess crosses over and lies beside him while she sings to the haunting strains of the arhu.

Then the action returns to the court of the Lord of the East, who misses his daughter and needs help dealing with the new intrigues of the court.

The History Teller hated it. It was so obvious that the only reason the scene was there was to allow time for the audience to believe that the Serving Man had recuperated from his injury enough to continue the journey. She watched and tried to contain her irritation. She knew the audience needed a break from the story of the Serving Man and the Princess, but she wasn't sure about returning to the Lord of the East. She knew that the reason she chose it was that the audience already knew the Lord of the East so he didn't have to be reintroduced. She wondered, though, if she could jump ahead in the story and bring on the Lord of the West. She had never seen a story jump ahead in its time sequence. She wondered how that would work. How would she get back to the chronological story after she did that? For a moment she was outside the event, looking down on it, as one would at a raw piece of ivory that awaited the sculptor's chisel.

The performance was now in its fifth hour but was only reaching the climax of its fourth of seven acts, in which the family who has joined the Princess and the Serving Man in their travels is threatened by the Monkey King in the high mountain passes. The Serving Man must choose between his duty to defend the Princess and his duty as a fellow human being to confront the Monkey King to save the helpless family. The interior conflict of the Serving Man is explored in a most extraordinary feat of juggling with throwing clubs that the actor performs while he sings his dilemma.

The next scene once again brought the audience to its feet, but this time not to cheer or cry — but in fear. Loa Wei Fen had arrived.

This audience had never seen the likes of Loa Wei Fen's performance as the Monkey King; no audience in the Middle Kingdom had ever seen its like. From his leaping entrance to his tumbling run across the stage to grab the child, to his race with the wife up to the highest point of the mountain — it was completely unique. At the exact place where reality and art meet.

The History Teller watched in awe. Loa Wei Fen had made the leap from form to feeling, but what he was doing was not really acting. There was no distance between performer and performance. The danger seemed real because it was real. For the hundredth time, the History Teller wished she had demanded more information about the strange boy/man when her mother had insisted she take him into her troupe. The performance was startling, grotesque but beautiful. To add to the shock of it, the History Teller had removed all the dialogue. Loa Wei Fen as the Monkey King never made a sound, but the music and the physical reality of his performance lifted the entirety of the event to another plain. A dangerous plain that both tantalized and appalled the History Teller.

The History Teller leaned back against the post to watch the climactic ending of the scene. Not only was the violence unexpected, but it came on what the History Teller thought of as the "offbeat," so that just as the audience relaxed, the Monkey King made a sudden, fatal lunge.

The Heavenly King clambered back up onto his raised throne, amazed that he, in response to the Monkey King, had actually leapt out of his seat. His feet had landed on the mud ground! The young girl in charge of the lower half of his body quickly knelt and swept up any part of the dirt that may have touched her lord's foot. The moon was now high overhead and the stars were in their early summer brilliance. The "brother of Jesus" readjusted his robes and returned his attention to the stage performance.

The final days of walking in the scorching desert challenge the Princess's and the Serving Man's endurance. Twice they come upon oases that are dry. In the intense cold of the desert night they huddle together for warmth — but also because they have now become lovers.

The History Teller was most pleased with this sequence. She had layered in physical clues throughout the play to lead up to their joining — and it was done simply, almost casually, as if their coming together was no more unusual than a man holding a door open for a lady.

As they approach the end of the act they begin to stagger, thinking they cannot go farther. They think of simply lying down side by side in the sand and allowing the carrion birds to find them, but the Princess's sense of duty to her father forces them back to their feet.

Shortly thereafter the clamour of horns and cymbals announce the arrival of the Lord of the West's cavalry. All forty of the actors, dressed as soldiers with the small bamboo switches in their hands to indicate they are riding horses, enter the stage, and once again an intricate dance of seeming randomness ensues that ends with the reveal of the interior of the court of the Lord of the West.

The Princess bows. "My Lord and husband, may I introduce the man who guided me all the way from the court of my father?"

"Enough!" shouts the Lord of the West. He is unconcerned with her and orders her brought to the house of his concubines. But as she is hurried out, she tries to get one final look at the Serving Man.

In the last scene the entire stage goes into tableau, forty actors perfectly still — a single note of the arhu sounds and the Princess floats out from upstage. She stands behind the Serving Man and reaches up. She grabs the feathers from her headdress and pulls them down into her mouth, arches her back, and lets out a cry that is a perfect third above the note of the arhu. The arhu moves up to her note and she pitches her cry up to the fifth. The arhu moves to the fifth and she moves to the tonic. The arhu moves to the tonic and she to the third, and on and on for what seems like a suspended moment in time. As if her broken heart has torn through the fabric of time itself — and they fall — and the audience falls with them.

The crowd rose as one and howled its approval.

Then the cymbals sound and the Princess steps in front of the Serving Man. "What will you do now?" she sings. He doesn't look at her, as he responds, "I will walk back to the lands of the East. Alone." The tableau breaks and the Princess is swept away into the anonymity of the house of concubines, no more important to the Lord of the West than a new horse for his stables, while the Serving Man takes his initial step on his two-thousand-mile journey back to the East — with only the memory of the Princess who loved him as company.

Later that night Nanjing was thrown open — a true oddity for the Taipingers — to celebrate the first complete performance of *Journey to the West*. But it was a strange kind of celebration. Men and women on the whole were kept apart, and there was no alcohol, as it was against one of the Heavenly King's God-inspired edicts. But, nonetheless, the city celebrated. Perhaps it would be more accurate to say that the city "released." There was something that approached dancing in the streets, music where there had been little before, and people chanced offending the authorities by shouting their joy to the night skies.

After the acting troupe had been introduced to the Heavenly King and his consorts they were allowed to join the revels — such as they were.

That evening the History Teller wandered the streets of this alien city — a city strewn with banners. Some exhorted the people to work harder for the good of Jesus's brother, the Heavenly King; others warned the people of dire consequences should they break the laws of the Heavenly Kingdom, especially the laws segregating men from women; other large banners spoke of the requirement of prayer and the rules against breaking the Sabbath; but the largest banners were devoted to the prohibition against the use of alcohol and opium — special emphasis was put upon this final prohibition.

Yet the people seemed to be happy. There was evidently enough money to go around. Unlike Shanghai, there were no beggars on the streets of Nanjing. Nor were there women with bound feet. Women also didn't seem to be subservient to the men, and many of them led both military and work units. All dressed modestly and were covered from the neck down, despite the warmth of the evening. All businesses inside the city walls were run by the Taiping government, although there were several private businesses outside the walls, often using the city wall as the back wall of the shop.

It was in one of these private businesses, a restaurant, that the History Teller looked up from her excellent noodles and found herself staring, across the room, into the deep pools of Maxi Hordoon's eyes.

The red-haired *Fan Kuei* nodded.

The History Teller pointed to the empty seat across from her.

Maxi walked across the restaurant. At her table, she pointed to the empty chair again and smiled. He sat. A young *Fan Kuei* soldier stepped forward and offered to translate for Maxi. Maxi knew the man as one of the mercenaries hired by the Taiping Kings. Maxi found the idea of being paid to fight distasteful but was grateful for the man's service.

"You have found a fine restaurant, History Teller," Maxi said through the translator.

"By accident, I assure you."

"I doubt that. The food inside the city walls is not very good."

"True." The History Teller smiled. "I left two government restaurants whose food was literally hard to swallow."

Maxi smiled, then asked, "Do you have a name?"

"I used to, Mr. Hordoon, but now people call me the History Teller."

"And that's what you want me to call you?"

"No."

"Then what?"

"I don't know yet, but I'll let you know, when I know."

Loa Wei Fen watched the History Teller leave the small restaurant with the red-haired *Fan Kuei*. The actors in the troupe didn't feel comfortable in his presence, and that was okay with him. He didn't feel all that comfortable with them, and when one suggested that there had to be "some real fun in this town" he left their company and began to wander the streets of the ancient capital.

Once he left the wealth and beauty of the compound of the Heavenly King things changed quickly. The old city was drab and grey; the people seemed drab and grey, too. There were no bright lights here, no bustle, no outward joy of being alive, and very, very few *Fan Kuei*. He quickly realized that he was being followed and it almost made him laugh, although Loa Wei Fen seldom laughed. He made a sharp turn down an alley and in a single step was running at full speed. A wall scaled, a window climbed up to — and his followers were gone.

But of course, now it was him following — following the History Teller and the red-haired *Fan Kuei* out into the countryside. The inky blackness of the night made his task simple. As they walked he often came within ten yards of them. With his keen eyesight he matched their footfalls and inhalations. They never sensed his presence — although he was acutely aware of them, of everything about them: their steps in perfect pace, her height equal to his, their hands touching, seemingly inadvertently, from time to time.

At the small but neatly kept farmhouse, the *Fan Kuei* and the History Teller removed their shoes, and Loa Wei Fen circled the building. Finding an open door to a dank cellar, he entered and stood very still. He heard them above. He felt his way in the darkness and found a ladder that led to a door in the floor, which he opened an inch. Through the crack he saw Maxi pour wine for the History Teller and a Hakka woman bring out a newborn and two young girls. It was obvious from the way that the red-haired *Fan Kuei* held the baby that the child was his own. The two young girls held their mother's hands, but when they were called over to be introduced to the History Teller they were happy to be with the red-haired *Fan Kuei*. *These must be stepchildren*, Loa Wei Fen thought.

After their wine and a sticky rice pastry that the History Teller proclaimed to be the finest she'd ever tasted, she and the *Fan Kuei* went out into the fields. Loa Wei Fen retraced his steps and followed them. The fields smelled of newly laid fertilizer, probably nightsoil. But the sky was clear and the wind blew gently. Loa Wei Fen climbed a small tree and watched the two of them walk side by side through the rows of sorghum and soya and then enter the dense field of tall bamboo canes. Something about their body language made Loa Wei Fen's heart ache. It was clear to him that these two, despite the *Fan Kuei's* Hakka wife and children, were destined to discover something Loa Wei Fen had never had — love.

That night the History Teller slept in the open room on fresh mats laid on the floor by the Hakka woman. But she was not alone. Up above her, stretched out on a rafter beam, was Loa Wei Fen, watching, protecting the woman for whom his heart ached, the History Teller.

35

DEAL WITH A DEVIL; DEAL WITH AN ANGEL

Various locales in the Celestial Kingdom
1860

The Dowager Empress, Tzu Hsi — also known as "Old Buddha" — looked at her beautiful feet and smiled. They were her pride, now that the glitter in her eyes had dulled and the skin of her face had spotted brown. Her feet remained her final claim to the great beauty of her youth. Ah, she had been a very great beauty — a famous beauty — and had taken full advantage of her exquisiteness to satisfy her gargantuan sexual appetites. Even the memory made her glow and waters move where they had not moved in quite some time. Was it the danger that quickened her, loosed her interior streams — gave her access to the lava flow? She didn't know, but she enjoyed the motion, the life within that even further curled her tiny toes beneath her perfectly arched foot.

"Majesty?"

She'd forgotten that the ugly man was standing at attention waiting for her to answer some question or other. She didn't know which. She'd almost forgotten that she was at a war council that she herself had ordered into session. These were ugly men, though, of that she was sure. The ugliest she had seen in some time. Still, they were better warriors than the pretty ones she had appointed at the beginning of this noisome rebellion.

"Majesty?"

"Report," she said with a curt nod. That was always a good thing to say.

"Yes, Majesty. The rebels approached our Shanghai positions in force. They were led by General Li Xiucheng."

Another cow-faced man, she thought. *This one I'll have boiled in oil when they catch the insolent pup.*

"Majesty, they sent letters in advance to the heads of each of the *Fan Kuei* groups guaranteeing the safety of their persons and property. All they wanted from the Round Eyes was a continuation of their neutrality while they attacked our positions."

But the Fan Kuei did not remain neutral, she thought. Her spies had already told her that the Taiping assault on the Chinese section of Shanghai had been repulsed by the guns from the *Fan Kuei* ships. But why? She stood, and the men in the room leapt to their feet. She smiled, inside this time. Her smile was not for the consumption of these ugly men. She walked with the oh-so-desirable hip-swivelling gait that was the natural result of the binding of her feet as a little girl. It had hurt terribly but she'd never cried, never showed the world the cost of attaining beauty — great beauty — celestial beauty.

When she came to a stop two servants rushed to place a satin stool behind her. Without looking down the Dowager Empress of China plopped her rump on the padded seat. As she did, she remarked, "Perhaps it is time to approach the Foreign Devils — perhaps it is finally time for them to join us in ridding the Celestial Kingdom of these heavenly fools." Then she thought of the ugliness of the Foreign Devils and momentarily the sweetmeats she had consumed an hour before threatened to move up her throat and out her mouth. She let out a breath that picked up the scent of the anise flower that she kept in her left cheek and listened to her stomach flip one last time. Perhaps it was better just to poison the *Fan Kuei*'s water supply and be done with them. She smiled at the thought — to rid the world of so many ugly people at one time pleased her. She glanced at her tiny feet in her tiny satin shoes and thought, *Beautiful. Truly beautiful.*

She looked up at her ugly generals and said, "Offer the *Fan Kuei* trading access to Beijing if they commit their forces to join ours to rid China of these Taiping fools." She looked away. How long could she bear to look at these unsightly men? Then she thought, *First the Fan Kuei will help us eradicate the Rebels, and then I will eradicate them.*

Maxi reached up and touched the tunnel struts beneath the Taiping stronghold. He gave one a yank and it didn't budge. He shook his head.

The three Taipingers with him hadn't seen their strange red-haired *Fan Kuei* behave like this before. His translator, a Hakka man whom Maxi called Cupid, asked, "Is something wrong, sir?"

Maxi called the man Cupid because he couldn't begin to pronounce the man's Hakka name, and the man also had a bizarrely tiny bow-shaped mouth. But Maxi had also been to battle with Cupid and knew him to be a man with a warrior's heart, and because of that he trusted him, not something Maxi did often or easily.

"They're getting better," Maxi said.

"The Manchus?"

"Yes, the Manchus, unless someone else built this tunnel," Maxi, uncharacteristically, snapped. Maxi had successfully defended several of the Taipingers' walled cities against Manchu attack. His strategy wasn't complicated. Once he was sure the city's walls were sound — and many of the walls were very sound — then he knew the attack would have to come from underground. That being the case he sent out spies to try to establish where dirt piles were accumulating. Then he drew what amounted to a straight line from the dirt pile to the nearest section of the city's walls. That was where the tunnel would be. In the night he'd instruct his men to dig down and intersect the Manchu tunnel.

Initially he'd simply diverted sewage from the town into the tunnels and allowed the townspeople to laugh at their filth-covered enemy as they emerged. Naturally the laughing citizens were safely behind their yards-thick walls. Then he'd begun to undermine the tunnels themselves, strategically removing solid struts and replacing them with hollow pieces of timber filled with blasting charges. When his spies told him that the Manchus had entered their tunnels he would set off the charges and the tunnel would collapse on them. The strategy had worked for quite some time, but this tunnel was different. It was built by a craftsman. Maxi, despite himself, admired the workmanship. Then he said, "Blow it up," and returned to the surface.

Once back above ground he turned to Cupid and said, "I want to go up." Cupid hollered a series of orders and a horse was brought. Maxi leapt on its back and cantered down the rickety streets to the hill on the west side of the city centre. Standing on the back of his horse he reached for a rope harness that hung from a sturdy, tall pole and fitted it about his waist — just as he had done years ago in India, when he had retrieved the Hordoon brothers' first opium supply. With one end of the rope dangling he grabbed the other and hoisted himself into the air. As he did, he admired the lightness and strength of the silk ropes and the efficiency of the knots he had learned onboard the ship that had first brought him and his brother to China. He had since sat with several Taiping craftsmen and they'd made porcelain block-and-tackle devices to direct the ropes, so that now he could hoist himself high in the air, and then switch harnesses and pull himself along an adjoining guidewire across the top of the crowded city.

The children ran beneath him trying to keep up, but this was no game. This city had been under siege for almost three months and the system he had developed allowed him to see the oncoming armies of the Manchus — the seemingly endless oncoming armies — armies that were getting better at their craft. The glint of light on the ground in the west fulfilled his worst fears — the Manchus were building a moat. They had made real advances in their ability to guide the course of rivers, and now they'd ushered the water into their moat, from which they would guide it toward the walls. Walls were nothing more than two stacks of bricks or stone filled with only dried mud between the masonry. If the Manchus were able to channel their moat water toward the walls, the dried mud would soak up the water and make the walls themselves unstable. And there was nothing Maxi could do about it.

The Manchus had finally found a way to besiege the Taiping cities. Maxi let himself down slowly. A grim smile was on his face.

"What?" asked Cupid.

"Nothing," Maxi answered, but he knew that the Taipingers couldn't win, and this brave man would undoubtedly die for a doomed cause.

It never occurred to Maxi to worry about his own safety. He was responsible for the safety of others, and that was all that concerned him.

Eliazar Vrassoon squirmed uncomfortably. It was quickly approaching sundown and it was Friday. But the two men standing in front of him seemed to be in no hurry to complete their business. If this had been opium business or silk business or rubber business or silver business, then Vrassoon would have put up his hands and called a stop to the proceedings. He had religious obligations that, unlike business negotiations, could not wait. But these men in front of him were not traders. They were emissaries sent directly from Tzu Hsi, the Dowager Empress of China. And they were proposing a most interesting arrangement — a deal to allow the traders full access to the very heart of China, to Beijing and its surrounds.

The interior of China had remained entirely off limits to the traders. They had entered the Yangtze and traded with varying degrees of success upriver until the Taipingers took over Nanjing, but never up the Grand Canal to Beijing itself. Few Whites had ever seen the interior of China's capital city. None had entered the Empress's Forbidden City. Despite the specific agreements in the Treaty of Nanjing, the Chinese had always refused to allow any foreigner into their capital, let alone permit *Fan Kuei* to trade freely in Beijing.

Vrassoon glanced out the window. The sun had not yet set — but it would shortly. He stood quickly and the Manchu Mandarins were shocked into silence. "Tell her Majesty in Beijing that I am very interested in her proposition and will present it to the other traders. Now, as you can see, the sun is going down, and I have religious obligations that call upon my time."

The translator stumbled over this last, since religious obligations linked to sunset were the result of ancient desert thinking — not the thinking of the Middle Kingdom that joins Heaven and Earth. Eventually he conveyed Vrassoon's basic meaning.

The Mandarins both raised an eyebrow creating a humorous picture of Oriental confusion — where in fact none existed. Both men had been fully briefed concerning the odd "religious obligations" of the Vrassoon Patriarch and had purposefully extended their meeting to back up against the setting of the sun. Both men then bowed slightly and canted their heads to one side — perfect bookends again. But Eliazar Vrassoon didn't notice. He had already left the room and was heading toward the Beth El Synagogue — a place he had built and that he found very good for the contemplation of both religious and strategic problems. If his mind had been so inclined he might have seen the similarities between the two — but the Vrassoon Patriarch's mind was not so inclined.

After sunset of the next day Eliazar Vrassoon presented the Dowager's offer to the heads of Dent, Oliphant, and Jardine, Matheson — he felt no need to contact the Baghdadi boy. The men listened in what Hercules thought of as a perfunctory silence. Then the Scot broke that silence with a single word: "Why?"

"Indeed," Percy St. John Dent added, "why bother? The rebellion has been a boon to our little town. Without it we'd still be lifting and toting our own goods and living without servants or retainers. Now, thanks to the violence in the countryside, Shanghai prospers — we prosper. Why endanger that on the promise of a Celestial? We all know how much such promises are worth. They still haven't lived up to their side of the Treaty of Nanjing and it's been more than fifteen years."

He didn't bother mentioning that the traders hadn't lived up to their side of the treaty either, but that wasn't the issue as far as Percy St. John Dent, now the head of Dent and Company of London, was concerned.

Vrassoon thought this all a bit short-sighted and said as much. But the traders were making money — lots of money — and were unwilling to risk the opium markets they had for those that they might get.

When she was told of the *Fan Kuei*'s refusal of her offer, the Dowager Empress gripped the arms of her golden chair so hard that she snapped the long nail on the middle finger of her left hand. She looked at the stub of the nail that remained. The blunt end was deeply yellowed. She knew that fungus was alive in the tissue and that it could not be eradicated. She hated the idea that something was growing in her. Something foreign. But then again, something infinitely foreign was growing in her country. Two foreign things! The damnable *Fan Kuei* in Shanghai and elsewhere, and the Taiping religious fanatics in Nanjing. *One at a time*, she told herself, *deal with them one at a time.*

She looked up at the waiting men. "Bring him in," she said simply.

A low-ranking officer turned and left the chamber. Moments later he returned, followed by an officer whose right eye drooped from its socket. He had been in charge of securing all the territories that the Manchu armies had wrested from the Taipingers. It was a hard job, since the filthy peasants and thieving merchants would turn around and sell their mothers for a bolt of cloth or a bucket of rice. And the Taipingers always returned, and by coercion or force or both often regained the support of the locals. Without local support there was no way to secure territory, and without secured territory there could be no reliable base from which to mount the final assault on Nanjing. It had been a serious problem until the man who stood before her, the man she'd heard them speak of as the Droopy-Eyed General, had taken control. The man's viciousness was the stuff of legend. His willingness to tie hundreds of men to piles of brush and then set them alight had changed the loyalties of many a peasant — and every merchant.

He had also conducted several successful sieges against Taiping-held cities by diverting water to undermine the defensive walls. The details of such things were both shadowy and of no concern to Tzu Hsi, Dowager Empress of China.

She looked more closely at the man. A tear had formed in the droopy eye and it was about to fall to his cheek when his hand viciously swiped it aside.

Good, she thought, *he is furious with any sign of weakness. I can use such a man.*

Maxi held the baby in his arms and looked at the deep, dark pools that were her eyes. *Mine*, he thought, *mine*. His Hakka wife held the hands of her two children as they all, as a family, walked through the tall canes in his bamboo stand. The wind blew gently through the stalks making them sway. And Maxi's family was in their midst so they swayed too — no different from the canes, all part of one great, moving thing, just as Maxi had felt all those years ago in India when he and Richard had worked with the opium farmers.

Then he saw them standing on the far hill — waiting for him. His wife saw them a moment later and grabbed at his hand and begged him not to go to them. But there was no real argument. These men were from the Heavenly King — no doubt this new general they called the Droopy-Eyed One had taken the field to the east of Nanjing.

Maxi held the baby close to him and rubbed his rough chin against her silky cheeks. The baby laughed. Maxi knew that he would have to defeat the Manchu General if he were ever to hear that laugh again.

If Maxi had known his Bible stories he might have been aware of the parallels between him facing the Droopy-Eyed General and David facing Goliath — but Maxi neither knew nor cared about such desert-inspired fairy tales. He appreciated them as stories, just as he appreciated the Shakespeare stories that Richard used to tell him, but he never saw Bible stories as morality tales, let alone stories with any portent.

The Droopy-Eyed General was backed by five times the number of troops that Maxi commanded — fine. *Just one factor in deciding the outcome of the day*, Maxi thought. He looked toward the rising sun and for a moment wondered what Richard was doing at that precise moment. He hadn't thought of his brother in a long time. Then he thought of the History Teller and a pang threaded through his heart, so sharp but so sweet that for an instant he wobbled on his feet. Finally he took the red kerchief from his pocket and wound it round his head — the signal for his left flank to charge the siege forces of the Droopy-Eyed General.

"What?" the Droopy-Eyed General shouted as he turned in the saddle of his desert pony.

The adjutant repeated the message from their right flank. They were under attack and requesting orders.

"Tell them to fall back slowly, and send me the commander of our centre."

The man arrived quickly and the Droopy-Eyed General told him of the slow pull back of their right flank. "Should we wheel on the rebels as they chase our troops?" he asked.

The Droopy-Eyed General stared at the man. Finally he spoke. "Why else would I have let our men fall back? Rouse yourself. The day is upon us."

Maxi's men advanced quickly against the enemy's right flank, and much to his surprise the Manchus didn't stand their ground but gave way under the attack. His adjutants were joyful but Maxi was unsure. He galloped to the highest hill and once again hauled himself up by a rope-and-pulley system — and what he saw terrified him. As his men advanced, the whole centre of the Droopy-Eyed General's army wheeled right and were setting up to attack Maxi's exposed flank. He hollered an order to his adjutant then loosed himself down onto the back of his horse and galloped at full speed to catch up to his left flank.

He managed just in time to get to the flag-bearers in the rearguard to signal a retreat — and not a moment too soon. Twenty minutes later and his forces would have been devoured by the massive power of the Droopy-Eyed General's centre.

"What?" screamed the Droopy-Eyed General as he was given the report of the escape of Maxi's left flank. "Bring that general here with his men."

A half hour later, the general of the Manchu right flank knelt before the Droopy-Eyed General, who looked past him and addressed the assembled troops.

"This man," he said as he ripped the general's silk robe, "failed you. He failed me as well." The Droopy-Eyed General drew his sword and with a scything motion cut at the man's neck. Much to his consternation his cut did not go all the way through. A tear built in his malformed eye, but before it came to his cheek he swung a second and then a third time, until the man's head fell from his shoulders. Then the Droopy-Eyed General swiped the tear aside with his sleeve and shouted at his men, "We are not here to fail. Is that clear?"

He leapt onto his horse and rode to the battle front. As he approached, the bannermen lifted their flags and horns sounded. As much from fear as from loyalty, the Manchus cheered their leader.

"He's vain," Maxi said through his translator to his assembled captains.

"And ugly," one of the younger captains quipped.

Maxi knew that the two sometimes went together, the physical deformity causing the overweening pride. He thought about that and the new tunnel structures he'd been finding. Pride. He had met many prideful men. Then he smiled. Prideful men often thought themselves excessively smart. He ordered his men to go on shifts to mark their way through the night. To Cupid he said, "Assemble the generals, we need a plan." To himself he added, *A complex plan for a vain man who thinks he's smarter than the rest of us.*

With the generals assembled, Maxi began.

"My brother used to read me stories when we were young. One, a play called *Cymbeline*, had a lot to say about deception and vanity. Vanity is all about appearance, and this Manchu General needs to be shown he is important because in his heart, and maybe this time in his eye, he knows he's not."

"So let's give him the tribute he wants, that Manchus have always wanted since they invaded the Middle Kingdom all those years ago. I think a huge trunk filled to the brim with silver and gold — and two of our most beautiful women should suffice."

The Taiping generals balked at that. Sex was an entirely forbidden subject in the Heavenly Kingdom. Maxi saw the resistance and said, "We all make sacrifices for the Heavenly King — some with our lives — these two but with their modesty." Maxi gave the generals only a moment to object. Then he went on. "Go tell the History Teller what we want. She'll know how to dress the women."

"How big should the trunk be?"

"I'll have designs for our artisans by evening. I want only our best craftsmen to work on this — and only men we trust."

"And the gold and silver?"

"Get it for me. If things work out properly it will just be a loan."

"But how does giving this monster money and women help us defeat him?"

"As in that play I mentioned, there will be something other than money and women in the trunk — on this, trust me."

The Taiping artisans stared at the crude design Maxi had presented them but did not speak. Finally Maxi asked, "Can you make this?"

"Do you have permission for us to make something like this?" the head artisan asked, pointing to the coitally entwined figures of a nude man atop a nude woman on the lid of the six-and-a-half-foot-long trunk. The man's face was buried in the woman's neck, his arms lost beneath her back, while the woman's face was turned out, her eyes open, looking outward while her left arm reached with her fingers splayed.

"I give you permission," Maxi assured them.

There was a lengthy silence that finally the head artisan broke. "And the man's figure is to be solid but the woman's hollow?"

"Yes."

"The woman's figure is rather large ... for a woman."

"Yes, it is," Maxi replied, "and the floor of the trunk should be four inches thick, made of mahogany."

The artisan nodded. He knew that no knife could penetrate a

hard wood to that depth. "What about the lid beneath the woman's hollow figure?"

Maxi thought for a moment then said, "No. No extra depth there."

"So there is no protection from below for whoever is inside the hollowed-out woman's figure?" the man asked.

"Either the deception works or it doesn't," Maxi said.

The artisan nodded slowly, then asked, "How long will the person have to be inside the hollowed figure?"

"A while." Maxi sighed. "Just tell me if it can be done."

The artisan looked quickly to the other craftsmen then shrugged as he said, "It can be built." The man hesitated.

"What?" Maxi demanded.

"How will the hidden figure get to the latch to release himself?"

Maxi thought about that. Then his toothy smile lit up his face. "Put a silk ribbon in the woman's hair and thread it into the cavity."

The artisan nodded, then asked, "But how shall it be tied?"

Maxi nodded, an old memory from onboard a ship sailing from India to China filled his head, and he said, "Leave the tying of the knots to me."

At noon the following day, emissaries were sent to the Droopy-Eyed General with a proclamation that did not surrender the city but requested: *the right to present to the most honoured General a token of our esteem for his greatness.*

Although two of the emissaries were kept as hostages, the third returned with a note outlining exactly how and where the "token" was to be delivered. Maxi was not surprised by the demand for much pomp and ceremony to accompany the delivery of the Taipingers' gift.

At the appointed hour Cupid led the small but stately group, who presented the massive carved chest filled with gold and silver, along with the two girls, to the Droopy-Eyed General. The Manchu was much impressed with both the gold and silver and the girls — or so Maxi was later told.

Maxi felt the trunk lid being flung open and he assumed the Manchu was examining the wealth. Then Maxi felt a heavy shock race through the wood and send shivers up his spine. It set his ears to ringing. As his hearing slowly returned it occurred to him that the Manchu must have thrust a knife, or more likely a spear, into the thick bottom of the chest.

Then Maxi felt the lid slammed shut and the whole chest being lifted. Maxi couldn't determine how long he was carried but the thump upon landing momentarily snapped his head up and then down, almost causing him to black out. After that he didn't remember much. The two hollow reeds in his mouth were slowly disintegrating from his spittle and he was worried that he wouldn't be able to get enough air from the tiny air holes without them. As well, his muscles had cramped badly, especially the muscles of his left arm that reached out toward the front of the chest. And he had a terrible need to urinate.

He held on as long as he could, then he reached for the silk ribbon that controlled the interior latch and pushed.

In his weakened condition the lid felt as though it weighed hundreds of pounds. But it opened smoothly and soundlessly as the artisans had promised.

The luxuriance of what he assumed was the Droopy-Eyed General's tent surprised him. In the dying light from the brazier, he saw a pair of feet extended past the end of the silk-swathed sleeping pallet. Maxi assumed the two Taiping girls were somewhere in the tent.

He hoped the Manchu had not hurt them. But that was all he could do for them — hope.

He slid his knife from his pant leg and allowed himself down from the large, carved chest. He thought about closing the lid then decided against it. He looked around the Manchu's tent and tried to discern exactly who was there. But all he could do was guess. Hope the girls were not hurt. Guess that the Manchu General preferred his sex in private. Too many variables, and he knew it.

The Manchu General saw the white-skinned ghost rise from the chest and smiled. Gold, silver, dead girls — and killing a *Fan Kuei*. A fine day.

On his raised bed the two dead girls lay in each other's arms. His little game of *show me yours and then I kill you* had been a great success as far as he was concerned. And then the ghost took out a knife.

Maxi whipped around and stared at the feet hanging off the end of the pallet bed. The feet had the slightest glint of nail polish. He spun quickly and threw himself to the floor.

The Manchu's knife sailed over Maxi's prone body.

The Manchu rose to call for his guards but he never got out a word as Maxi's fists crashed into his face and broke his nose. The droopy eye was no longer the most deformed part of the man's face.

Maxi grabbed the man's ceremonial sword from his sash. And as the General's droopy eye opened, Maxi raised the curved sword. The man turned his head to face his executioner and smiled.

Maxi's blow bisected the smile and the man's life leapt from his skull like a prisoner finally released.

Then Maxi waited. Shortly he heard it — the sound of shouting and the sound of gunfire, as he had ordered. Crouching in the recesses of the tent he watched the guards race in and discover the humiliation of their General.

As Maxi had hoped, word of the Manchu's death loosed chaos in the ranks, and as the Manchus tried to restore order in their midst, Maxi made his escape.

36

SHANGHAI PROSPERS

The City of Shanghai
May, 1860

Richard couldn't help smiling. He was selling units in his new four-storey apartment buildings faster than he could get them built. And they were being built with incredible speed. Bamboo scaffolds sprang from the ground in leaps and bounds. Peasants carried the world on their backs up the bamboo ladders to the masons and carpenters and framers above. And all of them — all the Chinese workers — now fought to work for the Foreign Devils. There were almost seventy thousand Chinese living in the Foreign Settlement, and many more awaited housing there. Richard almost laughed out loud when he remembered how he'd nearly lost everything he'd worked for because he couldn't find workers. Finding workers was no longer a problem.

His keen eye noted a set of bamboo canes lashed together along the front of the third floor that seemed to bow deeply when the workers set foot on them.

He felt a tug at his sleeve and looked into Lily's brutalized face. The ear holes, all that remained after her ears had been cut off by the Manchus, were carefully covered with her hair, but there was nothing she could do about the absent nose — the dark blotch in the middle of her face. She indicated the metal thermos bottle in her hand. He nodded, and she poured dark musky tea into an almost translucent porcelain cup, then covered it with an equally translucent porcelain lid and handed it to him. The skin of the underside of her baby finger just grazed his palm and she smiled — inwardly.

He took the lid from the tea and drank deeply. The dense flavour, once so foreign to him, was now comforting. He looked at Lily and smiled as he remembered her help in the village where he was millstoned. And she had been with him ever since. Always there. Never demanding anything from him except the odd smile. He smiled again, and she seemed to smile back. It was hard to tell with her features.

She tightened the cap on the thermos bottle and retreated a few steps — and awaited another opportunity to help the man she loved.

Then Richard heard the sharp report of bamboo cracking. He looked up and saw a workman, his back stacked high with bricks, slip off the tilting walkway and plunge toward the ground. Two other workmen threw off their loads and grabbed vertical struts just in time as the bamboo walkway snapped in two under their feet. Other workers tossed aside their loads and ran to help them.

Patterson, Richard's foreman on the project, raced over to him and pulled him aside. "There'll be trouble. You'd better leave."

"Is he dead?"

"The bugger who fell, him?"

Richard nodded.

"Aye. They're not built strong enough to take a fall like that."

"Why'd…?"

"Dunno, but it's suspicious."

"Sabotage?"

"Well, sir, there are those who don't enjoy your success."

Richard thought about that, then felt a familiar tug at his sleeve and looked down at Lily. "Go now. Must go now." She was eyeing the gathering mob of workers.

One stepped forward and pointed at Richard. "You killed him. You might as well have put a knife through his heart. You murdered him."

Patterson stepped forward and screamed, "No more monkey talkee! Back to workee! Chop chop!"

Richard touched Patterson on the shoulder and, much to the workers' surprise, stepped forward and spoke to them in the Common Tongue. "Was this man married and did he have children?"

Both questions, after a stunned silence, were answered in the affirmative.

"I will look after his family, since he died working for me."

A ripple of approval went through the crowd.

"Send for a Buddhist monk and have him buried properly. But I want to know why that scaffolding failed."

Half an hour later Richard stood beside the workers' leader and looked at the offending bamboo canes. For a moment Richard wished that Maxi were there, since he understood this kind of thing. But Maxi was far away and had been for a very long time.

Richard pointed to three long cracks in one of the bamboo canes. "Are these from too much weight on the walkway?"

The leader of the workers leaned down and ran his large, calloused hand along the cracks, then shook his head. He looked up, a scowl on his face.

Patterson moved to one side.

"Why is the wood so dry and brittle?" Richard asked.

The worker ran his finger along the edges and said, "Old. Needs to be fresh to be strong. Old is cheaper."

Richard nodded and turned. Patterson was gone.

Across the street the Vrassoons were tearing down an ancient courtyard building and putting up cheap tenements. He thought for a moment, then he strode forcefully across the street and demanded to see the foreman.

"Gonna be a fight, a real big fight, and the Brits are going to help the Johnny Rebs to get back at the Yanks, and the Yanks are going to invade the Johnny Rebs, and the cotton's going to burn or be blockaded and Europeans are going to wear scratchy wool for the foreseeable future. You gonna finish that beer, son, or wha?"

Silas passed his half-finished mug of beer over to the man who he assumed was an American, although he hardly seemed religious, which most Americans, in Silas's experience, were. How religious could he be sitting in the whorehouse waiting his turn?

"First time, lad?"

Silas wasn't interested in answering the man's question and was pleasantly surprised when a hand landed on his shoulder and a lilting, French-accented voice said, "Don't bother with the fool's questions. Your brother tells me that he is buying you a birthday present."

Silas nodded, intoxicated by Suzanne Colombe's perfume. He said, "Yes. It's my birthday," then added quickly for some reason, "my twenty-first birthday."

"Milo told me," Suzanne said, then added with a smile, "he celebrated his birthday a few days early."

"Did he? Why? We were born on the same day." Then Silas added, stupidly, "We're twins."

Suzanne smiled and said sardonically, "Really, I would never have guessed."

"Is Milo here?"

"Usually, but not tonight." She thought of telling Silas that his brother was in one of her opium dens but decided against it. She was enjoying speaking English. "Milo told me that you have never experienced the clouds and the rain?"

Silas didn't catch the reference and asked for it in Mandarin, which Suzanne supplied. He shook his head quickly, "No." Then he added, "Not yet."

Suzanne put an arm through his and walked him into the next room. The slightest trace of opium smoke scented the air. But Silas didn't notice. His eyes and senses were filled with the array of women sitting, lounging, laughing, playing cards.

Suzanne prodded him in the ribs with her elbow. "Is there anything here that you like?"

Silas had seen her the moment he walked into the room. Tiny compared to the French and English women, the Han Chinese girl sat quietly to one side. Her flawless skin drawn tight across her cheekbones, her beautiful tapered fingers arranging the cascade of her jet-black hair.

"Ah," Suzanne said, "I see."

The girl's skin was cool to the touch and her tongue a lightness almost indistinguishable from the air itself. But alive. Her mouth a warmth and her hands in motion, unbuttoning, caressing, pulling … then she stopped and stepped away from him.

Silas stood there, his pants and undergarments around his knees, not knowing what to do.

She pointed at his member.

For an instant he forgot how to speak Mandarin then finally found his words. "Is something wrong?"

Still pointing, she asked, "Did it hurt when you lost it?"

He tried to smile, never having spoken of his circumcised member before, let alone to a girl who was pointing at it. "No."

"Ah," she said, and placed her hand, light as a feather, on its cap. Then she guided him between her thighs and put her arms around his neck. With her tongue deep in his mouth she gently put him on his back and then placed his hands on her small breasts and murmured, "We'll bring the clouds and rain, together."

And her nimble body moved on his and heat came from her — and Silas felt all this happening to someone else — not him.

Patterson's report of Silas's twenty-first birthday celebration began with the charming phrase, "And there were all sorts of White whores and he chose the one Chinee twat in the place."

Richard ignored him, wanting to talk about how to keep their worksites safe, but Patterson insisted on continuing, "It reflects on me too, sir. What young Silas does reflects on all of us in the Foreign Settlement, it does."

Richard needed Patterson. The man knew building, and his willingness to mix it up with the Chinese contractors had saved Richard a small fortune. And although Richard never really trusted him, he paid him well enough that he expected some honesty from him. "So, my son's behaviour reflects badly on you, does it?"

Patterson drew himself up to his full height and said, "On all of us. All of us. We are as good as occupying their country, sir. And there are millions of them Chinee and only a few of us. How are we going to control them if we treat them like equals? They are not our equals. They are not Whites and we are. Simple as that." He looked away from Richard, whom he didn't consider a White at all but rather some kind of murky brown, then he muttered, "There are enough Chinee hotheads out there without shoving a hot poker up their butts by sleeping with their women. We need them to do what we say. We need them to work for us. We need them to accept our occupation. Your son doesn't seem to understand that."

Richard didn't completely disagree. He'd heard the rumblings before, and he was aware that it was a delicate matter to appease the upper-echelon Chinese so that they would continue to help keep the lower orders — well, in order. "Go find him and send him to me." Milo entered with Silas. "I would like to stay, father," he said.

"That might be, son, but this is between myself and your brother."

"But if it concerns him it concerns me, father."

"Sometimes, Milo, but not this time." Richard pointed toward the door of his office then made a "scat" gesture.

Milo turned to Silas, who shrugged his shoulders. "Go, brother mine," Silas said in Yiddish.

"What?" Milo asked in the Common Tongue.

"Go," Silas replied.

Milo left and Richard made sure the door was firmly shut, then he turned to his son. Before he could speak, Silas challenged him in Farsi, "You wanted to see me, father?"

"I did." Richard met the challenge in Farsi.

"Why?" Silas asked, switching to English.

"Because we have much to talk about," Richard replied in the Queen's tongue.

"Such as?" Silas asked in Mandarin.

"Don't question me, Silas," Richard replied in Mandarin.

"Well then, perhaps you need to question me, father," Silas said in Cantonese.

"Enough of the games!" Richard snapped in Shanghainese.

Silas corrected Richard's use of the idiom, then said, "Fine," naturally, in Shanghainese. They had at least agreed upon the language of the argument. "What is troubling you, father? I have done what you asked. I now spend time in the stables shovelling horse droppings, which was what you wanted."

"I want to understand what is going on with you."

That stopped Silas. For a brief moment he thought about telling his father his dark secret, but then he shrugged his shoulders and said, "Nothing is going on with me." Then he corrected Richard's word choice for the idiom "going on."

"Stop that. You know what I meant." Richard took a small cigar from a teakwood box on his desk and lit it. "You're not a boy anymore." A smile crossed his face. "How did you like your twenty-first birthday present from your brother and me?"

That surprised Silas. So his father had contributed to his night at the House of Paris. "It was a very thoughtful gift, father. Thank you."

Silas's formality brought a laugh to Richard's lips but he suppressed it. "Why with her? Come on, son, answer my question. With all the French and English girls there, why choose the Chinese girl?"

Because I was trying to find someone that could make me feel something, he wanted to shout, but couldn't. It would just sound stupid. So he said, "Did Mademoiselle Colombe report my choice?"

"In English or Mandarin. I don't speak French."

"Sorry. Did Miss Colombe tattle on me?"

"No. An American who was there told Patterson and he —"

"The drunk who claimed that every European would be wearing scratchy shirts soon?"

Richard stopped and put down his cigar. "What's that about scratchy shirts?"

Silas told him of the man's claim of an oncoming civil war between the North and South in America and the inevitable blockade that would stop the cotton trade out of the Americas to Europe.

Richard picked up his cigar and allowed the smoke to float up through his fingers. Then he said, "Tell me that again, but slower, and any detail you can think of, no matter how small, I want to hear it." He reached to the buzzer on his desk and pressed it. Instantly a secretary from the front office opened the door.

"Describe the man," Richard ordered Silas.

The boy did.

Richard turned to the secretary. "Find him. Bring him here. Take as many men as you need. Kidnap him if necessary. My bet is a bottle of whisky should do the trick. And bring me any other American you can find who has arrived recently."

The secretary nodded and left.

Richard turned to Silas. For the first time in Silas's life, he felt that his father actually wanted to hear him speak. It was possible that his father was actually smiling at him as he laced his hands behind his head and said, "Now tell me again about this drunken American."

After two days of interviewing Americans, Richard barged into Eliazar Vrassoon's private office. "There's no reason to buy cheap supplies and endanger the workers," Richard said to the stony visage of the Vrassoon Patriarch.

"Are you claiming...?"

"That your people have been selling my people the cheapest bamboo they can find? Yes, that's what I claim, but at this point in time I don't care about that. You win. I'm willing to leave the property game to you and your den of thieves." He recalled Milo advising him to stay abusive to avoid suspicion. That's why he was reeking of opium, despite the fact that he was stone-cold sober.

Then Richard threw the deeds to all of his properties on Vrassoon's desk. Just as he and Milo had planned it.

"Get out," the Patriarch said, with a steely cold that penetrated Richard's bones, and suddenly he wasn't sure he could pull it off, or that he wanted to pull it off. But he had lived his whole life walking on the edges of cliffs, going where others refused to go, and besides he was there — actually in Vrassoon's office — so he charged on.

"What? Is it Shavuos? Sukkott, then? Damn, I never remember when ... or is it Simchas Torah — fuck, I always miss Simchas Torah."

"Get out!" the Patriarch repeated, but Richard noticed that the man's eyes were devouring the property deeds on the huge mahogany desktop.

"Maybe you're right," Richard said, reaching forward and collecting the deeds together in a drunkard's pile. Then he felt a deeper coldness enter him as the old man's hand rested on top of his — the land deeds beneath both.

"How much do you want for these marginal properties? I'm willing to be generous but there is a glut of property now on the market and ..."

Richard slid his hand out from beneath the Patriarch's and, with what to Vrassoon was surprising dexterity, stacked the deeds and put them back in two large manila envelopes. "I think not. Perhaps I'd be better off with Hercules, or maybe even Dent's. I understand that both are angry that they didn't buy land when they could — that they left the field to us Yids."

The guards at the door made a move toward Richard but Vrassoon signalled them to back off. "How many properties are we talking about, son?"

Richard resisted saying, *I'm not your son!* and managed to smile as he enumerated the number, location, and potential revenue of each of his one hundred and seven properties without ever referring to the deeds.

The rest was just dickering. Since Richard knew exactly how much he needed, he refused to sell when the offer was too low and accepted when the offer rose to his needs. The whole process took less than three hours — substantially less time than it had taken him to buy up the entire cotton crop from the Shanghai delta lands — the cheapest fine cotton available in the world outside of Egypt and of course, the southern states of the United States of America, which just that morning had declared themselves independent from their federal government in Washington.

"How long should it take, father?" Milo asked as he went over the last of the warehouse contracts that he had settled with Chen.

"For what, Milo?"

"For the price of our cotton to go through the ceiling, naturally."

Richard lit a cigar and leaned back in his chair. Lily immediately came forward and supplied a fresh ashtray. Richard blew the blue-grey smoke into the evening air and shrugged his shoulders.

Milo stopped what he was doing with the warehouse contracts and stared at his father. "You don't know? Hell's bells, you don't know!"

"We're traders, son, not mystics. We invest and hope. Sometimes we win, sometimes we lose."

"And if we lose this time?"

"We lose it all. Warehouses, trading routes, steamships, even the house we're standing in."

"You mortgaged our house?"

"There's no point in having only *some* of the Shanghai delta cotton."

"You bought the whole crop?"

"And optioned the next two years', as well. I think the Americans will be fighting with themselves for a long time."

"Over slaves?"

Richard shook his head. "That war has nothing to do with slaves. It's got to be about money, control, and, you can bet your last *tael*, religion. And when religious nuts fight they fight for a long time. Usually until a new generation comes along and tells the old, bearded zealots to put their guns up their own arses, that no one cares whose God or gods are right or wrong. That it's time to recognize the obvious, that the world is clearly a place of random occurrences and whim. If there is a God up there, son, he's bored silly with us and awakens only periodically to tinker with our hearts and destroy our lives." Milo stared at his father. "Worried about my immortal soul, are we?"

"No, father, I don't give a damn about your immortal soul."

"Good, because I *have* no immortal soul, nor do you, nor do any of them."

"As you will."

"Fine, but what is it that is worrying you, then?"

"You cashed in everything that the Hordoons own, didn't you? Everything. If this goes bad we lose everything."

"Not true, son. Absolutely not true."

"Then you didn't sell everything we own?"

"Oh, that I did, son, that I did, every last item that had our names on it has been sold."

"Then I'm right, we could lose everything."

"Wrong."

"How am I wrong, father?"

Richard began to laugh so hard that he had to take the cigar out of his mouth. He sputtered with laughter. He rocked with laughter. He giggled and guffawed and roared with laughter. And Milo couldn't help himself and joined his father — and Lily thought the two had gone mad, quite mad.

Finally Milo got control of himself and pulled his father to his feet by the lapels of his waistcoat. "So, father, if you are wrong we end up with nothing."

His eyes streaming with tears of laughter, Richard shook his head. "Absolutely not — you'll have seventeen warehouses full of cotton!"

Within six months — six harrowing months in which Richard laid off his entire house staff, closed down all of his operations, and sold off the last of his ocean-going clippers — Richard's cotton gamble proved to be the single most successful commodities play the Middle Kingdom had ever seen. The cost of cotton doubled, then trebled, then doubled that — until finally Richard agreed to sell some of the only available cotton in the world — his Shanghai delta cotton — to keep the shirt factories of Manchester and the textile factories of Lyon and the clothing factories of Bremen afloat.

And money the likes of which had never been seen — more even than the wealth of the Kadooris' rubber monopoly in Siam — flowed into the coffers of Shanghai's Hordoon and Sons.

"Why aren't you happy, father? We won!" Milo asked.

Richard was still groggy from last evening's opium dreams. Groggy and haggard. He felt the snakes of opium trails in his blood, their slow, sinuous dance lingering where they were no longer wanted. He lunged toward the porcelain bowl in the water closet and doused his face with cold water, then looked in the mirror. The deep lines on his face surprised him. Behind him, in the mirror, his handsome son Milo stood waiting for him to answer his question. How handsome this boy was. How competent this boy was. How this boy loved him — how he loved this boy. He turned to face his adored son.

"Ask me again."

Milo did. "Why aren't you happy, father?"

Richard sighed deeply. *Because I'm haunted by whispers of a memory*, he wanted to say, but instead he put his hand on Milo's soft cheek and said, "The Vrassoons. The Vrassoons keep happiness from me."

"And me, father."

"Good. Now let us finally do something about that damnable family. Look, Milo, the source of much of the Vrassoons' power is the English parliamentary decree that grants them the sole right to sail ships directly from England to China. Everyone else has to figure out elaborate trade and counter-trade provisions at the various stops — Malay, India, Singapore, Ceylon, India, and finally the Azores before they land in England. This costs time and money and opens the vessels to danger from the pirates in the China Seas and the Straits of Malacca, and from other enemy vessels. Ships that need to make that many stops must also be lighter in weight so they can run before the wind and hence carry only limited cannon."

"I know all this, father, but —"

Richard charged on, "Not so the great Vrassoon boats of 'the Company.' Sometimes twice the size of ours and always armed to the teeth — the Company's ships are seldom the subject of attack. Their huge India Man sailing ships load in the safety of Plymouth and land in the equal safety of Shanghai, stopping in the six-month voyage only for food and fresh water. It's a tremendous — and vastly unfair — advantage over us and all the other traders. And why do they have this advantage? Are they better businessmen than us? Do they work harder? Do they risk more? No and no and no." He reached into the top drawer of his desk, slid a finger under the hidden panel there, drew out the doctored photograph of Vrassoon's eldest son with the little girl, and tossed it on the desk. "And why can a Vrassoon do this to a little girl and…?" That memory again tickled the back of his mind. But what little chance he had of retrieving it had been forever forfeited by his nightly opium voyages. "Why?" he demanded.

"Because they have the British Parliament behind them, father. This is nothing new."

"No, not new, but wrong, Milo. Wrong."

Milo reached across and looked at the photograph. He stared at the eldest Vrassoon son standing over the partially clothed Han Chinese girl with the flawless skin — maybe ten, maybe twelve years old — naked and bloody on the bed. The blood from between her legs had evidently sunk deep into the feather mattress.

Milo thought for a moment then tossed aside the photograph. "Okay, what do you need to get back at these bastards, father?"

"A way into the British House of Lords. Someone who knows those people. Someone who will do our bidding there."

Milo thought about that, and then about Mademoiselle Suzanne and all the people she knew. "Leave this with me, father. I think I know where to start looking for just such a man."

His father had called him, in his calmer moments, Lord Snivel. *Well, maybe I am*, thought the Third Earl of Cheselwich, Lyndon Barrymore Bartlett Manheim by name, as he looked at the young, naked boy asleep on the bed. *Such fine skin. Fine brown skin*, he thought as he ran his hand along the boy's back. He'd like to pay this fine

Chinese boy for the excellent services he'd so nimbly and obligingly rendered, but the Third Earl of Cheselwich had a problem. He was broke. Again.

The boy stirred, turned over, and stretched. Suddenly the boy was on his feet, seemingly not a boy anymore — and the knife in his left hand was no child's toy.

The boy's right palm was open and the chunky sounds coming from his mouth, the Third Earl of Cheselwich assumed, were a demand for payment. He'd heard that demand in many different languages since he had taken his father's unasked for advice and headed for "parts East to seek whatever fortune you can manage." His father had been right that he could play upon his title, and with the assistance of the three letters of introduction from his fathers' friends who were members of the British House of Lords many doors would open for him.

He straightened out his linen shirt and said, "Put down the knife. Don't be a silly bugger."

"*Gei qian!*"

"Ah, am I to assume you are demanding a payment for services rendered?"

"That's what he's asking for."

The Third Earl of Cheselwich spun around, his pudgy paw of a left hand flying to his puffy-lipped mouth, to find the source of the new voice in the room. After a brief squint his eyes discerned a dark-complexioned young man standing in the doorway. The young man, without so much as a by-your-leave, walked past him to the boy and said, "*Duo qian?*" — Mandarin for: How much?

The Third Earl of Cheselwich saw the boy's eyes narrow and shrink to small black marbles. Then he spat out, "*Wu shi gang bi!*"

The dark young man laughed a hearty chortle and replied, "*Wu shi gang bi?* Fifty Hong Kong dollars is pretty steep."

The boy whore shrieked a high-pitched wail that hurt the delicate eardrums of the Third Earl of Cheselwich. Then the boy whore proceeded to pull at his own hair with such force that literally a hunk of the thick black stuff came out in his hand. As he did his knife swung wildly, often close to his face, and he shouted in English, "No, no, no!"

"I comprehended his response. Perhaps my language skills are increasing," said the Third Earl of Cheselwich with a smile.

"I sincerely doubt that," said the dark young man, who then threw up his hands and continued in English, "If he is as he is, and this circumstance is evidently as it is, then I leave you to each other." With that he turned to the door and headed out.

The Third Earl of Cheselwich lunged to follow the dark young man but the boy whore shouted words that were clearly a warning.

"I don't think he wants you to leave before you pay him," said the dark young man, known to most of Shanghai's Foreign Settlement as one Milo Hordoon.

"My boy, I'd be in a state of unrelenting happiness if I had sufficient funds to cover the aforementioned expenses."

"Is that English you're speaking?"

"The Queen's own, and pure, I might add. The voice of Milton and Shakespeare, the ebb and flow of oral commerce, the tongue of the Sceptered Isle itself."

"Fine. But is it English, yes or no?"

"Put that way — English, yes."

"Fine. Did you agree on a price with the boy before you began?"

"Of course not. I'm a gentleman."

"And it would be too crude for ..."

" ... a gentleman to barter for intimacy as a fishmonger does with a peasant woman or a simple shopkeeper would with a kitchen wench. Matters of the heart are beyond financial recompense."

Milo stared at the Third Earl of Cheselwich and smiled. His father would be pleased, very pleased, but he couldn't resist a bit more fun before he paid the fool's bill and brought him back to see the head of the Hordoon clan.

"What did he do for you?"

"Do? Do? We, he and I, partook in ..."

"Did you fuck him? Did he fuck you? Did you suck him off? Did he suck you off? Or did you just use your hands?" Milo wished that Silas were at his side to see this.

"My good lad!"

"No. Two mistakes. I'm not your lad and I'm certainly not good." He couldn't wait to tell Silas about that retort. "So, exactly where was your prick in all this, or his prick — both of your pricks, where were they exactly?"

"Really!"

"This is China, sir. You may be in the House of Paris but make no mistake this is the Middle Kingdom and we here in the Middle Kingdom are not squeamish about pillow matters."

"How barbaric!"

"Not paying for contracted services is barbaric."

"Why, I've never in all my life ..."

"Cut it out or I'll leave you here with him and his very sharp, pointy knife."

After a moment the Third Earl of Cheselwich said, "Please don't."

Milo looked at the pathetic man. Probably closer to forty than thirty, pear-shaped and with a sickly pinky-white skin. The man's handcrafted leather shoes had clearly not been polished in some time and his expensive linen shirt hung limp on his frame, as if it had been left out in the rain. Milo looked carefully but saw none of the telltale signs of cholera. If this clown was sick he wasn't coming anywhere near the Hordoon household, no matter what level of nobility he came from.

"So what did you do with the boy?" Milo asked as nonchalantly as he could manage.

To Milo's surprise the older man leaned over and whispered into his ear a litany of sexual acts and positions of some considerable length and variety.

When the surprisingly long recitation finished, Milo took a step away and said, "And how long did all this take?"

"Just under fifteen minutes, I expect."

"Really, under fifteen minutes for all of that?"

"I would appreciate your confidence in these matters, as one gentleman to another."

Milo stuck out his hand. "Milo Hordoon."

The Third Earl of Cheselwich took the proffered hand limply in his and mumbled his name and title. Milo asked for it a second time, and this time it was delivered with a bit more enthusiasm.

"So what can I do for you, your Earlship?"

"Your Lordship ... and I seem to be in a slight financial predicament."

"Ah, you'd like me to pay the boy for his no doubt expert ministrations."

"If that were possible I would be forever in your debt."

Milo peeled off a series of bills and handed them to the boy as he said to the Third Earl of Cheselwich, "Yes, you will be in my debt."

Richard looked at the almost nude body of the Third Earl of Cheselwich as he collected the cards from the table and said, "I thought you were a gambler, sir."

"I was ... I've been trying to ... could I have some of my clothing back? It's chilly."

"No, I'm sorry, but you lost your clothing to me in this fine game of whist."

"But I have nothing ..."

"You have those three letters."

"But sir, they are introductions from family friends."

"Powerful friends?"

"I guess they are powerful, yes."

Richard got up and went to his desk drawer and removed

the doctored picture of the eldest Vrassoon son with the bleeding girl. He caught sight of Milo out of the corner of his eye. The boy nodded. Richard sat and threw the photograph on the tabletop. "Recognize him?"

"He's that Jew!"

"Careful. I asked you if you recognized him."

"I do what's he doing with —"

"I can arrange it that you have an income of seven hundred pounds sterling per annum from this day forward until you finally pass away. Would that interest you?"

"Well, yes, it would, but what…?"

"Would you have to do?" Richard pushed the picture into his hands. "Deliver that and several copies of it to your family's powerful friends. And your financial future is assured."

The British House of Lords might not have been the most exclusive club in the world, but it certainly pretended it was. And like all would-be important institutions, it could be stirred to defend its supposedly untarnished reputation with the same avidity that a lioness shows in defending her favourite cub from attack. But action was not the métier of the House of Lords. Slow, considered discussion and then assignment to committee were the normal patterns of this august body. Never starting a session before ten-thirty in the morning and seldom sitting past teatime, the House of Lords was a luxurious, courteous debating society for the indolently privileged. But when Richard's photograph of the eldest son of one of its members circulated in their private clubs and drinking dens, a strange thing began to happen. Outrage stirred these old souls to the most unusual of things in the House of Lords — action.

Naturally, taking action was easier when the offending member was not really one of their own. "These Vrassoons are Hebrews, aren't they?" A Hebrew was never really a part of British nobility.

A Jew was not one of them. A kike should watch his "p"s and "q"s — and those of his eldest son. The fact that many owed money to the Vrassoons simply added a certain zest to their enterprise.

Eliazar Vrassoon had responded to a cryptic message received from his headman in London by sailing on the first clipper from Shanghai to Britain. He had been back just over a month when he found himself sitting in the deep leather Windsor chair and resisting putting his head in his hands. He'd been shown the photograph that evening. The man addressing him was a younger member of the House of Lords, from the standards and procedures committee or some such thing, but it was clear to Vrassoon that the man had the full support of the House. The photograph explained the sidelong glances he'd received since his return to London, and why people left his club the moment he arrived. Even at Bedlam, there seemed to be a peculiar distance.

"Have you shown this to…?"

"Some of us in the House of Lords have seen it."

"How many?"

"More than enough!"

Vrassoon couldn't believe it. Members had seen and no one had contacted him. Not one of these creatures whom he had bailed out of financial straits of their own making, not one of them had had the decency to at least warn him.

The image of the little girl on the farm blossomed in his mind and the thunderous reality that this was God's punishment for his sins fell on him. His hands flew up and then just stayed there. Around him he noticed other men peering in his direction. Men he had thought were his friends.

The man was speaking but Vrassoon was having trouble focusing. Finally he heard a snippet, "We are considering asking the Queen to revoke your seat in the House of Lords."

"Can you do that?" he said before he could stop himself. The smile that came to the little man's face was one that Eliazar

Vrassoon — that all Jews — recognized. So it was about that, too. Finally he said, "What do these noble lords want?"

"Excuse me?"

"Has a sudden deafness taken you? You heard me. You came for something. What? These honourable members would like the world to believe that they are above bartering, but they are not! So, what do they want from me to keep this picture secret?"

After only the slightest pause the little man said, "They want you to renounce your monopoly on trade from England to China, so that the companies with which they are associated can receive the same benefits that you and yours do."

It stunned the Vrassoon Patriarch. Was that the reason? Why now? But he couldn't think about it. "And if I refuse to renounce what is mine?"

"The photograph will go to Her Majesty and then be given to the press. Many of whom would be only too glad to publish it."

"They wouldn't dare."

The young man stood. "Are you sure of that? Would you really be willing to risk the reputation of your entire family on the honourable intentions of our Fleet Street press? Are you willing to risk a pogrom in London?" He withdrew a formal document with a royal seal on the bottom and the imprimatur of Britain's House of Lords emblazoned across the top.

Eliazar Vrassoon scanned the document — "fully renounce" — "as of the signing of" — "all title to and assumption of" — words. Words that would bring him to heel, like a disobedient dog who was finally muzzled tight enough that he could be whipped.

"Sign it, Jew."

The young man was enjoying himself.

The Vrassoon Patriarch looked at the document and forced his mind to race through the possibilities. Then took the proffered fountain pen from the young man and signed away the source of his greatest wealth in a single pen stroke.

CITY RISING

Two hours later the eldest Vrassoon son stared down at the rail tracks beneath the bridge. He felt strangely calm. Almost light-headed. He'd taken this very train several times to Paddington Station and from there ... He decided not to think of where he went from Paddington.

The rain had finally stopped and there was an inkling that the sun might come out. *Come out and bless the day*, he thought. Then he heard the Paddington-bound commuter train in the distance. He looked at his watch. *Right on time.* The sound of the approaching train grew louder behind him. He climbed up to the railing of the bridge and balanced himself against a strut. He looked up. *I will know, presently*, he thought. The train whistle sounded shrilly as it charged toward his bridge. He thought, just before he jumped, that he heard a young girl call his name. But he may have been mistaken.

In Shanghai, news of the Vrassoons' loss of their monopoly set off one of the biggest parties that even this town, very used to big parties, had ever seen. Jiang and Suzanne marked the occasion by cutting the rates on their wares, and the clear, cool evening was ideal for an all-night drunk. All of Shanghai participated. Those who had never been in the Foreign Settlement or the French Concession came with their whole families. Fortune-tellers set up shop on every corner, and there were no constables to be seen. Store owners stacked bales of hay in front of their stores for protection from the inevitable window-breaking and looting, then joined the party. The whole city sang and staggered and drank and danced.

As the old clock in Richard's room clanged three bells, Lily knelt and lit the opium ball she'd prepared for him. It was the fourth Richard had inhaled that evening. Outside there was the sound of revelry — the odd gunshot and the subsequent sound of sirens. Richard propped himself up on an elbow to inhale the sweet smoke and muttered to Lily, "Sirens outside, sirens inside, it's all one, Lily, it's all one."

Later that night the Shanghai *Star Standard* dropped its stack of morning papers on the corner of Nanjing and Henan Lu. The crowds were still out and the drink was still flowing so no one noticed the banner headline: "TAIPINGERS THREATEN TO ERADICATE OPIUM FROM THEIR TERRITORY." The subhead read: "TAIPINGERS CLOSE DOWN OPIUM DENS AND ARREST TRADERS."

#

FINAL JOURNEY

*The City of Nanjing and the City of Shanghai
1863–64*

No one ever claimed that the Taipingers were sparing in their use of the rod, or that the Taiping Kingdom of Heaven, Nanjing, was a place of peace and tranquility. But even the hardest of the hard hearts of the Taiping faithful were shocked by the display that awaited them when they reported for work on the cold morning of April 21, 1863. Despite the horror, they stood and gawked without saying a word, knowing that any show of sympathy or revulsion would be taken as an act of sedition against the state of the Heavenly King. So there was just a profound silence in the ancient city — a silence broken only by a periodic whimper of pain from one of the seven hundred men who had been crucified upside down on wooden crosses and were now on public display in the central square of the city. The seven hundred men now awaited, with various degrees of patience, the balm of death that was still several days and nights away.

Hung from the feet of each of the inverted, crucified men was a placard proclaiming the victim's involvement with the *Fan Kuei*'s devil drug, opium.

None of the shocked spectators doubted that the men, now impaled through their feet and hands and dripping blood from their ears and eyes, were involved with the opium trade. In fact, many of the onlookers began to make plans to escape Nanjing and Taiping control, since they themselves were either storing, supplying, importing, or using the *Fan Kuei*'s tar-like bringer of dreams.

But these crucifixions were only the beginning of the Taiping campaign against opium. These crucifixions were literally for local consumption. The ones that followed were unapologetic threats — threats to the entire *Fan Kuei* community.

Hercules's gout had returned with a vengeance after his night of drinking. *Damn*, he thought, *a little pleasure, a tiny little pleasure, and He takes his revenge.* Hercules was in such pain that he almost missed the commotion on the Bund promenade down below him. He carefully placed his gout-afflicted foot on the cold flagstones of the floor and made his way over to the large, leaded window that overlooked the Bend in the River. Pushing open the large pane, he was at first unsure what it was that he saw — then he recoiled in horror, and in so doing slammed the gout nodule on his foot against the wall. But he was in too much shock to feel the pain.

Percy St. John Dent was returning from a night at the House of Paris when he first saw them, and before he knew it he had thrown up his entire extravagant dinner into the murky waters of the Huangpu River.

Jedediah Oliphant, head of the House of Zion, called to his assistants to get horses. They galloped past the American guards at the crossing point of the Suzu Creek and down to the Bund river- promenade, where a huge crowd had formed. Jedediah at first couldn't discern why this particular large crowd was so disconcerting, until he figured it out. There were literally thousands of souls here but there was total silence. There was never silence in Shanghai! Then he heard a moan from the river and looked at the six ships there — and froze.

Jiang had been the first to see them and had immediately sent for the Fisherman and the Confucian — and there they stood at the far end of the promenade at the Bend in the River and stared at the six ships, their tall masts denuded of sails, slowly swaying — like a stately matron at a lavish ball who had consumed one too many glasses of fine Champagne and was somehow disoriented in her own home. But these ships were not matrons at a ball. They were warnings — graphic warnings etched in the blood and the pain of the hundreds of men who hung, head down, nailed to the masts of the boats in mockery of the Crucifixion. Even from a distance their cries for help could be heard when the wind blew shoreward. Then the wind would shift, throwing their voices away from the shore toward the Pudong, and the onlookers would have the odd sensation that the pain had suddenly ceased and that the men were somehow just acrobats holding unusual positions on the tall masts. Then, just as unexpectedly, the wind would blow shoreward and the cries of pain would fill every ear.

Just as mysterious as the arrival of the boats was, so was the seemingly magical and very sudden appearance of thousands of pamphlets in the crowd of onlookers.

Jiang grabbed one of the poorly printed things from the rickshaw boy beside her and read it quickly: "Behold what befalls those who have traffic in the Devil's drug. See and take warning what happens to those who do the Devil's work in the Heavenly Kingdom." It was signed by the Heavenly King.

The Confucian looked at Jiang and said, "We'll meet tonight in the Warrens. Inform the Carver."

"Not exactly an understated message, that," remarked Percy St. John Dent as he poured himself a healthy glass of Hercules's very fine sherry.

"Well, no one ever claimed that the Taipingers were fond of any form of subtlety," replied Hercules from his high-backed chair.

Percy took a tiny sip of the sherry and said, "Oh, very good, Hercules, very good indeed. So what exactly was the message meant to say, gentlemen?"

"Can't your interpreter read the pamphlet for you?" asked the Vrassoon Patriarch from behind his steepled fingers.

"Oh, that part of the message was clear enough. It's the other part of the message that bothers me," said Richard abruptly reminding the others that he was in the room.

"What other part?"

"The unwritten part. The part that says that they can come and go whenever and wherever they please. That they have only left us alone up until now because they wanted to, not because they had to. That they live amongst us. They cook for us, clean our houses, move our goods, look after our children. That we are in their country not they in ours."

What followed was a silence unlike any that the traders could remember. Their meetings were complicated, bombastic affairs, not contemplative meetings of minds, which suddenly this conclave had become.

Finally Oliphant asked, "Whose ships were they?"

"What does it matter?" asked Vrassoon. "The message they carried was evident and clear."

"Perhaps, but if we knew …"

"Are you suggesting that we track down the shipowners and see who's doing business with the Taipingers? Look around you, here. We are all doing business with them. If we didn't, we couldn't exist," said Hercules.

"This is mad. This is the act of a madman," Percy said.

"Of a madman who thinks he is the brother of Jesus Christ," scoffed Oliphant.

"Not a madman, just a religious man, like several of you in this room," said Richard flatly. Then with a smile he added, "So madness is to be taken for granted."

Oliphant immediately rose to the bait, but Vrassoon signalled him to sit down and turned to Richard. "We have had our differences in the past."

"Really? What differences?"

"Fine, even had we been friends of the heart for years it makes no difference. We are both now facing a real danger to ourselves and our families and our businesses."

"I am in the cotton business."

"Ah, yes, the cotton business. A safe business. But what is to stop the Taipingers from next suggesting that all trade from the Middle Kingdom is to be done only by Chinamen? What's to stop them from doing that? Then what happens to your brilliant speculation and your tons of cotton? Do you think your Chinese workers would defend your cotton against the Taipingers? Would they risk being nailed to posts for your cotton?"

Richard reluctantly nodded agreement.

"Good," said Eliazar Vrassoon, "then you'll contact your crazy brother? He's a man of some power and suasion in Taiping circles, I'm told. Go to him. Talk some sense into him."

Richard looked out the window at the gathering clouds, then finally nodded again and said, "I'll set out tonight."

"Why does Milo get to go and I have to stay?" complained Silas as he backed into a paddock to allow a large black horse past him.

Richard patted the animal's shining flank, then stroked the boy's hair and said, "Next time I'll take you."

"But I want to see Uncle Maxi. It may be the last time —"

"It won't be!" Richard's voice was hard as granite. Then he

softened as he said, "Don't worry. Your Uncle Maxi is indestructible. He'll be around for a long time yet. Patterson, are the supplies waiting for us?"

"They're all aboard, sir. Are you going to take horses, too?"

"Just these two."

"Done, sir."

"Good. Come on, Silas, cheer up. With Milo and me gone, you're the head of the House of Hordoon, that's got to be worth something." The boy tried to smile but managed only a rough approximation. His father grabbed him to his chest in a bear hug, then turned on his heel and left Silas alone with Patterson.

"Why couldn't I go too?" Silas whined as he kicked at the hay in the stables.

"Probably because monkey-lovers aren't wanted on the voyage," Patterson said smoothly as he picked up the shovel and tossed it to Silas, with a simple command that made it perfectly clear who was in charge of the House of Hordoon while Richard was away. "Muck up, monkey-lover."

Richard's trip with Milo to Nanjing was closely monitored by the Manchus. Their patrol boats, which controlled the lower stretches of the Yangtze, accompanied Richard's large junk right up to the disputed waters just west of the Grand Canal across from Chinkiang, the City of Suicides. Thereafter, for twelve hours, the junk sailed without escort. But on the following morning Taiping ships came up on either side of their boat and silently stayed to starboard and port all the way to Nanjing, the seat of the Heavenly King.

To Richard's surprise the welcome in Nanjing, although not effusive, was openly friendly. A modest banquet was set for him, followed by a performance of the History Teller's Peking Opera company's final act of *Journey to the West*. The entirety of the piece's seven acts took almost nine hours to perform, so usually only sections of it were acted at any given time. The section they showed this evening was the end, entitled "Partings."

As the sun set, the presentation ended with the Serving Man turning away from the falling sun and striding off — back to his home in the East. The crowd was on its feet applauding the elegantly understated sorrow. As Richard leapt to his feet the actors stepped forward, turned, and applauded to their right. And there, to Richard's shock, was his brother Maxi — that damned red kerchief around his neck — stepping forward to accept the applause of both actors and audience as the patron of the company.

"So, I assume you are here to talk some sense into your wild, red-haired sibling, is't so, brother mine?"

"Aye."

"Well, that could be something in the doing," Maxi said, showing his full mouth of large, white teeth.

And then, suddenly, they were in each other's arms, hugging each other with an ardour that surprised them both. Then, just as suddenly an odd embarrassment came upon them and they each took a step back. An awkward silence followed, which Maxi finally broke.

"Milo looks a fine young man."

"He is. Strong like you, and wild like you."

"And Silas, why'd you not bring him, too?"

Richard looked away. He really didn't know why he hadn't brought Silas with him, just a feeling. At last he said, "Someone has to look after the shop while I'm gone."

"So you finally turned him into a businessman?" Maxi asked with open astonishment.

"Not really," Richard replied. "He's a fine linguist, though, and could be of real use to us."

"To you. There is no *us* any longer, brother mine."

"But Maxi ..."

"Do I have to set you on your keister in front of your son to prove my point? 'Cause I will, if that's necessary. You promised me that I could go back if I didn't find what I wanted in our new business. Well I didn't find it, brother mine, so I moved back, to here." He indicated his ripening fields of sorghum and soya beans and his large stand of bamboo. "And I'm happy here. Happier than I've been since we left India."

"I see," Richard said.

"I don't think you do. Look at this place. Look at my crops, and my wife, and our child. Look — allow yourself to really see, brother mine. This is the kind of place that could rid you of the opium addiction that rules you. I could help you. We could all help you here — and love you here, brother mine."

His final night in Nanjing, Richard dreamt of the old Hindu man who had surprised them in the alley of the town outside the Opium Works at Ghazipur — and the man's curse of one brother murdering another rang in his ears until he forced himself from sleep and watched for hours as the sun rose over another dangerous day. He longed for the escape that only opium could offer him. But it was not only the opium he wanted. He felt somehow incomplete — was it Maxi he missed? Perhaps. But more likely it was the constant, silent presence of Lily for which he longed.

Maxi kissed Milo on the cheek, then said to him, "Tell your brother I look forward to meeting him, now that he is a man like you." He turned to Richard and said, "There is still time for you to decide to stay with us here."

"There is still time for you to convince these people to stop this madness."

"Stopping the selling of a drug that kills people is madness in your way of thinking? Opium is the Devil's drug."

"You've been with these fanatics too long."

"Perhaps. But you've been with your fanatics too long too, brother mine."

The History Teller watched the parting of the two White men on the south Nanjing docks. As their leave-taking proceeded, words flew into her head:

> *On a dock, in sallow light,*
> *Brothers say final goodbyes,*
> *As men do to the world*
> *From their death beds.*

The Assassin watched the History Teller watching the two *Fan Kuei*, and for the first time in a long time he felt blood fill the hood of the cobra that had been carved into his back after he killed his cousin. The snake arched up, and the Assassin's head snapped back as his arms pulled tight to his sides. To his surprise his right hand came forward holding the swalto blade that glinted in the fading light. The only word that came to him as he looked at the killing instrument in his hand was "hunger." Yes, the snake on his back and the knife in his hand were hungry — hungry for blood.

Richard and Milo travelled back to Shanghai in almost total silence. A silence that was broken only by the few words needed between father and son to allow a day to proceed. Both felt the heavy weight of failure on their shoulders and the ominous movement of history. Milo even smelled the reek of ozone.

When they finally docked in the Pudong, Richard took a bumboat to the Bund and reported his failure to the traders gathered there. His report was greeted by another kind of silence. He stood there waiting for their comments. None was forthcoming. Finally he turned on his heel and left. No one moved to stop his going.

"What does it matter?" the Vrassoon Patriarch said to Hercules and Percy St. John Dent. "We will still need the Royal Navy — actually, we deserve the Royal Navy's support in this little matter. Her Majesty makes a fortune by taxing the tea we sell in England, tea that can only be bought from the Chinese with the money we make by selling them opium. And that tea tax accounts for just under 32 percent of Her Majesty's annual taxation revenues."

"That much?"

"Perhaps more. And that tax money pays for roads and schools and hospitals and orphanages and more ships for the Royal Navy. It pays for England itself. England is paid for with the proceeds from the opium that we sell to the Chinese. Make no mistake about that. And now it is time for England to do its fair share in this joint enterprise."

"But with the Royal Navy?"

"Why not? What else are they doing at anchor in Hong Kong and Macaw? It's time to show these rebels that it is one thing to defeat the Manchus but quite another to take on the forces of the British Empire."

Percy smiled, and then added, "Perhaps a Sikh regiment would be a useful addition. I understand that they hate Celestials with a passion — something to do with religious differences."

"Perhaps," Vrassoon said, "perhaps Sikhs would be the ideal people to show these rebels what violence really looks like." He paused and then added, "They might be of use should our dear Queen decide that the Manchu Empress needs a lesson as well."

When the Royal Navy began to arrive in force at the Bend in the River, Richard headed down to the Shanghai docks. He was pleased to find Admiral Gough was in charge of the military side of the mission. He was even more pleased when the Admiral remembered him and willingly took him onboard as an extra translator, and then insisted that he wear the uniform of a British lieutenant.

As Gough turned to more pressing business, Richard took the opportunity to explore the ship. There had been definite advancements from the vessel upon which he had sailed upriver in 1841. But the intent was the same — to terrorize. Every available space on the great sailing ship was devoted to armaments — every space except the forward hold, where, much to Richard's surprise, there were four billiards tables stacked one on top of another.

"The men need to be entertained, Mr. Hordoon," said Gough from behind him.

"Sorry, sir," Richard said. "I didn't know you were there."

"Well I am." He hesitated for a moment, then asked, "Is it true that your wild brother is a commander with the Taipingers?"

"So it would seem, sir."

"Ah," the Admiral said. "Well, a siege can be a very long process, and the greatest impediment to success can be boredom amongst the troops. Hence these billiards tables."

"Ah." Richard smiled, then mused, "The click of billiards balls give dreadful note of preparation."

The Admiral smiled and responded, "The country cocks do crow, the clocks do toll …"

"… and the third hour of drowsy morning name. Proud of their numbers and secure in soul, the confident and over-lusty English do the low-rated Taipingers play at billiards."

"Very good, Mr. Hordoon. You know your Shakespeare."

"Some. A certain Thomas De Quincy suggested it as an antidote to a bad habit of mine."

"Interesting, Mr. Hordoon." It was evident that the Admiral wanted to pursue the topic but decided, out of decency — one gentleman to another — to let it go. "We'll take Nanjing, Mr. Hordoon, of that you may be sure. It's just a matter of time. But during that time there's only so much building and toting to be done. Basically a siege is a matter of starvation. And a big city like Nanjing can take many months to starve."

Richard thought about another conversation on a similar ship about starvation. But that seemed a lifetime ago.

"These are also very helpful in passing the time," the Admiral said, holding up a broad cricket bat. At first Richard assumed that the Admiral was referring to the bat as an enforcer of discipline, then he realized that the man was talking about entertaining the troops again.

Richard looked at the Admiral holding the cricket bat and said, "Is this a party or a war, sir? Surely the Taipingers will mount a counterattack against your positions both on land and sea."

The Admiral smiled. "I doubt that."

"Excuse me, sir?"

"Do you know what those are?" he said, pointing to several large cannon-like weapons that had eight narrow barrels attached together and a crank behind them. "They're called Gatling guns, and they'll change everything. A single man can now fire hundreds of rounds a minute by turning that handle. These guns will protect our heavy cannon batteries so no force on earth can get to them. With these Gatling guns as protectors, our cannon can fire day and night without fear of assault — even from that crazy brother of yours. Think of it, Mr. Hordoon: one man can kill hundreds in a few minutes. Forget about sallies from Nanjing. They may try it once, but certainly not a second time."

Richard stared at the awful thing.

"Things change, Mr. Hordoon. Things change."

Richard found himself breathing deeply — and for the first time smelling something acrid in the air.

Two weeks later Maxi found himself roused from his bed by Cupid, and the look on the man's bow-shaped mouth was grim.

"British," he said, clearly. "Many British."

Maxi threw aside his blanket and kissed his wife goodbye. Then he went to the children's room. His wife's two little girls slept in one bed, entwined with each other, thin limbs around and through and about each other, loosed hair a combined tangle of dark beauty. He touched each of their faces, then moved to the small bed of his daughter. To his surprise, her eyes were wide open despite the early hour. When he went to kiss her, she turned her head aside. Her mane of red-tinged black hair fell across her face. Her mouth that never smiled opened and closed but said nothing.

"Say goodbye to your Daddy."

She turned, tears in her eyes, and said, "Come back, Papa, come back to me."

Two hours later Maxi walked the south walls of Nanjing with Cupid and three of his most experienced commanders at his side. There, arrayed like lines on a canvas, were six brigades of British troops. In their centre was a regiment of Sikhs in full battle dress. The entire assembly stood stock-still while behind them four British men-o'-war came about and positioned themselves to shell the walls of the ancient city.

"*Ta men ma shang jiu kai shi wa jue ma, xian sheng?*" asked one of his commanders.

Maxi's translator said, "Commander Wu asks if they will start digging soon."

Maxi shook his head.

"*Na hao, mei shi me hao pa de. Wo men de cheng qiang jian bu ke cui.*"

"He says then there is nothing to fear as the walls of our city are strong. Unassailable."

"Tell him that's not true. Look over there," he said, pointing to the west. There the Manchu bannermen were planting stakes in the ground. "How many?" he asked.

"I count fourteen banners, sir."

"Fourteen Manchu legions, four British men-o'-war, and at least six brigades of British troops — our walls have never been challenged by such a force."

"But —"

"Open the evacuation tunnels out of the city for the women and children."

Cupid took a step aside, and Maxi said, "What?"

"I already looked, sir. They've all been blocked in the night. No one in the city is leaving. Besides, the Heavenly King wouldn't permit retreat from the seat of the Heavenly Kingdom, would he?"

Maxi ignored the comment about the Taiping King, who no doubt had his own way out of the city. But it shocked him that the attackers had bothered to block routes that were clearly to be used by women, children, and elders. Maxi had made sure that the routes were narrow so that any attacker would know that they were not exit or egress routes for soldiers and armaments. They were just wide enough for a person carrying a load on his back.

"Are you sure?" Maxi asked.

"About the escape routes? Yes, sir. Two were blasted closed in the middle of the night, three others have cannon stationed facing them. They seem to have a new weapon, sir." He pointed to the crest of a nearby hill and handed Maxi a spyglass.

Maxi looked through the glass and saw a large, mounted gun with several barrels and a crank on it. He panned down to the mechanism and gasped. His keen mechanical mind quickly saw how the rotation mechanism worked the rifle barrels. He panned across the field and spotted six more of these instruments of death. Each of them was set between Nanjing and the batteries of heavy cannon that were aimed at the city walls.

He was about to ask if anyone had seen these weapons work when the first of the British batteries on the north side of the city loosed a barrage of cannonballs aimed at the walls, and scrap metal aimed high over the walls to lacerate and slice and terrorize the inhabitants of the seat of the Heavenly Kingdom.

Maxi turned to see the damage caused by the first barrage and was amazed to see fires spring to life in the city. A turret on the south wall was leaning dangerously as its supporting brickwork caved in under the onslaught.

Maxi turned to Cupid and said, "Is your family safe?"

Cupid shrugged his shoulders. "Is yours?"

Maxi turned his head away from the man. Then the four men-o'-war fired all ninety-six cannons at once — and the terror grew.

For three days the English batteries thundered without let-up. The destruction in the city was manageable but it would undoubtedly get worse with time. What took the most serious toll on the city was the lack of sleep. Through his spyglass Maxi saw the head gunners looking at pocket watches before signalling their men to fire. Maxi surmised that some inventive person had organized it so that the cannons didn't fire in any sort of regular, repeating pattern. Instead, they fired intensely, then stopped, then fired sporadically, then stopped altogether, then fired intensely again. Maxi timed the intervals and they were never the same. Someone understood that people could adapt to noise so long as it occurred in some sort of regular pattern, but random loud blasts robbed the city of Nanjing of sleep. After three days without sleep, the fabric of discipline a city needed to survive a siege was already beginning to fray.

In the early evening of the fourth night of the siege Maxi gathered his most trusted men. Men with whom he'd been to war. Men who had trusted his decisions. Men who had followed him and, under his leadership, had defeated the best units of the Manchu bannermen.

Maxi tried to smile but he was troubled. He hadn't seen those strange guns work so he didn't know exactly how to attack them. He'd sent out several small decoy parties but none had been able to draw fire from the things. As well, most were placed far enough from the city walls that the Taiping cannon couldn't reach them.

"Sir?" It was Cupid. He was holding out Maxi's red kerchief.

"Thanks," Maxi said, as he took the thing and put it around his neck. Then he turned to his men and said, "One more time, gentlemen — and I use the term loosely."

A cheer went up — and Maxi finally smiled.

Maxi and his men emerged from the sewage drain and assembled along the side of the stinking cesspool. Cupid touched Maxi on the shoulder and pointed at the sky. A large, dark cloud was moving slowly across the new moon. Maxi nodded and the word was passed. When the cloud obscured the moon they would charge the British southern battery, which continued its barrage of the city.

Maxi looked up. The edge of the cloud tipped across the point of the new moon. He tapped Cupid's shoulder and the men emerged from the tall reeds of the cesspool and crept toward the southern battery with the strange gun in front of it.

Suddenly they were running.

Maxi felt the wind on his face and his blood surged. His senses moved forward to his skin and his eyes became bright. A fight! He'd always loved a fight.

Four hundred yards and still no resistance.

The large black cloud completely obscured the slender moon. The lanterns from the British tents in the far distance were the only points of light in the pitchy dark.

Three hundred yards and the British hadn't spotted them. They increased their pace to an all-out sprint.

Suddenly light.

A trench of oil on his left sprang to life.

Maxi looked. *That can't be right. The trench should be in front of the battery to protect it. Not to one side. What was the point of having it to one side?*

Then something spat bullets — hundreds of them pinging off rocks, whizzing past his ears, thudding sickeningly into the flesh of his men. Cupid whirled around and crashed into Maxi, his right arm almost severed from his body, a bloody blotch where his left eye should have been. Maxi held him. He took the kerchief from his neck and wrapped it tightly around Cupid's face, trying to staunch the bleeding from the empty eye socket. Another bullet had hit a vein and blood was raining down.

Cupid's hot blood quickly coated Maxi's face. Through the blood he stared ahead at the thing spitting bullets. A single man stood there cranking something that fired the bullets. Behind him British officers drank beer. Some carried pool cues. All of them cheered.

Maxi looked to the fire trench and he understood why it was there to one side, not in front of the gun battery. It was there to light the scene! As though it were a play. The fire wasn't for protection, it was for illumination. His men were dying to provide entertainment for the British!

Three more slugs hit Cupid hard in the back and yanked him from Maxi's arms.

Maxi took a quick look at his old friend then yelled to the others, "*Che! Che!* — Back! Back!" It was one of the few Mandarin words he knew, and he'd never had occasion to use it on a battlefield. But with this new weapon he had no choice.

Of his just under two hundred men, only seventeen made it back to the sewage drain. As they gathered, the dark cloud cleared the new moon, and in the thin moonlight the men saw their comrades littering the field while the British toasted the man who had cranked the strange new weapon.

Maxi felt liquid on his face. At first he thought it must be Cupid's blood, but then he realized he was wrong. It was his own tears.

Richard witnessed the appalling slaughter. He never saw Maxi, although after the firing stopped he ran out on the battlefield and spotted a red kerchief on one of the dead Taipingers.

And then he heard them and looked up. Vultures. Their dark forms filled the sky, obliterating the stars. Battlefield dead always attracted carrion birds, but somehow this carnage, this open field charnel house, drew more of them than Richard had ever seen. More and bigger. It disgusted him that the British returned to their games of billiards as the great birds tore lobes of gray livers and purple strings of intestines from the dead and dying.

He reached down and retrieved the red kerchief from the body, which had been badly mutilated by the Gatling gun's large-calibre bullets. As he folded it carefully he began to think of how to get into Nanjing and save his brother and his family from the inevitable bloodletting that was about to befall the capital of the Heavenly Kingdom.

Richard stood at the crest of the hill looking over the farmland to the south of the city, where Maxi's farm … had been. All that remained were the burned stubs of field crops and the lonely hearthstones of burned-out farmhouses. It took Richard a while to orient himself so that he could find what remained of Maxi's farm.

Roving Manchu warriors were everywhere. On occasion a woman's cry would cut through the sound of burning. Rape was never a silent activity, and in war it was often a spectator sport. Oddly, the screams of the victims seemed to intensify the fury of the Manchus.

Richard was challenged by Manchus several times, but with his British officer's uniform and his command of Mandarin he talked himself past every checkpoint.

It wasn't until dawn that he picked up a trail from talking with two terrified farm women. They pointed to a hill to the west.

It took Richard two days to find Maxi's wife. One of her daughters had been dragged from her arms by Manchu soldiers and she hadn't been seen since; the other had been viciously raped and now hid behind her mother's skirts. Maxi's wife held their little girl in her arms as if frightened to let the child out of her grasp. But the girl just stared, seemingly unafraid, into Richard's eyes.

Maxi's wife suddenly drew in a sharp breath and pointed at Richard. It was only then Richard realized that he was wearing Maxi's kerchief around his neck. "No. No, don't think that. I didn't find his body. If anyone can stay alive in this hell it's my brother Maxi."

He gave her the red kerchief and she clutched it to her breast. Then he gave her all the money he carried, although he wondered if currency was of any value in a war zone. He questioned her about Nanjing. About exits and entrances. About refugee routes. About where she should meet up with him and her husband. They agreed on a place. She asked, "When?"

Richard didn't know what to say, then it occurred to him. "Watch the Manchu banners in the field. When they head toward the city you go to that place to meet us. Once the Manchus are in the city it's all but over."

But the siege wore on and on. Dogs and cats were the first obvious victims in the ancient capital. They simply disappeared. Then the plants and grass were gone. Eventually even the weeds disappeared from the park lands. Stomachs distended. Envy caused fights to break out everywhere. And finally the most unwelcome, although most common, of guests came to visit the terrorized, weakened citizenry of Nanjing — cholera.

And yet the city did not fall. The walls were punctured during the day and repaired at night. Fires roared through the city from incendiary bombardments but were put out by organized, although depleted, teams of Taipingers.

A strange, unofficially sanctioned kind of trade began between those under siege and those doing the sieging. At first it was just the trading of creature comforts from the homes of the Nanjing residents for food from the soldiers. Then began a brisk trade in antiquities for food. Finally, anything of any value in the city was traded for food. It was under this rubric that the History Teller's troupe was traded to the Manchu Commander for two fat sows.

"Welcome," the Manchu Commander said to the History Teller as he openly admired her beauty.

"Are you a follower of the arts, Commander?"

"If they are your arts, I am sure that I am a follower."

"Then shall we perform this evening?"

"Indeed."

The troupe performed that night, literally for their dinner — and every other night the Commander felt like being entertained by a troupe of Peking Opera performers.

In the fourth month of the siege, rumour spread through the city that the Heavenly King had left with his son, and finally the inevitable revolt of the dispossessed and exhausted brought the city to the brink of surrender.

Maxi pleaded, through his interpreter, that to open the gates was to allow in destruction. "The Manchus will be let loose to avenge themselves on you. The British already have what they want. They've broken our prohibition on opium. All that remains is the slaughter. You open the gates and that is what will happen."

Three days later, the front gates of Nanjing, China's ancient capital, were flung open and a committee of twelve officials, all dressed in white silk robes, strode out in the time-honoured fashion, to surrender the city. The Manchus beheaded them and raced toward the open gate.

From the hills, Maxi's wife saw the Manchu banners begin to move and she knew the end was near. She picked up the toddler and held her other daughter's hand as they made their way carefully to the meeting place she had agreed upon with Richard.

Richard raced into the city with the first wave of Manchus. There were screams everywhere. Limbs literally littered the streets and old men were nailed to the doors of their ancestral homes. The Manchus were drunk on revenge. For over a decade they had fought the rebels and lost. Now was their time to get back at those who had shamed them.

But the Taipingers were not finished. They fought for every street, every alley, every building of the capital of the Heavenly Kingdom. They held back the Manchus for four full days and nights — then they could hold out no longer.

Maxi's Hakka wife waited at the assigned meeting place, with their little girl and her daughter, for a day and a night. The frozen dawn of the second day presented her with stern choices. What little food she'd managed to buy with Richard's money was quickly running out, and she didn't know when or where she could find more. As well, Manchu soldiers — drunken Manchu soldiers — had begun to frequent the hill. They dragged girls there. Raped them. Then slit their throats.

By noon of that second day Maxi's wife was forced to make a choice. She had very little food. Soldiers were everywhere. This place wasn't safe — and her daughter cried all the time.

She took one last glance at Nanjing below them, then tied the red kerchief on the toddler's head and laid her gently on a bed of ferns as far back in the stand of trees as she could go. Then she took her traumatized daughter by the hand and began down the far side of the hill. They got only half a mile before the taunting calls of three Manchu soldiers stopped them — once and for all.

Richard saw the last line of the Taiping defence sunder and run — and he knew the end had finally come. He looked desperately for the high ground of the city. Finally he spotted silk overhead lines and ran furiously, following them until they brought him to an open clearing in a park in the north end of the city. And there, sure enough, Maxi was organizing a group of wounded men for one final charge.

"It's no use, Maxi. The Manchus are in total control of the city. If you fight on it will be suicide."

"If we don't fight it's suicide, brother mine."

"There is an alternative."

"What? To run?"

"No. To see your family. To protect them. You've given years of your life to this cause. Now at least offer something to your family."

Maxi opened his mouth but no words came. Richard put his hand on his brother's shoulder and said, "Now it's time for me to save you, brother mine."

Two hours later, Richard found the History Teller helping the actor who played the Serving Man redesign his makeup. They were deep in discussion about the performance they had just given. The History Teller noticed Richard and stepped aside to address him.

"The Manchus let you into their camp, Mr. Hordoon?"

"I'm a resourceful man."

"So it would seem."

"I need your help. Actually, my brother and his family need your help."

The History Teller allowed her breath out slowly, then turned away from Richard. Finally she asked, "Where is your brother?"

"Getting his family from their hiding place."

The History Teller lowered her lovely head and tried to still her heart but she did not speak. For all her time in Nanjing she'd been careful, after that first night, not to get too close to the red-haired *Fan Kuei*, and now here was his brother asking her to hide Maxi and his family.

"They need your help."

"So you've said. What would you like me to do to help your brother and his family?"

She listened closely as Richard outlined his plan. Unbeknownst to Richard and the History Teller, however, someone else was listening as well. Someone with extraordinarily acute hearing and a cobra carved into his back.

Maxi raced to the assigned meeting place but found no one. Following tracks he eventually came upon a clearing in the woods — jackals had eaten away what little flesh had been left on his wife and her daughter's bodies. But where was his daughter?

He retraced his steps and searched the area carefully. Nothing. He sank to his knees in the middle of the clearing, then something, something out of place, caught his eye. A spot of red amidst the greenery in the copse of trees. He stood and walked cautiously toward the patch of colour.

He found his little girl playing quietly with two sticks while lying on her back on the bed of ferns.

She touched the red kerchief on her forehead then looked at her father — but she did not smile.

The sacking, pillaging, and raping of Nanjing took almost a week. Well before it was over, the British had left Nanjing behind and headed back to their bases in Hong Kong and Macaw. Eventually sated, the Manchus reorganized their troops and headed out into the countryside to rid the rest of China of the "scourge of the Taipingers."

One morning, unceremoniously, the History Teller was called to the Manchu Commander's tent."

"Sir?"

"It is time for you and your troupe to go."

"Go where?" she asked.

The Manchu just laughed. "Go wherever you can. But watch your pretty head, History Teller. There are bandits everywhere, and roving bands of Manchu bannermen who are hunting down the last of the Taipingers. Both the Heavenly King and his son are still at large. And of course, the red-haired *Fan Kuei* general. Until they are all caught and executed, the rebels are dangerous. There are bounties on all of their heads. Should you see them, you might consider what that kind of money could do for your little company of players." The Manchu Commander turned to leave, then stooped to lace his boot. As he did he mentioned, "Stay away from the river. Any boat that does not belong to the Manchus will be boarded, and the people onboard put to the sword."

"Really?"

"A word to the wise."

"Why do you tell me all this?"

An odd smile crossed the man's hard features. "Because I enjoyed your performances. They touched me." He stood. "But be careful, History Teller, or your beautiful head will end up on the end of a pike. What kind of History could you tell from that vantage point? Not much, I'd guess."

The History Teller gathered her people and they — along with Maxi and his daughter — started the dangerous journey back to Shanghai.

That very night the Chosen Three met with the Carver in the deepest section of the Warrens beneath the Chinese section of Shanghai. The Confucian already looked twice his age, and something was definitely wrong with the Fisherman, the uncle of the Assassin. The young Carver had taken over from his ancient father but carried himself with the dignity that all representatives of the Carvers managed to display.

Jiang was unsettled by the distant stare of the Fisherman. "What draws your eye so far away, old friend?" she asked.

"Just my age," he said unconvincingly.

"We all age, Fisherman, but some of us have bad dreams as we near our end. Do you call out in your sleep these days?"

The Fisherman had no idea how Jiang knew that, and he was appalled that his privacy had been so breached.

"Are they dreams of your son whom the Assassin dispatched?"

The Fisherman slowly nodded. His whole life had collapsed since the passing of his gentle son. The birds refused to fish for him. His wife had contracted the palsy and died amidst howls of pain. Now he was alone in his bed — alone with the nightly pleading of his beautiful boy: "*Help me, father, help me.*"

The Confucian stepped forward and put a hand on the

Fisherman's shoulder. "We have all sacrificed for the future of our people. For the Seventy Pagodas."

Again the Fisherman nodded, although he kept his eyes down.

"The three of us carry a heavy burden," the Confucian continued, "and that burden takes many forms. My grandmother —"

"We are not here to bemoan our present state," shot back Jiang, viciously. "We have a duty to carry out, and at this time a momentous decision to make. My people tell me that the Heavenly King is trying to contact the red-haired *Fan Kuei*, and that the people in the countryside are so enraged by the treatment they have received at the hands of the Manchus that if those two were able to unite the rebellion could well start again."

"Do we want that?" asked the Fisherman.

"That's why we're here, to decide if defeating the Taipingers will complete the prophecy of the White Birds on Water, or if supporting the Taipingers will complete the prophecy."

"What does it matter what we think? We have no control over the Heavenly King or the red-haired *Fan Kuei*."

"Not over the Heavenly King, true. But over the red-haired *Fan Kuei* — yes, we have something to say about his life and death." The others looked at Jiang as if she were speaking in riddles. She sighed and said, "The red-haired *Fan Kuei* is being kept safe by my daughter, the History Teller, hidden by makeup and costume in her troupe."

"And my nephew the Assassin is in the same troupe?"

"The very same," Jiang said. "So you see, gentlemen, we have a choice. The Heavenly King is nothing without the red-haired *Fan Kuei*. If the *Fan Kuei* lives, he will no doubt rejoin the Heavenly King and the rebellion will swell once more. However, if our Assassin rids the world of the red-haired *Fan Kuei* …" Jiang allowed her voice to trail off as the others felt the weight of their choice in the still air of the deepest cavern of the Warrens.

But the Carver wasn't listening. He was staring at the Narwhal

Tusk — at the still-closed second window of the Ivory Compact.

The History Teller's troupe made its way slowly eastward, performing when they could to raise enough money to feed themselves. Several nights they slept in the open air without having eaten that day. But despite that, they rehearsed a new, centre section of *Journey to the West*, adding a scene for a new comic actor and his unsmiling little girl. They rehearsed that section so often that some of the actors stayed in makeup and wigs almost all the time — especially the new comic actor playing the Lost Peasant, an actor that only the History Teller knew was the red-haired *Fan Kuei* general who had led the defence of Nanjing for the Taipingers.

After a long nighttime rehearsal, the History Teller sent the company back to their beds, then said, "But not you."

Maxi stopped in his tracks.

"You have made some progress with this role but you have a much longer road to travel before you have any mastery of it."

Maxi didn't doubt that, but he chose to say, "Your English is very good."

"You are generous. It is only good because your Mandarin is execrable."

"Execrable's a serious word for a new English-speaker."

"Execrable sounds like what it is — sluicy, loose shit."

Maxi nodded. "Never thought of it that way. Don't actually think I've ever heard the word 'execrable' used in a proper sentence."

"Do you miss your wife?"

The question surprised Maxi. He'd managed not to think about her. "I was unable to keep her safe."

"Yes. That's true, but it's not what I asked. Do you miss your wife?"

Maxi thought about that for a moment, then said, "Have you been married?"

The History Teller nodded as a sadness crossed her lovely features. "A long time ago, and only briefly. Typhoid took him from me."

"I am sorry to hear that."

The History Teller shrugged her slender shoulders. "So, do you miss your wife?"

"We were very different. She never learned any English or me very much Hakka. We communicated …"

"With touch?" the History Teller suggested.

Maxi nodded. "Yes. She was a good woman. Honest and hard-working, and she loved the children." He paused for a second, then added, "She was assigned to me by the second King of Heaven. The King of the West."

"Ah, Jesus's other younger brother."

Maxi nodded.

"And why do you think you were assigned this wife, while most Taipingers were kept strictly away from the opposite sex?"

He looked at the History Teller. At her strong features. The elegant way she held herself. Her full lips.

"Answer my question, please."

Something deep inside Maxi opened and a long sigh escaped his lips. He knew the answer to her question, had known it from the beginning, but had never admitted it, even to himself. But here, with this beautiful, mature woman sitting before him, he said simply, "To report what I was doing to the authorities."

The History Teller nodded. "So you don't really miss her in your heart?" Maxi didn't answer. He didn't have to. Suddenly tears came to his eyes. "Don't," she said, "your makeup will run and you don't know how to put it back on yourself."

"How long do you think I can get away with this charade?" Maxi demanded.

"That, my friend, depends on how well you learn your part. Play your part well and no one will guess that the man beneath the hideous makeup of the Lost Peasant is in fact the second most wanted man in the Middle Kingdom."

The Assassin had been expecting an order since the night, two days back, when he had seen a man in the front row of the audience stand on his entrance and signal with his fingers the same way his father had taught him all those years ago. Loa Wei Fen had waited for an order — longed for it. And there it was, on the underside of his writing stone, etched by an unknown hand but with his uncle's chop affixed to it to lend it credence: "The Lost Peasant is the red-haired *Fan Kuei* — he and his daughter are to die — but it must be a very public death so the rebellion will never reform and terrorize the people of China again."

The cobra on his back uncoiled slowly as he took his swalto blade into his right hand and slid it slowly across the writing. Thin, even sheets of soapstone came away, and with them the message, until all that was left was his uncle's chop, and the yearning to fulfill his destiny.

At the end of the week the troupe approached Chinkiang. Sitting on the north-east bank of the Grand Canal and the Yangtze, the strategically placed city had been handed over back and forth between the Manchus and the Taipingers. It was now a highly fortified city, fully in Manchu control.

When the troupe approached the west gate they were ordered to stop and lie face down on the side of the road. The company — and Maxi, who, like about half the company, was in full makeup and costume — did as they were ordered. The springtime sun became slowly hotter and hotter as the day progressed, and still they were left face down by the roadside. Maxi was afraid that his makeup had sweated away and hesitated when, after a Manchu officer's shouted order, the troupe slowly got to their feet.

Maxi carefully moved behind the tallest of the actors and bowed his head.

"So, History Teller, we meet again!" The voice belonged to the Commander of the Manchus to whom the troupe had been traded for two sows at Nanjing. "And I see your pretty head has avoided finding its way to the end of a Manchu pike. My congratulations. Welcome to my new posting as Commander of the Empress's Manchu forces here, in Chinkiang. Well, enough of that. What are you going to do for your …. ah, I know," he said with an odd tilt of his head. "I command a performance — a full performance of your masterpiece."

"It is a very long play."

"The people of Chinkiang need something to take their minds off their misery. What better than the misery of the characters in your play? Right?"

"When would you like this performance?"

"Tomorrow, starting at midday and going for as long as it takes." The Commander of the Manchu forces turned to leave, then stopped and turned back to the History Teller.

"Yes, Commander?"

"Just this, History Teller — welcome to Chinkiang, City of Suicides."

"When will you learn how to put on your own makeup?"

"Maxi, my name's Maxi."

"I know your name," the History Teller said. "I've known your name since you first arrived to watch a rehearsal in my mother's establishment."

"Brothel. Your mother's brothel."

The History Teller bobbed her head in acknowledgment, then took the small metal trowel and scooped out the white paste and began to apply the base to the *Fan Kuei*'s face. As she continued to work the makeup deep into his skin, she looked down and saw Maxi staring up at her. "Why do you stare?" she asked.

"You're very beautiful."

He said it so simply that it took her by surprise. To cover her embarrassment she said, "Your Mandarin is awful."

"You ought to hear my Hakka, if you think my Mandarin is awful. How's your English today?"

"Eloquent, erudite, and acute," she responded in highly accented English. A smile creased her face.

"Sounds like English but I've never heard those words before. What do they mean?"

"You are staring again. It's impolite."

"I don't care, unless it bothers you."

"It doesn't."

The simplicity of her response caught him off guard.

"I've been staring at you since the first time I walked into your rehearsal, what was it, nine or ten years ago?"

"Nine years and two months. On the second day of the month of the Rat." She tilted his head back so she could apply the dark eye makeup. "Look over my shoulder."

"Can't."

"What?"

"Can't stop looking at you." Then he slid a hand up her thigh, and she pivoted her hip to allow his hand access to her as she squeezed her legs on either side of his knee and allowed herself to be moved as the world is moved — by the restless winds of a lonely heart.

"What's your name?"

"I'm the History Teller."

"I know that, but what's your name? Or perhaps you don't know your name."

"Oh, *I* know my name — it's you, Maxi, who doesn't know my name."

The audience was crammed into every available space as the play, under the blazing sun, began. The excellence of the company's performance brought the audience to its feet over and over again. The play continued as dinner was served to the Manchu nobles. Others had brought their own repasts, but the crowd was quiet. A true rarity for a Chinese audience.

The History Teller sometimes did her best writing in the presence of her own work. And it was so that day, as *Journey to the West* began its meandering but inescapable voyage toward heartbreak. She allowed the sights and sounds of the play to move past her, and forced the enthusiastic crowd response into the background. And there she stood, apart from both the play and the audience, facing her new project, a story that she'd been tinkering with for months — that of an arhu player whose music is so rapturous that those who listen fall in love. The musician is surrounded by love — but he himself is utterly and totally alone. He is called to the homes of the great and powerful, to the deathbeds of the lowly, to the arranged weddings of merchants. And everywhere he plays, love flowers.

The History Teller didn't have to be told how close this was to her own life.

At the beginning of the fourth hour the Monkey King made his first entrance, and every person in the audience knew that something serious about the evening had changed. Even the actors, who were used to the odd energy of the private boy/man who played the Monkey King, were startled by the height of his tumbling and the energy that seemed to flow from him.

By the sixth hour the Serving Man was approaching a high mountain stream with his Princess of the West in tow, and he was met by the Lost Peasant, his wife, and little girl.

Maxi was having trouble in his costume. The costume mistress had changed one of the straps and it restricted the mobility of his left arm — his sword arm. The plump actress playing his wife followed him onstage carrying Maxi's daughter in her arms. She stopped and threw her sleeves high in the air to signal her distress. Maxi executed the moves he'd learned and the crowd howled with laughter. Maxi was always surprised by that. He thought he was doing exactly what the History Teller had taught him, but the audience immediately pegged him as the comic relief. Fine, just so long as they didn't peg him as the red-haired *Fan Kuei*!

The History Teller had outlined the basic scenes of her new play about the arhu player and several had already been committed to paper. But she knew her own process and she knew that she was stuck. She also knew that the way forward was to find the very centre of the idea, the cry of the heart that propelled everything else — and that cry would become the title.

She knew the final song of the musician as he tossed aside his ancient arhu and left the realm of men and women. She knew the lyric of the chorus was:

The raindrops fall
One, then another
On the hard ground
Until finally wisdom,
The true gift of the gods,
Blooms.

She also knew that although this lyric was close to the very centre of the idea of the evening, it was flawed — fell somehow short of what she wanted to say. She repeated the lyric in her mind as she allowed her attention to return to the performance.

Maxi opened his arms, as he had been taught to do, to indicate that the Lost Peasant's wife and child should follow him. Suddenly the crowd stood as one and pointed toward upstage left. Maxi turned to see what had taken the audience from him and there he saw the boy/man who played the Monkey King in full makeup, hanging from an overhead beam by one hand as his other hand reached inside his tunic.

The swalto blade turned in the Assassin's hand and found its purchase. The boy felt his head swivel on his neck and heard the *click click click* of his vertebrae, one at a time, twisting past their previous locked positions. Then the sharp tang of the acid from the snakeskin on the swalto's handle filled his mouth. His tongue traced the length of the smooth snakeskin handle as his testicles retracted into his body — ready.

"Papa!"

Maxi spun around and saw that his little girl was crying, reaching for him, and calling his name loudly. He took one step toward her then heard the sharp whine of wood yanked clear of its nails. He looked up.

"*Always attack from above. Always from above*," the voice of his father, who for all those mornings had taught him the skills of an assassin, whispered in his ear. He felt his father's hand on his shoulder. "*Do your duty for China*," the voice said, as it had at the end of every morning's training session. But this time the boy heard not only the words, but also the loneliness in the voice and a desire to reach out and touch.

"I will, father. I will do my duty," he said aloud.

The History Teller rose from her seat at the back of the audience and shouted, "No!" and pushed her way through the thick crowd that separated her from the stage.

Maxi saw it happening right in front of him but somehow in unnatural slowness, in the way that shadows emerge from deep caves. The boy/man Monkey King had a knife in his teeth as he dropped from the beam. In midair he turned his body in a full somersault and fell face first toward him — the knife a shard of death pointed at his heart.

Joy surged through the boy. He felt his own elegance. He was a thing of inestimable beauty. A god falling to himself. Something worth the love of the History Teller!

Maxi felt a weight in his arms and time snapped back to the frenetic present. His daughter was in his hands. How had she gotten there? The girl wasn't looking at him, but at the knife plunging toward her.

The History Teller climbed over three people who wouldn't let her through and flung herself toward the front of the stage.

Maxi lifted his left arm to defend the girl from the blow but his arm snagged on the newly fitted costume. He tugged and the new tie snapped free just in time for him to slide his daughter to safety before he fell to his knees on the hard stage floor.

The red-haired *Fan Kuei*'s sudden fall caused the Assassin's perfectly aimed dagger to miss its target and slice cleanly through Maxi's shoulder and upper arm. Then it cut straight down the outside of the man's leg and lodged several inches deep in the stage planking.
    The Assassin touched down with his left hand then somersaulted and began a tumbling run across the stage.
    The audience cheered wildly.
    At the end of his tumbling run he snatched the red-haired *Fan Kuei*'s little girl from the stage floor and then, holding the girl in one hand, cartwheeled off the other. When he once again stood erect, the swalto was magically back in his hand.
    He turned to the audience and struck a pose, the girl in one

hand and the knife in the other.

The musicians awoke from their stunned silence and cymbals smashed and horns blared.

The audience shrieked its approval.

Then Loa Wei Fen stuck his knife deep into the chest of the girl.

And time stopped.

Maxi threw himself at the Monkey King. The wig covering his red hair fell to the stage floor as he smashed into the blood-covered Assassin.

The History Teller leapt onto the front of the stage and ran toward the Monkey King. Maxi saw her and shouted, "No!" But the Monkey King spun and his swalto sliced cleanly across the History Teller's neck.

Words flew into her head:

Crimson line,
Across my soul
Invites flights of angels.

For an instant she saw the Monkey King's face and, through the miracle of Peking Opera makeup, finally saw, saw so clearly, the boy's longing for her — and she at last knew the title of her new opera:

The Tears of Time.

Then she heard whistling — from beneath her nose, beneath her chin — air, whistling out of her.

Maxi saw the History Teller's face take on a strange expression, as if something were suddenly clear to her. Then her head fell from her neck, hit once on her shoulder, and landed on the stage and stayed there, staring at him.

The Monkey King spun to face Maxi, his love gone. All that was left was his *chi* screaming to be set loose upon this *Fan Kuei*.

Maxi stood did not move. He'd seen a lot of death in his life. He'd caused much of it. But his own death was something that he'd not prepared himself for. He looked at his dead little girl, then at his dead love. He was partially aware that people were screaming, that the audience was running — but it didn't matter. He saw the terrifying keenness of the swalto blade.

The boy/man turned from him and slowly removed his silk costume. The cobra on his back, its hood gorged with blood and its eyes a flat black, spoke of endings. All Maxi remembered was thinking, *Such anger. So much rage.* Then he was back in India, the gentle opium farmer's hand on his, guiding the knife across the casement of the opium plant.

"See, it oozes, it's life."

"Like me, father," Maxi said.

"Indeed," the opium farmer said, "indeed, like you, my son."

The cobra leapt from him and his swalto cut deep into the *Fan Kuei*'s chest, but the man's eyes were strangely calm. The Assassin jerked the knife up and heard the breastbone crack beneath its pressure. Then he cut down and ripped the man's ribcage open.

He turned. He knew that the audience must be screaming but he couldn't hear them as he cut the red-haired *Fan Kuei*'s heart from his chest, slit it in two, and bit deeply into one half. And then he heard it. Faintly at first but then stronger, the voice of his friend, his cousin: "*Don't kill me, Loa Wei Fen, don't kill me.*"

The Assassin turned toward the stunned audience and raised his hands — he made no attempt to catch the objects hurled at him and felt only relief when the bullets thudded into his body and threw him to the stage floor like a discarded child's toy.

38

A PROPHECY

Virginia, USA, and Shanghai
1864–65

On the same day that Richard was told about Maxi's death, in a small church several thousand miles away, in a place called Virginia, an ostracized but unbowed woman named Rachel Oliphant walked beside her white-skinned, red-haired boy up the aisle of a small Episcopal church to receive his First Communion. Later that day Rachel sat down with her son and told him of his father, a wild, red-haired Jew named Maxi.

"My father's name is Maxi," he said without a hint of comment. "Maxi," he repeated, "is a fine name — a fine name for a man."

Rachel smiled at her red-haired son, whose rugged Hordoon features were clearly underlying her own, more delicate looks.

"Yes, he was a very fine man."

"Is he dead, mother?"

With a surprising certainty she said softly, "Of that I'm sure."

Silas felt a cold breeze move across his face and he thought someone had called his name. He looked up into the high ceiling of the sixth floor of the Hordoons' massive new department store on Bubbling Spring Road, which his father had built directly across from the Vrassoons' newest emporium.

"Did you say something?" Silas asked the accountant with whom he was setting up the store's books.

"No, young sir," the man said.

"It's cold in here, isn't it?"

"I don't think it's cold, sir. Perhaps you have a chill."

Then Silas saw Milo at the far end of the aisle, his face a mask of pain, tears streaming down his cheeks — and Silas knew, just as surely as Rachel had known, that the force of nature that had condescended to take the human form of Maxi Hordoon was no more.

Silas looked out the window and for a moment thought he saw the silhouette of a man dancing on the roof of the Vrassoons' department store, a silhouette of a man that somehow wore a red kerchief around its neck.

Richard rejected all offers of sympathy and was especially harsh when the Vrassoons offered to sit shiva for Maxi. Although he had the body brought from Chinkiang to Shanghai he refused any religious rituals, Jewish or otherwise, and had Maxi's body buried in a simple pine box, beside the graves of the two White men who had been strangled to death by the Manchus all those years ago when the traders needed a sacrifice to force them into a united front.

The day of the burial was clear and cool. All anyone said that day was, "Maxi would have approved of the weather."

That night Richard sat alone in his office and stared out the window at the Huangpu River and remembered. Remembered the boy who had allowed Teacher to sodomize him so as to save Richard; the boy who had danced and laughed around the bonfire at the opium farm; the young man who had donned the red kerchief and led his irregulars into battle after battle; the grown man who had saved him with a trick of guns attached somehow by silk threads; and finally the man who had tried to convince him to stay with the Taipingers, saying, "This is the kind of place that could rid you of the opium addiction that rules you. I could help you. We could all help you here — and love you, brother mine."

Richard reached out and pulled the drapes together. In the darkness of the room only one thought offered Richard any solace: at least he had not been the cause of Maxi's death. The old Indian's prophecy that brother would kill brother had not come to pass.

While the Hordoons went into mourning, Shanghai celebrated the end of the dreaded Taipingers. The country was open for business once again, and opium began to flow upriver as it had never flowed before.

Stores opened and new streets were built. The city expanded south and west. People from the four corners of China, and then from the four corners of the world, flocked to the economic miracle that was Shanghai.

The Confucian's eldest son now joined his father at the meetings of the Chosen Three. It was clear he would soon take over his ailing father's place in the Compact. Jiang knew him by sight but had never conversed with him before. *The Fisherman is not long for this world either*, Jiang thought.

The Carver flipped the latches on the cabinet that protected the Narwhal Tusk and they leaned down to look at the image of the Seventy Pagodas in the third "pane."

"We prosper," said the Fisherman.

"Indeed," replied the Carver, enigmatically.

"But are we near the age of the Seventy Pagodas?" asked the young Confucian.

Jiang couldn't tell if the young man was being sarcastic or not.

Finally she said, "We have all given up much to bring and then intensify the darkness of the Age of White Birds on Water — much," she added, thinking of the last time she'd seen her beloved daughter, the History Teller. She'd been offered her daughter's body but she had declined to have it transported to Shanghai. She'd simply instructed them to follow the rituals, then scatter her ashes. "I'll see her soon enough," she'd said.

The Fisherman was deep in thought about his lost son and worried who, now that his nephew was gone, would lead the Guild of Assassins. He had another son, and perhaps he had the years left in him to complete the boy's training.

The Confucian thought of his father's bent frame and the book of ancient writings he'd been given. All the weight of the family's addiction to opium had been carried on his father's back as surely as a coolie carries water on his carrying poles. Heavy, painful — always there.

"I doubt it is so simple," the Carver said.

No one had to ask to what he was referring — the city at the Bend of the River was becoming large and powerful. But it was a large and powerful European creation. Europeans built cock-proud buildings on the Bund, but not pagodas — pagodas were light and tall, they were Chinese buildings. The Age of Seventy Pagodas was not yet upon them.

"No doubt we need to discover how to open the second window before any pagodas can be built."

No one argued with the Carver's statement.

For just under a year Richard saw almost no one. He handled his business dealings almost exclusively through Patterson.

Silas threw himself into his Chinese language studies and Milo threw himself at as many women as he could find — and being a handsome young man, as well as the wealthiest potential husband in all of Shanghai, he had many takers.

A year after Maxi's death, Richard called his sons to have dinner with him in the big house. Lily sat to one side — she was the only other person in a room that was designed to sit forty comfortably for dinner.

"It's been a year, now," Richard began.

"It was a year yesterday, father," Silas corrected him.

"What does that matter?" Milo asked.

"If it's a year or a year and a day — it's enough. It's time for the House of Hordoon to re-emerge. To come back to life."

"I agree," said Milo.

"I didn't notice that you had particularly retreated from life's delectations, Milo," Richard said.

"Well, one of us has to continue to fly the flag."

"Enough. What have you got in mind, father?" asked Silas.

Richard reached beneath the table and withdrew a large set of blueprints and spread them out on the table, then said simply, "The Shanghai Racetrack."

"So that's why you never built on …"

"I don't know why I did it, Milo, but it seems to make sense to me."

"A way to honour Uncle Maxi that Uncle Maxi would approve of," said Silas.

"Are we agreed, then?" Richard asked.

They mulled over the blueprints well into the night. Only as the light began to dawn through the windows did the three agree upon the last details, and Milo said, "How shall we open Uncle Maxi's racecourse?"

"With the biggest, richest horse race in all of Asia, naturally."

"A single race. One horse from each of the great houses. Each house puts up fifty thousand pounds sterling and one horse. Winning horse takes all."

Only in Shanghai, with its access to literally thousands upon thousands of workers, could a racetrack have gone up with such astonishing speed, and the talk around the town grew from excited to ecstatic as the date of the opening race approached.

A month before the scheduled opening, Silas waited for his father at breakfast.

"Silas? To what do I owe the…?"

"I have to speak to you, father."

"Speak, but pass me the porridge first."

Silas ladled some into a fine crystal bowl for his father and handed it over. "I have an idea, father, but I don't think you'll like it."

"About the race?"

"Yes."

"You don't want us to race?"

"No, father, I want the race to go on as much as you do."

"So what is it?"

"We are Shanghainese."

"Absolutely, we are. This is our home."

"Right, not rotting Shanghailanders who just come here to rape —"

"Your point, Silas? The day's upon us."

"Make the race open to everyone."

Richard looked at his son for a moment, then said, "But it is. The French, the British, the Americans, the Germans …"

"The Chinese?"

"Now you know better than that, Silas," he said, throwing aside his serviette and rising.

"Better than what, sir?" Silas stood to meet his father's wrath.

"Listen to me, Silas. You can spend as much of your time as you like with them. I've never said a word about that."

"Do you not approve, father, of me spending time with — ?"

"It's not for me to approve or not. That's not that point! We cannot allow ourselves to socialize with …"

"Monkeys. The word you're looking for, father, is monkeys."

"Aye, monkeys, damned monkeys I say, lad!"

Silas whirled around and stared into the florid face of Patterson, who had somehow gotten into the room without Silas noticing. "I'll not ride in front of monkeys and neither will any of the other riders. If you want a race, your damned monkeys had better not be there."

Richard put a hand on Silas's shoulder. "See, son, even if I wanted to, my hands are tied on this matter. What kind of race would it be without riders?"

Silas remembered standing for what seemed like hours with his father's hand on his shoulder. He didn't remember leaving the room — or when the rage came upon him.

The night before the race, Silas slipped into the Hordoon stables and moved to the stall of the family's prize mare. The animal eyed Silas with a barely concealed menace, but Silas walked into the paddock and slapped the horse hard on the rump. The animal hesitated, then shuffled aside.

"Good," Silas said, careful to keep his voice down and his tone stern. He walked to the back of the stall where the hard tack was kept and pulled out the hand-carved leather saddle that Patterson loved so dearly. Then, using a small, sharp knife, he carefully cut several striations at various points of the saddle's cinch strap, which was meant to secure the saddle to the horse's belly. He held the thing to the light and his rage abated. Without the tension the strap would experience once around the horse's midsection, his cuts could not be seen, even if someone was looking for them. Replacing the saddle in the hard tack box he said, "A little treat for you, Mr. Patterson, from your 'lad' — and his monkeys."

The day of the race dawned crisp and clear, with a breeze from the east that brought the smell of the ocean to the thriving small city at the Bend in the River. The celebration began early with Champagne breakfasts all over the Foreign Settlement and the French Concession. Suzanne was surprised to see customers arrive just after breakfast. *A little something before the race*, she thought. Jiang made ready for early customers, knowing that many Chinese, despite the fact that they were not allowed to attend, had wagered heavily on the race and were trying to guarantee their success with an early-morning session of clouds and rain.

The racetrack itself threw open its doors at ten o'clock and the *crème de la crème* of the English, American, French, German, and even Russian communities pushed their way into the lavish facility. They oohed and aahed at the luxury all around them and quickly made their way to the betting windows.

By ten-thirty, over a quarter of a million British pounds had been shoved through the windows. But the real betting was on the side. Richard had taken bets from both Percy St. John Dent and Hercules McCallum, but they were minor compared to the bet with the Vrassoons. And their bet was unique. It had nothing to do with which horse won the race. It had only to do with which of their two horses outdid the other — a grudge match.

By eleven o'clock the few bars that had closed the night before had opened and the excitement in the city ratcheted up as whisky added its own unique acceleration to human joy.

At noon the horses were finally walked out on the track to take their pre-race workouts and a hush fell over the gathering crowd. Shanghai was used to superlatives — the best wines, the sheerest silks — but the horseflesh on the track in the bright morning sunshine was the finest collection of Thoroughbreds that hundreds of years of careful breeding could produce.

The Vrassoon rider walked beside the large, almost pure-white stallion and offered up sugar cubes as they promenaded around the track. The stallion stood a full two hands taller than any of the other horses on the track. The Vrassoons had kept their animal in a secret paddock all the way downriver at Wusung, so that no one knew much about the stallion. But everything necessary to know was openly on display as the powerful animal pulled hard at the reins, clearly anxious to race.

The Dents' rider noted the muscle of the Vrassoon stallion and then looked at his fine grey gelding, as the Jardine, Matheson colt pranced by with its jockey holding the reins tight on his Orkney-bred steed.

The American horse was technically the entrant of Russell and Company, but as Russell's representative, a Mr. Delano, later confessed, "We at Russell's were just a front. Jedediah Oliphant was the money behind our entry. Because of his religious convictions he is opposed to gambling in all of its forms, but he would have killed himself if he'd been left out of the race, so he contacted us and, for a modest fee, Mr. Roosevelt and I fronted his Kentucky pony." And the animal was a marvel — sleek and light of foot and probably the most beautiful animal on the track.

The Hordoons' mare was the last to make its entrance, surprisingly late, and the chocolate-coloured animal seemed to shy away from its rider to the point that the man dismounted and tried to coax it into walking by his side.

At twelve-thirty the bar at the racetrack opened, serving Champagne on ice to all comers — and it did a brisk business — as did the betting windows, which by that time had taken in more than three quarters of a million British pounds.

Then the first set of betting odds were posted, and the lines in front of the betting wickets doubled.

The Vrassoon horse was almost even money, followed by the American horse, then farther down the other three horses.

Side betting came out in the open as the water trap jump was filled and the three hedge jumps were pulled into position. The horses left the track for their final preparations.

The day grew hot but no one even thought of leaving as the clock clicked slowly toward race time: one o'clock.

Silas noted that he was the only non-Chinese on the Bund promenade that day. Across the water, the challenge of the Pudong stared back at him. He'd never been there, but there were stories, such stories about that bit of Shanghai! He approached a five-spice egg seller and purchased one of her products. The old seller was pleasantly surprised with Silas's fluent Mandarin and told him as much. He balanced the hot thing between the tips of his fingers as he took a bite out of the top. His teeth scraped just the edge of the hardened yolk, as he had been taught to, allowing the flavoured white of the egg to mix with the dense taste of the yolk. He smiled as he heard the chatter around him. And he took it all in: the peasants squatting on their haunches, planning the next moves in their complicated lives; the rickshaw boys sitting in the shade of their conveyances; the old man on the ground surrounded by the heels of women's shoes while he cobbled an ancient shoe back into use; the four elderly men moving like shadows across the pavement as they performed the moves of their T'ai Chi exercises in perfect unison; the man selling delicate wrens and hummingbirds in bamboo cages; the two young men playing Go on a board drawn on the pavement itself, surrounded by other men offering unsolicited advice; a woman carrying a large wreath of flowers destined to be draped across the doorway of a new business for good luck; men, their backs stacked high with parcels or furniture or equipment or cages of live animals or garbage pails or water on poles — men carrying the world itself on their backs. And Silas took it in and it made him smile. Shanghai — his Shanghai — his home.

He turned toward the Pudong and a shiver went up his spine. Instantly he turned back toward the city and heard the roar of hundreds of voices from the direction of the racetrack. He ran to the nearest rickshaw and in rapid Shanghainese shouted, "To the racetrack as fast as you can!"

A loud gunshot started the race. As soon as the horses hit stride, the Vrassoon rider pulled hard on his stallion's left rein, forcing him to cross in front of the Hordoons' mare. The smaller animal veered, then shied away toward the rail. For a moment the mare lost her gait, then she sorted herself out and headed after the pack of horses that was now several lengths ahead of her.

The other three horses wisely moved away from the big white stallion and raced toward the first of the three hedge fences, with the American horse the first to reach the low hedge.

Oliphant was cheering so loudly that the other members of the House of Zion were taken aback. But he turned to them and screamed, "God's horse! Cheer on God's horse, for God's sake!" The fact that, through Mr. Delano, he had placed what he called "a modest, truly modest wager" on his horse — some seventy thousand British pounds — had nothing whatever to do with his enthusiasm.

The low hedge posed no problem for the American pony, which leaped over the obstruction as simply as a child skips a step while running down stairs. The Vrassoon stallion seemed to gain as he left his feet to clear the obstruction, followed closely by the horses from Dent's and then the Orkney pony of Jardine, Matheson, which cut toward the rail as soon as it cleared the hedge and quickly passed the Dent's horse. Then, five full lengths back, the Hordoon mare approached the hedge.

Hercules managed to step on his own gout-afflicted foot when his rider did as he had ordered and passed the Dents' pony on the rail. "Ride," he shouted, "ride for Scotland!"

The Hordoon jockey felt his mare find her stride on the far side of the first of the three hedges and smiled as he thought back to the day's events in the Hordoon stable. Then he whooped a characteristic whoop and grabbed a handful of the mare's mane and shouted, "That'a girl. Good girl, Rachel."

The second hedge, about twice the height of the first, was approaching quickly as Silas threw money at his rickshaw boy and ran toward the entrance of the Hordoons' racetrack.

The American horse was the first to the hedge and just cleared it, with the top of the obstruction rubbing across the animal's belly. The American rider adjusted to the change in midair and the horse landed perfectly balanced and shot forward toward the third obstruction — the water jump.

The Vrassoon stallion sailed over the second hedge, its powerful flanks providing more than enough lift to clear the barrier. His front hooves hit ground only half a length behind the American pony.

Quickly after the Vrassoon stallion, the Jardine, Matheson Orkney pony raced toward the barrier, then suddenly ducked its head, throwing the rider into the hedge. The hooves of the Dent's horse just missed the fallen rider's head, and when the Dent's rider looked back he was surprised that the Hordoon mare had passed him in midair — and raced after the two front-runners.

The third obstacle, the water jump, was approaching quickly, and much to everyone's surprise, while the American pony was in midair clearing the water, the Vrassoon stallion made no effort whatsoever to jump and instead raced through the pool, which the Vrassoons had made sure was only six inches deep rather than the traditional three feet. Seeing the Vrassoon stallion, the Hordoon rider let out his reins and urged his mare on through the water.

They were now on the far side of the track beginning the long turn toward home. Only the large hedge remained. The Vrassoon stallion led by two lengths but the Hordoon mare was closing fast.

Silas spotted his father and ran up the aisle to him. With all the noise, Silas couldn't hear the words his father was shouting. Then he looked past his father and saw Patterson. Patterson! Silas whipped around to face the track and over his shoulder he heard his father's voice shouting, "Milo! Yes, Milo! Catch him Milo! Ride that mare, Milo!"

And Silas's heart sank as the horses made the last wide turn,

Milo now only a length behind the Vrassoon horse as they headed toward the large hedge.

Milo, no, not Milo.

Milo sensed it. He didn't know what but something was different. Some odd smell in the air. Then he dismissed it — it was the anticipation of the race. All the planning, all the excitement. Each of the great trading houses backing a horse, and the mammoth purse that his father had put up and all the betting and all the people — it must be that, just that. Then he smelled it again, and so did the Hordoons' prize mare in her stall.

"Easy, Rachel," Milo said, but the powerful animal's eyes were wild and she reared, kicking out with her front legs against the wooden slats of the paddock. "Easy," Milo cooed to the animal. Suddenly the horse turned in the stall and slammed her powerful back hooves against the stall's gate. "No, Rachel, no," he shouted. Then he smelled it again. A dry, musky, acidic smell in the air.

Had Milo asked a Chinese peasant, he would have been told what the reek was — the smell of change. But there were no Chinese workers in the Hordoons' stables. All the work there was done by the Hordoons, some of Maxi's old irregulars, and of course Patterson, who even now came running down the centre aisle of the stable, shouting, "Leave that animal alone, boy."

Milo took a step back from the mare. Patterson opened the gate and swacked the horse hard across the nose. "No, me lovely, we'll have none of that." Then he moved past the horse and got his prized saddle out of the hard tack box.

"Trouble, gentlemen?" Richard said as he came into the stable.

"No, sir, no trouble."

"I hope not. It's race day. Race day," he repeated happily. "Where's your brother, Milo?"

"I don't know, father."

The mare shied away from Richard. "Easy Rachel, easy," he said as he put his hand on the animal's smooth flank. As he did, he continued to speak softly to the animal and run his hands along her back. Then he slipped the bit into her mouth and tossed the reins over her neck. "What's gotten into her?"

"She smells something," said Milo.

"Nonsense," snarled Patterson. "What does an animal smell, do you suppose, lad? She's just excited about racing, like me." Patterson hoisted the saddle up on the mare's back.

Milo looked to his father and was about to ask, "Don't you smell it, father?" when the mare reared suddenly and kicked out. Her right fore hoof caught Patterson beneath the chin and the man crumpled to the ground like a puppet whose strings had been cut.

Milo grabbed the reins and yanked hard, turning the powerful animal's eyes to his. The mare immediately calmed. Milo ran his hand up the horse's muzzle.

Richard pulled Patterson to his feet. The man had a hard noggin and, unlike those whom he called monkeys, his bulldog Scottish body was built to take a fall. But the blow to his head had left him woozy and disoriented, so, over the man's vociferous objections, Richard sent him back to his home and turned to his son.

"Be honest, you wanted to ride for the family all along, didn't you?"

"I always did, father," Milo said as a smile bloomed on his handsome face.

"Well, now it's not a matter of wanting." Richard straightened Patterson's leather saddle on the mare's back and said, "Cinch her tight, son, then mount up. We'll walk her slowly to the track."

Milo reached under the animal's belly, grabbed the cinch strap, and pulled it tightly through the catch. Then he swung up into the saddle. From his perch on the fine animal he looked down at his father, who was looking up at him with a peculiar smile on his face.

"What?"

Richard wanted to say, *What a wonderful son you are*, but he didn't. He just chuckled and said, "Son, ride like the wind."

"I'll make you proud, father."

Richard smiled and said softly, "You already have, son, you already have." He thought for the briefest moment of his promise to Milo's mother and vowed that he would, at long last, write something about Milo — just for her.

"Ride, Milo! Ride, son!"

Silas strained to see his brother as Rachel pulled even with the Vrassoon stallion just before the large hedge.

Milo pulled back, then loosed the reins on Rachel and she flew — flew over the large hedge and landed at the exact same time as the massive Vrassoon stallion.

Milo heard the crowds screaming as he leaned into the final turn in the track's back stretch, Rachel neck and neck with the larger Vrassoon stallion. Then stride for stride, just waiting to break out of the turn and into the home stretch. Milo knew that Rachel could outrun the heavier animal on the straightaway, all he needed to do was stay even on the curve. Just a few more yards!

He leaned hard in the saddle — and felt something — shift. Had Rachel missed a stride? He leaned forward to settle her when he felt the saddle move. Then he heard it — something snapping — something metal hit him — and he fell.

As his limber body fell toward the track he smelled it again. That dry, musky reek. Then he saw them only inches from his face — hooves — the massive hooves of the Vrassoon stallion.

There was no funeral. No rites. Just a simple pine box and an unmarked grave over which stood a beaten man and a guilty son.

Silas never told his father what he had done to the cinch strap of the saddle that had loosed his brother to his death. Never admitted his guilt. But he knew that he had fulfilled the prophecy that

Richard and Maxi had heard from the mouth of the ancient Indian man in the alley in the town near Ghazipur: *Brother will kill brother.* Knew it, and didn't know how he was going to live with it.

Richard actively retreated from the world. Even his writing, which always brought him peace, was a torment. He never was able to complete the journal entry about Milo. He refused to see anyone but Lily, until one night he awoke with a start. There was someone in his room. He lit the oil lamp by his bed and was shocked to see Eliazar Vrassoon in the flickering light of the lamp.

Richard had no idea how the old man had gotten into his bedroom, but there he was — the Vrassoon Patriarch — at one time the most powerful man in all of Shanghai, now a bent thing leaning on a walking stick. But evidently the man was not so powerless because he had gotten into his bedroom, unannounced and definitely uninvited.

The old man coughed. Something red flecked his lips. Then he smiled.

"What are you doing …?"

"In your bedroom? Well you might ask, but I've been in your bedroom before. In one way of thinking, I've been in your bedroom every night of your life."

Richard swung his legs over the side of the bed and grabbed a silk bathrobe which he wound around himself.

"The other time I was in your room you wore only dirty underclothes — but perhaps you don't remember."

"Remember what, you —"

"Careful. No need to insult the dying. Whatever reward awaits is already prepared in a manner unforeseen on this earth."

"More gobbledygook!"

"Really?" Eliazar Vrassoon said under his breath.

"So you're dying?" Richard remarked brightly.

"So it would seem. Then again, we are all dying, my boy."

"I am not a boy. I am not your boy!"

"You've been my boy since the first night we met. In another bedroom a long time ago — in Baghdad."

Suddenly Richard knew what kept beckoning him in his opium dreams. The door that always awaited his coming. Not the door, but what was behind the door. Not what, but who.

"You took my sister?"

The Vrassoon Patriarch seemed to sway for a moment, then, through a coughing fit, asked, "Took your sister? You think I took your sister, Miriam? You believe I stole her?"

"What else could you call it?" Richard screamed at him.

"You are shouting, boy. Why are you shouting, boy?"

"I killed your son," Richard announced triumphantly.

Eliazar Vrassoon nodded slowly. "With the picture?"

"Yes."

Vrassoon continued to nod. "By that token you could say I killed your father. But neither claim would be true. My son threw himself from a bridge. You may think you caused it with your photographic invention, but my son was so filled with remorse for his sins that his jumping was just the final act in his tragic life. Just as your father's death was no more than the final act in his comic existence." Eliazar Vrassoon shuffled his feet, then turned to Richard and in a loud voice said, "Come with me, boy. Your father has agreed."

Richard felt himself falling. As if the world were suddenly upside down. "What?"

"You heard me, boy. Your father has agreed and you are the price. Grab your trousers and come with me. Now, boy!"

Richard breathed deep. The smell of spicy chickpeas was in the room. The cry of the muezzin calling the faithful to morning prayers entered from the window. But how? This was Shanghai, not ... the sound of a peacock shrilly screaming a warning ... and he was back. Back in Baghdad in his room as a four-year-old boy and this big man was in his room saying, "Your father has agreed, boy."

Richard staggered two steps closer and smelled the odour deep in the man's gabardine coat. He looked up into the man's eyes and the Patriarch was young. Powerful. Full of fury. "Your father has agreed. Now come, boy."

Richard heard his knees hit the floor but felt no pain. He looked up at the old man leaning on the cane. "You were in my room in Baghdad."

"Yes."

"You had come for my sister, Miriam."

"No."

Richard felt his insides fall again and suddenly he was tumbling, plummeting down an ancient well, backwards, on a moonless night — falling.

"No, boy. I came for you. As your father had agreed. You were to be my apprentice, in return for which I was to make sure your family survived and got safely out of Baghdad. I came for you, boy. For you."

Richard nodded slowly and looked up at the old man. "But I was afraid and I pointed toward my sister's bed."

"You were afraid, perhaps. But you didn't point toward your sister's bed."

"I did — toward her bed."

"No."

"I did!" Richard was screaming again.

"No. What Jewish family would put two sons in the same room with a daughter?"

The truth of that pierced Richard's heart. Something was falling away. His skin? His bones? His heart?

"You took my hand, walked me to her door, and opened it for me. Then you traded, boy. You traded your sister Miriam to me so that I wouldn't take you. You even offered me your brother Maxi as part of the deal. You traded like any stinking kike of a Jew boy. You made a deal. You sold her to me. Four years old and already swinging deals. What a Jew you are!"

"Go to hell," Richard managed to say weakly.

"That's not really your decision to make, now, is it? Besides, you don't believe in a heaven or a hell. Be that as it may, boy, wherever I go, I'm sure you'll shortly follow. Oh, by the way, — you seem to have pissed your trousers, boy." Then he laughed and made a motion with his hand as though tipping his top hat. "Good night, Richard Hordoon. I'm sure we'll meet again in another bedroom another time — of that I have no doubt."

After that night Richard seldom chanced sleeping. And with an ever-increasing frequency he turned to opium for relief from his waking dreams of opening a door and pointing at his baby sister and begging, "Take her. Take her, not me."

And opium, Richard Hordoon's true love, opened her arms to him and he succumbed to her — completely.

END BOOK ONE OF SHANGHAI, THE IVORY COMPACT

SPECIAL PREVIEW

CITY RISING

The Bend of the River
THE SHANGHAI TETRALOGY | BOOK 2

DAVID ROTENBERG

The following is a special preview of *The Bend of the River*, the second book in the acclaimed 'Shanghai Tetralogy'.

⳼2
ARISE THE ASSASSIN

December 31, 1889

Wang Jun stood naked astride the grave of the man he thought of as his noble ancestor—the First Assassin, Loa Wei Fen—and grimaced as his aged father carved the first line of the cobra on his back. He watched the shadow of the moonset as it crept along the Bend in the River, casting deep shadows on the elaborate gargoyles and geegaws on the facades of the European buildings across the river on the Bund.

The second cut was longer and wider than the first, demarcating the outer line of the fully spread hood of the serpent. He knew the third and fourth cuts would be small but very deep—the eyes of the cobra's hood were the heart of its fury.

His blood ran in narrow, viscous streams down his back and pooled momentarily on the rise of his backside before it sought the eternity of the earth whence it came.

His father picked up dirt from Loa Wei Fen's grave and worked it deep into the cuts on his son's back. He had taught his son well, as his father, the Fisherman, had taught him after his gentle brother was put to death in the bamboo canes. He forced more dirt into the cuts. The dirt would cause the wounds to welt upon healing—or cause infection and death—either way, his son would fulfill his destiny. But he knew in his heart that his son would not die from the wounds. And his son would outshine even the First Assassin. His son would revive the ancient Guild of Assassins and help his people to the Seventy Pagodas. He was proud to have such a son. A son who did not cry out at the pain he caused as he dug deep into his flesh to carve out the first eye on the cobra's hood.

The left eye, Wang Jun thought as he resisted the impulse to pull away from the knife in the flesh of his back. He watched a trail of blood curl around his hip and proceed down the front of his left leg, then around the knob of his ankle, and finally between his toes onto the sacred ground of the grave of Loa Wei Fen. It was for this ceremony that he'd had the First Assassin's remains brought from Chinkiang to this side of the Bend in the River—the wild side—the Pudong.

The first of the new year's fireworks lit the newly darkened sky and shadows seemed to leap briefly from the dense forest.

The final cuts were quick and shallow, following the ancient design first seen on the wrist of Q'in She Huang's Body Guard on the sacred mountain, the Hua Shan. He heard his father sigh deeply and sensed the last of the older man's chi enter him as the knife fell to the ground of Loa Wei Fen's grave.

"It is done," his father said in a hoarse whisper.

"As it is decreed," Wang Jun replied. He hugged his father, surprised by the man's sudden frailty. It was as if he had aged twenty years in a day.

As he walked his father to the small boat that would take him back to the Shanghai side of the Huangpo River, he wondered if he'd ever see him again. This stern, strong, righteous man who had taught him the art of the assassin.

"Do you know the sign…?"

"For the Chosen to meet? Yes, father, we meet this very night. It was all arranged before we came to the Pudong. Now, father, forget me—as you have taught."

"Will I never see you again?" the man asked, his voice cracking.

"No. Wang Jun is no more. But you will hear of me. You will hear of your son, Loa Wei Fen."

His father looked at him closely. Suddenly a brightness came back into his eyes. "You have taken his name, the First Assassin's name?"

"Yes, father, as befits one who will revive the ancient Guild of Assassins."

This concludes our special preview of *City Rising, The Bend of the River,* available Spring, 2024, wherever At Bay Press books are sold.

Photo: Christopher Grove

DAVID ROTENBERG is a professor emeritus of theatre studies at York University, where he taught graduate students for over 25 years. He has released 12 novels which have been published by Penguin, Simon and Schuster, McArthur and Company, St. Martin's Press, and ECW. His novels have been optioned in the past for major motion picture adaptation. *City Rising* is presently in negotiation with London producers. He is the founder and artistic director of the world-renowned actor training institute - Pro Actors Lab. *City Rising, From the Holy Mountain* is the first of four books in the 'Shanghai Tetralogy'.

OUR AT BAY PRESS ARTISTIC COMMUNITY:

Publisher - **Matt Joudrey**
Managing Editor - **Alana Brooker**
Substantive Editor - **Kiki Yee**
Copy Editor - **Priyanka Ketkar**
Proof Editor - **Danni Deguire**
Graphic Designer - **Matt Stevens**
Layout - **Matt Stevens and Matt Joudrey**
Publicity and Marketing - **Sierra Peca**

Thanks for purchasing this book and for supporting authors and artists. As a token of gratitude, please scan the QR code for exclusive content from this title.